# DAMAGED

# DAMAGED

## KIM PRITEKEL

SAPPHIRE BOOKS

SALINAS, CALIFORNIA

# Dedication

This book is dedicated to those who survived, prevailed and soared.

# *Prologue*

Then what?" the five-year-old asked, green eyes wide with excitement at the story she was being told.

"Well," Shannon said, sitting at the child's bedside, her hand resting on top of the tiny body tucked beneath the covers, her voice hushed, "when they got to the top…they found the pencil!"

"They did?" the child whispered in awe.

"They did. And what they found was a golden pencil."

"So Peter can do his homework!"

"Exactly!" Shannon cuddled the child and rocked her, leaving a kiss on her head. "You sleep well, dear, sweet Bella," she said quietly. "I love you."

"I love you, too, Mommy," the girl said with a jaw-cracking yawn.

Smiling and filled with love, Shannon tucked in her only child and left the tiny bedroom in the two-bedroom apartment, closing the door, the cloud nightlight painting the room with a soft white hue.

Heading down the short hallway to the bathroom, Shannon shed her robe, walking nude until she reached the tub. She turned the knobs until the water temperature was what she wanted before tugging up the stem to send water streaming down from the finicky showerhead. She nearly growled as she stepped into the tub, throwing the flimsy plastic shower curtain closed behind her. She hated that she had to essentially run around the tiny space to get wet. But, eventually she was able to smooth back her short, bottle-black hair and begin her washing.

A quick shower later, she stood in front of the mirror, yet again naked, preferring to air dry as she began the intricate dance of makeup and hair. She had been shocked to hear from him and wanted to look her best. She smelled good, would look good, and at the end of the day, she knew she *was* good.

Standing back from the mirror, ignoring how shadows from two of the five burnt-out light bulbs made her look, she saw herself in the mirror surrounded by bulbs, ready to head out on that stage. She grinned, admiring the red slash of her lipstick. She used to love her smile, but she hadn't had a lot to be truly happy about in a while. As she closed her lips, she also closed the door on the questionable choices she'd made from time to time. She hoped he wouldn't notice or mind. She hoped he still saw what he did on that stage seven years before.

"You've got this," she murmured, a smoky-eyed wink backing her claim.

Looking in on Bella once more, she stepped into her stilettos and grabbed her handbag, keys, and cell phone then headed out.

# *Chapter One*

Jesus, who told her *that* was a good idea?"

"Jamie, if you make me tell you one more time, I'm going to kill you, okay?" Nora Schaeffer said, looking up from her camera, a sickeningly sweet smile on her lips.

"God, you can be such a grouch." He followed her out of the venue and to the elegant landscaped yard where the wedding party was gathering. "But come on, Nora," he whispered, shrugging her heavy camera bag higher onto his shoulder. "That dress is awful."

"Shut it," Nora growled.

After the wedding, Nora and Jamie got some dinner and she dropped him off at his downtown Pueblo apartment, handing him a check for his work that day as her assistant. Leaving Jamie, she headed out to what was referred to as "The County," the farmland area of Pueblo, Colorado where families had lived and farmed for generations.

As she took a right on Thirty-Sixth Lane, right across from Pueblo County High School, she headed on deeper into farmland, a small smile coming to her face as she thought of her home. Since she'd been a child, there was a particular house she'd always loved and had dreamed about one day owning. She took several more turns before she was on her own street—a dirt road to keep her Jeep constantly covered in dust—and a picturesque old farmhouse at the end of her journey.

It was a two-story and the bottom level had been built nearly 130 years before, the second story to follow thirty years later. The white house with black shutters, dormers, and a wraparound porch sat on four acres, and the clincher was the 700-square-foot studio apartment in the back—that's what sold her on the place. Originally a barn for farm equipment, it was now her home studio.

The tires of her red Jeep Wrangler Unlimited crunched on the gravel of the driveway to her home, the four-door pulling up in front of a detached one-car garage, original to the house. At one time, buggies, a carriage, and buckboards had been parked inside. Now, the hot engine of her Jeep ticked as it cooled and she climbed out, heading to the back to retrieve her equipment.

With a grunt, Nora heaved the heavy camera bag onto her shoulder so she had two free hands to gather up the two tripods she'd brought for the shoot. She walked down the flagstone path to the studio and unlocked the door, letting herself in. With a yawn, all she wanted was to unload everything and soak in her claw-footed tub, also original to the house. The farmhouse wasn't large: three bedrooms, living room, laundry room, and a small kitchen with the one bathroom off to the side. It was maybe twelve hundred square feet, but for her alone, it was perfect.

The old plaster walls were lined with exquisite framed and matted pictures from all over the world from her days as a photographer working for *National Geographic*. She'd started out carrying equipment for Ralph Dalstrom, one of the best in the business, following him through the mountains of Nepal. Eventually, she'd worked her way up to one of their senior shooters with awards to back her work.

She entered the house from the back door, which opened into the kitchen, and sat on the small stool right inside the door to remove her shoes. She let out an almost obscene moan—her feet ached from so many hours on them. It had been a long wedding and an even longer day. Sighing heavily, she pushed to her feet and made her way into the bathroom, not bothering to close the door. In the eighteen months she'd been back living in the country, she had to get used to living alone again. While living overseas, she typically had a roommate, be it her assistant to lug her equipment as they moved around from assignment to assignment or a producer who organized the trips.

She plugged the tub and turned on the hot water with a bit of cold before pouring in a little lavender-scented bubble bath. Water running and fragrant bubbles forming, she turned to the antique cabinet topped with a container sink. She glanced into the oval mirror on the wall above it as she reached into the vanity to grab her cold cream. During a regular day, she wore little to no makeup, but during a job, she did. Now, all she wanted was for it to be gone.

Nora had been told that she was a beautiful woman, but she didn't agree or care. Her dark brown hair was cut into a short bob, one side usually tucked behind an ear. She had bright green eyes, which she knew were entirely too expressive. They got her into trouble. She had an average build and was a tad shorter than the average height of a woman, but she made up for it with a feisty attitude and loner mentality.

Smiling at her own thoughts, she pulled her hair back from her face with a headband then washed her face. Finished, she wiped up the water around the basin then stripped as she stepped into the tub and sank down beneath the suds.

Resting her head back against the warming cast iron, she closed her eyes and allowed her body to ease, her aches and pains from a bad back clenching from time to time until they began to release when the heat absorbed into her muscles.

As she began to relax further, her cell phone rang where it lay on the kitchen counter. Annoyed, she cracked her eyes open and glanced in that general direction. There was no way in hell she was going to leave paradise for a phone call.

⁂

Nora cringed as she took a closer look at the shot she'd taken two days before. Though Jamie had been inappropriate to comment on the bride's dress at the event, he wasn't incorrect. It honestly looked as though a burlesque dancer's outfit and that of Laura Ingalls decided to mate and Debra Spencer's wedding dress was the fruit of their passions.

Shaking her head, she continued through the shots. Despite the…interesting…outfit choices and the fact that the groom sported several facial tattoos, the couple somehow managed to be incredibly photogenic. They were playful and willing to try new things, which was always fun for Nora, as wedding shoots could get awfully boring and cookie cutter.

"Okay, Debra," she said, snatching one picture in particular, which she thought the bride would be thrilled with, "let's get this puppy looking perfect."

So involved with what she was doing, Nora flinched in startled surprise when her phone rang.

Sparing a glance to where it sat on the table behind her, she reached and her fingers stumbled around the tabletop until they touched it, her attention still on the computer screen.

"Hello?…Yes, this is Nora, who's this?…I'm sorry, I don't know a Penny Garcia, I think you've got the wrong num—" She sat up a little straighter in her chair, airbrushing forgotten. "Wait, what? How long?" She brought a hand up to her forehead, eyes falling closed. "What's the address?"

# *Chapter Two*

Jill Lacey laughed into the phone. "Edward, if you don't have the caterer from Oliver and Bethany's anniversary party, I'll never forgive you." She laughed again as she headed into the master bathroom, which was larger than most studio apartments. Her opened silk robe flowed behind her. "Yes, I realize the birthday party isn't until October 20, but there is no way I'm letting Paige have a better party for that ugly little daughter of hers than I'm having for the twins. I mean, come on, Edward," she said sweetly, observing herself in the large, wall-length mirror. "Sylvia and Tyler will only turn sixteen once." She smiled at what she'd heard on the other end of the line. "Good boy."

Ending the call, she tossed her phone onto the newly installed marble countertops with the double sinks. The exquisite white stone was also used on the floor and the walls of the standup shower, large enough for a party of four, should that be an interest.

For now, her thoughts were on the fact that the twins were back in school and it was a gray, rainy day, perfect for a lunchtime quickie. Right on time, she heard the front door open and the heavy tread of work boots heading up the massive winding staircase.

"Robert," she said, looking herself over one last time before hurrying back into the bedroom.

He was such a handsome man. Though she'd never found redheaded men attractive, there had been something about him that drove her wild, with his deep red hair and deep blue eyes. His smile, however, clinched it for her. That and he was a fantastic lover.

Reaching down to open her robe, she posed herself on the bed, a welcoming smile on her lips.

❧❧❧❧

Sated and freshly-showered, Robert had gone back to work, and Jill moved through the 6,500-square-foot house. Earlier that morning Ezra, the housekeeper, had been by, and Jill wanted to make sure she'd gotten to everything Jill had asked her to do. She'd noticed over the past couple months, the woman who had been working for them for just shy of two years wasn't doing as thorough of a job. It was a big house, yes, but Ezra was paid fairly well for her efforts.

Pleased with what she found, she headed out to meet Bethany for their planned lunch.

"Hey, sorry I'm late," she said in a rush as she breezed into the bistro where Bethany was already seated and had a red wine sangria sitting in front of her. "I had issues with Ezra." A lie for sure, but she was embarrassed at the true reason for her tardiness. She set her purse down on the empty chair to her right as she sat across from Bethany. "Oh, that looks good!" She waved down a waiter who hurried over to them. "I'd like one of those, too, please."

"Yes, ma'am," he said before scurrying off to do her bidding.

She brushed blond hair away from her face and let out an exasperated breath. "What a day." She took the menu in her hands and opened it, glancing over the selections. "But," she added, glancing at the African-

American woman who had been her friend for a little under five years, "I did manage to get Eddie on the phone. I threatened to essentially neuter him if he didn't get me Carol and her people."

"Their food is so amazing," Bethany said, sipping her drink. They were quiet as the waiter lowered Jill's drink to the table then went on to take their food order. Once he'd left, Bethany raised her glass. "To a successful party for the twins."

Jill grinned and lightly clinked her glass to her friend's. They each took a sip, and she set her glass down. "It's going to be spectacular, best on the block, for sure."

"Are Sylvia and Tyler looking forward to it?"

"They are. Oh!" Jill exclaimed, slamming her palms against the table. "One of Tyler's teachers had the audacity to call me yesterday and tell me she's worried he won't graduate if he doesn't get a handle on his study habits now." She rolled her eyes. "Can you believe the nerve?"

"He's what, a sophomore? God," Bethany said, taking her drink in hand again. "Maybe if she'd do *her* job Tyler would be able to do his."

"Exactly what I told her. Bitch." Both their attentions were drawn to Jill's purse as her cell phone rang. She dug it out and rolled her eyes. "Not answering that."

"Who is it?"

"Nora."

"Are you guys fighting again?"

Jill chuckled. "When aren't we? She feels it's perfectly fine to criticize my life and my marriage." She leaned slightly forward. "Can you believe she bought that old run-down farmhouse on Nicholson Road? I mean, who does that?" The phone rang again, Nora's name showing up for a second time. "Figure it out, Nora," Jill said, sipping her drink. The two women continued chatting when Jill's phone rang again. This time it was Sylvia. With an annoyed sigh, she answered. "Hey, honey. I'm at lunch with Bethany. What's up?" She used her free hand to pick her fork through her salad as she listened to what her daughter was telling her. "Honey, she tried to call me already. You know we're not talking to Aunt Nora right now, so—" She put the bite into her mouth and chewed. Finely arched eyebrows drew together. "What do you mean, it's important? I'm not calling her, Sylvia...I see." Jill let out a heavy sigh. "Yes, I'll call her back."

# *Chapter Three*

Downs!" Coach Schaeffer yelled, his voice booming in the large gymnasium. He blew his whistle, and the entire football team came to a stop from their forced run around the perimeter, many of them bending over with hands on knees as their chests heaved. "Get over here!" The varsity player jogged over to where the coach stood behind the podium in the corner where he was working on plays for the first game in a week.

"Yeah, Coach?"

LJ Schaeffer looked at the kicker over the rims of his reading glasses. "Seriously, Randy?" he asked in a quiet, yet firm voice. "You're going on your third year on this team and you decide it's a good idea to walk during a run?"

The kicker crossed his arms over his chest and glanced away, one hand coming up to stroke his attempt at a beard, which was more like patches of scraggly hair than a badge of masculinity.

"And another thing, if you want to be on this team," the coach growled, "you're going to look like a man, not a homeless person. Get that crap under control, or I'll find someone who would be happy to be a respectable face of this team." When Schaeffer felt he wasn't being heard, he grabbed the teen by the front of his shirt. "Got me?" Noting the player's quick nod and wide eyes, he dropped his hand and turned away from him, effectively dismissing him.

Lawrence Schaeffer, Jr. noticed a figure walking toward him across the gym, shined Gucci shoes reflected in the polished wood floor. He dropped his pencil and watched the man approach, a man who looked as though he'd stepped out of a Jos. A. Bank commercial. "Andrew."

"Lawrence," the man said, offering a hand in greeting as he reached the coach, who took his hand, eyeing him uncertainly. The walking Armani model looked around at the players. "What, these boys too good to run out on the field?"

LJ glanced at his players. "Well, unless you want an entire team of lightning rods with the storm outside." He gave him the best smile he could.

Seeming to ignore his retort, Andrew said, "I dropped by to pick up Sylvia after theater practice, on my way home from work. Jill wanted me to let you know she received a call from Nora."

Heavy medium-brown eyebrows drew together. "Nora? I thought Nora wasn't talking to her."

Andrew Lacey grinned, his dark good looks striking in his unwavering deep blue gaze. He looked more like John Stamos than the high-powered attorney he was. "When *are* they talking?"

"True enough. So, what did she want?"

"Well"—Andrew rocked on his heels for a moment as he tucked his hands into his pants pockets—"some sort of family matter, an emergency of sorts. Not exactly sure."

LJ reached up and rubbed the back of his neck before he readjusted his baseball cap, which bore the logo of the high school he coached and taught at. "Okay. Where? When?"

"Tonight at Nora's place, seven thirty."

LJ blew out a breath, thinking of what he was supposed to be doing that night at home. At last, he nodded. "All right. I'll be there."

"Wonderful. I'll let Jill know. See you there, Lawrence," Andrew said as he headed out of the gym, walking right through the crowd of running football players, a few of the boys running into each other to avoid running into him.

LJ watched him go then grabbed the whistle that hung down his chest. He brought it to his lips and blew, the shrill sound echoing in the cavernous expanse. "Hit the showers!"

⚜⚜⚜⚜

LJ pulled his black Dodge Ram extended cab into the driveway of the four-bedroom house he shared with his wife, Adrienne and their daughter, Kristie, who was a senior at Pueblo West High School, where he taught.

Cutting the engine, LJ removed his baseball cap and ran a hand through his hair, making it stand up at strange angles. He glanced up at the house—the light was on in the master bedroom. He sighed, trying to will his hand to remove his keys from the ignition and get his other one to pull the handle to open the door. Neither happened.

Distantly he noticed a pair of headlights wash across the back of his truck and into the cab before they were gone. A moment later, he jumped, startled at the tapping on his window. There, grinning at him, stood his seventeen-year-old daughter.

He rolled his eyes and opened the door. She moved aside then returned to her place. "Hey, you."

"What up, Dad?"

"Well, apparently you're trying to give me a heart attack," LJ responded.

"Lord, you better not," Kristie said dramatically. "Then I'll be stuck with her." She nodded toward the house.

"Hey, be nice," LJ said, as much "dad" in his voice as he could muster. He climbed out of his truck and slammed the door closed, exactly as Adrienne had asked him to do. How else was she to know he was home? That is, since he wasn't allowed to park "that huge, hulking truck" in the garage next to her beloved BMW.

He followed his only child inside, noting her baggy black cargo pants and fitted quarter-sleeve shirt with horizontal stripes. Her naturally medium-brown hair, now dyed black—which nearly got her crucified by her mother—was cut into a short, choppy style. Most of the time he wasn't sure what to make of her style, but if it was up to him, he'd let her just be her. Kristie was in a constant battle with her mother, though.

They entered the house, which was nicely appointed, but not too extravagant. Adrienne's car was what they'd spent the most money on in the past five years of their twenty-year marriage. They'd met their senior year of high school and, after going off to college together and five years of dating, Adrienne had given him an ultimatum: either he propose, or she find someone else to put a ring on it. Feeling he'd never find anyone else, he'd dropped to one knee.

Father and daughter went in opposite directions as Kristie headed to her bedroom in the basement and LJ climbed the stairs to his own bedroom on the second floor.

"I don't know, Karen," Adrienne said into her cell phone, walking by in her silk slip as LJ reached the bedroom doorway. "I still think we have a huge problem with Jorge for Tuesday's school board meeting." She walked over to her walk-in closet. LJ's was on the opposite side of the room.

Heading to the bed, he sat down, exhausted after a long day. He removed his baseball cap and set it on the comforter next to him. His attention was caught when his wife let out a bark of laughter.

"Oh! Right?" she grabbed her discarded blazer and tossed it into the bin for dry cleaning. "Can you seriously imagine that old bastard actually signing off on a new textbook committee next year?" She glanced over at LJ, hard brown eyes on his baseball cap.

Mapping the direction of her glare, LJ let out an irritated sigh and grabbed his hat, holding it in his lap. After all, it might get sweat on the expensive comforter. Tired of waiting for her to get off the phone, he pushed up from the bed and walked over to his own much smaller closet and tugged open the door. His hamper sat right inside the door, so he tugged his T-shirt off over his head and tossed it haphazardly inside.

Shirtless, LJ walked toward the master bath for a quick shower only to be stopped by his wife's sharp words.

"No, Larry. I need a soak."

He turned to her still standing at her closet, the phone held to her neck. "And I need a quick shower. It'll take me like two minutes."

"Larry," she said with a heavy sigh. "I've had a long day dealing with teachers, school board members, and budget issues. I don't want an audience. Okay?"

Hands on hips, LJ turned away, irritation making his jaw muscles pulse.

"Larry, you get to play all day—"

"Fine!" he exclaimed, hands up in supplication. He didn't even look at her as he stormed back to his closet and grabbed a pair of jeans and fresh T-shirt and underclothes then headed out of the room.

After a quick shower in the guest bath downstairs, LJ dressed and smoothed his hair back with a comb before exiting. He found Kristie sitting at the kitchen island, phone in hand and chomping on chewing gum.

"Mom texted," she said absently, scrolling through her text messages.

Standing at the Sub-Zero fridge to grab a cold bottle of water, LJ glanced back over his shoulder at his daughter. "What?"

"Yup," the teen affirmed. She glanced up at him over her phone. "Said you need to get the pork chops started. She's tired and not cooking tonight."

"When does she?" he muttered, running a hand through damp hair. He turned to her. "Tell her..." He shook his head, slapping his palm on the granite countertop as he made his way around it. "Never mind."

Heading upstairs, he was ready to tell Adrienne what he had to do. He entered the bedroom and heard drips of water as Adrienne moved around in her bubble bath. As he stepped into the large master bath, he glanced down at his wife who lay with her head resting against the raised back, eyes closed.

Leaning back against the wall, he crossed his arms over his chest and adjusted his stance a few times, trying to pump himself up for added confidence.

"What, Larry?" Adrienne murmured, eyes still closed. "I told you I don't want an audience."

"Kristie got your message," he began, voice weaker than he'd like. He cleared his throat. "Andrew came in tonight."

"What does that have to do with dinner?" she asked, opening her eyes to glance at him.

"I have to head out to Nora's place."

"What? Jill said Nora was blowing off the entire family."

"Who knows." LJ moved over to sit on a small stool where Adrienne put her folded towel, ready for when she exited the tub. He placed the fluffy softness on his lap. "But, I guess something has happened. We're all supposed to meet at Nora's."

"And, what about dinner?"

He hung his head for a moment, managing to keep his ire in check. "I can grab something on the way home."

"Do you know how hungry we'll be, Larry?" she said, partially rising out of the suds, exposing the tops of her breasts.

"Well, then why don't you guys come with me? Or better yet, Kristie can handle it. Why don't you come with me?" he said, growing excited by his idea. "We can deal with whatever at Nora's place then go to dinner, just us. It's been forever since—"

Adrienne waved him off. "Forget it. You crawl off to do your sister's bidding and Kristie and I will figure it out." She met his gaze with a pointed one of her own. "Maybe we'll go out and grab a nice dinner."

He looked away, stung.

She sank back into the bath. "You might as well ask Nora if you can crash in her guest bedroom while you're at it. She seems to be the family you give two shits about tonight, anyway."

Without a word, for fear of what he'd say, he tossed her towel back onto the stool and stormed out of the bathroom.

# *Chapter Four*

Nora glanced around the lower level of her home, knowing it would be looked over with a fine-tooth comb. She stood in the middle of the living room, hands on hips. Her cheeks blew out for a moment like a squirrel gathering nuts before she let out the nervous breath she was holding.

She could smell the coffee brewing in the kitchen and the remnants of the blueberry muffins she'd baked earlier. Tucking her hair behind an ear, she headed into the kitchen when she heard tires crunching on the gravel of her driveway.

Running her hands down over her red fitted tee, she headed to the kitchen door as she heard footfalls and voices coming closer. Not wanting to seem too anxious to answer the door or like she'd actually been waiting, she ducked into the bathroom for a moment. She closed her eyes and grounded herself, taking several deep breaths. Not surprised to hear a firm knock at the screen door, she waited a second before stepping over to it with a broad smile.

"Sorry," she said, pushing open the door to allow Andrew and Jill inside. "Wasn't sure I heard you guys knock."

Jill gave her a weak smile before passing in front of her followed by her husband. Both were dressed casually, yet they still managed to look like they'd stepped out of a magazine. Though not the biggest fan,

Nora was glad to see Andrew with her older sister—the oldest of the Schaeffer siblings. He'd acted as a buffer more than once.

"Uh," she said, feeling unsure in her own home, which pissed her off to no end, "would you guys like some coffee? Muffins?"

"Coffee would be great, Nora," Andrew said with a charming smile.

"Sure. How do you like it?" she asked, ignoring her sister's glare at her husband.

"Black is fine."

Nora was preparing his coffee when she heard more tires crunching. The window above the kitchen sink showed her father's gunmetal gray Escalade pull in behind Andrew's Mercedes. She had to smirk—her country driveway had been turned into an insecure man's parking lot. She turned away from the window, steeling herself from the vacuum that was her father's presence.

"Here ya go, Andy," she said softly, setting the steaming mug down in front of her brother-in-law where he and Jill sat at the kitchen table. She mentally counted down to seven before the kitchen door burst open and her father appeared.

"What the hell is all this nonsense about?" he roared, dressed in the tracksuit that Nora had known him to wear since she was eleven. Before that, it was pads and cleats, Denver Broncos blue and orange. "Why the hell are we out here in the damn boonies, squished into a goddamn shoebox instead of at Jill's place or mine?" He walked over to where his eldest daughter was seated, cupping the side of her head as he pressed it to his side. Leaning down, he left a kiss on her crown. "Hello, sweetie," he said. He looked to Nora with questions in his small hazel eyes.

"I need you to keep your voice down," she said evenly, despite bubbling with irritation inside. When she heard a knock, she glanced at the kitchen door and waved LJ inside.

"Hey, sis." He walked over to stand near her. "Hey, all. So, what's going on? Why are we all here?"

"Because I didn't want to wake Bella," Nora responded, eyeing each of them.

"Bella?" Andrew said, hands on his hips. "Is Shannon here?"

Nora shook her head, meeting his gaze. "No. That's why I called you guys here."

Lawrence, Sr. took a step forward, his stance wide. "Where the hell is she?" he boomed. He gave Nora a contrite look when she glared at him.

"She's missing." The silence that followed would have been amusing in the typically loud, boisterous family if the situation weren't so serious. She looked at each of them, her gaze going back to Jill as she pulled her cell phone out of her purse.

"I don't know what you're in such a fuss about, Nora," she said, perusing something on the large screen. "She's probably off with one of her boyfriends or something."

"Leaving her five-year-old daughter alone? For two days?" Nora challenged, her anger building. She felt LJ's hand on her shoulder. She didn't look at him, but it did calm her.

"This is ridiculous," Jill said, running her finger over the screen of her phone before pressing the device against her ear. Everyone watched her as a moment later she pulled it away. "Straight to voicemail."

"You don't say," Nora drawled.

"How did you end up with Bella?" Andrew asked, reaching for his cup of coffee.

"A woman named Penny Garcia. She's one of Shannon's neighbors. Apparently she gave Mrs. Garcia my number in case…Well, I guess just in case."

"In case of what?" Lawrence, Sr. barked. "She ain't gone at night. She's working for that car dealer or whatever. Daytime stuff. Jill here helped her get that job."

"My contractor, Daddy," Jill interjected.

"Contractor," the patriarch corrected. "Answering phones and stuff."

"Guys, I know exactly what you do right now," Nora said, folding her arms across her chest. "I don't know. I thought she was doing okay, too."

"She's upstairs now?" LJ asked softly, pointing to the ceiling. At Nora's nod, he pardoned himself and headed up the narrow, steep staircase to the second floor.

"Jill, call your contractor friend and see if she's been to work. Dad, if you can, head up to Colorado Springs and see if you can check out her apartment."

"Yes, I can see if Robert is available to chat." She eyed Nora. "And, what exactly are you going to be doing?" Jill asked, arching a brow.

"Raising her kid."

❧❧❧❧

"Those were some seriously good muffins, sis," LJ said, loading the last of the coffee cups and saucer plates into the dishwasher.

Nora smiled. "Thanks. Figured if I could plug some pieholes, might make tonight easier."

LJ chuckled, closing the dishwasher after he added a soap pod and pushing the button to start the load.

"So, how's Kristie?" Nora asked, glancing over her shoulder as she wiped down the table.

LJ shrugged as he crossed his arms over his chest and leaned back against the counter. Finished with her task, Nora stood and studied him, watching his face. She knew he and Adrienne had struggled to understand their daughter—Adrienne far more than her brother.

"She's her own person, I guess," he said. "Not sure what else to say."

"Is that a bad thing, LJ?" She rinsed out her dishrag before slapping it on the rim of the farmhouse sink to dry.

He let out a heavy sigh as he stared down at his tennis shoes for a minute. "I don't know. I honestly don't know anymore, Nor."

Nora studied him for a long moment. "I've missed you, Larry," she said softly. When he met her gaze, she gave him her usual smile. "Have you eaten? Well," she said with a flamboyant wave, "other than my amazing muffins, that is."

"Nah, I was going to grab something on the way home." He looked away.

She let out a heavy sigh and shook her head. "Adrienne again, huh? What, did she send you out into the woods on your own, pissed that you weren't there to wait on her?"

He glared at her, fire in his eyes. "You don't understand, Nora."

"What's not to understand? When are you going to stand up to her? When are you going to allow you and your daughter a peaceful life without the authoritarian making every move for you?" Nora regretted her words as soon as they were out of her mouth. She quietly cursed herself when her big brother stormed out of the house. She knew she had to follow. "LJ—"

"What the hell do you know about dealing with it, Nora?" he said, halfway to his truck, standing little more than twenty feet from her. "What the hell do you know about having to come home and there's someone else there that you have no choice but to answer to? Think about? Who has to rely on you, huh?"

She hurried over to him, her face inches from his. "Our little sister's five-year-old daughter!" she hissed. She pointed to the second story of her house. "That little girl up there has no idea what happened to her mother, Lawrence. And guess what? Neither do I! She's missing!" Nora felt the tears sting behind her eyes. She looked away, bringing up a hand to swipe at her emotion. "She's vanished and I don't know what to do about it."

Without a word, LJ turned away and stormed to his truck. He gave her a final glance before he climbed in and drove away, leaving her gravel drive empty.

"Damn," she whispered, hoping that of anyone, she'd have an ally in LJ.

Turning to the house, she exhaled in a whoosh. She was suddenly tired and wanted nothing more than to go to sleep.

❧ ❧ ❧ ❧

LJ slowed his truck as he pulled into the drive-thru of the burger joint. He was truly an asshole. Braking behind the car ahead of him, he ran a shaky hand through his hair. As right as his little sister was—

as usual—he struggled dealing with her directness. He always had.

But still, he knew she meant well.

Pulling out his phone, he studied his apps. He remembered Kristie had been messing with his phone a few weeks ago and mentioned something called Snapchat. Glancing up, he moved up a bit as the car ahead of him did. When he looked back down at his phone, he remembered what his daughter had told him about it.

"Okay, I can do this," he said, logging into the app. Again, he lifted his head to move the car mere inches and returned to the app. He typed out the message.

*"Hey, sis. Sorry about earlier. Here's my chef for the night."*

Nora chuckled as she got a round-robin shot of the fast food drive-thru line and menu. "Stupid son-of-a-bitch," she said from her bed. "Could have had a home-cooked meal."

*"Love you, Nor. I'm sorry."*

"Me, too."

# *Chapter Five*

LJ maneuvered his truck into the parking lot of the apartment complex, which consisted of three three-story buildings with a walkway that ran along the dark brown-painted doors and stairs on either end to the lower or upper floors. He pulled the large truck into a parking space and cut the engine.

"Damn," his passenger said. "Pretty run-down."

LJ glanced over at his daughter and nodded as he returned his focus to the building before them: Shannon's building. "Yeah. I guess let's go have a look-see."

LJ had gotten Penny Garcia's number from Nora, and they'd scheduled a time for LJ and Kristie to pick up the spare key to Shannon's apartment so they could check things out.

"Okay," Kristie said, following her dad up the stairs to the third floor. "Apartment thirty-four."

Glancing over at his daughter, her expression as concerned and uncertain as his, LJ raised his hand and knocked firmly on the door before them. A moment later, a Hispanic woman answered, her long, black hair tucked up into a messy bun. She looked from father to daughter with a question in her dark eyes.

"Yes?"

"Hello, Mrs. Garcia," LJ said, extending his hand. "Larry Schaeffer and my daughter, Kristie. We spoke on the phone?"

"Oh, yes! Come in, please."

LJ stood aside to let his daughter enter before him then stepped inside, closing the door to the small two bedroom. A cursory glance showed him a run-down unit, though it was obvious the tenant was doing her best as it was clean and fairly neat.

"You two can sit here," Penny said, her Spanish accent thick. "Coffee?"

"No, thank you." LJ gave her a polite smile, wanting to get into the apartment. He did have questions, though. "Do you mind if I ask a few things?"

"No," Penny Garcia said, leaving the room briefly before reentering with a solitary key, which she held out to him.

He took it, enfolding the brass object in his hand, almost as though he were enfolding his youngest sibling's hand within his own. "What happened?" he asked sagely, still looking down at the hand that held Shannon's key.

"Well, Shannon told me she was going out and she'd be back. Promised she'd text me when she got back, so I knew the baby was safe. Anyways, I never heard nothing from her and fell asleep. Next day, I was out all day with my son, Ronnie, and his girlfriend and forgot about it. You know, Ronnie is a truck driver, so he's all over the place, so when he's in town, I grab him for some time." She reached over and snatched a tissue from the box of Kleenex on the side table, lightly dabbing at her eyes. "I didn't know," she said quietly. "But, next morning, I heard the baby crying."

LJ cleared his throat softly as he felt his own emotions rising, his concern for Shannon growing. "It's okay," he said, reaching over and patting Penny's knee.

"I didn't think nothing of it," she continued. "You know little kids, they cry. But, when I kept hearing her, I knew something was wrong. I tried calling Shannon, but it went to her voicemail, so I was worried, you know? Bella really began to cry when I knocked on the door." Tears rolled down her cheeks. "I came back here and got the key," she said, indicating LJ's closed hand. "I went back and Bella was all alone." She began to full-out cry.

Kristie met her dad's gaze before she moved over to sit next to the upset woman, a hand on her back. "It's okay," she said softly.

Penny met Kristie's concerned gaze. "I didn't know she was all alone, Miss Kristie."

"I know."

Penny took several deep breaths before wiping her eyes and face. "So," she continued, "I brought her here and called Nora."

LJ stroked his chin. The stubble told him he needed to shave. "Where was she going? Did she say?"

Penny Garcia looked away. "A date," she said, though there wasn't a lot of conviction behind her tone.

"A date?" LJ asked, confused. Then, his stomach dropped. "She's not…"

"I won't talk badly about Shannon when she's not here to defend herself," the neighbor said, looking down at her fidgeting hands in her lap, as though unable to meet LJ's gaze.

❧ ❧ ❧ ❧

LJ was so afraid to see what lay beyond the brown door, but he knew he had to. He felt better that his daughter was with him. Turning the key he'd inserted into the lock, he turned the knob and pushed. This time, however, not sure what they'd find, he entered first, holding up a hand behind him to halt Kristie. He took a step or two in, eyes everywhere. He listened and heard nothing but a ticking clock somewhere deeper inside the apartment.

Allowing Kristie to join him, LJ walked into the small living area, shocked at the mess he encountered. He knew his youngest sister wasn't the greatest housekeeper on the planet, but this was even beyond her. Toys everywhere, as well as opened boxes of cereal and cookies. He figured that was from Bella, finding easy things to eat while alone. He also spotted several empty juice boxes littering the floor and couch.

"Damn," Kristie said. "I've never seen Aunt Shannon's place this gross before."

"Well, I think a lot of this was Bella," LJ said quietly. They both spoke in hushed tones, almost as though afraid to disturb something. "She was alone in here for at least a day and a half."

They headed farther inside back to the hallway, which led to the bedrooms and one bathroom. Bella's bedroom was like any five-year-old's bedroom. Shannon's bedroom, however, looked as if she'd left in a hurry. Her bed was made, but it was messy, as though Bella had been rolling around on it or something had been lying on the comforter. The bathroom was a disaster, makeup scattered all over the small vanity top.

"Looks like she was in a rush," Kristie said, leaning in from the hallway.

LJ nodded. "Yeah." He sighed and met her gaze. "Ready to go?"

"Yup."

❧❧❧❧

In the truck on the way back to Pueblo from Shannon's apartment in Colorado Springs, LJ's mind was filled with thoughts, worries, and consternation. He sensed his daughter's gaze on him, which helped to break him out of his thoughts. He glanced over at her.

"What?"

"What did Mrs. Garcia mean by 'date'?" she asked, the word in air quotes. "The look on your face told me it wasn't exactly meeting the guy down the street for dinner."

LJ let out a heavy sigh and reached up, readjusting the baseball cap he wore. He'd never spoken to Kristie about Shannon, who was only eleven years older than the high school senior. Very much a late-in-life baby for his parents.

"She's had a rough go of it," he began, sparing her a glance as he pulled up to a red traffic light. "Starting when she was around your age."

❧❧❧❧

Pueblo, Colorado – 2005

"Damn! Great game. Love me some Pats!" Larry, Sr. exclaimed, slapping his son so hard on the back LJ nearly took a header into the wall.

Annoyed and so ready to go home after a long day watching the Super Bowl with his father and his friends, LJ gave his dad a weak smile. "Yup. I was rooting for the Eagles, but yes, your Patriots did their thing." He walked over to the chair where he'd left his jacket when he'd arrived earlier that evening. "Where's Shannon?"

"Out with friends," Larry, Sr. said, taking a swig from his fresh beer.

"Dad, it's after eleven. Isn't it a little late for her to still be out?" LJ said nothing else as his father waved off his concern. "Well, I gotta get. See you later, Pops."

Stepping out into the brisk early February night, LJ headed for the minivan he and Adrienne had bought after the birth of their daughter, five years before. He dug his keys out of his jacket pocket when he noticed a sedan parked across the street with a man sitting behind the wheel. His head was resting back against the seat, and it looked as though he were in complete rapture.

"Jeez, dude," LJ muttered to himself. "Couldn't even wait until you got home, huh?" He chuckled and walked across the snow-covered lawn to his minivan when he saw that, not only did a woman sit up straight in the passenger seat, a tissue in hand as she wiped her mouth, but that woman was his fifteen-year-old sister Shannon. Stunned, he watched as the man handed her what looked to be money.

Outrage overtook him as he stormed across the street and yanked open the car door, pulling the startled man out of the sedan before he'd even buttoned and zipped his pants. LJ sent him reeling with a left hook to the guy's jaw.

"LJ!" Shannon shrieked as she hurried out of the car as quickly as her tight skirt and high heels would allow.

LJ grabbed the man by the front of his sweatshirt and pulled him to his feet, only to send him flying back into his car with a haymaker. "You sick son-of-a-bitch!" he roared at the bleeding man, who was at least thirty. "She's a fifteen-year-old kid!"

The man looked at Shannon with wide eyes before nearly diving into his car, the door barely closed before he squealed out of the neighborhood.

He turned to Shannon who looked defiantly up at him. "What the fuck do you think you're doing?" he said, his voice nearly a roar. "Please tell me that was not what I think it was." He reached down and ripped the twenty-dollar bill out of her hand and waved it in front of her face. "*Is* it?"

It was only then that Shannon looked contrite. She glanced down at her shuffling feet but said nothing.

LJ let out a heavy sigh and knelt down to pick up Shannon's purse, which she'd dropped when she'd run over to the man. He reached out to gather the scattered things that had come out upon impact: a pair of sunglasses, tube of lipstick, her house keys, and a clear plastic sandwich baggie. He picked it up and examined the contents.

"Is this why you were doing that?" he asked, holding the baggie up for Shannon to see. "Pot? Is that what this is for?" he asked, again waving the money. Disgusted, he unzipped the baggie and shoved the money inside with the three rolled marijuana joints and stuck it in her purse before handing it all back to her.

❧ ❧ ❧ ❧

Three days later, LJ was in his classroom where he taught English and Literature when he was coaching football. The day was over and the kids had all left, leaving him to finish up grading a few of the tests they'd taken the previous period. He glanced up when the classroom door was opened.

Shannon walked in, dressed casually in a pair of jeans and a loose button-up shirt. She truly was a stunning young woman with delicate features, a petite frame, and long, auburn hair that flowed down her back.

"Hey, LJ," she said quietly, walking over to his desk where she set down the two textbooks and notebook she was carrying.

"Hey, kiddo," he responded, voice calm and even. He was still deeply troubled by what had happened the previous Sunday and what he'd witnessed and discovered. He hadn't mentioned anything to his wife because, frankly, he was deeply embarrassed for Shannon. "How'd you do on that math test?"

She shrugged, resting her hip against the edge of her desk. "Okay, I guess. I know Mr. Nunez doesn't like me, so…We'll see, I guess."

He nodded, not sure what to say. Truth was, he didn't like Troy Nunez at all.

"Look, the reason I stayed after today was to come talk to you without Adrienne being around."

LJ sat back in his chair. "I understand."

Shannon briefly met his gaze with her emerald-green eyes before looking away, her fingers playing nervously with a dry-erase marker from the whiteboard mounted on the wall behind LJ's desk. "I want to apologize for the other night. Like, I don't even know how that happened or how I got caught up in it with that guy, you know?"

"Who is he?"

"His name is Alex or Allen, something like that. I don't really know him. Sunday was I think only the second or third time I'd ever seen him."

"He's obviously not a student here," LJ said, indicating the school around them.

Shannon shook her head. "No. He's old, like almost thirty-five or something." She glanced up at her older brother, who was thirty-one. "Sorry," she said, giving him the smile that had melted his heart since she'd been a little girl. She quickly sobered. "I promise that'll never happen again, LJ. Honestly."

He nodded, sitting forward in the squeaky wooden chair. "Shannon," he said softly, reaching across the desk to take the marker from her fidgeting fingers and tuck them in his larger hand. "You are an absolutely beautiful young woman. I was thinking that right when you walked in. You have the singing voice of an angel and, even though you're only halfway through your freshman year, Mrs. Barr already wants you for the starring role in the end-of-year play."

"Really?" she asked, eyes wide. He nodded and grinned. "Oh my God!" she gushed, hurrying around the desk to plop down in her brother's lap and hug him so hard it hurt.

He hugged her back and gave her a noisy kiss on her cheek, like he had since she was a baby. His smile grew when that made her giggle. "You've got a lot going for you, kid. Don't screw it up or I'll have to hunt you down."

She grinned and looked at him. "I love you, LJ."

"Love you, too."

※ ※ ※ ※

LJ looked down into his cup of coffee, his daughter sitting quietly across from him at the small diner they'd stopped at. He hadn't thought of that time in Shannon's life in a lot of years, and in all honesty, it kind of hurt, even now.

"Dad? You okay?"

He glanced up at Kristie, who was halfway through her piece of banana cream pie. He nodded. "Yeah. I guess."

"How come nobody told me about all the issues Aunt Shannon has? Had….Has, I guess."

"I don't know," he said with a heavy sigh, sitting back against the vinyl of their booth. "I guess partly because it wasn't exactly my story to tell or share, but mostly, if I'm honest with myself and with you…mostly I think we all hoped she'd eventually pull it together. Especially after Bella was born."

"I thought she had," Kristie said, forking herself another bite of pie.

"So did I."

# *Chapter Six*

Ma'am, I've told you, as a twenty-seven-year-old woman, your sister has the right to walk away, disappear, or anything else. Since she's an adult, we cannot open a missing person's case until she's been missing for—"

"She left her five-year-old daughter alone in the apartment for more than two days! Is that something a grown-ass woman would do to disappear or walk away from her life?" Nora exclaimed, palms flat on the front counter at the Pueblo Police Department. "My sister is missing, damn it, and I need someone to listen to me!"

The officer at the desk eventually sighed, raising his hands in supplication. "Okay. Hold on." He pushed up from his chair and stepped away.

Left alone, Nora hugged herself and let out an agitated sigh. She walked over to a wall in the lobby that was filled with plaques dedicated to officers killed in the line of duty. She absently read the names as she waited.

"Miss Schaeffer?"

Nora turned to see the officer she'd been speaking to standing at a solid metal door that led deeper into the police department and required the person to be buzzed in from inside.

"If you'll follow me."

She was led through a maze of hallways until they ended up in front of a small room. A sign next to the opened door indicated it was Interview Room 2.

"Go ahead and have a seat, Miss Schaeffer. Someone will be with you in a minute," the officer said before heading back the way they'd come.

The room was small and square with a partial wall serving as a two-way mirror, a metal table at the center, and three chairs—two on one side, one on the opposite. She took the single chair and sat down. She assumed this would be the room a suspect would be taken to for interrogation and couldn't help but think of all the cop shows she'd seen over the years.

Tucking her hair back behind her ear, she removed her phone from her purse, which she'd set on the table. She sent off a quick text to check in with Jamie, who was sitting with Bella for her. Based on his response, she was confident that all was well, and she set her phone aside and waited, though she didn't have to wait long. A few moments later, the door was opened and someone stepped through.

"Sorry to keep you waiting, Miss Schaeffer, but I—"

Nora was struck dumb as she looked into dark, chocolate-brown eyes. She took in the long, nearly black hair that was pulled back in a chignon. The trim figure dressed in a women's-cut suit. The lovely face that had haunted her for far too many years, still stunning.

The detective closed the door softly behind her, keeping her back to Nora for a moment longer than necessary before turning around and walking confidently to the chairs across the table from Nora. She sat, placing her notebook and capped pen on the tabletop before meeting Nora's shocked gaze.

"I'm Detective Sarah Sanchez. I work in the

missing person's unit." She looked away and cleared her throat before a brief smile touched her lips, and she shook her head at whatever she was thinking. At last, she met Nora's gaze again. "Hello, Nora."

"Hi," Nora said softly, mentally shaking herself out of her stupor.

"I hadn't heard you came back home."

Nora was surprised at the avalanche of guilt that crashed over her but did her best to shake it off. This wasn't the time or place. "Yeah. A couple years ago."

"Well," Sarah said, all business as she flipped her notebook open to a blank page. She uncapped her pen and looked at Nora expectantly. "What's going on?"

"Shannon is missing."

Sarah began to write but stopped midsentence. She glanced up at Nora. "Shannon, little Shannon?"

Nora smiled. "She's not so little anymore. She's a twenty-seven-year-old mother."

Sarah's smile was brief before she was back to Detective Sanchez. "Okay, so tell me what happened."

❧❧❧❧

"That's Mommy?" Bella asked, eyes wide and excitement in her voice.

"It sure is. Here, she was only a little bit older than you," Nora said, lightly touching the five-year-old on the nose with her fingertip, making her niece giggle. "And, in this one"—Nora turned the page of the photo album as she and Bella sat cuddled together on the couch—"she was a snowman in the play she was in."

"What's a play mean?" the girl asked, looking up at her aunt.

"Well, it's..." Nora thought about it, wondering

how on earth to explain this to a five-year-old. "Okay," she said, inspired. "You know when you and your friends are playing house or Barbies? You make up a story?" At Bella's nod, Nora continued. "That's kind of what a play is. It's a story that somebody writes and other people pretend and act it out."

"Oh!"

Nora brought up a hand and smoothed back messy brown hair. Bella's smile was so much like her mother's, as was her charm. She truly was the spitting image of Shannon but with a different hair color.

"I think it's time for bed, little one," she said softly. "We can look at more pictures tomorrow."

"Can I sleep in your bed?"

Nora left a loud kiss on her forehead. "Yes, you can."

"Aunt Nora?"

"Yeah, sweetie?" Nora asked, closing the photo album and setting it on the coffee table. She stood and reached upward as she stretched out her back.

"Is Mommy coming back?"

She stopped midstretch and looked down at the little girl who still sat on the couch. She gave her the bravest smile she could. "Absolutely."

❧❧❧❧

With Bella tucked safely and comfortably into Nora's bed, she headed back downstairs to clean up dinner dishes. She'd made spaghetti, and to her relief, Bella loved it, especially the homemade meatballs. She'd babysat her nieces and nephew before but hadn't been around a little one in quite some time. It was exhausting but definitely rewarding. Bella was a sweetheart and a joy.

She thought of Bella's question to her, and she too wondered if her mommy was coming back. Obviously she couldn't speak her own fears. There was no way for Nora to possibly know where her sister was, what had happened, and if she would return. All she could do was try to stay strong and positive for an innocent five-year-old girl who had no idea what was going on.

She'd spent twenty to thirty minutes with Sarah that afternoon telling her story as the detective wrote it all down. She'd had to shut her mind off about who she was talking to. Trying to forget was, of course, an impossible task.

"So, you became a detective, huh?" she said, smiling as she rinsed the last dish and loaded it into the dishwasher. "You always were ambitious, Sarah."

⁂

Pueblo, Colorado – 1995

"I am so sick of that woman, Shane," Nora sighed, sipping her Coke. "I honestly despise her. She's fairly okay with Shannon I guess, but she treats the rest of us like absolute shit."

"Yes, your dad unquestionably has some shit taste in women, that's for sure. I mean, like what's up with your mom? Who up and leaves her kids, especially when Shannon was all of what, like three?"

"Shane, can we please not sit here and bash my mother? It's already a fucked up enough situation as it is."

Nora's high school friend looked away. "Sorry." He dipped a couple French fries in his small paper cup of ketchup. "So, what are you going to do? Can you afford your own place?"

Nora shook her head and flung her long, brown hair back over her shoulders. "Nope. I don't get consistent hours at the library, and there's no way I can leave my apprenticeship with Layla to go full-time anywhere." She let out a frustrated sigh.

"Well," Shane said, wiping his fingers on the napkin that bore the fast food logo where they ate. "Darryl works with a chick who's a rookie cop, and I know she and her roommate are looking for a third. The last guy moved out a month or so ago and they're actively looking for someone to rent his room."

Nora rolled her eyes. "I do *not* want one roommate let alone two, Shane."

He shrugged, crumbling the wrapper that had been around his cheeseburger. "It's an option. It'll get you out of your dad's place." He reached for Nora's purse and dug out a pen and random envelope. "Here's Sarah's number. If you decide it's something you want to think about, give her a buzz. My brother said she's really nice."

❧ ❧ ❧ ❧

"So, obviously the place is furnished," Dr. Daniel Liu explained, the second-year resident indicating the mismatch of furnishings in the living room. "All you'd need is your own bedroom furniture." He led her through the small kitchen to a medium-sized room off of it, near the back door of the smallish three-bedroom house. "Now, this room does get more noise considering it is off the kitchen, but you do get your own bathroom." The handsome Asian man showed her the empty bedroom. "It's only a shower, so if you're a bath kinda girl, the bathroom Sarah and I use down the hall is always an option if we're not home. Which," he added, "is often. I work crazy hours at the hospital and Sarah works the night shift at the police department, so when she's home, it's usually to sleep during the day."

Nora nodded in acknowledgment, looking around the bedroom. It was easy to imagine her stuff in there. In a way, she kind of liked that it was away from the other two bedrooms, felt more private. "What's the rent?"

"We split everything three ways from rent to utilities, so rent is two seventy-five and utilities average between fifty and sixty bucks apiece." He gave her a winning smile and crossed his arms over his polo shirt-clad chest. "So? What do you think?"

Two days later, Nora used the key Daniel had given her after she'd signed the lease and paid her first month's rent to get into the quiet house. The first of the month was Sunday, but he'd told her it wouldn't be a big deal if she moved in Friday or Saturday. So, Friday night found her moving her limited items into her new home. Tonight she'd be sleeping bagging it. Shane would help her move the bed and dresser from her dad's house the next day.

With a grunt, she took her last load into the dark house, only her bedroom light on to show the way. She was excited. She'd only met Daniel thus far and liked him well enough. He seemed quiet and grounded, which was great. Though only nineteen, Nora was far too focused to be a party girl.

She reached the bedroom and, once inside, dropped the overstuffed trash bag of clothing she'd been lugging and allowed her heavy backpack to slide down her arms and hit the carpeted floor. With a relieved groan, she adjusted her shoulders and rolled her neck. This was the third trip she'd made. The only thing left was her sleeping bag and a pillow.

She hurried back through the house and out into the cool early autumn night to her car to grab the last of her stuff, only to realize it would take two more loads as the sleeping bag was so large and bulky.

"Damn it."

Grabbing it up in both arms, she hurried back awkwardly to the house, leaving the front door open as she made her way to her bedroom and dropped the packed sleeping bag on the floor. Turning around to head back out, she nearly had a heart attack.

"Freeze!"

Her hands instantly went up and eyes grew wide as she was presented with a woman blocking the doorway, legs in a wide stance and both hands wrapped around a pistol. She was dressed in police blue, her badge and name tag glinting off the overhead light.

"I'm a statue!" she said, barely daring to blink let alone breathe.

"Who are you?" the woman demanded, not moving a muscle.

"I'm Nora Schaeffer," she said. "My wallet is over there in my purse by the backpack. I live here."

The woman relaxed her stance somewhat, lowering the pistol but not putting it back in the holster. "Are you the new roommate?"

Nora nodded vigorously. "Daniel told me the house would be empty, so I could move in today or tomorrow if I wanted to. I came over after I got off work."

The woman grinned, securing her weapon before

sliding it back home on her utility belt. She stood up straight and walked over to Nora with her hand extended. "Sorry about that. I haven't seen him in the last few days, so I had no idea he'd said you could move in early. I wasn't expecting you until Sunday. I'm Sarah."

"Nora."

"Do you need help with anything?" Sarah asked, looking around at the scattered bags in the room.

"Nah. I need to grab my pillow and another duffel bag and I'm done. My friend and I will bring my bed and stuff tomorrow."

"Awesome. Well, welcome and again, sorry I scared you."

"Yeah, same here."

"Good night."

Left alone, Nora watched the policewoman go, noting a tall, shapely frame, her dark hair short and stylish. She looked to be a few years older than Nora and nice enough. She let out a heavy and tired breath before heading out for her final load of the night.

# *Chapter Seven*

Jill sat in her car, which was parked outside the country club where she knew her father was playing golf. She honestly had no idea why she felt as nervous as she did, but she knew she had to talk to him, get his thoughts.

Glancing in the rearview mirror before she exited the car, she saw that her hair and makeup were perfect, and the dangling diamond earrings her father had given her two years before were in place. Letting out a sigh, she opened her door and stepped out of the luxury sedan.

She looked more like she was about to play tennis than drive a golf cart for her father as she made her way to the white sidewalk and the building. Inside was a health club, swimming pool, restaurant and bar, and locker rooms.

"Good afternoon, Mrs. Lacey," the receptionist said, her thin, red-painted lips smiling to reveal extremely white teeth.

"Hello, Laura. My father is already out there, I'm guessing?"

"I believe he's out hitting some balls, Mrs. Lacey."

"Excellent."

Jill moved on, waving to various members of the community on the way. She and her husband, Andrew, had belonged to the country club for about four years, of course at the invite of her father. Larry Schaeffer was quite the fixture there.

"Jill! Wait up."

Jill stopped and turned as she stepped outside behind the large building, tennis courts to her left, golf course beyond a copse of trees to her right. She smiled instantly and put on the charm.

"Well, hello, William."

The tall, handsome blond reached her, tennis racket in hand. He was tanned and looked every bit the living Ken doll. He flashed his pearly whites at her. "I never got your call," he said, resting a large hand against the brick wall a foot behind where she stood.

"Well," she hedged coyly, "maybe that's because I never called you."

"But," he drawled, "I thought you wanted a quote on the new landscaping in your backyard. Remember? We spoke about the pool, water fountain feature…"

She glanced down at the gold cross he wore around his neck, visible in the open V of his white-and-blue-striped polo shirt. She reached up and ran her painted fingernail up and down the length of it. "I know but Andy is being cheap," she said, sparing a glance up into his eyes. "He had the audacity to mention that we just had the kitchen redone." She pouted. "So mean."

"I can certainly give you a good deal, and I do good work, you know," he said, lowering his voice enough to send a little twinge to her belly.

"I bet you do," she said, returning his smile. "Why don't you come by Wednesday afternoon, say around one thirty?" She dropped her hand from his cross and turned away, hips swaying enticingly as she headed to where she figured her father would be.

She spotted him in a golfing outfit she'd never

seen before, replete with baggy cotton pants, a pastel pink polo, and white golf cleats.

"Nice one, Daddy," she said, walking over to him once it was safe to not get beamed in the head by his club. He glanced over his shoulder at her.

"Thanks, Jill. Not as smooth as I like, but hey, only my fourth hit of the day." His leathery features broke into a smile as he gave a one-armed hug and kiss on her blond head. "You come to drive for me?"

"Of course."

"Where's Andy?" he asked, loading his clubs into his bag so they could walk over to his golf cart, which he owned and kept stored in the clubhouse.

"Oh, working on some new case," she said, waving off the question. "But, when isn't he?"

"Well, he's got to," Larry, Sr. said with a laugh. "How else are men like us supposed to keep women like you lookin' so good?"

"Daddy," she said, lightly pushing on his arm, the large man immoveable. They wandered on toward the golf cart, and her father loaded his clubs into the back before he hopped into the passenger seat, organizing his score sheet as she climbed in behind the wheel. As she got them moving, she glanced over at him a few times. She tucked her bottom lip beneath her upper teeth, trying to get the courage to ask.

"So, how're the party preparations coming?" he asked, glancing over at her briefly before reaching into the breast pocket of his polo to remove a pair of sunglasses, which he slid into place on his face.

"Good. Really good." She glanced at him again as she headed toward the first hole. "Daddy," she began, "are you worried about Shannon? This whole thing?"

"Nah." He glanced away as he pulled his golfing

gloves out from the small glove compartment of the cart. He looked at her, a smile on his face. "She'll turn up."

"But, Daddy, she left Bella all alone." Jill hit the brakes, bringing the cart to a stop.

"So says your sister, who," Larry, Sr. said as he climbed out of the cart, "I think is making a big to-do about nothin'. She's jumping the gun and getting everybody all worked up over a weekend tryst."

Not sure what to say, Jill glanced out over the lush emerald-green sea of lawn before them. Slightly nervous, she cleared her throat softly.

"Your youngest sister is a real beaut," Larry continued, tugging the club free that he intended to use to tee off. "Who wouldn't want to spend a long weekend with her, you know?"

Again, Jill cleared her throat. She sat and waited while her father set up his shot, wringing her hands in her lap. She winced when the large diamond of her wedding ring dug into her other hand.

"Oh, that was beautiful," Larry said as he watched his *thwacked* ball sail into the air. He walked back to the cart. "You know women leave, Jill." He eyed her over the tops of his sunglasses.

Jill looked away from him, hurt. "That's unfair, Daddy," she said quietly. "That was only two weeks and we were having problems."

"Yes, well"—he climbed back into the cart—"point still stands." As they headed toward the second hole and her father's ball, Larry, Sr. continued. "Like *your* mother, for instance. What the hell am I supposed to do with a damn kid, basically a toddler, let alone you guys? I'm a man. What the hell am I supposed to do?" he asked again.

"Be a father?" Jill nearly whispered, shocked the words had come out of her mouth.

"That's women's shit. I ain't no damn caretaker!" He seemed to ignore her comment. "As a man," he said, thumping himself in the chest with his thumb, "I bring home the money. Give a woman a house, all the shit she wants and give her something to do all day." He glanced over at his oldest. "Not my job."

Jill turned away, not sure what to say. All she knew was she wasn't there to talk about her mother who, twenty-five years before had packed up and left, but about her youngest sibling who had disappeared almost a week before.

"Good luck on your shot, Daddy," she said.

❧❧❧❧

Pueblo, Colorado – 1989

Jill leaned over and gave her boyfriend, Chris, a quick kiss before climbing out of his white Fiero. "I'll call you later," she said, rolling her eyes as she glanced up at her family house. "So lame I have to be back so early."

"Yeah. See you."

She hugged her purse and bag with the new shoes Chris had bought her that day on their Saturday afternoon date then closed the door of the small sports car and trotted up the front walk of the family home, which the Schaeffers had moved into eight months before. The family had lived in Cherry Hills, a wealthy area of Denver during their father's NFL career. He'd retired at the end of the previous season after an injury cut his thirteen-and-a-half-year career short.

Her new town, Pueblo, was okay, she supposed. Not like she or her siblings had a choice. So, now they lived in a posh—she supposed—area called University Park, which was near the university. She stepped up onto the large porch to the double front doors and pushed open one side to enter. Immediately she heard her father yelling at someone. She wondered who the lucky recipient was this time.

Deciding she didn't want to join in on the fun, she ducked out to the back stairs that would lead to the second floor she and her fourteen-year-old brother and twelve-year-old sister shared. Their parents had an entire suite on the third floor, where they weren't allowed.

When she saw LJ sitting in his room, she figured the yelling that echoed throughout the house had to be Nora or their mother. She stopped at his open doorway. "What's going on?"

He glanced up from a notebook he was writing in. As soon as he saw her, he flipped it closed and stashed it behind him. "Dunno. Some announcement or something. Dad's gonna be pissed that you're late."

She glanced down at her Swatch. "He told me to be here by three. It's like, three-twelve."

LJ met her gaze. "As I said, you're late."

She rolled her eyes and continued down the hall to her own bedroom. She'd just pushed open the door when she heard her father bellow up the stairs.

"Is she here, yet? Goddamn it, we don't have all damn day!"

"Yes, she's here, Dad," LJ said, his voice seeming to flow down the hall and to the top of the stairs. "She's been here for almost fifteen minutes."

Jill tossed her shoes towards the bed and ducked

her head into the hallway, sending a grateful smile to her brother's back.

"Oh. Well, you two get your asses down here."

Nora sat on the couch next to their mother, who was working on her ever-present needlepoint. Framed works hung all over the house. Nora was messing with the small, pink camera she'd been given the previous Christmas. The two older siblings pounded down the stairs and plopped down into the two fluffy armchairs. Larry, Sr. held court standing at the center of the room in front of the fireplace, long legs spread wide and big hands placed on his hips. His short-cropped hair was slicked back from his strong features.

"Judy," he said, his wife's head popping up from her task. Without a word, she set it aside and squeezed between the large square coffee table and Nora's legs to stand by him. She reached up and tucked some dark blond strands behind her ear, her green eyes dull and not focused on anyone or anything. His arm protectively, almost possessively, around her shoulders, he spoke. "We wanted to announce to you kids that we'll be adding another member of the family sometime late winter."

Jill glanced over at LJ then Nora then back at her parents. "What?"

"Havin' a baby," Larry, Sr. said with pride, standing up a little taller at a job well done. "Your mamma is going to be a mamma again."

Jill's gaze fell upon their naturally quiet mother to see her looking down at fidgeting hands that rested in front of a belly that would be growing soon. "Well, congratulations," she said, at a loss.

"This is great news, guys. Maybe I'll have a son to toss the ball around the backyard with."

LJ looked down at his hands before meeting Jill's eyes, which were already on him. She gave him a quick smile but didn't dare reach over to touch his leg or arm.

"So? What the hell do you all think?" the patriarch boomed.

"Uh," Nora said, leaning forward, feet spread and arms resting on her thighs. "I guess it's great." She glanced at her older siblings. "Right, guys?" She shrugged before glancing at their parents. "Maybe it won't be so bad being the youngest. I guess."

❧❧❧❧

The months went by and Jill's life continued as normal. She was about to turn sixteen and enter her sophomore year of high school as their mother entered the final trimester of her pregnancy. Judy Schaeffer had always been quiet, certainly one to keep to herself. But, in the ensuing months since the Schaeffer kids had been told about the coming baby, she'd become downright remote.

After a few outbursts from her, Larry, Sr. felt it was best for Judy to stay with her beloved aunt in Aurora, a suburb of Denver for the final trimester.

It was a Tuesday when Larry, Sr. knocked lightly on Jill's bedroom door. She was lying on her stomach on the bed doing homework. She glanced at the door. "Yeah?"

The door opened and her father stepped in, giving her a quick smile before shutting the door behind him.

❧❧❧❧

Jill's wedding ring glinted in the overhead light

as she brought the glass to her lips, the wine sweet yet intoxicating. She glanced at the clock, noting Andrew was nearly two hours late. She knew he had a big case that he'd been working on for months, but tonight she truly needed him. She needed to talk.

Setting the wineglass down, she grabbed her phone and went to her contacts. Fingering through them, she looked for a name, *any* name, to jump out at her. Name after name flew by, and she was shocked at the realization that not a one could she talk to tonight. Not for what was on her mind. None of them would understand, she knew instinctively. Her eye and finger stopped on Nora's name. She chewed on her bottom lip, trying to decide if she should press down or not.

Shaking her head, she stubbornly put the phone aside and picked up her wineglass.

# *Chapter Eight*

"Come on, sweetie," Nora said, opening the car door to let Bella out of the backseat. She seemed to know how to unbuckle herself, but it took her a moment to climb down out of her car seat. Nora smiled down at the adorable little one and took her hand.

"Where is this place?" Bella asked, looking around.

"This is your Aunt Jill's house," Nora explained, waiting as short little legs climbed the high stairs to the front porch. "You get to spend some time with her for a little bit while I go to work." Bella looked up at her with wide, frightened green eyes. "It'll be okay, sweet girl, I promise. And, your cousin Sylvia even stayed home from school today to spend some time with you!"

"Really?"

"Yup. Sylvia's awesome and has some pretty cool stuff in her room." Reaching the front door, Nora extended her free hand to ring the doorbell. After a few moments, the clickity clack of high heels on the marble floor of the foyer grew louder. Butterflies batted at her rib cage as nerves hit her. The door opened and Jill stood before them, looking as stunning as ever. "Hey," Nora said as pleasantly as she could. "Thanks so much for doing this. What I have to do today isn't exactly kid friendly."

"I understand," Jill said coolly. She knelt down to

Bella's eye level. "Well, hello to you, sweetheart." She opened her arms to take the small girl into a quick hug. "I am so excited you're here today."

"Aunt Nora said Sylvia has a cool room," Bella said shyly, holding her beloved teddy bear, Sam, closer to her chest.

Jill gave her a charming smile. "She sure does. She's excited to show you, too." Jill pushed to her feet and reached down to take the hand that had been in Nora's. She looked into the younger woman's eyes. "She'll be fine."

Nora nodded, knowing she would be even as she was loath to leave her. Bella still cried nightly and slept many nights in Nora's bed or ended up there at some point in the night. "I'll text you when I'm headed back to town. Shouldn't be longer than a few hours." Nora gave her niece a tight hug and kiss on the cheek before turning and trotting down the steps. She stopped halfway down the path when she heard her name.

"Do you think it was odd how Mom left?" Jill asked.

The question was so out of the blue and random, Nora wasn't entirely sure what to say for a moment. "I suppose," she said at last.

Without another word, Jill turned and she and Bella disappeared inside the house, one side of the etched double doors closing softly behind them.

Letting out a sigh, Nora headed back to her car. After she climbed in, she sat in front of Jill's car for a moment and thumbed through her emails to find the address of the shoot, so she could plug it into the GPS. At the advertising shoot today, she'd be taking photos for a business's new brochure. She chewed her bottom lip at the realization that the shoot she was heading to was in Manitou Springs, a little more than twenty minutes from Colorado Springs. She filed that information away for later.

❧❧❧❧

"Are you guys happy with the shots?" Nora asked the business owners as they leaned over her shoulders to look at the screen of her tablet. She had uploaded all the shots she took of their café, the gorgeous mountain scenery of the small town around them, and anything else they'd asked her to take.

"Yeah, fantastic," one of the owners commented, standing erect. "You said we'll get copies in a few days, right?"

Nora slid her tablet back into its bag and stood from where she'd been sitting at one of their outdoor tables. "Yes, a week at most, but honestly," she said, looking each in the eye, "two days, likely."

"Excellent." He extended his hand, which Nora shook with a firm, confident grip. "Thanks so much."

"No problem, Mr. Hagaar." She brandished a bright smile. "Talk to you both soon."

On the road again, Nora wove her way through the small hilly town, trying to get back to the highway. She pulled up behind a Cadillac at a red traffic light and chewed on her bottom lip, trying to decide if she should head back to Pueblo and spend the afternoon with Bella or head to Colorado Springs and Shannon's apartment. She needed to grab a few more things for her niece, and though she could easily buy her new clothes at Wal-Mart, she figured Bella would feel more secure with clothes she knew were hers.

Decision made, she headed toward the Springs.

Her mind was wandering all over the place. One thought pattern landed on Jill's words right before Nora left her house. Yes, Shannon's disappearance had made her think about her own mother, but she hadn't allowed herself to focus or dwell on it. But now, she wondered why Jill asked that question. Where did it come from?

※ ※ ※ ※

Pueblo, Colorado – 1992

Shannon giggled uncontrollably as Nora tickled her three-year-old little sister with merciless precision, the sixteen-year-old knowing all the best sweet spots. She was giggling right along with the adorable redheaded toddler until their father's booming voice interrupted their play on the couch.

"Shut that kid up!"

Stunned, Nora instantly gathered the girl into her arms as she looked up at the looming figure who'd stomped into the living room. "Sorry."

He let out a heavy sigh and ran a hand through his hair. "Where's Larry, Jr. and Jill?"

"LJ called about ten minutes ago. He's waiting for Jill to pick him up from practice and they'll be here. So, should be any time, now." To her relief, the front door opened as her words still hung in the air like a dialogue bubble.

"Get in here, you two!" he bellowed, the words followed by two sets of harried footsteps.

"Sorry, Daddy," Jill said with an exasperated sigh. "Roger didn't come in on time, so I had to wait until he arrived—"

"I need you to quit that job, Jill," Larry, Sr. said, interrupting her explanation.

"What?"

"Your classes, too."

"Daddy," Jill said, jaw falling open. "I can't. I've only got three semesters to go, and I can move on to graduate school—"

"What the hell do you need a degree for?" he asked, waving his hand in the general direction of her left hand. "What the fuck do you think that rock is on your finger for? Andy is supposed to end up being some rich lawyer or something, ain't he?"

"What is this all about?" LJ asked, seated between his sisters.

Without a word, Larry, Sr. left the room only to return a moment later. He tossed a piece of paper at his son. "Read it aloud."

LJ bent down to grab the page that had floated down to the floor to land atop his right shoe. Holding it in both hands, he read, "'I can't do this anymore. I will contact you once I get settled. Love, Mom.'"

Nora felt her heart stop. Still holding Shannon, who chewed on her first two fingers on her left hand, she reached over with her free hand and snatched the page from her brother. She read it three times before the note was taken from her, their father crumpling up the paper before throwing it into the lit fireplace.

"See what she's done?" he boomed, looking at all three of the oldest kids. "She left me! Packed all her shit and left. Left all the shit I've done for her all these years, left this beautiful house, and left you guys." He waved a dramatic arm to indicate the four of them. "You"—he pointed at Jill—"are moving back home. There's a house to be cleaned, meals to be made, and a kid to raise." He indicated Shannon.

"Wait, Dad, LJ and I can—" Nora began.

"No! You got high school to finish and Larry, Jr. has got football to play. She ain't got nothing to worry about. High school's done and she's got a lawyer fiancé to take care of her."

Nora glanced past her brother at her older sister, who looked absolutely crushed. "Jill," she said softly and shook her head when Jill sent a watery gaze her way. "We can take care of all this. Don't leave school or Andrew."

"It's done. This is how it's gonna be. Jill, I want dinner by six thirty tonight," Larry, Sr. said before storming out of the room.

꧁ ꧂

Nora shook her head to clear it. She hadn't thought of that day in many years, as it had led to the worst year of her teenage years. Jill had been turned into essentially a slave overnight, but, always wanting her daddy's approval, she'd done it all, anything he asked of her. Finally, Andrew came to the rescue and moved their wedding up by more than a year to get her out of there.

She pulled into Shannon's parking lot and found a spot. It was fairly full, which she found interesting for a Tuesday afternoon. She had to wonder if anyone who lived there worked. She cut the engine and pulled her ignition key loose as she stared up at the building, then Shannon's apartment door. LJ had mentioned to her that the place looked pretty much like that of a busy single mom, save for the extra messes presumed to be made by a frightened five-year-old.

Unhooking her seatbelt, she climbed out of her car and slammed the driver's door shut, automatically clicking the alarm button on her key fob. She pocketed her keys and cell phone as she walked across the parking lot and up the stairs to the third floor. Remembering she needed Shannon's key, which LJ had returned to her in case she needed more things for Bella, she retrieved her keys and picked out the one that fit the apartment door.

Nora stepped inside the dark, stale-smelling apartment. Nobody had been there for a week nor had any windows been opened. She wanted to air the place out but thought perhaps it wouldn't be a good idea. She needed to be careful of anything she did and mindful of what she touched, should the missing person's investigation come to the apartment.

She closed the door behind her and, from habit, locked it. Flicking on the light switch, which was connected to the floor lamp tucked into the corner by the couch, she saw the cereal mess LJ had mentioned, and it broke her heart. She couldn't even imagine how terrified Bella must have been. She almost wanted to call Jill and ask her to put Bella on the phone to hear her voice. She'd always loved her niece but had certainly become incredibly protective of her in the last handful of days.

Picking her way through the apartment, she ended up in Bella's bedroom. She found a duffel bag and stuffed it with some clothes and a couple more stuffed animals before zipping it up. She hitched it over her shoulder and headed back to the hall, stopping at Shannon's bedroom door. Setting the duffel on the floor right inside the room, she walked in, still able to smell her sister's perfume and the scent of lotion.

Shannon was a notorious lotion user. Her dresser top was half-filled with various scents. She also noticed a framed picture of Bella grinning from behind the glass, a picture of them both together, a couple snapshots of Shannon with a few women, whom Nora assumed were friends, and one that surprised her.

Nora picked up the picture, studying her sister's lovely face and the handsome man she was cuddled up with. She recognized him as Richard—or Rick— Stanton, Bella's father. He was an actor Shannon had met doing community theater seven or eight years before. Nora had only met him a time or two, but LJ had told her he didn't like him. Said the guy seemed slimy. Either way, Rick had absolutely broken Shannon's heart, taking off when Bella was a baby. Obviously Shannon never got over him.

Putting the picture back, she glanced at the bed, noting several outfits lying there. It looked almost as though Shannon had been trying to decide what to wear on her night out. In the corner, tucked between the bedside table and the wall, was a faux wood cardboard box with handle cutouts and a lid. Written in thick black letters on the top was Precious Memories.

Squatting, she pulled the box toward her and lifted the lid. She smiled when she saw Bella's baby blanket that the hospital gave her to swaddle the baby in before taking her home. Bella's tiny hospital bracelet was there as well as a few other memories of that special day in March 2012. She saw a thumb drive tucked into a large spool of thread.

As Nora dug down a bit farther, she was surprised to find a couple scripts and playbills from a few of the plays Shannon had done in high school. Beneath those, and toward the bottom of the box, she came across something wrapped in a towel. As she unwrapped the covering, her breath caught. It was the four Sarah Brightman CDs she'd given her baby sister over the years, including the first two, her own words still inked on the dust jacket tucked inside the jewel case cover.

"Shannon," she murmured, lovingly stroking the smooth plastic cover of *Phantom of the Opera.*

Replacing everything exactly how she found it, she walked over to the bed, her heart heavy and emotions rising. She plopped down on the sagging mattress, hands in her lap as she looked around the bedroom. She couldn't help but think that what she was looking at was what Shannon saw every morning when she woke up.

Reaching behind her, she grabbed one of Shannon's pillows and placed it in her lap. She rested her hand on its soft fullness before she lifted it to her face, closing her eyes as she inhaled the scent that was a combination of her sister's shampoo and the smell of the other products she used in her gorgeous auburn hair. She was the only one in the family whose hair wasn't some shade—natural shade—of brown. The tears came swiftly as she hugged the pillow to her chest.

"Where are you?" she whispered.

As though her question had been answered, Nora froze. She heard a key being inserted into the deadbolt and then the doorknob. Tossing the pillow aside, she ran into the living room.

"Shannon?" she called out desperately as the door was being pushed open.

Briefly, she saw a male figure dressed in jeans and a black hoodie, but then he turned around and ran.

"Hey!"

Nora ran to the door and swung it open the rest

of the way, eyes wide as she scoured the walkway and stairs. She saw a flash of dark clothing jump over the last five stairs of the first floor, nearly losing his footing as he continued running.

Pushing off the doorframe, Nora ran down the walkway and almost lost her own footing as she took the stairs as quickly as she dared. She barely felt the scrape to her hand grazing the brick of the building as she rounded the corner where she'd seen the man flee. The building backed up to a dense copse of trees, and there was no way she'd be able to follow or see him.

Out of breath, she turned around and headed back to the third-floor apartment, the key still in the door that had been used to unlock it. Nora's heart froze in her throat when she saw the keychain dangling from it. It was a little clay heart that Bella had painted for her mother in daycare for the previous Mother's Day. She knew better than to touch it in case there would be fingerprints on it.

"What are you doing here?"

Nora whipped around to see Sarah taking the last couple stairs up to the third floor, her eyes locked on her.

"Nora, you can't be here." Sarah walked up to her, dressed similarly to how she'd been on their first encounter in Interview Room 2. "You can't."

"Someone tried to get into her apartment," Nora said, ignoring Sarah's admonishment.

"What?"

Nora pointed at the key, though she now noticed Shannon's car key was missing. "I was in the bedroom and I heard someone coming in. I hurried to the living room and it was some guy."

Sarah's expression instantly transformed from

irritation to the professional she was. "Come with me."
Nora followed Sarah into the apartment where she was
told to sit down. Nora did and watched as Sarah pulled
an evidence bag out of the pocket of her blazer and a
pen. She used the pen to hook the loop of the keychain
and gently tugged the key loose from the lock where
it dangled. Sealing it up, Sarah closed the door and
walked over to Nora, sitting beside her. She pulled her
cell phone out of her pocket and made a quick call for
a CSI unit to fingerprint. Turning her attention back to
Nora, she asked, "Who would have a key to Shannon's
apartment? Besides obviously *you*."

"Nobody, that I know of," Nora said, hugging
herself. She felt sick. "The key I have came from the
neighbor who initially called me."

"Can I have that key, please, Nora?" Sarah asked
softly, holding out her hand.

Nora placed it in her palm, noting the long,
beautiful fingers she had once known very well. She
looked away. Clearing her throat, she returned her
gaze to Sarah in time to see her tuck the key into her
pocket and pull out the same notepad she had used
when taking notes that first day.

"Tell me everything," Sarah said, pen poised
above the page, an expectant look on her face.

Forty-five minutes later, Nora was almost to her
car, the duffel bag she'd packed when she'd gotten there
in hand. She reached into her pocket and removed her
keys, pressing the button to unlock the doors.

"Hey."

She turned to see Sarah walking up to her. Nora
pulled open the back driver's side door and tossed the
duffel bag inside before turning toward Sarah.

"Are you okay?" Sarah asked, leaning a shoulder

against the side of the vehicle.

Nora considered how she felt as she glanced back at the building before returning her gaze to the woman standing on the other side of her open door. "I suppose so. I don't think I've fully processed this all yet. I mean, the bastard who I chased down may be responsible for why my sister is missing. As you said, how else would he have her keys?"

Sarah nodded. "I know and I'm sorry. I mean"—she blew out, bringing up a hand to brush long strands of her dark hair out of her face that the slight breeze had picked up—"though I don't want you or anyone else in Shannon's place right now, I guess it turned out good that you were." She gave her a small smile. "You may have given us a lead and no doubt at least something to chew on."

Nora nodded, shoving her hands into the back pockets of her jeans. "Well," she said softly, troubled by how comfortable she felt around Sarah, "I'd better go. I need to pick Bella up from Jill's place. I didn't expect to be here so long."

"I understand." Sarah backed away from her car. "I'll be in touch if I need anything or learn anything, okay?"

Again, Nora nodded. "Okay. Thanks, Sarah."

Sarah gave her a quick smile and a wave before she turned and headed back to the building.

Nora watched her go before she tore her eyes away.

# *Chapter Nine*

*G*rab my hand!" he roared, hoping to be heard over the rage of the inferno below, the flames licking their way up the ruined elevator shaft, turning the square metal tube into an Easy-Bake Oven. Sweat beaded on his forehead, plastering dark bangs to his skin. "Take it!"

She looked down then back up at him, panic in her eyes. "I can't."

"You have to." He looked beyond her, reaching up to swipe at the sweat puddling above his upper lip. "You can do this, Amanda." He glanced back over his shoulder. "Hold on tight!"

Without even finding out if he'd been heard, he grunted as he climbed down as far as he dared. He reached both hands down and snagged the terrified woman's wrists. The heat was unbearable and the noise, noise like he'd never heard before. It sounded like a freight train and it was gaining speed.

"Hold on!" he yelled. Again, he glanced behind him. "I got her! Pull! I said pull, goddamn it!"

He gritted his teeth as slowly, oh so slowly, he was pulled back to the open maw of the elevator door. Amanda inched up with him.

"We're going to die!" Amanda sobbed, the tears pale trails in the soot on her exquisite face.

For that moment, everything disappeared for him except her. He smiled at her, holding onto her even *tighter.*

"No we won't," LJ said, fingers racing across the keypad of his laptop. "In that moment," he said, typing as he spoke, "Jack knew he'd never leave her again. The end."

He grinned, sitting back in his black leather captain's chair in his home office. He reread the last few paragraphs and dialogue and, thrilled with what he read, he grinned, punching himself in the arm for a job well done. He clicked on the Save feature in time for Kristie to burst into the office.

Annoyed, he quickly slammed down the top of his laptop, trying to look as nonchalant as possible.

"Looking at porn again, huh?" the teen smirked, throwing herself sideways into one of the two chairs on the opposite side of the desk.

He was irritated with himself as he blushed. As innocent as what he'd been doing was, he felt ashamed. "What do you want, punk?" he asked instead, his tone light and friendly.

"Well," she drawled, swinging the leg that was tossed over the arm of the leather high-back chair she was sprawled in. "I was wondering if I could borrow the Volvo." Her gaze fell to her grape-purple-painted nails. "Me and Julia want to go see a movie."

He leaned forward, moving the laptop aside as he laced his elbows in its place. "Did you ask your mom?"

Kristie blew out a sarcastic breath, bringing her hand up to swipe black bangs out of her eyes. "Would *you?*"

"Touché," he chuckled. He studied his daughter for a moment. "What's the occasion?" he asked.

"Nothing, God!" Kristie growled. "Can't I go out

with my friend?"

He smirked. "I suppose so." He reached into his pants pocket and removed the key to the spare car, which the couple intended to give to Kristie upon graduation. He tossed it to her, Kristie catching it in midair.

"Thanks!" she gushed, popping up from the chair.

"I expect it to be full of gas when you return *by* ten thirty."

"Ten thirty? Dad..." she whined.

"Kristie..." he mocked her. "It's a school night."

She sighed dramatically. "Fine." She pocketed the key. "Thanks, Dad." She turned to leave.

"Wait." LJ grabbed his ring of keys again and found the small brass one that fit the bottom drawer of his desk. He quickly inserted it and pulled it open. Inside was a small lockbox filled with cash. He pulled out two twenties and closed the box then relocked the drawer. Getting to his feet, he walked over to her, holding the money out. "Here," he said quietly, glancing over his daughter's shoulder to make sure his wife wasn't anywhere around. "You girls have a fun night on me."

Kristie looked down at the bills as she took them before she looked up into his sad gaze. "Dad, I can't take this," she said just as quietly. "I know how it works, and I know that's all you've got to spend."

LJ cleared his throat and looked away, embarrassed.

"Come on, I know that's why you always want scratch tickets for your birthday." She grinned up at him and gave him a quick but tight hug. "I love you, Dad."

He smiled as he hugged her back. "I love you, too, Bug." He gave her a noisy kiss on her cheek. "Tell Julia I said hi."

"'Kay. Love you!" she called as she hurried from the room, grabbing her leather jacket from the coat closet near the front door before she nearly jogged out of the house.

He stood where he was for a long moment, shaking his head. He loved that kid more than he ever knew it would be possible. After he and Adrienne were married and decided to try to get pregnant, he made up his mind then and there that he'd do his damndest to be the kind of father he always wished he'd had. The truth was, he was terrified. He was terrified he was a Junior for a reason and he'd be exactly like him.

Deciding to call it a night, LJ opened his laptop and logged off before shutting it down. He cut the light in the office and headed to the kitchen. It was only 7:40 p.m., but he was in the mood for a snack.

Padding across the wood floor in sock-clad feet, he opened the fridge, scanning the shelves for anything that looked good. His gaze fell on the chocolate cake Adrienne had brought home with groceries the day before. Pulling the confection out of the fridge in its clear plastic container, he butted the fridge door closed and set the cake on the island countertop.

He reached into the cabinet next to the fridge to grab himself a plate.

"Grab me one, too?"

He glanced over his shoulder and was shocked to see Adrienne standing on the opposite side of the island. Without a word, he grabbed a second plate, closing the cabinet before returning his focus to the cake.

After an awkward silence, the District 70 Superintendent spoke. "How's practice going at P-Dub for the Pigskin Classic against County High?" she asked, P-Dub the nickname adopted for Pueblo West High School.

He nodded. "Good. I mean, it's not like County is that hard to beat." He gave her a quick smile.

"That's wonderful. It's so important for us to have a winning team and, well you know, a winning coach."

LJ said nothing but felt his stomach begin to roil.

"Martin Murphy called today."

"Oh?" LJ responded, placing a piece on a plate and sliding it across the granite to his wife. "How are things in Cherry Creek?"

"Good," she said taking the fork he offered her. "He said George is definitely going to retire next year and wants me to go ahead and send in my resume."

He sighed, annoyed as he placed his own slice on the plate before replacing the plastic cover onto the plastic tray and returning the cake to the fridge.

"LJ," Adrienne said, "it's the best district in the entire state. He's already told me the money would be near double what I'm making here."

LJ held his fork in tanned fingers that matched extremely tanned features from so many hours outside training his players. "Adrienne, it's never been about the money for us."

She cocked her head slightly to the side, long, naturally curly brown hair falling over her shoulder, and studied him with a hard, dark look. "No, for you it's always been about what Daddy wanted. What about what *I* want, Larry? What *Kristie* wants?"

"What Kristie wants?" LJ said, his tone

incredulous. "What Kristie wants is to stay where her friends are. To stay where her family is. She wants to go to school here at CSU – Pueblo, Adrienne. She's fine with that, and it's a damn good school."

Adrienne cut a bite of cake with her fork. "You can be so selfish, Larry," she said, shaking her head. "Absolutely selfish and have absolutely no vision for a good future for us."

"In Cherry Hills," he said, palms resting on the cool stone of the counter. "I've lived there, I think you forget that. As much as you want all the status and stature, your 'doubled' salary"—he used air quotes—"won't matter. This house"—he indicated the structure around them—"this place would be two to three times the cost." He snorted. "On second thought, that price and not near this much house" Munchies vanished, he shoved his plate away. "How does that make sense? And, forget helping Kristie with school."

"I'm done with this conversation," Adrienne said sharply, gathering her plate and fork and heading to the stairs.

He watched her go and leaned back against the counter behind him, arms crossed over his chest.

❧ ❧ ❧ ❧

Colorado Springs, Colorado – 1994

"This is a bad idea, Nora," LJ said, glancing over at his sister who was expertly maneuvering her Honda through evening traffic as they entered the city at last. "I mean it."

"Nah, you can do this, LJ," the eighteen-year-old responded, glancing over at her brother. "Nobody will know you and you're really good."

LJ felt like he was about to throw up as he scrubbed his sweaty palms on the thighs of his jeans. He looked around, not recognizing where they were. "Nora, where are you taking me?"

She grinned at him. "Don't worry about it. You said you didn't want to be recognized. You won't be recognized."

Twenty minutes later, Nora pulled the small car into a packed parking lot. The building at the end was painted in dark colors with a bright rainbow neon sign announcing, Aqua Splash. He glanced over at his sister.

"Why do I feel like I'm going to be slightly out of place here?"

Nora pulled the parking brake and killed the engine. "Come on, stud," she said with a chuckle.

As they neared the building, LJ noticed the marquee said OPEN MIC NIGHT. "Oh God," he whispered.

She paid their three-dollar entry fee, and they both received a stamp on the back of their hands denoting they were underage so couldn't be sold alcohol. LJ lamented that fact, as right then, he would have done anything for a shot.

The club looked like any other club, save for the smattering of very tall women, who after a closer look, LJ realized were men. He turned on Nora, eyes wide and panic in his voice.

"You've brought me to a gay bar?"

Nora laughed. "Hey, if anyone knows you here, somehow I think they've got the bigger problem."

"Ladies and gentlemen! Fags, hags, and beautiful boys." The voice boomed over the club, and out of nowhere, a spotlight was on the flamboyant man on the stage, his glittery gold blazer nearly blinding. He held a microphone in one hand, the other resting on a hip. "It is my great pleasure to MC our open mic night tonight. So, all you singers, dancers, criers, and buyers, it's your night!"

LJ swallowed audibly. He allowed Nora to take his hand and lead him through the crowded club to a table in a corner. He felt nauseous, nervous, and overall, like he essentially wanted to die. The letterman jacket he wore suddenly felt hot and tight.

He looked at his sister. "You are going to get me raped!" he hissed, noting a lot of men in leather who were checking him out a bit too affectionately.

"Stop being such a pussy," Nora hissed back.

"First off, we have Jezebel!" the MC announced with a flourish, the crowd cheering.

LJ watched, wide-eyed as "talent" after talent went up on stage.

"And now, a super-duper special treat for you beautiful boys out there," the MC spoke into the microphone, his ice-blue gaze aimed at LJ. "Our very own poet laureate, LJ Schaeffer!"

LJ's eyes nearly popped out of his head. He looked at Nora, ready to throttle her.

"Come on, LJ," she said, her voice barely heard above the roar of the crowd. "Nobody knows you here." She shoved at his bulk. "Go do your thing!"

Nearly growling, LJ pushed to his feet and walked to the stage, taking the three stairs up as though he were walking to the gallows. He walked over to Mr. Flashy and took the microphone as well as the once-over the MC gave him.

Alone on the stage, LJ looked out over the crowd, which was hard to see due to the intense light shining on him. He was, however, able to see Nora, which helped. He cleared his throat and turned his attention back to the crowd.

"Um, hi." He waved, feeling lame and totally alone. "I'm LJ." He wasn't sure whether to laugh or cringe at the catcall sent his way.

"Take it off, frat boy!" someone yelled from the darkness.

"Oh, uh, no. Um…" He swallowed. "I tell stories." His heart fell when the audience began to complain and jeer at him.

He looked to Nora. Her unwavering look of adoration and pride gave him the courage to continue on. He swallowed hard; then, with a flourish, he whipped the letterman jacket off broad, muscular shoulders, revealed by the tank top he wore, as well as muscular, well-built arms as the leather sleeves slid down them. Finally, the jacket fell with a heavy clang to the floor, weighted down by endless achievement patches and pins.

The crowd went wild, cheers, whistles, and more catcalls raining down on him. He grinned. Though not particularly his crowd, he was beginning to have a good time. He decided on the very short story—more like a vignette—that he'd scribbled down earlier that afternoon.

"This is a story about Joel, a guy sitting in his room, trying to decide what he wants to be, who he wants to be, and how he wants to do it."

"Doggy style!" a woman's voice yelled out from the darkness, laughter following.

LJ laughed along with them, sending out a salute in the general direction of the suggestion. "You see, all of Joel's life," LJ began, a bit more comfortable as he moved around the stage, "he's felt like he had a world of expectation on his shoulders. He felt, why, maybe even like there was no acceptance, no place for him, and nowhere to be. So"—he raised a finger for emphasis— "maybe I'll become a singer!" With that, he belted out a terribly off-key C note, making the crowd laugh. "Or, maybe I'll become an All-Star hitter." He used the microphone to mimic the motion of a swinging baseball bat. He scrunched up his face and brought the microphone close to his mouth. "Fuck sports."

He grinned over at Nora who was laughing wildly with everyone else, considering he was Mr. Sports in the flesh and he knew it.

"Maybe, just maybe," he said, falling to his knees, sending up a whole new round of cheers. "Maybe I'll be Father Joel." He pressed his palms together and spared a glance out into the audience. "Praying for all you sinners." He was loving the playful energy of the crowd. He stood. "Maybe—"

"A drag queen!" someone yelled.

LJ put a hand on his hip and did his best "gay man's" voice. "Honey, I ain't *that* lost." Even he lost it on that one. He got his laughter under control and pretended to be looking in the air for the pigskin spiral coming his way. "Maybe," he said, running toward the edge of the stage, misjudging the end as he flung himself right off, landing hard on his shoulder. Stunned for a moment, he put the microphone to his lips. "Maybe I'll be an All-American like my dad." He purposefully filled his tone with pain. A scary bull dyke and scrawny bleach blond twink helped him to his feet and, as he climbed back up on stage, hurting and out of breath, he plopped down, legs dangling over the apron. "Or, maybe I'll just be me."

The roar of applause was deafening as every person in the place shot to their feet, Nora yelling and whooping loudest of them all. LJ grabbed his jacket, grinning as he got to his feet. "Thank you," he said and handed the microphone back to the MC, who was applauding as he stepped up onto the stage.

❧ ❧ ❧ ❧

With one too many offers for a drink or a dance for comfort, LJ and Nora had opted to leave. LJ whooped and ran his way through the parking lot to Nora's car.

"Holy shit, that was so much fun!" He pumped his fist in the air, excitement and adrenaline thundering through him.

"You rocked it, dude," Nora said, unlocking her door before opening it and leaning over to tug on the lock pin on the passenger's side door.

LJ climbed in and shut his door. He looked over at his little sister before leaning over and leaving a kiss on her cheek. "Thanks for believing in me, sis."

"Of course." She slapped him on the thigh. "Let's get something to eat."

They drove back to Pueblo with LJ going on and on about the experience, shocked that first of all, he was able to do it and second, he was able to do it in a gay bar.

"We're not monsters, ya know." Nora laughed.

"Yeah, yeah. They actually seemed pretty cool."

An hour later, they sat in Denny's, one of the few restaurants still open. Dinners eaten and plates taken away, the two sat drinking coffee.

"I think you should write more, LJ. You absolutely are a good storyteller."

"God, can you even imagine what Dad would say? 'Not manly, son,'" he said, imitating Larry, Sr.'s voice. He glanced over and saw a lovely brunette with long, curly hair sitting alone. She was eating a piece of pie and looking over what appeared to be a textbook. As though she sensed she was being watched, she looked up, meeting his gaze. He smiled, and she looked back at her book.

"Oh, she so dissed you!" Nora crowed.

He glared at her before getting the attention of the waitress. "I'd like to pay for that young lady's pie and soda," he told her, nodding in the brunette's direction.

The waitress walked over to her table, and they spoke for a moment before the waitress returned. "I'm sorry, sir, but she's refused your offer."

LJ felt like an idiot. He cleared his throat and rubbed the back of his neck.

"However, she did say," the waitress continued, placing a folded napkin and pen on the table, "if you write your phone number down, her words, she *might* call you."

Glancing over at the young woman, who quickly looked away, he picked up the pen and scribbled down his phone number and his pager number before handing the napkin and pen back to the waitress. "Thanks."

A few moments later the young woman packed up her books, sliding them into a backpack before standing. To LJ's delight, she walked over to his and Nora's table.

"Well, I figured it might be a good idea to ask

your name, I mean, after all, in case I manage to find some time to perhaps call, it would be a good idea to know who I'm asking for," she said.

LJ leaned back, running an arm along the back of the booth, as casual and suave as he could make it. "I'm Larry, but everyone calls me LJ. This is my sister, Nora. And you are?"

"Adrienne." She glanced over at Nora. "Nice to meet you." Back to LJ. "And, nice to meet you, Larry."

With that, she was gone.

❧ ❧ ❧ ❧

LJ lay on the living room couch in the dark, one hand resting on a more rounded belly than it had been in those days, the other resting casually above the throw pillow where he leaned his head. He was smiling, as he hadn't thought of that night in a long time.

He tore his mind out of the past when he heard a car engine and saw the wash of headlights sweep the front of the house. A moment later, the engine grew silent and footfalls up the rocks that bordered the grass could be heard. Key in lock, door opening then closing.

LJ glanced at the clock on the mantel, barely making out the numbers in the dim light. "You're late," he said softly to the dark figure heading in his direction.

"I know, I'm sorry. The movie got out late," Kristie said, flipping on a lamp before she sat on the coffee table in front of the couch where LJ lay. "It did!" she exclaimed to his raised eyebrow. "Some kid had a seizure or something, so they had to stop the show. When they started it again, it was like, almost forty minutes later." She extended her hand to him, a medium-sized Dairy Queen cup in it with a long, red plastic spoon sticking straight up. "But, I did get you your favorite."

LJ sat up with a groan, his knees bothering him from entirely too many football and wrestling injuries. "Oreo Blizzard?" he asked, taking the icy cold cup.

"Is there any other kind?" she drawled. "Though I guess in all honesty"—she uncapped her own Peanut Buster Parfait—"technically *you* bought you an Oreo Blizzard."

LJ chuckled, enjoying his first bite. "Well, then I thank myself." He glanced over at his daughter, noting what looked to be yet another earring in her left ear. He didn't understand it, but at least those could close up when it came time for her to get a real job or career.

"How's Julia?" he asked, licking a large chunk of cookie off his spoon.

"Good," Kristie said simply, no additional information offered.

LJ studied her for a long moment, sizing her up. "Good. That's good."

# *Chapter Ten*

S arah!"

"*Hola, abuela.*" Sarah smiled as she was taken into such a tight hug, she was positive her much-shorter grandmother was going to pull her head right off.

"*Pensé que no ibas a poder venir?*" the ninety-year-old said accusingly, pulling back enough to look up into her granddaughter's face.

"*Y perderme tu cumpleaños? Nunca.*" Sarah endured another hug before she was released.

"Sarah?" You came!"

Once word got out that she'd arrived, Sarah was inundated by her family in her grandmother's tiny home, which consisted of her mother, four brothers, and two sisters and a small army of nieces and nephews. But, what made her smile was when she saw the twinkling dark blue eyes of the man with mostly gray strawberry blond hair. He held his arms open to her, and she immediately went to him.

⁂

Pueblo, Colorado – 1979

A seven-year-old Sarah was curled up on the couch holding her little sister, Ernestine as their mother, Paola, answered the front door. Two policemen stood there, one a short African-American man with a graying mustache and the other, a younger, tall white man with bushy strawberry blond sideburns and kind blue eyes.

"Hello, Mrs. Sanchez. I'm Officer Gaines and this is Officer Browne. May we come in, ma'am?" he asked, removing his peaked cap by the shiny black bill.

"Yes, come in. What is this about, officers?" the young mother of two asked, stepping aside to allow the men to enter.

The fair-haired officer glanced over at Sarah and Ernestine and gave the girls a kind smile before returning his attention to their mother.

"What's happening?" four-year-old Ernestine whispered.

Sarah shook her head as the two men spoke quietly to their mother in the entryway of their small home near CF&I, the steel mill where their father, Ernesto, worked. All of a sudden, Paola let out a howling cry and began to fall, but Officer Gaines caught her before she could fully collapse.

"No!" she wailed.

Sarah held Ernestine a little closer as the young child began to cry, too. Sarah remained strong—she had to. She watched her mother and the officer closely, noting as again, Officer Gaines glanced over at the girls again, a warm smile on his lips.

After a moment, their mother, with the two officers helping her on either side, walked over to the couch. Sarah looked over at her mother with big, dark eyes.

"Something bad happened, didn't it?" she asked.

Paola nodded, tears still streaming down her cheeks.

❧❧❧❧

Sitting next to Chuck Gaines, the man who had been in her life since she was seven and held her heart since she was eight, she glanced over at him. They'd enjoyed a wonderful early dinner with the entire family, including homemade tamales and of course, Chuck's favorite, Texas-style baked beans. It always made for an interesting combination.

"You know," she said, watching as he eyed her. He took a swig of his Coors as they sat on the back stoop. "I used to be so confused why this policeman stuck around so much. My teachers taught us you guys were supposed to protect and serve, but it seemed a little extreme."

He chuckled. "Yeah, well, initially I felt so bad for your mom, a young mother, her husband doing something so innocent as walking home from an honest day's work." He lowered the beer bottle, letting it dangle between spread legs by two fingers around the neck. "Coward bastards and their gang drive-bys." He shrugged. "Somewhere along the way, guess I fell in love with all you girls."

"Yes, the Gringo and the Salsa Mamma," Sarah said with a grin, playfully shouldering him.

He chuckled and took another sip. "Gringo, indeed. Man, the way your grandma used to look at me like I was a cockroach."

Sarah nodded. "Yes, I'm glad you won her over, though. I think especially once you and Mom had the boys and Kylee."

He smiled. "And, it only took nearly fourteen years," he added, his gold wedding band glinting in the setting sun.

Sarah smiled, sipping her own beer.

"You know, Sarah, your dad would be so proud of you and Ernie. Here she is, working with babies at Parkview Hospital every day as a pediatric surgeon, and then there's you."

She met his gaze. "And then there's me."

"Finding the bad guys."

Chuck's pride in her meant everything, and she sensed a slight tug in her chest for a moment. "Well," she said, clearing her throat, "it is because of you that I became a cop, ya know."

He leaned over and reached a hand up, steadying her head so he could leave a kiss there. "So," he said, releasing her. "How's this case going? I know you've said you're struggling with it. Why?"

"I know the one missing and I know the family," she said softly, taking a long swig.

"Oh. That's tough. Had that happen only once. It was the year before I retired when I was working Homicide. Went to school with the guy. Did you talk to Price about recusing yourself?"

"Yup," she said with a nod and a grin to him. "He told me to stop whining and get my damn ass to work."

Chuck laughed. "Sounds about right. So, what do you have?"

"Nothing. Not a goddamn thing," Sarah said with a sigh.

"Nothing came back on the key chain?"

Sarah shook her head. "Nope. We did get a print from one person and a partial from another, but no matches. No DNA, no security camera evidence of places nearby. I mean, Chuck, it's like this poor girl just vanished."

"How well do you know the family?"

Sarah met his gaze again. "It's Nora's little sister, Shannon."

"Oh boy." He glanced away. "Well, as I've always told you, kiddo"—he turned back and stared her down—"sometimes you have no choice but to think outside the box."

❧❧❧❧

Tired after a long day, Sarah pulled her '68 black-and-chrome Mustang into the driveway of her townhouse, the classic car coming to a stop as she reached up to press the button for the electric garage door opener and waited to pull into the single-car garage.

Letting out a tired sigh, she cut the engine and grabbed her phone and purse before climbing out of the car that Chuck and two of her brothers—Ray and Mac—had rebuilt for her as a congratulatory gift upon making detective eight years before.

She loved her family dearly, but lordy they could be draining. Hitting the inside garage door opener, she unlocked the door to her home as the big door moaned into place.

She stepped into the laundry room, which doubled as a mudroom and extra storage for the small townhouse. From there, she made her way through the kitchen, headed to the stairs.

"Sarah? Is that you?"

She paused two stairs up, eyes squeezing closed for a moment. "Yup. It's me."

Leslie appeared at the top of the stairs, looking down at her with a wide smile. "I was cleaning today."

"Great," Sarah said absently, continuing to climb.

She gave the blonde a hard look as her path forward was blocked. "I'm tired, Leslie. I'm not in the mood for games."

"What are you talking about games, Sarah? All I said was that I cleaned. I thought you'd be thrilled."

Sarah looked the taller woman in the eye. "You never gave two shits about cleaning when we were together. One of the many reasons why you're living here until you can find a new place." With that, she turned and headed to her bedroom, slamming the door behind her.

Standing in the master bedroom, Sarah bared her teeth and screwed up her face, yelling silently in frustration. She rested her hands on her hips and raised her closed eyes to the ceiling.

"How the hell did I let her move in here?" she whispered. "Jesus."

As if in answer, music suddenly blasted from below. She knew Leslie was pissed and was doing her immature passive-aggressive bullshit and Sarah had nothing to give, no desire to fight anymore. She'd spent far too many years—*wasted* far too many years— so decided to lock her bedroom door and grab her iPod and headphones.

⁂

Sarah wasn't keen on having to wash her baby once she made it back into town, but she was enjoying the long, country roads on her way out to Nicholson Road and the old farmhouse. She slowed the muscle car down to turn when she received a phone call. Stopping at the stop sign next to the small, white chapel on the corner, she picked up the phone.

"Sanchez." She listened, her heart beginning to race. "Okay. I'm on my way right now."

In a plume of dust, she whipped the car around, almost landing in the ditch, then sped back the way she'd come toward Highway 50 and the long drive to Canon City, roughly forty-five minutes away from Pueblo, proper. Keeping one eye on the road, she managed to find Nora's cell number and called it.

"Hey, it's Sarah. Listen, change of plans. I had to turn around and am headed to Canon. I'll call when I'm on my way back out, hopefully tonight."

❧❧❧❧

Sarah slowed the Mustang as she headed toward Skyline Drive, a local hangout for teens who wanted privacy as well as those looking for a spectacular view and others for more nefarious acts. She pulled up beside the three police cars parked at the entrance, cutting off public access.

"Hey, Detective Sanchez," one of the officers said, walking over to her. "Glad you're in casual clothes. We've got a bit of a hike. Follow me."

"Thanks, Pete."

They walked up the steep, winding dirt road that led to the top. Sarah looked at the incredible mountain views all around them.

"Damn, this is pretty," she commented, slightly out of breath.

At long last, they arrived where the rest of the crew was, including her Canon City counterpart, Detective Patrick Holdsted.

"Hey, Pat," she said, walking up to them. "What do we have?"

"Over there," he said, pointing in the general direction. Couple hikers found it."

Sarah's stomach churned, the sick sensation spreading like vine weeds. She let out a heavy breath as she ducked under the yellow tape to the spot where everything had been found. The department photographer was snapping the scene.

"Joe, I need you to send those to me as soon as you're done, 'kay?" she said absently, zeroing in on the scene.

Before her was the taped-off area, the foliage peppered with a few items. She saw a black clutch, smeared with mud, as well as a black stiletto, the thin heel partially snapped off. Off to the left of the shoe about four feet was a smeared Colorado driver's license, the smiling face of Shannon Schaeffer looking back at her.

"Oh man," she said, accepting the pair of latex gloves that were handed to her. She wiggled her fingers into them as she knelt down. It was then that she noticed a car key. "Do we know what Shannon Schaeffer drove?" she asked those around her.

"Honda Civic," one of the officers supplied.

"So, why does this belong to a Subaru, then?" She held up the thick key, the maker's logo spelled out on the plastic grip. She looked out into the fading afternoon, her mind reeling. Handing the key to a CSI member, she got to her feet. "We need to find out what model that key belongs to then find out where an abandoned car is. Without a key, you ain't gettin' too far."

# *Chapter Eleven*

L J walked the small apartment, noting the galley kitchen and somewhat aged tile. There was one small bathroom for the one decent-sized bedroom, considering the square footage of the apartment. The finishings were dated and some worn, but the fridge was clean upon inspection, as were the oven and stovetop.

"So, does this seem like something that would work for Kristie?" the building manager, Sally asked standing in the middle of the empty living space.

LJ turned around in the narrow kitchen and rested his arms on the serving bar in the opened-up space that looked out on the living room. "It's nice," he said, trying to sound noncommittal. It was, and he knew Kristie had an incredibly limited budget, but he wanted to keep his cards close to the vest.

"Well, let me remind you, the university is literally up the hill, and not far in the other direction are shops, restaurants, bus stops, things that might be useful for a college student."

He nodded, walking out of the kitchen and meeting the older woman in the living room, the brochure she'd handed him upon meeting in his hand. "I'll speak to my wife and we'll get back to you."

LJ made his way back to his truck, which was parked in the small parking lot of the U-shaped apartment complex, a small courtyard in the middle of the ground floor. It wasn't bad, he had to admit. He'd looked at a handful of properties that day in the price range he and Adrienne had agreed on. They weren't willing to pay for Kristie's entire life during her college years, but they had been wise and had saved for it. So, now the agreement was they'd pay the rent, and the rest was up to her, from her car payments, insurance, utilities, and anything else that popped up.

He grabbed the other brochures and printouts he'd gathered that day, each detailing costs and amenities. Tossing the paperwork into the console between the two leather bucket seats, he started the truck and was on his way. At least he'd gotten the ball rolling.

After their argument a few nights before, Adrienne had come to him a couple days later. She told him she'd thought about things and, even if she and LJ moved to Denver for her career, perhaps they could consider letting Kristie remain in Pueblo. In other words, it was her way of apologizing. In all their years together—more than twenty—he'd only ever heard her apologize one time, and that was to her mother because they were late to Christmas dinner.

As grateful as LJ was for her olive branch, which was more like an olive twig, he knew it was a large part of what was wrong with their marriage; it always had been.

Shoving all that aside, he pointed his truck in the direction to hit Santa Fe and head out to the county, where the superintendent's office was in the administration building. He stopped at a Starbucks along the way, intending to pick up coffees for Adrienne and himself. He pulled in behind an old station wagon, which surprisingly still ran, when something caught his eye.

Glancing behind him, he saw there was nobody waiting, so he thrust the truck into reverse and plowed out of the drive-thru, turning the wheel as hard as he could for the hairpin turn out of the parking lot.

He spared a glance at the sign that had caught his attention in the first place: OPEN HOUSE! BEAUTIFUL NEW TOWNHOUSES BY MELODY HOMES. Pulling the large black truck into the fresh black asphalt of the parking lot, he slowed as his gaze scanned the beautiful structures. Though new, they were Victorian in design.

Pulling into a parking space next to an original orange Volkswagen Bug, he killed the engine and sat there for a moment. He ignored every thought in his head and climbed out of the truck and walked toward the building.

There was a small group ahead of him, all speaking excitedly to each other. They were met at the open front door of a unit by a woman, who LJ presumed was the real estate agent in charge of the event. They passed and it was his turn.

"Welcome!" she said brightly, giving him a large smile. "Each unit is about thirteen-hundred square feet, hardwood throughout, your choice of three bedroom or two bedroom and a dedicated office. Enjoy your tour, sir, and here's my card if you have any questions."

"Uh," he said softly, taking the card and giving her a weak smile, "thanks."

LJ stepped inside, his eyes everywhere as he reached up and adjusted the baseball cap on his head. It was easy to admire the high ceilings, and the big, beautiful fireplace, which was obviously a feature of the open-concept first floor. The kitchen was filled with upgrades and easy access. He made his way to the dedicated office, which could be closed off to the main floor by French doors. A small, gas fireplace was tucked into the corner.

As he stood in the staged room—large walnut desk and leather chair—it was easy to see his own things in the room, including him sitting there with a fire going, soft music playing in the background, maybe a little Josh Groban, as he worked on a new story.

He violently shook himself out of his thoughts, storming out of the room then out of the townhouse, sick to his stomach. He could think of nothing but getting to his truck. Once there, he slammed the door shut, cutting him off from the world outside. He closed his eyes and took several deep breaths. Feeling like an idiot, he stuffed the material the woman had given him in the console and started the engine.

"Starbucks," he whispered. "Yeah. Got to get back to Starbucks."

❧ ❧ ❧ ❧

Two hot paper cups in hand, LJ walked into Adrienne's office, who he was glad had read his text and left it open for him. He entered and, knowing his wife's preference for privacy, used the toe of his boot to lightly tap the door closed.

"Hey," he said, walking across the medium-sized office to the desk, where Adrienne was sitting in front of the computer, her reading glasses firmly in place.

"Hang on," she said absently, moving the mouse for whatever she was working on and seeing on the screen.

LJ set her cherry vanilla latte—extra hot—near

the mouse pad and sat in the chair across from her desk after he pulled the brochures he'd tucked into his back pocket out. Crossing an ankle over the opposite knee, he sat back and relaxed as he sipped his mocha breve.

"I hadn't realized a new coffee shop was opened out here," he said conversationally. "Nice gals who own it, too. One is a pilot and the other is—"

"An author, I know. It's been around for a couple years, Larry."

"Oh. Well, I'm not out here all that often." He glanced out the window as he waited for her to finish and give him her attention. He gave a side glance to the apartment brochures on the edge of the desk and couldn't help but think of the townhouse he'd seen. He kept seeing that fireplace in his mind's eye, so magnificent and with awesome light for writing by the fire.

"Okay, sorry about that."

Torn from his thoughts, he focused on his wife, guilt causing him to clear his throat. "No worries. I know this budget thing has been a beast for you this year."

"God isn't that the truth," Adrienne said, pulling her glasses off and tossing them to the desktop before grabbing her cup. She took a careful sip, eyes closing. "Good stuff. Those ladies certainly know how to make a good latte."

"So, I picked up some brochures for you today of the places I saw," LJ said, pushing the small pile toward her across the large desk. "The one in Pueblo West is the best priced, but honestly, I'm not sure it's a good idea."

"Too far," Adrienne agreed, looking at the brochure for that property.

"Yeah. But, figured I'd show you anyway. So, we agree this one's out?" he asked.

"Agreed," Adrienne said with a nod, tossing the brochure into her desk-side trashcan. "What's next?"

"This one is the most bang for the buck, but I'm not keen on Kristie living on the west side—"

"What's this one, Larry?" Adrienne asked, holding up a brochure for another property. "It's a two bedroom."

LJ cleared his throat and readjusted himself in the chair. "Yes. It's a hell of a deal, very centralized between her job and school and, she's talked about maybe having Julia as a roommate."

Adrienne glared over at him. "She doesn't need a roommate."

He met her gaze, somehow managing to keep his tone even. "She doesn't need a roommate, or she doesn't need Julia Donovan as a roommate?"

Adrienne looked back down at the options before her. "I hardly think it's a discussion worth having when seeking a good place for our daughter to live in during college," she muttered.

LJ rolled his eyes as his wife's gaze was on the provided paperwork, not on him.

"So," she said, getting his attention. "What are your plans for the night?"

Confused, he shook his head. "What do you mean?"

"I have the retirement party for John tonight."

"Ah, yea," he said, grabbing his breve. "The event you didn't invite me to join you for."

"Larry," she said with a sigh, hands coming to rest on her forehead, "you never even worked with John."

"Is Sherry going?" he asked casually, meaning the wife of one of the teachers going to the event.

Adrienne looked away. "Why does everything have to be a fight with you, Larry?" She glanced at him. "I figured you would enjoy a quiet night, both Kristie and I out of the house." She reached for her glasses and put them on, turning back to her computer, effectively dismissing her husband.

❧ ❧ ❧ ❧

LJ slowed his truck so as not to slide before he turned into Nora's long, gravel drive. He pulled up beside the house and pulled the brake, killing the engine. He glanced over at the back of the house where Nora and Bella sat on the back stoop, their attention on something in the child's lap.

He climbed out of the truck and made his way over. "Hey."

"Hey, yourself." Nora pushed up from her place and met him halfway on the path to the back stoop. She gave him a one-armed hug, which he returned. "Glad you called."

"Glad you were home and wanted company," he said with a small smile.

She looked up into his eyes. "You okay?" she asked quietly.

He gave her a quick shrug. "So, what do we have over here?"

Bella looked up at him, and for only a second as the sun shone in her eyes, he swore he was looking down into the face of his baby sister. Taken aback for a moment, he cleared his throat and reached up to readjust his baseball cap. He felt a hand on his lower back and turned to see Nora giving him an understanding look. He had to assume she saw it, too.

Turning back to the little one, he knelt down. "Hey, kiddo," he said cheerily, reaching over and mussing her hair. "Who's this?"

"It's a kitten," Bella said, indicating the tiny bundle in her lap.

"Is it your kitten?" he asked, reaching over and petting the white and black fluff ball that looked back at him with huge green eyes.

"No. Aunt Nora said she needs to stay with her mommy."

He smiled. "That is important."

"But, Aunt Nora said she hasn't seen Oreo's mommy."

He glanced up at Nora for clarification. Nora moved around the two to sit behind Bella on the stoop. "Oreo here is the kitten of one of the feral cats around here," she explained. "I used to see her and the three kittens around, but I haven't seen her or the other two in a couple days."

"Well, that's not good, huh?" he asked, looking back at the girl. He smiled when he saw that the kitten was attempting to chew on one of Bella's small fingers.

"Are you hungry, LJ?" Nora asked. "I was going to make us Bella's favorite."

"What's that?"

"Mac 'n cheese and hot dogs."

"Yup, kid cuisine."

Two hours later, Bella tucked in with her arms wrapped around her stuffed bear Sam, Nora and LJ sat at the kitchen table, dishes taken care of and loaded into the dishwasher.

"Man, she reminds me so much of Shannon," LJ

said softly, indicating the bedrooms above their heads on the second floor.

"Me, too." Nora looked down at her hands, which rested on the table, fingers interlaced. "This has been so hard on Bella. God, she cries, LJ," she almost whispered, unshed emotion in her tone.

"Any news? Have you met with the police who are dealing with Shannon's case?"

Nora grinned. "Well." She pushed back from the table. "That one requires a beer." She walked over to the fridge and opened one side. On the top shelf—far out of the curious hands of a five-year-old—sat a six-pack of Blue Moon that had been there for months. "Want one?" she asked, wiggling a glass bottle in front of her.

He chuckled. "I don't know. With everything going on, you got anything stronger?"

Nora nodded. "I believe I do." She put the bottle back and closed the fridge, turning back to her brother. "Help?"

LJ walked over to her and reached up into the cabinet above the appliances, grabbing a bottle of Grey Goose vodka, which still held most of its contents. He set the bottle on the counter and closed the cabinet door.

"Okay, Coke or cranberry juice as a mixer?" Nora asked, opening the fridge once more.

"Who needs a mixer?" LJ teased, reaching over Nora's head to grab two glasses. "I'll take the juice."

"Coming up." Moments later and with a drink in each hand, she nodded toward the large front porch. "Come on, let's sit outside before it gets too cold to do that."

Settled and each with their drink, Nora eyed her

big brother. "What?" he asked, uncomfortable by the scrutiny. In truth, he'd been enjoying the quiet peace of the evening.

"You know I love seeing you, LJ, but let's face it, it's not often that the warden turns you loose, especially on a Saturday night. I mean, Lawrence, your obsequious nature with her hasn't been the greatest in life choices."

"Cheers to that," he said, raising his glass to lightly clink against Nora's. "I got paroled for the night. She's at a retirement party for a colleague."

"Why aren't you there with her?"

"I'm not a colleague."

"No," Nora drawled, "but you are her husband."

He gave her a rueful smile. "I tried to remind her of that today."

"Oh, ouch. And, how did that go over?"

"Like a lead balloon." The siblings were quiet for a moment before LJ looked over at where she sat in a chair that matched his, a small square table between them where her drink sat. "I wanted to ask you a favor, sis."

"Sure. What's up?" She took her drink back in hand for a slow sip.

"I was wondering if you'd be willing to spend a little time with Kristie."

Nora met his gaze, surprise in her eyes. "Oh? Is everything okay?"

"It is." He nodded. "But I think she needs a little…Aunt Nora guidance." He grinned over at her. It took a moment, but Nora's eyebrows rose.

"Oh?"

He nodded. "Oh."

# *Chapter Twelve*

## Beulah, Colorado – 2002

You said here, right?" Nora asked from behind the wheel of her rental car. She had a small break between shoots. She'd be heading to South Africa next.

"Uh," Shannon said, studying the screen of the GPS system in her hands. She glanced out the window of the sedan to the wooded area to the right of the car. "Yeah. It looks like it should be in there somewhere." She indicated a general area.

"You know Dad is going to kick your ass for taking his TomTom, right?"

Shannon smirked as she brought up a hand to tuck long auburn hair behind her ear. "He's always angry about something, Nora. I mean, come on."

"True." Nora found a place to park on the side of the road and turned the car off, facing her sister. "Okay, now what exactly are we doing again?"

"Geocaching," Shannon said simply, as though that explained it all. She reached down to the backpack that she had stowed between her feet and tugged it onto her lap.

"Again, what exactly are we doing again?"

Shannon grinned over at her big sister. "It's basically a treasure hunt where people hide stuff and I use Dad's GPS to find it."

"Okay, so then why did you have me stop to buy a bunch of erasers and stickers and stuff?" Nora asked, unbuckling her seatbelt, accepting the printed page she was handed.

"That has a few clues on it," Shannon explained. "The erasers and stuff are to put in the geocache. You take stuff and leave stuff."

Nora nodded, looking over the text on the page. "Okie dokie." The two headed into the woods, Nora watching her step. She was lamenting wearing tennis shoes now, rather than the hiking boots Shannon had worn. "So, how do you like the new house?" she asked, glancing over at her sister, reaching up to move a low-hanging branch out of their way. The thirteen-year-old was still several inches shorter than Nora, but even Shannon would have been smacked in the face.

Shannon shrugged, glancing down at the GPS. "It's okay, I guess. It made me mad that I had to switch schools." She glanced up at Nora. "I liked Heaton. It was awesome to be able to jump on my bike and ride up to the college and spend the day reading or playing on the computer or whatever. I don't like Pleasant View that much." She let out a sigh. "Kinda feel like I'm out in the middle of nowhere."

"I know, kiddo." Nora wrapped an arm around Shannon's shoulders. "I'm sorry. I was only a little bit younger than you when we moved here, so I understand." As they continued through the heavily wooded area, she asked, "Do you like Minnie?"

Shannon sent a glare her way, which made Nora chuckle. "She's a hag, and she's the reason we had to move. *Not* happy with Minnelia Turk." She scrunched her lovely young face. "Who on earth names their kid Minnelia?"

Nora shook her head slowly. "You've got me on that one." She chuckled. "Just when I thought Minnie was bad. So, are you still singing?"

"Of course!" Shannon exclaimed, as though Nora should know better than to ask.

"Well good, 'cuz, it would break my heart if you ever stopped singing, kiddo."

Shannon smiled with pride. "I'd rather sing than just about anything, Nor. Way more important than boys."

"What? You mean, you're not engaged, yet?" Nora teased.

Shannon rolled her eyes. "Duh, I'm only thirteen. Boys can wait."

"Yes, indeed," Nora said, the two continuing to follow the GPS signal.

"Over that way!" Shannon exclaimed, excitedly pointing toward three trees that seemed to be in a distinctive and natural huddle. "Come on!"

Nora followed, startled as the teen took off running. Once she caught up to her, out of breath, Shannon was on her hands and knees, pushing foliage aside. She glanced over her shoulder at Nora. "Read the clue."

Nora lifted the page she'd been given in the car. "Uh, okay. 'To find me look for the green, but don't let your eyes fool you.'" Nora's eyebrows drew together. "What kind of clue is that?"

Shannon didn't bother to answer and instead, set the GPS unit aside and began to really dig in, leaves, twigs, clots of dirt, and even a lizard all flew until Shannon whooped out in victory.

Curious, Nora moved to her side and squatted down. She watched as Shannon pulled out a neon green case that appeared to be for holding glasses or sunglasses. She chuckled. "Well, I guess the clue makes more sense now."

Shannon fell back to sit on her behind in the leaves and opened it. She pulled out a long, narrow slip of paper rolled up like a scroll. It sat atop various little gizmos, including half a pencil, plastic coins, a couple "dollars" from a Monopoly game, and a handful of plastic farm animals, including a chicken with a plastic wire necklace attached to it.

"Pick something," Shannon said, handing Nora the eyeglass case as she unfurled the scroll and jotted down the date and her name.

Nora picked through the contents until she decided on the chicken on a plastic string.

Nora removed an eraser shaped like a duck from Shannon's backpack and placed it inside the case, as well as the rerolled scroll. She put the green case back where they'd found it. Shannon grinned up at Nora as she stood, wiping any loose dirt off the butt of her jeans.

"Congratulations," she said. "You've now officially been part of finding your first geocache."

Three hours, seven more finds, and a lunch later, Nora pulled up in front of her father's ranch-style house, a mile past the Mesa Drive-In.

"I'm so glad you came home for my choir concert," Shannon said, glancing over at Nora from the passenger seat where she had unbuckled her seatbelt.

"Oh, course! It's not every day my little sister gets not one solo, but *two*." She smiled as Shannon blushed slightly. "Listen, I have something for you." Nora reached past her sister to the glove compartment and grabbed a square wrapped package from within.

"With your incredible talent, I wanted to introduce you to an incredible talent."

Shannon took the package and with the look of a child on Christmas morning, tore into the wrapping paper revealing the two-disc CD set of *Phantom of the Opera* and *Eden*, which had a handwritten note on the dust jacket inside the plastic jewel case cover.

*No matter what happens in life, always remember to be you and that you're loved.*

*Love your big sis,*

*Nora*

"Wow," Shannon whispered, her fingers running over the smooth plastic. "I've heard of *Phantom of the Opera* before, but who is this Sarah Brightman person? She's pretty."

"Yes, and she's in both of those. She plays Christine Daae in *Phantom* and the other one is her own album. I saw her in Milan two years ago. You actually sound a lot like her."

Shannon glanced over at her. "Seriously?"

"Yup. If you like her stuff, I'll send you more." She reached over, resting her hand on the back of the headrest of Shannon's seat. "Listen, missy, next time I come back here, I fully expect to be serenaded by your favorite Sarah song. Got me?"

Shannon grinned and nodded vigorously. "I got you."

❧ ❧ ❧ ❧

Nora stood at her dresser, jewelry box open. She dug through a few trinkets she'd brought back from her travels until she found what she was looking for. A small smile spread across her lips when she found the plastic chicken on a plastic, smooth and tubular rope like a strand of red licorice.

Closing her eyes, she brought the plastic chicken up to her lips and left a soft kiss there, almost as though sending up a silent prayer. Her attention was taken by the chirp of her phone lying on the dresser, which she instantly silenced, not wanting to wake Bella who was asleep right across the hall. She'd asked Sarah to text when she arrived rather than knocking or ringing the doorbell.

Pocketing the chicken, Nora headed toward her bedroom door, flicking off the light and, as quietly as possible, trotting down the steep staircase.

"Hey," Sarah said as Nora let her in through the kitchen door. "I know it's late and I'm sorry. It's been some very long, chaotic days."

"It's okay. There's coffee going if you want some," Nora said, keeping her hand on the glass door as it closed so it wouldn't slam and wake her niece.

"Yeah, that would be great." Sarah stood in the middle of the kitchen holding a blue folder and looking rather uncertain.

"Sorry," Nora said with an apologetic smile. "Have a seat."

As Nora moved around the small kitchen, gathering mugs, spoons, and coffee fixings, Sarah pulled out a chair at the wooden square table and sat. "As I said on the phone earlier, I have a slight update and I have some questions."

"Okay," Nora said, butterflies batting ruthlessly at her insides in anticipation of what she was going to hear. She brought her offerings to the table and took the seat across from Sarah.

"Nora," Sarah began, her expression serious,

"does Shannon have any connection to Canon City?"

Nora considered the question as she poured Sarah a mug of coffee. Eventually, she shook her head as she slid the steaming mug over to her. "No. I've never heard her mention it before, at least. I'm not even sure she's ever been there." She eyed her warily. "Why?"

Seeming to ignore Nora's question, Sarah opened the folder that lay on the table and presented Nora with an eight-by-ten color photo of the ruined high-heeled shoe they'd found. "A couple hikers found some things. Do you recognize this shoe?"

Nora took the proffered picture and studied it. Instantly, tears stung the backs of her eyes. She nodded. "I was with her when she bought these shoes," she said softly, recognizing the small patch of rhinestones at the top of the stiletto stem. She gave Sarah a small smile. "I used to call this shoe her hooker shoes because of how high they are." She looked back down at the shoe. "There was only one?" She noted Sarah's nod. "Are these scuff marks? It almost looks like…" She had to stop, unable to say it out loud.

"I know it looks like drag marks," Sarah said softly, taking the picture back. "We're not sure yet." She handed over another glossy.

Nora looked at it and shook her head. "I know Shannon is the ultimate girly girl, all bags and shoes, but I don't recognize this purse. That doesn't mean anything, though," she clarified. "It could be hers, but I don't know."

"Okay. What kind of car does Shannon drive, Nora?" Sarah took the opportunity to pour some cream and add a bit of sugar to her coffee, lightly stirring with the provided spoon.

"Uh…" Nora glanced off into space to think.

"Subaru. An Impreza, I think. Why? Did you find her car?" Nora asked, not entirely sure what she wanted Sarah's answer to be.

Sarah shook her head. "No, but we found what we believe to be her car key with the purse. It's a key for a Subaru."

Nora buried her face in her hands for a long moment before blowing out a breath, her hands dropping to the table. Sarah reached across the wooden surface and covered Nora's hand with one of her own.

"I know this is hard," she said softly, kindness in her dark eyes. "I'm so sorry. I'm doing all I can to find her."

Nora nodded, swallowing hard before she was able to speak. "I know. How, how do you know for sure these are her things? I mean, could it be coincidence?"

Sarah let out a breath of her own before she removed a third picture from the folder and handed it to Nora.

A sob tore from Nora's throat when she saw the image of her sister staring back at her from her very own driver's license. As her vision became blurry with tears, she heard the scoot of a wooden chair on the floor as Sarah moved from her chair to the one next to Nora. Nora allowed herself to be taken into a hug, her head cradled against Sarah's shoulder and soothing fingers running through her hair.

"I know," Sarah whispered into the hug. "It's okay."

After several minutes, the tears began to slow then stop. Nora sniffled, feeling stupid and entirely too comfortable. She moved away from Sarah, giving her a rueful, albeit watery smile. "Sorry."

"You have nothing to apologize for," Sarah said

with a smile of her own. She reached a hand up and tucked some hair behind Nora's ear. "Do you want to stop for tonight?"

Nora shook her head, pushing away from the table to grab a paper towel from the roll mounted under the cabinet. "No," she said, wiping her face before blowing her nose. "I'm sorry. I didn't expect that to hit me so hard."

Sarah moved over to where Nora stood by the sink, her back leaning against a perpendicular counter as she crossed her arms over her button-up shirt-clad chest. "It's completely understandable that it would, Nor," she said.

Nora glanced at her, not used to hearing the name Sarah used to call her. She had to push that aside. "Was that blood smeared on her license, Sarah?"

"We don't know, yet. The lab hasn't gotten back to us. It was pretty muddy up there, so it could be mud, but we don't know."

Nora threw her soiled paper towel into the trash next to the stove. "What does this all mean, Sarah? I mean, that guy with her apartment key that day, that was in Colorado Springs obviously, but then this stuff found in Canon City which is what, like forty-five minutes away?"

"Yeah. The thing that has me concerned is, they're two different counties, El Paso and Fremont Counties. I have to wonder if whoever is responsible for Shannon's disappearance did that on purpose."

"What do you mean?"

Sarah shrugged as she moved back to the table and took her seat. She sipped from her coffee before she said, "Typically the police aren't going to communicate unless some sort of link is found, a connection to another county or town. I'm guessing the person or persons behind this were hoping that would work in their favor."

Nora walked back to her seat, as well. "Sarah, do you think Shannon is still alive?"

Sarah let out a heavy sigh as she sat back in her chair. "I can't say that, but I can't say that she isn't. The only thing I *can* tell you is, the more time that goes by, the more dangerous the situation becomes."

Nora nodded. "I understand." She grabbed her own cup of coffee and fixed it how she liked it. She grimaced when she took a sip as it had cooled. "Do you want yours warmed up?" she asked, getting to her feet.

"Nah," Sarah said with a grin. "I'm used to drinking cold coffee all day."

Nora smiled and made her way over to the microwave.

"Would you be willing to look at some folks for me? Help me identify them?"

"Sure. Whatever you need."

"Okay," Sarah said, digging through her folder and pulling out several more pictures, placing one in front of Nora's chair. "Do you know this guy?"

The microwave beeping to a halt, Nora retrieved her coffee and rejoined Sarah. She set the mug down as she lowered herself into the chair, her gaze on the man in the picture. "He looks familiar, but I don't know his name. I think I saw him a few times at a club Shannon hangs out at in Denver." She spared a glance to Sarah. "I used to go with her sometimes."

"Do you know the name of the club?"

"It was called The East Room, but it closed down last year."

"Okay, this guy?"

Nora looked at the new picture presented to her, this one a Hispanic man. "No idea."

"Okay, and finally this guy."

"Oh, that's Rick Stanton," Nora said immediately, tapping the picture of the smiling man. "Bella's father."

"And, he died two years ago, right?" Sarah asked, putting the three pictures back into the folder.

Nora looked at her with confusion in her eyes. "Rick? No. I just saw him, maybe six months ago at Sam's Club. He looked alive and well to me. I mean, I don't know if something has happened since, but he's definitely been alive in the past couple years. Why would you think he was dead?"

"Do you know Ronnie Garcia?"

Nora thought for a moment. "Isn't that the neighbor's son? Penny?"

Sarah nodded. "Yup. He told me Shannon told him Bella's dad was dead."

"That's weird," Nora said, stroking her chin. "Why would she tell him that? She loved Rick."

"Mommy! Mommy, no!"

Nora nearly knocked her chair over backward in her haste to get to the stairs, which she raced up, Sarah hot on her heels. Nora was breathless with concern and exertion by the time she reached Bella's bedroom. The little girl was sitting up in bed, eyes wide and tears running down her cheeks.

"Bella?" Nora hurried over to her bed. "Hey. What's wrong, honey?" Nora glanced over at Sarah, who stood at the foot of Bella's bed as the child clung to her. "Did you have a bad dream?" she murmured to the girl, who nodded, her face buried in Nora's neck.

"Can I get her anything? Some water or something?" Sarah asked.

"Do you want some water, sweetie?" Nora rubbed comforting circles across Bella's back. At Bella's nod, Sarah turned and hurried from the room. "What happened in your dream, hmm?" Nora asked softly, gently pushing the little girl away from her so she could look into her tear-streaked face. She used the edge of the sheet to dry her cheeks.

"Mommy got hurt," she said, her voice as tiny as she was.

"How did she get hurt?" She glanced up when Sarah reappeared, an unopened bottle of water in her hand. "Thanks, Sarah." Nora twisted off the cap as Sarah took a seat at the foot of the bed. "Here, sweetie. Take a drink."

Bella grasped the bottle in her small hands and took several long gulps before handing the bottle back to her aunt. "A big doggie ate her."

"A big doggie?"

"Like we saw in the field that day."

"Ah, the coyote. Oh, sweetie. I'm sorry." Nora gave her a small kiss on her forehead.

"Is Mommy okay?" she asked, looking up at Nora with big, green eyes.

Nora glanced over the child's head to Sarah, not sure how to answer that. "Bella," she began gently, "I want you to meet someone. This lady is Sarah." Bella glanced at Sarah, who was sitting a couple of feet away and waving a few fingers at her. "Can you say hello, sweetie?"

"Hi," Bella said quietly.

"Hi, Bella," Sarah said. "I'm working to try to bring your mommy back home to you, okay?"

"Are you magic?" Bella asked, two fingers finding their way into her mouth.

Sarah smiled and shook her head. "No, but I'm a police officer. I'll do all I can, okay?"

Bella nodded, eyeing her. "'Kay."

"Let's get you tucked back in, okay?" Nora said softly, standing from the bed. "Lay down, sweetie." She got the girl settled and leaned over to give her a kiss on the forehead. "Goodnight, sweet girl. I'll see you in the morning."

"Bye, police lady," Bella said sleepily to Sarah, who was moving to the door.

The two women headed back downstairs.

"She is such a beautiful little girl," Sarah said, walking to the table and gathering her things together. "I see so much of what I remember Shannon looking like as a child."

"Yes, she's a spitting image, really. She's a good girl. So often, I honestly have no idea what to say, how to answer her questions."

Sarah nodded. "I can only imagine. You're in a tough spot, Nora, but you truly are doing a wonderful job with her. You're so good with her."

"Thanks for what you're doing, Sarah. I mean, I know it's your job, but thank you, from me, from Bella, from my entire family."

Sarah studied her for a long moment before looking away, tapping her folder on the table to right all the pictures inside. "No need for thanks." She gave her a small smile. "Listen, do you know of any places where Shannon spent a lot of time at any restaurants, stores, anything like that?"

Nora nodded. "Yeah, quite a few."

"Can you email me a list of them, by chance?"

"Some I can, but honestly, most of them I simply remember how to get there, I don't know the names or addresses. Especially since some were private homes."

"Okay. Well, how would you feel about going on a little field trip with me? It's a bit different, but we can head to the Springs and hit some of these places."

"Absolutely. Let me know when so I can make sure I have care for Bella."

"Okay. I'll text or call you tomorrow to work out the details."

Nora nodded. "Sounds good." She watched as Sarah drained her coffee mug and set her empty cup into the sink. "Drive safe," she said lamely.

Sarah walked over to her, folder tucked in her hand against the side of her thigh. Nora met her gaze, an awkward silence flowing between the two.

"Well," Sarah said at length, moving past Nora to the door, "talk to you soon."

# *Chapter Thirteen*

Andrew Lacey sat in his comfortable leather chair, bouncing slightly on the chair back's spring as he held the phone to his ear. He chuckled at what had just been said. "Nah, Brian, I honestly think they're going to cave the minute they hear we got Alex Ferris on our side. I mean, come on, Ferris gave us information that will bankrupt this company." He laughed outright at the response. "Okay." He glanced toward his office door after the soft knock. A moment later his secretary, Mary, poked her head in. "Hang on, Brian." Andrew held his hand over the mouthpiece. "Hey, Mary, what's up?"

"Sorry to bother you, Andy, but there's someone here to see you. Do you have a minute?"

"Sure, have them come on in. I've got a few minutes before lunch." Once Mary disappeared, he said his goodbyes to his friend and colleague and cradled the phone.

Pushing away from his desk, Andrew glanced in the mirror next to his bookcase quickly, bringing up a hand to smooth back his hair. He didn't bother to don his jacket, choosing to remain in his starched white button up with tie and fashionable suspenders.

He took his place behind the desk again as the door opened and a woman stepped in. She was dressed simply in a peasant skirt and ill-fitting blouse. Her brown hair was pulled back from her face with a headband, and plain sandals finished the outfit.

Andrew turned on his usual charm, rising from his desk as she neared him. "Hello. I'm Andrew Lacey. How can I help you?"

The woman, who looked as though she were about to cry, looked away before meeting his eyes with her own pained blue ones. "Mr. Lacey," she said softly, "My name is Laura Caffey. My husband is Robert Caffey, and I believe he and your wife are having an affair."

The smile froze on his face as he looked into the devastated woman's face. "Excuse me?"

She indicated one of the two leather chairs before Andrew's desk. "May I?"

"Please." Waiting for the woman to sit, he also took his seat.

"Listen, Mr. Lacey," she said softly, "I didn't come here to upset you or hurt you, I came here because Robert is all I have." She looked down at her hands, which fidgeted in her lap. "Three years ago, I was diagnosed with MS." Her gaze remained firmly on her hands. "I can no longer work. Some days I can barely take care of our three children." She looked up at last and met Andrew's concerned gaze. "Mr. Lacey, I love my husband, I do. Fourteen years is a long time to give to someone."

He nodded slowly. "It is." His heart pounded in his chest. He forced his mind to stay clear and hear her entire story before he allowed himself to think or feel.

"To be honest, I'm not sure if my illness drove him to your wife." Again, she looked down at her hands. "I'm not always able to be the wife he needs, I know."

"Mrs. Caffey," Andrew began gently, resting

his hands on his desk and lacing his fingers together. "What makes you think your husband is sleeping with my wife?"

"Well, you see I was suspicious. Robert is like clockwork." She gave him a weak smile. "He's so predictable, I always told him I could literally set my clock to his routine." The smile slid from her face. "Suddenly, he wasn't coming home for lunch anymore. He had all sorts of excuses, but I knew." She gave him a rueful look. "A woman always knows." She cleared her throat. "Anyway, I followed him one day from the trailer where he runs his contracting business, and he went directly to your home."

"How do you know who lives there?"

"Because I'd been there before. You see, Mr. Lacey, Robert and his crew did the renovations on your house. I brought them lunch several times while they were working on your kitchen."

Andrew felt as though he'd been punched in the stomach. He fell back against his chair, mouth slightly open. He remembered the redheaded man who had led the charge on his house. He'd been polite, hard-working, and extremely efficient and professional. Andrew had even passed his name on to some of his friends for their own home projects.

"I don't know what to do, Mr. Lacey," the seemingly-frail woman before him whispered, her face dissolving into tears.

"Hey," he said, quickly hurrying around to her side of the desk. He knelt next to her chair, reaching up onto the desk for a tissue, which he handed her. She sniffled several times, dabbing at her eyes and nose. "Listen, I was about to head to lunch."

"Oh! I'm so sorry—"

"Why don't you join me, okay? And we can talk about this."

⚜ ⚜ ⚜ ⚜

Pueblo, Colorado – 1990

"Hey, Andy!"

Andrew, then a college sophomore, turned at his name, yelled over MC Hammer's, *U Can't Touch This.* "Hey, Neil!" he called as he tried to make his way into the party, his girlfriend, Kayla holding tightly onto his hand, so they wouldn't get separated in the throngs of college kids.

They managed to reach Roger, Andrew's old high school friend, whose parents owned the house but were away for the weekend.

"Hey, Andy! Glad you guys could come," Roger said, already well on his way to being drunk. He wore his typical dark Wayfarer sunglasses, which Andrew knew was how he hid bloodshot eyes from far too much partying. The guy had barely managed to graduate high school because of a constant hangover. Once Andrew realized his friend was a raging alcoholic at the age of nineteen, he'd pulled back from their friendship. "Hey, Kayla," Roger greeted the brunette with a leer. "Looking hot as ever."

She rolled her eyes and said nothing.

"Get a beer, man. There's plenty."

"Thanks," Andrew said, leading Kayla past his friend and to the backyard where he knew there would be an old bathtub sitting in the middle of the yard filled with ice, beer, and bottles of hard liquor.

"Andy," Kayla said, moving up beside him once

they'd reached the tub. She looked around at the throngs around them. "How long do we have to stay?"

"Not long," he answered, handing her a Zima while grabbing a beer for himself. "Babe, he's been asking me for months to come to one of his parties." Andrew moved in close to his girlfriend of two years so she could hear him over the music. "I've put it off."

Kayla nodded as she twisted off the cap of the slightly carbonated alcoholic drink and took a small sip. "I know. It's only...I don't like the way he looks at me."

"Want me to say something to him?" Andrew asked, cracking open his can of Budweiser.

"No. We're not around him enough to bother. I simply don't like him."

"Hey, there's Toby and Myra. Let's go talk to them," he suggested, noting a couple that he knew Kayla liked.

As the two couples chatted about their classes for that semester, Andrew's attention was caught by a gorgeous young woman who stood by herself at the tub of booze. She wore a summer dress with a flowing skirt. Her sandy-blond hair was pulled back away from her face, and she was stunning without wearing a bit of makeup. When she glanced over at him with big, brown eyes, he couldn't help but smile, which was returned. But, as she turned to walk away from the tub, her heeled sandal caught on some ice that had been dumped from the tub and down she went.

"Crap," he said as he and other partygoers hurried over to her. "Are you okay?" He knelt down next to where she lay, her hand reaching down to grab her ankle.

"I think I twisted my ankle," she said shyly with

a rueful smile.

"She okay, man?" Roger asked, shoving his sunglasses to the top of his head.

"She hurt her ankle," Andrew said. "Can we get her to the couch?"

"Yeah, totally." Roger stood. "Everybody move!"

Andrew slid his arm beneath her knees and circled the other around her back. "Ready?" At her nod, he got to his feet, easily lifting her petite frame and carrying her along the path Roger had made for them. He brought her into the house and to the living room where Roger was shoving some discarded jackets aside for her to lay down.

"This is so humiliating," the young woman murmured.

Andrew grinned down at her. "Hey, look at it as an adventure." Her smile nearly melted him where he stood. He lowered her to the couch as gently as he could. He felt strangely cold as her arm slipped away from where it had been wrapped around his neck. "I'm Andy, by the way," he said softly.

"Jill," she said.

Knowing full well he needed to return to his girlfriend, who was giving him the evil eye from the back door, Andrew smiled down at her. "See ya around, Jill."

* * * * *

Andrew hitched his backpack up a bit higher onto his shoulder as he headed toward the front door of The Pantry, a local greasy spoon with decent food at cheap, college-kid prices. He knew he would be the first to arrive—his two classmates, Martin and

Felix, were always late. They preferred to study at the restaurant together because he had a roommate who was far more interested in playing loud video or role-play games than studying. Martin lived at home and had a helicopter mom and Felix was couch surfing, every cent he made working at Albertsons supermarket going to his tuition.

The restaurant was abuzz with chatter as customers packed into the torn vinyl booths and uncomfortable chairs at tables. He stepped up to the sign that read, PLEASE SEAT YOURSELF.

"Hi. Just you?"

Andrew turned, shocked to see the young woman from the party the week before standing before him, a smile on her lovely face. "Uh, no, there will be three of us," he managed.

"Okay." She stretched to reach behind the abandoned cashier's desk to grab three menus. She smiled up at him, reaching up to brush some strands of hair that had come loose from her ponytail. "Follow me."

Andrew did exactly that, noting the way her well-fitting jeans hugged a shapely behind. He was so focused on said behind he nearly ran into her when she abruptly stopped. He looked up, eyes wide in surprise and guilt as he came to an abrupt stop.

"Um, this is your table, Andrew," she said softly, though an amused smile crossed her full lips.

"Oh. Uh, thanks." He gave her a winning smile to cover how stupid he felt. He slid into the booth and accepted a menu from her.

"Um," she said, looking down shyly at her feet before she spared a glance back to him. "If you need anything, ask for me."

"Okay. Thanks…Jill."

Her smile nearly blinded him. "You remembered."

"How could I forget?"

Laura Caffey broke off a piece of her taco shell bowl and popped it into her mouth. She was quiet as she chewed. "You know, that's funny," she said at length. "Robert and I met in a similar way." She gave Andrew a small smile from her seat across the table from him. "It was a church function. We were both in high school, and Robert was in a car accident and broke his leg, so he was in a cast." She looked down at her half-eaten lunch. "He was so handsome."

"I'm truly sorry, Laura," Andrew said softly, wiping his mouth with the paper napkin provided. He liked this woman, thought she was a fine human being and deserved better. "How old are your kids?" He accepted the fresh Diet Coke the waiter brought him, the finished drink taken away.

A smile of pride spread across her face. "Michael is twelve and the twins, Abby and Beth are six."

"You guys have twins, too?" Andrew said, eyes wide as he sat forward, intrigued.

"Oh, yes. It was a difficult pregnancy with our son, so it was a shock that I got pregnant again, let alone with twin girls." She gave a small chuckle. "Honestly, I felt it was a gift from God. I knew instinctually I wouldn't be able to have any more kids." She let out a heavy sigh as she sat back in her chair, sparing Andrew a glance. "Robert always wanted a big family. He's one of nine. Though I never wanted that many, I knew he wanted a lot of kids, yet all I could give him was three."

"Hey," Andrew said softly, waiting until she met his gaze, "you don't owe him anything. I hate men who make women feel like broodmares." He took a sip of his fresh soda.

"How old are your twins?"

"They'll be sixteen in a couple weeks," he said with a sad smile. "Sylvia, now that girl has the world by the tail, you know?" He shook his head, pride quirking his lips into a small smile. "Lord only knows what she'll end up deciding to do."

"What about the other one?"

"Tyler." Andrew pushed his plate away, only a smear of refried beans and a small bit of Spanish rice remaining. "My son…struggles. I honestly don't think he has a clue who he truly is. You know?"

Laura nodded. "I do. I was very much that way."

"It's hard for me to understand. I knew from such a young age what I wanted to do, where my life was headed. I knew I wanted to be a lawyer, eventually a judge."

"Isn't it interesting, Andrew," Laura said softly, "all that planning, all those years understanding yourself, knowing what you wanted and going after it, yet"—she indicated the Mexican restaurant around them—"here we are, sitting at the Cactus Flower."

He studied her for a long time before looking away.

❧❧❧❧

Pueblo, Colorado – 1991

"I love this time of year," Jill said softly, her hand tucked into the pocket of her peacoat, her other hand laced with Andrew's as they walked through City Park. "Can you smell the smoke in the air? Everyone burning their fireplaces and woodstoves." She gazed up at her boyfriend with a happy smile.

His heart was pounding, he was sweating and, on such a gorgeous October morning, he was nervous. After that day at The Pantry, he and Jill had begun spending time together, talking, getting to know each other. Once he'd discovered her heart, he knew he was barking up the wrong tree with Kayla. He'd ended a two-year relationship to give it all to Jillian Schaeffer.

He shoved his hand into the pocket of his jacket. He was a twenty-year-old man about to graduate from college—a year early—on his way to law school. But, something in him knew he had to act. He felt the hardness of the small box inside the fabric. He glanced at her a couple times, noting the loveliness of her delicate features, the way her hair blew in the autumn breeze.

Clearing his throat, Andrew placed a hand on Jill's arm stopping her forward movement. She looked at him with a question in her eyes. "I've never met anyone like you, Jill," he said quietly, his heart pounding so hard he worried she could hear it. "You're so kind and an incredible woman. You're loyal, absolutely beautiful and—" He took a deep breath and brought out the ring box as he lowered himself to one knee. He was pleased when Jill gasped and covered her mouth with her hands, tears shining in her eyes. He opened the box, revealing a simple, yet exquisite diamond ring. "Will you marry me?"

"Yes!" Jill exclaimed, grabbing Andrew by his jacket to bring him to his feet, instantly falling into his arms.

Andrew strolled through the same park, the open ends of his London Fog flapping lightly in the early autumn breeze. His Armani wingtips crunched on a few fallen twigs from the trees above. He could still hear Jill's cry of excitement when he placed that engagement ring on her finger, even if it was a little bit too big and he had to get it sized. She wore it with pride, showing it to all her friends.

He came upon a bench and sat down, knees spread with his hands resting on his thighs. He saw a young couple, two women, strolling hand in hand down by the lake. It was bittersweet for him to watch them: sweet to see such young love but a bitter pill to swallow, to be sure.

In the time he'd spent with Laura Caffey that afternoon, he believed her, and thinking back, he knew she was right. Deep down, he'd suspected for quite a while. As he sat there on that park bench, he had never felt lonelier. He was too ashamed to call anyone and in truth, wasn't sure that he even wanted to talk about it.

With a heavy sigh, he pushed to his feet and turned in the direction of his car.

Andrew pulled his Mercedes into the garage, annoyed when he saw Jill's car was gone. "Figures." Now he was *really* pissed.

He slammed his way to the garage door that led into the house, noting the sound of the TV in the kitchen. He shrugged out of his jacket as he headed in that direction and saw Sylvia sitting at the island eating chips.

"What exactly makes you think Doritos makes a good dinner?" he demanded, his voice far more harsh than he intended it to be.

The teen glanced up at him from where she'd been staring at her phone screen. "No food in the house. Mom was supposed to get groceries today but didn't."

"Where is she?"

"Dinner with the girls," Sylvia said before crunching another cheesy chip.

"Yeah, right," he said, removing his wallet from the inside pocket of his suit jacket. He removed a fifty-dollar bill and tossed it on the counter. "Order some dinner. Where's your brother?"

"Upstairs," she said, shoving the bag of chips aside as she grabbed the money. "Killing something on his video game, I'm sure."

"Did he get his homework done?" Andrew asked, eyebrows drawn.

Sylvia snorted as she met her father's gaze. "That would require him to actually go to school, Dad."

"What? Again?"

She nodded, grabbing her cell phone. "Again. Pizza or Chinese?" she asked, phone ready to dial.

"Whatever you want," he said with a heavy sigh as he continued through the kitchen to the winding staircase. He tossed his coat over the banister and dropped his briefcase on the floor before he stormed to his son's bedroom, reaching for the doorknob only to find it locked. Raising a fist, he pounded three times on the thick wood. "Open the door, Tyler!"

"Fuck off!"

"Little bastard," Andrew growled and marched off to the bedroom he shared with Jill and grabbed the skeleton key from its hiding place in his bedside table drawer. Sadly, he'd learned long ago to not only hide the key but make sure it was always handy. Marching back to the locked door, he easily disengaged the lock and threw the door open. Tyler, who was lying on his unmade bed, held the controller for his Xbox One in his hands.

"Jesus!" he yelled, sounding startled. "Get the hell out of here!"

Andrew glanced over at the screen of the mounted flat-screen, noting the gore and blood splattered across the animated world. "Turn that shit off, Tyler."

"No. Get out of my room." Tyler turned his back on his father as he returned his attention to his game.

Enraged—by both his son and his afternoon—Andrew stormed over to the bed and grabbed the wireless controller from Tyler's hands and threw it across the room, only for it to slam against the wall.

"What the fuck did you do that for?" Tyler enraged, scrambled to his feet.

"First of all, you will *not* use that kind of language in my house! Second of all, why the hell weren't you at school today?"

"She fucking promised," Tyler said, glaring at his open bedroom door.

"How many times do we have to cover this, Tyler? You're failing your classes. You don't show up, and when you do, you disrupt the class."

"Who the fuck do you think you are?" Tyler yelled, moving farther into Andrew's personal space. "You don't know one whit about me, don't give a shit about me, so fuck you!"

"Who do I think I am?" Andrew was incredulous, shocked by the outburst. "I'm your father!" he roared.

"Yeah?" Tyler smirked. "Then maybe you should actually stick around and act like it."

As though physically punched, Andrew took a step back, his hand coming to rest on his stomach. No idea what else to say, he turned to leave. "You miss one more day of school and that game box disappears," he said, slamming the door shut behind him.

He stood there for a moment on the landing, hands on hips before he ran his hands through his hair in frustration. He grabbed his coat and briefcase and headed to his office, bypassing the bedroom. As he plopped down in the chair behind the desk, his phone alerted him to activity on his Facebook account. Grabbing his tablet, he went to the social media site and saw that he had a new friend request from Laura Caffey.

He stared at her name for a moment before, with a small smile, he brought his hand up and tapped the screen, accepting the request.

# *Chapter Fourteen*

## Cheyenne, WY

The constant drone of the Bobcat's engine was drowned out by the music blaring in Tony's ears. The fifty-five-year-old was a twenty-year veteran of the Cheyenne Landfill. It was decent pay, good benefits, good enough to send his daughter off to college. She was a med student and had given him the best Father's Day gift ever two years ago of a bandana and a bottle of peppermint oil. She'd learned in some of her classes working with cadavers to put a few drops of the fragrant and strong oil on the material then tie it around her face, bank-robber style. It sure helped keep the stench of the dump at bay.

His head bobbed to Johnny Cash's "Ring of Fire" as he pushed hundreds of tons of trash toward the area where later he'd come through with a grader to dig trenches for the garbage to be buried.

He put the powerful little machine in reverse before pushing forward again to gather what his first pass had missed. His music list switched to Alabama's, "Roll On (Eighteen Wheeler)." He was singing along when he spotted something he couldn't quite make out.

Bringing the Bobcat to a stop, he turned off his music and removed the earbuds. As he hopped down, his worn work boots crunched on gravel before he made his way to what had caught his eye.

"What the hell is this?" he said, reaching out to touch the strange object. "Holy shit!" He scrambled away. His crab crawl back to the Bobcat would have been amusing under different circumstances. He climbed up enough to reach his cell phone. Flipping the antiquated phone open, he dialed 911.

❧ ❧ ❧ ❧

### Beulah, Colorado

Nora grinned as she glanced over at her niece. "You know, you look about how I felt the first time I went to find this geocache. I promise you're not off to the firing squad."

Kristie met her aunt's gaze. "Sorry. Guess I see this as dorky as hell."

"It is dorky," Nora said, bringing up a hand to brush a branch aside. "But, since I consider myself quite the dork, I feel at home doing this." She laughed at the dramatic eye roll she received. "You know, it was your Aunt Shannon who introduced me to this. She was only a kid, then. But, she got me hooked, and once I went back to work, I did this all over the world." She glanced down at her phone and the geocaching app, which was guiding them to their target.

"Do you think she'd dead?" Kristie asked, sidestepping a fallen log.

Nora's heart stopped every time she was asked that or every time she, herself thought about it. "I don't know," she said quietly. "I hope to hell not." She let out a heavy sigh, reaching up to readjust the strap of the backpack that was hitched up on her right shoulder.

Inside she had packed bottles of water for the pair, a lunch, as well as a bag of her geocaching swag, items to be left behind. "I know Sarah is doing all she can to find her or find out what happened to her."

"Who's that?"

Nora looked over at the teenager, noting her style, the attitude of "screw you" that radiated off of her and wished, not for the first time, that she could have had half the kid's spunk and confidence at the same age. She also understood what LJ wanted her to get to with the girl, so she decided to be honest and open to get the conversation started.

"Well, she's the detective who is looking for Shannon, but she was also my first girlfriend."

Kristie stopped abruptly. "Wait, you're gay?"

Nora glanced back at her, fighting the urge to burst into laughter. "Yeah," she said nonchalantly, continuing in the direction her phone GPS led them. She was surprised at how overgrown the area had become compared to her first time there so many years ago. She did grin when she heard Kristie jog to catch back up to her.

"You're a lesbian?"

"Tried and true."

"How did I not know this?" There was shock in her voice. "Oh wait, maybe it's because you've been everywhere else but here for most of my life," Kristie said dryly.

Nora felt those words to her core. She watched the girl who walked by her side for a long moment. "I'm sorry, Kristie," she said, meaning every word. "Your dad put me up to this today, to talk to you, but to be honest, I'm so glad he did." She stopped walking and touched her niece's arm to get her to stop as well.

"Listen, having Bella with me for almost two weeks, I've come to realize how much I missed with you and with Tyler and Sylvia." She looked away, fighting back tears of regret. "I mean, shit, I don't even know your favorite color." Shaking her head in self-recrimination, she continued on, silence filling the air for several minutes

"Red."

"What?"

"My favorite color," Kristie clarified. "It's red."

Nora grinned. "Mine, too."

"Get out! Very cool." Kristie eyed her. "Your first girlfriend, huh? Were you in high school together?"

"God, I wish I'd been brave enough to have a girlfriend in high school." It was her turn to study her companion. "Like you." Nora grinned. "Yes, your dad knows, and yes, he's totally fine with it. He does wish you'd be open with him about it, though."

"I can never tell my mom," Kristie said with a sad sigh.

"I know. That's how it was with my dad."

"How old were you? Like, when you came out?" Kristie asked, hopping over a small stream, Nora following.

"I don't remember that being here," she said, glancing back at the water. "Uh, well I knew I was a lesbian pretty much from the age of four, but I had no idea what it was called." She gave Kristie a leering grin. "I only knew I wanted Brooke Shields's hair to move out of the way in the movie, *The Blue Lagoon*."

Kristie burst out laughing. "God, that's sick."

Nora chuckled. "Hey, I was four, okay? But, I guess I always knew."

"Did you date guys?"

"A few, never slept with them, though," Nora said, her face twisting into a grimace. "Gross."

Again, Kristie laughed. She raised her hand for a high five. "Woohoo! Fellow gold star."

Nora slapped her hand. "What's her name?"

"Julia."

Nora recognized that smile and knew her niece was absolutely in love. "Pretty name."

"Pretty girl." Kristie brought out her phone and scrolled until she found what she was looking for and showed her aunt.

"Wow. Total knockout," Nora said, looking at the selfie of the two girls, Julia a beauty with long blond hair and bright blue eyes. She handed the phone back. "Is it serious?"

"Yeah, it is." Kristie gave her an adorably shy smile. "I kinda think I want to marry her."

Nora's eyes grew huge. From what she knew about teenage love, it was pretty much seasonal then moved on to the next season. "Wow," she said, glancing down at her phone. "This way." She indicated they needed to turn left. "That's quite a statement."

"She gets me, you know?" Kristie said, following Nora in their new direction

Nora gave her a sad smile. "Yeah, I get it."

⚜ ⚜ ⚜ ⚜

"Okay, you're sure you're okay with this?" Nora asked, nervous. "I mean, she's five and can be a handful."

"Uh, sis," LJ said, an eyebrow raised. "You do know that Kristie was once five, right?"

Nora covered her face with her hands for a

moment before looking at him with apologetic eyes. "I'm sorry."

"Why the hell are you so nervous, anyway?" he asked.

Nora glanced out the window above the sink and ran her hand through her hair. "I don't know."

"Is it the fact that you're spending the afternoon with Sarah Sanchez to find information out about Shannon or is it that you're spending the afternoon with Sarah Sanchez?"

She glanced at him. "Yes."

LJ walked over to her from where he'd been leaning against the wall and took her in a hug. "It's okay."

Nora smiled as she rested her head against his chest, just like she used to do. It had been a long time, Adrienne cracking the whip more and more the longer they were together, isolating him from her, from all of them. Well, and then she ditched the entire bunch and ran away to every other country but her own.

"You know," LJ said softly, his deep voice resonating against Nora's cheek. "Kristie couldn't stop talking about you last night at dinner."

"Yeah?" Nora grinned.

"Yeah. Seems you had quite the impact on her. She even downloaded the geocaching app on her phone, she said."

Nora chuckled at that. "Guess she's a dork now, too." She pulled out of the hug.

"What?"

"Nothing. She's an amazing young woman, LJ. You've done a helluva job with her."

"I've tried. I honestly don't think I would have survived this situation without her."

Nora gave him a sad smile, rubbing his arm in comfort. "Everything happens for a reason, LJ," she said. "Without Adrienne, you wouldn't have your daughter."

"Very, very true." He glanced through the window over the sink. "Sarah's here."

Nora peeked out the window as Sarah's Mustang pulled up behind LJ's truck. After several deep breaths, she took mental stock of herself. She was dressed casually in jeans, boots, and a sweater. It was a cool, late September day. She nervously tucked her hair behind an ear as she watched Sarah climb out of her car and walk to the house.

During her time with her niece, Kristie had asked her several questions about Sarah, which had brought her back to memories she'd been desperately trying to avoid since Sarah had come back into her life. She felt antsy and nervous about the afternoon she'd be spending with Sarah, and in truth, she was terrified what they may or may *not* find out about Shannon's disappearance.

"Hey," Nora said with a forced smile as she opened the door to Sarah's knock. "Come on in."

"Thanks," Sarah said, entering the kitchen.

"Hey, Sarah," LJ said, walking over to her.

"He's going to be staying with Bella," Nora explained.

"Oh my God! LJ, it's so good to see you."

Nora watched as the two hugged and felt a strange mix of pleasure and sadness. At one time, LJ and Sarah had been close. For a time, it had been a point of contention between the siblings as Nora had suspected the two had kept in contact even after she'd left the States. In her immature and sanctimonious mind as a twenty-one-year-old, it seemed like LJ was betraying her.

"You, too. Hey, congratulations on the incredible career." LJ stepped back after the hug. "I'm so proud of you."

"Thanks, LJ." She reached out and squeezed his forearm. "And hey, congratulations to you on the incredible job you're doing with the Cyclones. My nephew, Caleb, said you were the best coach he's ever had."

"Your nephew is Caleb Sanchez, as in the greatest punter P-Dub has ever had?" LJ asked, eyes wide.

"The very one. I spent more time in the stands during those four years than I have in my entire life," Sarah said with a laugh.

"Well, damn. You should have come and said hello or something."

She shrugged then looked down at her shuffling tennis shoes. "Well," she said softly.

In that moment, Nora felt like an ass. She turned away, deciding to get her coat and purse in hand to leave.

"Ready to go?" Sarah asked. Almost out of nowhere she now stood by the kitchen table next to Nora.

She glanced at her and gave her a small smile. "Yeah." Nora cleared her throat to clear her head. "LJ, I should be back before dark."

"Take your time, ladies," LJ said, stepping over to Nora to give her a hug and kiss on the cheek. "Sarah, again, great to see you."

"You, too."

"You gals be safe and good luck."

Sarah led the way outside, Nora sliding her arms

into her jacket as she followed. It was chilly and the coming winter was already making itself known. She gave the magnificent muscle car a once-over before climbing in.

"Gorgeous car," she commented, reaching for the seatbelt.

"Thanks. I love it." Sarah gave her a quick smile as she too belted up. "I have to say, that was a bit surreal."

"What?"

"Seeing your brother again." Sarah started the car and backed out of the long gravel drive.

"Yes, it was. He always liked you."

"He's a great guy. I hear he and Adrienne had a daughter," Sarah said, sparing a glance at Nora as she got them on their way.

"Yes, Kristie. Now, she is a great kid. I actually spent the day with her a couple days ago. She has a good head on her shoulders."

"How old?"

"She'll be eighteen in the spring. Can't believe it."

"You know what's amazing to me is you were only a little bit older than that when you moved into the house."

Nora looked at her, studying her profile. "Yes, that's true."

Sarah pulled the car to a stop at the stop sign and met Nora's gaze, which she held for a long moment before she looked away. "So, where to first?" she asked, her voice a bit gruff.

After nearly two hours of driving around Colorado Springs, Nora doing her best to remember every possible place Shannon might have frequented, she was out of ideas. The two decided to stop for a late lunch.

"Will this work?" Sarah asked, indicating an Arby's.

"Yeah, great."

They sat in silence as they settled in and ate their lunch. Nora munched on the last of her curly fries as she studied Sarah, who was studying her fountain drink cup like it held all the secrets in the universe. She took in the dark features, hair pulled back into a casual ponytail. Her skin looked so soft and lovely, definitely touchable. Sarah was a gorgeous, sexy, and deeply passionate woman, but she was also kind and her heart knew no bounds.

At least, if that's how she still was. Twenty years could change someone, especially after what Nora had put Sarah through.

She shook her head as she studied what was left of her lunch. "Damn," she whispered, surprised she'd said anything out loud.

"What? Everything okay?" Sarah asked, taking a sip of her drink.

"Yeah. So"—Nora shook her thoughts out of dangerous territory—"what do you think? About the places we saw today and the people you talked to?"

Sarah let out a sigh as she sat back in her seat. "Well, honestly there wasn't a lot that was helpful, but I did find that Ellis White guy interesting. The bouncer at the club."

"Why do you say that?"

"Something about him," Sarah said, grabbing a napkin and dabbing at the corner of her mouth before tossing it onto the flattened wrapper that had held her sandwich. "Shifty fella. I also found it interesting that he's the best friend of Ronnie Garcia."

"Son of Penny," Nora added.

"Neighbor lady. I know that Penny and Shannon seemed to be sort of close, or at least Penny was trusted enough to keep tabs on Bella, but do you know if Ronnie hung around there much?"

Nora shook her head. "No. From what I understand, he's not around much at all. He's a truck driver so isn't in town much."

"What about—"

Sarah was interrupted by the ringing of Nora's phone. "Crap, it's LJ. I better take this." Nora put the phone to her ear. "Hey, LJ, everything okay?" She listened to him, her eyes cutting to Sarah who looked on. "Okay, I'll tell her… No, I think you did the right thing, that's what she'd prefer, is my guess. Okay, yeah, see you soon, bye." She ended the call and set her phone down.

"What's wrong?"

"Something was hidden inside of Sam," Nora said softly. "LJ thinks you need to see it."

"Who's Sam?"

"Bella's favorite teddy bear."

❧ ❧ ❧ ❧

The women arrived back at the farmhouse in record time, once again Sarah pulled the Mustang up behind LJ's truck.

"I have to say," Sarah said with a grin, "I love your house."

Nora chuckled. "Finally somebody does. My family says it's too far out here."

"Nah." Sarah pulled the key from the ignition and undid her seatbelt. "It's so quiet and peaceful out here. I think that would be fantastic after a long, hard day at the department."

"Well," Nora said quietly, sparing her a glance before opening her door, "you're welcome here anytime."

Shocked she'd said the words out loud, Nora quickly climbed out of the car and hurried toward the house. It was already dark, the dashboard clock in the Mustang claiming it to be after seven thirty.

"Hey, LJ," Nora greeted him as he stood on the back porch.

"Bella's asleep, so we have to keep it down," he said, raising a hand in greeting to Sarah who was coming up the walk. "Come on, I'll show you."

Nora's brother led them inside and to the living room where a pink plastic thumb drive box lay open on the floor next to the couch, a thumb drive just visible inside.

"When it fell out, this is where it landed," he explained, looking from Nora to Sarah. "I didn't touch it."

"That's great, LJ," Sarah said, squatting next to the plastic box, no bigger than a Zippo lighter. She pushed to her feet. "I'll be right back."

Left alone, Nora looked at LJ. "How did it fall out of a teddy bear?"

"Well, uh," LJ hedged, glancing over at her as he readjusted his baseball cap. "Oreo's claws kind of ripped a seam."

"And, why exactly *was* Oreo in here?" Nora asked, hand on hip and eyebrow raised.

"Well, I just might have gotten her shots and just might have gotten her a litter box and might have even gotten her food and toys."

Slowly, Nora folded her arms over her chest.

"And, where *might* this kitten be now?"

"Upstairs in bed with Bella," LJ said with a boyish grin.

"Damn it, LJ!"

"I know and I'm sorry, sis. I promise, I wasn't trying to pull shit in your house, but..." He glanced toward the stairs that led to the second floor. Lowering his voice, he continued. "I came across the bodies of what I assume to be Oreo's mom and one of the other kittens today," he explained. "Torn to shreds."

"Ah, damn," Nora said with a heavy sigh. "I was worried about that. Did Bella see it?"

"No, I distracted her first. But, I knew that kitten didn't stand a chance on her own, Nora. If you want, I'll take her home or whatever, but I couldn't leave her out there alone as prey."

"No, you did good. Let me know how much I owe you for the vet and everything."

LJ waved her off. "Bella adores Oreo. It was cute as hell to see her excitement when she was brought inside. They played for hours, which is why they're both conked out now."

Sarah reentered the house, a plastic evidence bag in her hands as well as a pair of latex gloves. She was also on her phone. "Yeah, about an hour and I'll be there. I'm clear out past County High School, so it'll take me a bit to get there. Oh, hey, have Carmen meet me outside so I can drop this off and she can get it to the lab ASAP." She hung up the phone and hurried over to the little plastic box and thumb drive.

"Everything okay?" Nora asked, stepping back to get out of her way.

Tugging the gloves on, Sarah carefully placed the items into the bag, sealing it and tugging off the black cap of a marker with her teeth before labeling the bag with time, date, and location. Getting to her feet, she capped the marker and pulled the gloves off.

"Shannon's apartment has been set on fire," she said softly.

"What?" LJ asked, voice raised in what sounded like shock.

"Oh God," Nora gasped, hands covering her mouth. She swallowed back her emotion. "Wow. Okay."

"So, I'm heading there now—"

"I'm coming with you," Nora said, hurrying over to the kitchen table where she'd set down her purse.

"No," Sarah said firmly, suddenly right behind her. She met Nora's angry gaze. "No, Nora." She softened her voice as she reached a hand out, briefly resting it against Nora's cheek. "You'll be in the way." Her hand dropped and she rushed toward the door, her evidence in hand. "I'll call you guys and let you know what I find out." She hurried from the house.

Nora was close to crying, the emotions behind her eyes stinging, her stomach threatening to revolt, yet she was absolutely powerless.

"Hey," LJ said, stepping up to her. "It's going to be okay."

Nora fell into his arms, the tears coming fast and hard.

# *Chapter Fifteen*

S arah arrived at the scene, the night shattered
by swirling red and blue. She exited her car
and walked over to a group of uniformed officers,
recognizing her partner, Mark. "Hey, gang."

"Hey," Mark said, turning to her. Unlike Sarah's
casual attire from her day with Nora, Mark wore his
typical and completely stereotypical wrinkled suit.
"They put the fire out before it spread too badly to
other units."

Sarah nodded, looking up at the building,
the front wall of the third floor blackened from the
flames. The acrid stench of smoke filled the night air.
"Anybody hurt?"

"Nah. The neighbor wasn't home, and hers
was pretty much the only other apartment that was
affected."

"Good. When can we go in?" Sarah asked,
looking around for the person who was in control of
the situation for the fire department. She knew the
Pueblo guys but wasn't familiar with the Colorado
Springs crews. She saw a woman in personal protective
equipment who seemed to be barking out orders to the
guys, also dressed in their PPEs.

"Not sure. Chief Hurley said she'd let us know."

Sarah figured the woman she was looking at was
Chief Hurley so walked over to her. "Excuse me," she
said, getting the short woman's attention. "Are you

Chief Hurley?"

"Yes, who are you?" the woman said, her tone harried.

"I'm Detective Sarah Sanchez. We need to get into that apartment, so when do we have the all clear?"

"When I tell you," the woman quipped.

"Look, I'm investigating the disappearance of the woman who lives there in conjunction with El Paso County. We need to check out the scene."

"Well," the fire chief said, reaching up and removing the yellow fireman's hat before running a hand through short, blond hair. "If you and your guys want to chance falling through the floor to the apartment below, go for it. But I'd seriously suggest waiting until I tell you folks it's safe."

Sarah let out an irritated sigh but nodded. She'd been here before and knew there was no reason to argue with the experts. "All right. I'll be over there," she said, indicating the group of police she'd just spoken with.

"Hey Detective." She turned and met the woman's gaze as the sound of her voice caught Sarah's attention. "We'll hurry."

Mumbling to herself, irritated by the wait as well as the woman's rudeness, she walked back toward the group when her phone rang. Stopping next to a faded yellow seventies-era Volkswagen Bug, she put the phone to her ear.

"Sanchez."

She glanced over her shoulder to see the fire chief weaving her way through the police cars over to her. Her reflective yellow heavy jacket had been unbuckled and hung open revealing a white fitted tee beneath.

"Hang on," she said to her unknown caller as she turned her focus to the woman stepping up to her.

"Your team can head in. Our guys found it sound, but be careful," the woman warned her. "The heat is still fairly intense. I'd recommend getting a look-see and then getting the hell out."

"Great, thanks," Sarah said with a smile, lifting her phone back to her ear. "Call you back." No idea who the caller was, she disconnected the call and pocketed her phone.. She waited until the attractive woman walked away before turning to her partner.

Once inside the ruined apartment, Sarah was stunned. She shone the beam of her high-powered flashlight across what remained of the living room, the walls black from smoke and soot. What was most disturbing however, was that the place had been tossed before lit aflame. Furniture was thrown around, the couch overturned. Books and toys had been thrown, one even making a hole in the wall upon impact.

"Looks like either someone had one hell of a party in here or they were looking for something," Mark said quietly.

Sarah nodded "I agree and wonder if it was stuffed in a teddy bear."

❧ ❧ ❧ ❧

Fort Collins, Colorado

Detective Leland Masterson carried his third cup of coffee back to his desk, and it was only eight twelve in the morning.

"Leland, you got a call on two from a Detective in Cheyenne about a Jane Doe."

"All right, thanks, Max." Leland sat down behind his desk with a grunt, his overweight body harsh on damaged knees. He set the Styrofoam cup aside and grabbed for the receiver, pressing the blinking line. "Masterson here…Nah, I don't have anything right now matching that description. Where did you say she was found?" He shook his head as he sat back in his squeaky chair. "Jesus, that's terrible. Let me do some digging and I'll get back to you…You have a good one, too." Replacing the receiver into the cradle, he turned to his colleague. "We got us a Jane Doe out of Cheyenne. He's gonna email me the details. Let's call around to see if we can find a match."

❧❧❧❧

LJ stood in the laundry room with piles of freshly washed clothes folded atop the long countertop that ran the length of the long, narrow room. He was folding his and Adrienne's clothes but had left Kristie's unfolded for her own delight. He hated doing laundry, but mostly, he knew it was something his daughter needed to know how to do.

As if on cue, he heard the front door open then slam shut and the nonstop talking and giggles of a teen's one-sided conversation.

"Hey, kiddo," he called out, leaning slightly out of the room so she'd see him.

"Jesus! You scared me, Dad. Gotta go," she said into her phone and hung up. "I didn't know you were home. Your truck isn't outside."

"Yeah," he said, reaching over for her laundry, which he'd put into a plastic white laundry basket. "Here." He handed it to her. "Your mom's car needed the oil changed, so she took my truck. I'm working on the car for her."

Kristie nodded, looking forlorn as she accepted the basket of clean clothes. "You know I hate doing this right?"

"You know I hate doing it, too, right?" he quipped with a raised eyebrow. They folded together in silence for a moment, Kristie taking the empty, far end of the counter. "So, how did things go with Aunt Nora the other day?" Nora had spoken to him a little about it, but he hadn't poked and hadn't sent out a fishing expedition.

Kristie shrugged and spared him a glance as she folded her zombie pajama pants. "Good. She's dorky like you. I can see why you guys used to be close."

LJ chuckled. "Yeah." What he didn't say was, he intended to get close with his sisters again.

"You knew she's gay, didn't you?"

He nodded. "Yup."

"And," she hedged, "You knew I was gay…didn't you?"

"Yup," he said again, giving her an easy, open smile.

"Which is why you sent me to hang out with her all day."

He nodded. "Yup." He shared her full-on smile and accepted the hug she offered. It actually felt good holding his little girl. He rested his chin on the top of her black head, remembering so many times over the years when he had to hold her and rock her when she was crying because she skinned her knee or got her first bad grade or experienced her first broken heart. Now, he held her because he was so proud of her and the woman she'd become. "And," he added, leaving a kiss on her head before she pulled away, "you can bring Julia around anytime you want, okay? I kinda like the girl."

Kristie beamed, nearly blinding him. "Cool."

"All right, kiddo. I'm going to take all this upstairs, and you finish up, got me?"

"Yes, sirree Bob."

Gathering the folded piles, LJ loaded them into the laundry basket he and his wife used and headed upstairs to their bedroom where he left her neat piles on her side of the bed and began to put his own clothing away. He glanced out the window when he heard his truck pull into the driveway and felt the slight nervousness in his gut that always occurred when he or Adrienne arrived home.

As he headed to his side of the closet to hang some jeans, he heard the two women downstairs swap a few words before Adrienne's advancing footsteps. When she entered their bedroom, she looked tired. He knew she worked long days and had to put out many, many fires in the district throughout the day.

"Hey," he said, heading back to the bed for an armful of shirts to hang, which he flipped over his arm.

"Hi," she said in return, heading into the bathroom.

LJ rolled his eyes. By the clipped tone she used, he knew this wasn't going to be a family night playing Uno around the kitchen table. "Everything okay?" he called to her.

In lieu of responding, Adrienne walked out of the bathroom, high heels missing and blouse partially unbuttoned. She walked over to where he hung his shirts and tossed something on the shelf where he kept the handful of baseball caps he owned.

LJ looked down at what she'd left there and groaned inwardly, noting it was the brochure and business card from the townhouse he'd spontaneously decided to look at the day he'd checked out apartments for Kristie. He'd forgotten about it after tossing it into the center console of his truck.

"What's this?" she asked, standing near the side of the bed, hands on her hips. "A townhouse for Kristie and eight of her closest friends so they can afford it?"

He finished hanging his shirts and ran a hand through his hair. "Adrienne—"

"Or, were you looking at this place for a more nefarious reason? Maybe Jill isn't the only whore in the family?"

"That's enough!" he roared, pushed to his limits. "We certainly know she's not the only bitch, don't we?" LJ's world rocked for a moment after the vicious slap to his left cheek. His jaw clenched, and he followed Adrienne into the bathroom. "What is your deal? Why do you have to make every goddamn thing so difficult? Our entire marriage, everything is a fight."

"Maybe because you either embarrass me or fail me at every turn, Larry. Did that ever occur to you?" she bit back, standing at the counter and reaching up to remove her earrings. "How many damn years did I have to bug you to get your master's?"

"And I did, if I recall," LJ said, feet set wide apart in the doorway and thick arms crossed over his chest.

"In Literature, Larry!" Adrienne yelled. "Who the hell spends the money and time getting a higher education in Literature? You might as well have gotten a damn degree in finger painting, as helpful as it's been! I told you." She turned and pointed a finger in his direction. "I told you to get your master's in something like Leadership!"

LJ was incredulous. "Why on earth would I get

my master's in Leadership? Sounds like a damn daycare worker."

"Because at least you could move up." She removed her necklace and tossed it angrily onto the vanity. "I want a man who has ambition, who knows what he wants to do," she continued, sending him a glare. "And mostly"—she walked over to him, standing within a few inches—"I want a man I can be proud of."

He knew his face was beet red and his anger was reaching a very dangerous place. "And I want a woman who isn't a fucking cunt," he growled, quickly turning away and slamming out of the room and ultimately, the house.

❧❧❧❧

Kristie could only stare at the front door her father had stormed out of. She had definitely heard her parents scream at each other over the years, as she had only moments before, but she'd never seen him so upset.

Pushing up from the couch where she'd been flipping through channels, she glanced up the staircase to see if her mother was going to follow. When all remained quiet—other than the music her mother began to blast, no doubt running her bath in the giant soaking tub—Kristie hurried to her father's home office. She knew just enough about computers to get herself in trouble, but right now, she intended to use that knowledge.

Turning her father's laptop on, she waited for it to boot up then went to work.

# *Chapter Sixteen*

Okay, no, no, no!" Nora gently took hold of the kitten, who was already nearly six feet up, using the front window curtains as a ladder. "Let go, Oreo. Let...go." She held the soft little body with one hand and used the other to pick all four little packs of razors out of the material. Finally free, she held the kitten up and looked her in the eye. "You're gonna be the death of me, kiddo," she said, before grinning and bringing the tiny bundle in for a kiss on her furry head.

At the sound of the knock on the door, she set the kitten down and headed to the kitchen, cursing softly when Oreo attacked her ankle as she passed.

"Shit, now I'm bleeding," she muttered, snagging a napkin from the holder in the middle of the kitchen table on her way to open the door. "Hey. Sorry, Oreo decided she wanted to become a podiatrist."

"Who's Oreo?" Sarah asked, stepping into the kitchen, glancing down at where Nora held the napkin to her bleeding ankle.

"That little monster," Nora said, pointing to the adorable black-and-white kitten who was batting at a toy hanging from the cat tree Nora had picked up for her.

"Oh my God, she's adorable as hell." Sarah chuckled, walking over to the kitten and giving her some loves. "Are you okay?"

"Yeah. The other day I was in the grocery store,"

Nora explained, pushing up the sleeve of her long-sleeve T-shirt to reveal several long scratches. "I had to convince the clerk I wasn't a forty-one-year-old cutter."

Sarah tried to hide a smile behind her hand but failed. "Well, I'm glad you're okay. So, I have some news."

"Okay," Nora said, moving past the kitchen and toward the living room couch. She plopped down on one end, Sarah the opposite. Oreo wandered over to the women, hopping up on the couch, and in her usual fearless way, climbed up onto Sarah's lap. "Sorry," Nora chuckled, reaching over for the kitten only for Sarah to playfully wave her hand away.

Sarah smiled. "How can she call you a little monster?" She tucked the kitten into her lap and ran her fingers over the soft fur. "I always wanted to get a cat, but Leslie is too allergic."

Nora felt her heart skip a beat, surprising jealousy rising to form a rock in the pit of her stomach. "Your partner?" she finally managed, knowing she had no right to ask, let alone feel the way she did.

Sarah glanced at her, still absently petting the purring kitten. "Ex. She's occupying the spare bedroom right now until she can move out." She looked down at the kitten, sparing Nora a glance before returning her focus to the fur ball in her lap.

Nora nodded at this new bit of information. Even though the two were obviously broken up, it still hit her that they'd lived together. It was all that Sarah had ever wanted from her and she could never give her. Fighting against a bit of emotional guilt that threatened to well up in her eyes, she smiled as bravely as she could and turned to Sarah. "So, news."

Sarah nodded and let out a breath, almost as though relieved to get back on track. "First, Shannon's apartment. We haven't gotten the report back yet from the Colorado Springs folks, but I'd wager it was arson. The place had been ransacked ahead of time."

Nora's stomach fell. "Oh, wow," she said softly, covering her mouth with her hand. "Okay."

"I have to ask you a difficult question, Nora," Sarah said gently.

"Okay. What is it?"

"Is Shannon involved in drugs?"

Nora could only stare for a long moment. "Drugs?"

☙ ❧ ☙ ❧

Parkview Hospital – 2006

Nora paced in front of the window, feeling both angry and worried as hell. She glanced at the bed, the form lying there pale and incredibly thin. She noted the red-rimmed green eyes that watched her and the dirty, stringy auburn hair.

"I can't believe this happened," Nora said, her tone filled with exasperation. "When I told you I wanted to come back here for you it wasn't because my seventeen-year-old sister was found in a goddamn flophouse overdosing on heroin!"

Shannon's eyes squeezed shut for a moment, tears in them when they opened once more. "I'm sorry," she said, her voice barely above a whisper.

Nora ran her hands through her short brown hair, having chopped it four months ago and regretting it ever since. "Look, I need to go. Seeing you lying there hooked up to God knows what…" She hurried toward the door but stopped when she heard the soft voice of an angel. Tears coming to her eyes, Nora turned to look at her sister, the beginning lyrics to, "Wishing You Were Somehow Here Again" from *Phantom of the Opera* and sung by Sarah Brightman floating through the air.

As soft as it was and as strained as Shannon's voice was from her ordeal, it still brought tears to Nora's eyes.

Halfway through the song, Shannon stopped, giving her a weak smile. "I promised you I'd learn one," she whispered.

Nora brought a hand up and wiped at her eyes. "Why now? Why would you sing this now, Shannon?"

"Because you never came back to hear me."

⁂

Nora hadn't even realized that Sarah had moved closer to her on the couch until she felt the warmth of her hand on her knee.

Feeling foolish, Nora turned away from her, reaching for a tissue from the box on the end table. "Sorry. Just a bad memory." She cleared her throat and turned back to the other woman, trying to push away her guilt from so long ago. "So, why do you ask about Shannon and drugs?"

"They went over that plastic box and thumb drive LJ found," Sarah began gently. "Shannon's fingerprints, and someone else's we're trying to source, were on the plastic box. Her prints weren't on the thumb drive itself, but cocaine residue was."

Nora buried her face in her hands, the tears

coming fresh. She knew LJ would be as devastated as she was. Again, Sarah's comforting touch was felt, this time on her back.

"I'm sorry," Sarah said softly. "I have to be honest with you so we can find her."

Nora nodded, wiping her eyes even as more tears came. "What does this mean?"

Sarah shook her head slowly. "We don't know. As we speak, my partner Mark is looking over the contents on the drive." A quick ding rang out, and Sarah grabbed her phone from where she'd left it on the coffee table. Glancing at it, she turned back to Nora. "I have to go. Mark just texted me."

Again Nora nodded. Without a word, she stood along with Sarah, who gently placed the sleeping kitten on the couch where she'd been sitting. Together they walked to the kitchen and the back door.

Sarah turned to Nora at the door and, without a word, gathered her into a hug.

Nora hung on to her, clinging to her warmth and familiar scent as she buried her face in Sarah's neck. Their bodies pressed together, and Sarah's breasts pushed intimately against her own. She sensed Sarah's breath against her neck and heard the slight hitch in it, like her own.

Slowly Nora's head rose from Sarah's neck, and she looked up into Sarah's eyes, the dark depths usually so guarded. Now there was so much swirling in there, none of which Nora could discern. Her verdant gaze fell to full lips that were slightly parted. A shudder went down her spine when Sarah's hands moved to her shoulders and slid slowly down her arms before they were gone.

"I need to go," Sarah whispered, pushing out of

the glass door into the chilly night.

❧❧❧❧

Pueblo, Colorado – 1995

Nora had lived in the house with Sarah and Daniel for four months, and true to what her friend, who had given her the lead in the first place, and the doctor told her, her two roommates were rarely home. It was turning out to be the perfect situation, though she was noticing a bit of extra—and unwanted—attention from Daniel when he was home.

This morning, Nora had woken up early as she had a shoot to do for a family portrait that had been set up for her by Layla, the woman she was interning for, who promised her that she could help lead her to bigger and better things. According to Layla Spencer, Nora was one of the best she'd ever seen.

She had showered and dressed and was cleaning up her bedroom when she heard someone moving around in the kitchen right outside her closed bedroom door. Rolling her eyes as she wasn't in the mood for small talk with Daniel, she gathered her gear and created a plan for a quick exit.

Shrugging into her jacket, she shouldered her heavy camera bag and headed for her door, pulling it open only to stop short.

Standing at the stove was Sarah, her short dark hair smoothed back from what looked to be a recent shower. She was dressed in a pair of black lace panties with matching bra. Her exposed legs, arms, and back were covered in smooth-looking skin that held a beautiful glow. She was cracking eggs into a frying pan.

"Uh, I'm sorry," Nora said, about ready to scurry out of the room.

"Hey, you're fine," Sarah said with a blinding smile, glancing at Nora over her shoulder. "Sorry, when Daniel isn't here, it's just kind of nice to do me."

Nora nodded dumbly, not sure what to say and not able to take her eyes off of the gorgeous body before her.

"Want some?" Sarah asked.

It took Nora several seconds to realize she was being offered scrambled eggs. "Oh, uh, no thanks. I've got a shoot that I uh, yeah." She quickly ducked out of the kitchen, nearly sprinting to the front door.

"Have a great day," Sarah called behind her.

"You, too!"

She didn't see her police officer roommate again for a week and a half, their schedules entirely incompatible. But, if Nora was honest with herself, she hadn't gotten the image of Sarah's half-naked body out of her mind, the way her incredible shapely ass looked in those panties and even better, the way her breasts were lovingly cupped in black lace and satin. Though she was nearly twenty years old and had known she was a lesbian for several years, it was the closest she'd ever been to a woman that unclothed who wasn't Jill.

The episode had made quite the impact and had been fodder for endless dreams and fantasies. Regardless, she was keeping her eye on the ball, her ultimate goal being to someday work for *National Geographic*.

One night, Nora knew she was alone in the house and was sitting on her bed with a packet of pictures she'd developed with Layla earlier that day. She glanced over the top of her computer to her closed bedroom door when she heard someone in the kitchen, a chair being scooted out and then soft talking.

Stomach roiling in fear, she looked around her bedroom for a weapon of some sort. As quietly as she could, she grabbed a shoe but quickly set it back down, knowing it wouldn't do much. Next, she decided on her bedside table lamp, tugging the plug free from the wall and holding the glass piece in her hands, high over her right shoulder as she neared the door. To her surprise, she heard a sniffle and then a sob.

"It's okay, Sarah," was murmured, somewhat muffled through the door.

Feeling foolish, Nora tossed the lamp to her bed and opened her door a bit, enough to peek out into the kitchen. There, she gasped when she saw Sarah sitting in a kitchen chair still in her uniform, blood spatter on her face and across a couple patches on the dark blue uniform shirt.

The fellow police officer standing nearby with a hand on her shoulder glanced over at Nora. "You live here?" he asked.

Nora nodded, unable to take her gaze off the distraught woman sitting before her, a woman who was usually so strong and stoic.

"Good. She's gonna need you to be there for her tonight," he said. He turned back to Sarah and said something to her before turning and leaving the house, closing the front door behind him.

Nora took a few steps out of her bedroom, standing halfway between the doorway and the table. "Um, are you okay?" she asked hesitantly.

Sarah said nothing but nodded. She grabbed a napkin from the plastic holder in the middle of the table and worked at wiping some of the blood off her face, fresh tears catching on it, making her look as though she were crying blood.

"Hey." Nora kept her voice soft and stepped closer to Sarah, who was crying harder now. With no response from Sarah, Nora walked over to the sink and squirted a few pumps of dish soap onto a cloth and ran it under warm water enough to activate the suds. She fully saturated a second cloth and walked back to Sarah, scooting a second chair so she could sit in front of her, their knees touching. "How ya doing?" she asked quietly, no idea what had happened as she gently began to wash away the dried blood from Sarah's face.

"Been better," Sarah said with a small, rueful smile.

"Do you want to talk about it?" Nora asked, switching to a different part of the washcloth that wasn't already stained with blood to continue her cleaning.

"No."

Nora stopped what she was doing and met her gaze. "Are you sure?" Without waiting for a response, she continued what she was doing, not wanting Sarah to feel like she was being interrogated.

After a moment, Sarah closed her dark brown eyes as Nora wiped a small smear near the right one, and she softly began to speak. "We got a call about a guy who was threatening to kill his eight-year-old son," she began.

Nora said nothing but grabbed the other towel to wipe the soapy ministrations away. She looked her in the eye to let her know she had her full attention. With a sense of dread, she thought of Shannon, who was close to the same age.

"We talked to him. Really tried to get him to see

reason," she said with a small sniffle. "He put the gun down," she whispered, pursing her lips. "So, I moved in to grab the little boy." Her eyes welled again. "Never saw it coming." She shook her head. "Never thought he'd put the gun...he'd..." The tears came strong and fast.

Giving up the cleaning, Nora stood and moved to Sarah's side, cradling her head against her chest. "It's okay," she whispered.

"He shot himself," Sarah managed through her tears.

Nora felt her own tears gather, easily able to imagine what happened, what Sarah saw, and certainly how it physically affected her. "It's okay," she whispered, holding her tight, cheek resting on top of her crown. "It's okay." She felt Sarah's arms wrap around her waist and pull her in tight.

❦❦❦❦

After that night, the energy between Nora and Sarah changed. They'd always gotten along after their first precarious meeting but had never hung out as friends. Even so, Nora had noticed when Sarah was off or wasn't sleeping, she spent more time out of her bedroom and oftentimes was in the kitchen, either cooking or working on reports for work.

It was a Friday night when Sarah had a few friends over and, as Nora sat in her room—as usual—working on her word processor to stay out of the way, she could hear their laughter coming from the living room. She glanced up from the screen when she heard a soft knock on her door.

"Yeah, come in."

Sarah opened the door enough to peek her head in. "Hey. Why don't you come out here and join us?"

"Nah, I don't want to get in the way," Nora said, nervous about the idea.

Sarah pushed the door open farther and stepped inside. "Come on, Nora. Come play with us and have a beer."

"A beer, Miss Police Officer?" Nora said with a raised eyebrow. "You know I'm only nineteen, right?"

Sarah grinned as she sat on the side of the bed. "Then don't tell anyone and I won't lose my job."

Nora chuckled, shaking her head.

"Come on. Come have some fun."

Nora sighed, able to see the hope in those dark eyes. At last she nodded, closing the top of her machine and pushing it aside. She was surprised when Sarah jumped to her feet and grabbed her by the hand, tugging her out of her bedroom, over to the fridge to grab them each a beer, then to the living room where Nora sat next to Sarah on the couch.

"Hey, she does exist!" one of the two guys exclaimed from his position sitting on the floor on the opposite side of the coffee table.

"Be nice, Cal," the girl sitting on the other side of Sarah said to him, tossing a throw pillow at him. "Hey, I'm Tanya." She reached around Sarah to shake Nora's hand.

"Nora."

It was after a short round of introductions that Nora noticed a plastic orange pumpkin pail sitting on the coffee table, along with scattered beers and drinking glasses filled with what she assumed was the whiskey from the bottle sitting on the floor next to the guy named, Chad.

"Okay, Cal, it was your turn," Sarah said, sitting back on the couch and sipping the fresh beer she'd opened, along with Nora's, with a church key.

"Okay," he said, leaning up to reach inside the pail and retrieving a folded piece of paper. "All right, Chad, in one belch, see how far you can go in the alphabet."

The group groaned in unison, making Nora wonder what would happen. She watched as the blond man took a long swig from a beer then, in one amusingly disgusting breath, belched from A to Q. Nora wasn't entirely sure whether to grimace or laugh, so decided to simply smile.

"God, you're so gross," Tanya laughed. "Okay, Nora, your turn."

Nora took a swig from the beer, more hoping it would make her feel less nervous than because she wanted it, then grabbed her own paper. She read it and groaned inwardly. "Um, am I supposed to read it aloud then answer?" she asked Sarah quietly. At her roommate's nod, she cleared her throat. "Um, it says to say how many people I've kissed and were they girls or guys." She could feel Sarah's eyes on her as she took a second swig of the foul-tasting beer. "Um, it was a girl."

"So, one?" Cal asked, sitting slightly forward from his spot on the floor.

"Um, yeah. We kissed."

"Holy cow! Not only are you the elusive roommate but you're a virgin, too?"

"God, dude. Lay off her," Chad said.

Cal smirked before taking a swig from his drink, wincing as the liquor went down. "Sounds like everyone has laid off her."

Nora was ashamed, and her blush was quick and hot. She glanced over when she felt a hand on her thigh. Sarah was smiling at her.

"Ignore him," she said softly. "He can be an ass when he drinks."

Nora nodded and gave her a small smile, not sure what to think when that hand remained there for a few more moments before it was taken away. It was only when it was gone that she was able to breathe. She took several quick swigs from the beer, regretting it as her head began to feel funny. A small giggle escaped her lips, making the group burst into laughter. Suddenly, she felt like laughing with them.

"That is one helluva lightweight." Chad laughed. "Your turn, gorgeous," he said to Sarah.

The group took several more rounds of questions and answers, all the while drinking, and to Nora, each question and its following answer got funnier and funnier. Some of the questions or directives were silly, some embarrassing, and some all-out lewd. All in all, she was admittedly having a good time. And now, on her third beer, it was Chad's turn.

"Okay, what we got here?" he said, unfolding his paper. He burst into laughter after reading it over quietly. "Okay, toots." He pointed at Sarah. "I pick you for this one. 'Choose a player to also choose a player to pantomime a sexual act, replete with grunts and groans.'"

"Oh God," Sarah groaned.

"I think you're supposed to groan *during*, not before." Cal grinned.

"Oh, fuck off, Cal. And, I know you wrote that one. Only you would use the word 'replete.'"

"Guilty!"

"Crap." Sarah pushed to her feet and reached down and grabbed Nora's hand.

"What, me?" Nora asked, eyes huge at the implication.

"Come on, stud." Sarah chuckled, moving past Tanya to the center of the small living room, only a few feet from the closest member of the group. "Come on, woman," Sarah said loudly in a lame Texas accent. She hitched her thumbs suggestively in the waistband of her thin, cotton yoga pants. "Let's get to the last of them dozen brats you wanted."

Nora laughed with the group, even as she felt like she was about to vomit and her nerves and uncertainty beat at her rib cage.

Sarah fell to her knees and tugged Nora down with her, pushing her to her back. Nora giggled when Sarah put her hands on her knees and, with a dramatic flourish, spread them wide.

"Oh my God!" Nora laughed, her pickled brain beginning to take her nerves away.

Sarah moved on top of her, holding herself up on her arms, her hands planted on either side of Nora's head. With exaggerated movements, she pretended to thrust into Nora, her hips moving high above her with each "out" motion. The group laughed at the raucous display.

"Damn, Sarah." Chad laughed. "You must have a ten incher!" This, of course, sent a new round of laughter and giggles.

"Jealous?" Sarah asked with a grin as she glanced briefly over at him.

There was a small part of Nora's brain that was sober enough to realize what was happening and that her stunningly sexy roommate was on top of her, lewdly moving between her legs. Her giggles came to a slow stop when Sarah looked down at her and, for a moment, something passed between them. Sarah's movements stopped briefly, and Nora gasped when she pressed down into her, sending sensation sprouting through every cell of her body. Her hands, which had been resting against her sides, tightened.

A catcall and whistle from someone in the room seemed to break Sarah out of her daze, and suddenly she was back to her obnoxious movements and grunts, Nora taking a second to shake herself out of what had happened and get back into the ludicrous fun of it. She too began to groan and grunt loudly, her hips bucking wildly with Sarah's crazed movements.

With a loud, obscene groan, Sarah collapsed on top of Nora, panting loudly. "Was it good for you?" she asked.

Nora giggled, wrapping her in a loose hug. "I'm feeling very knocked up."

Chuckling, Sarah left a quick peck on Nora's cheek then jumped to her feet, reaching a hand down to help her up. The two shared a quick but meaningful look before returning to their seats.

# Chapter Seventeen

From the locked door of room 213 was a trail of clothing across the maroon carpet with an art nouveau design through it. The pieces of a Gucci suit were strewn along with a simple dress of dark blue with tiny white dots decorating it. A pair of white high heels were intermingled with a pair of black Armani wingtips. A cream-colored purse hung halfway off an armchair, and an iPhone sat atop a briefcase that lay on its side, the phone lighting up as it vibrated its way to the floor with an incoming call. Navy satin panties were crumpled next to a matching bra. Finally, a pair of men's briefs hung haphazardly off the king-sized bed that squeaked with a rhythm as old as time.

❧❧❧❧

Jill sat in the uncomfortable chair, one of her high heel-clad feet tapping nervously on the tiled floor beneath it. One arm was crossed tersely over her chest as the other held her phone to her ear, and her usually delicate, lovely features were turned hard and sharp.

"Damn it," she muttered, disconnecting the unanswered call. She scrolled through her contacts until she found the other number she'd already tried and called again. "Mary, this is Jill Lacey again, I'm sorry to bother you again. He's not answering. Would you please have him call me the absolute moment you hear from him or he returns from his lunch appointment? Thank you, and you, too."

She glanced back over at the counter where the desk officer was typing away on his computer. She left him until her gaze landed on the closed door that she was told he would be coming out from. Nothing, still nothing. She'd been sitting there for more than an hour, bail already paid.

"What the hell's going on?"

Jill turned to see Larry, Sr. storm into the lobby, dressed for golf. "I'm about ready to hit the damn green when I get you boo-hooin' on the phone."

Jill pushed to her feet and walked over to him, accepting a quick hug from her father. "I'm sorry, Daddy. It's Tyler."

"What? What did he do this damn time, and where the hell is *his* father? Why do I gotta be here?" he asked, looking around, his features tanned and leathery as usual.

"Andrew is at some sort of lunch appointment. Tyler has been arrested—"

"How much?" Larry, Sr. asked, bringing his wallet out of the back pocket of his cotton pants.

"No," she said, feeling exasperated, placing her hands over his. "I don't need your money."

"Then, why the hell am I here?" he boomed, looking down at her with confusion in his eyes.

Jill hugged herself, regretting calling him now. "I'm sorry, Daddy," she said quietly. "I'm just"—she let out a heavy sigh, her shoulders falling—"I just don't know what to do anymore. Neither Andy nor I know where to go with him."

"What did he do?" he asked, voice slightly calmer.

"In his infinite wisdom, he and his friend thought

it would be a great idea to steal a car from the school parking lot and go joy riding." She glanced up at him and was shocked to see amusement in his eyes. "Daddy, this isn't funny."

"No, no it ain't. What that boy needs is a swift kick in the damn ass from that husband of yours. But, since he can't bother to be around, he's coming home with me."

"Daddy—"

Jill's words fell on deaf ears as Larry, Sr. marched up to the front desk officer.

"What the hell do I have to do to get my grandson out of here?"

❦❦❦❦

Able to sit at last, Sarah let out a sigh of relief and plopped down in her desk chair. She picked through the various messages and reports that had been left there for her. As she sifted through them, she grabbed the desk phone to check her voice messages. Hitting the appropriate buttons to dial in, she cradled the receiver between her ear and her shoulder.

Listening to one message after another, she deleted those that weren't important and grabbed a notepad and pencil to scribble notes down for a few that were. The message that caught her attention, however, was from Devon Hurley.

*"Hello, Detective Sanchez, this is Chief Devon Hurley. We met the other night over a torched apartment. Just wanted to say I hope you guys got what you needed and I'll have a report sent to you directly of cause. I can tell you this, though, everything is pointing to arson,*

*but I'm sure if you're as good as your reputation says you are, you knew that. Oh, and how about lunch next week?"*

Sarah's finger hovered over the delete option, but she hesitated. Instead she listened to the message again, this time taking down the provided cell phone number. She sat back in her chair and looked at the number, taking in the ten digits. With a shake of her head, she crumpled it up and tossed it into the trash can next to her desk. Turning to a report that had her interest, she gave a side glance to the trash can before she reached over and plucked the scrap of paper out, pocketing it.

Once she'd pushed thoughts of the cute little fire chief out of her mind, she redirected her attention to the mess on her desk, reaching blindly to her desktop computer to turn it on as she made piles based on importance.

"Good morning, Sarah."

She glanced up. "Hey, Mark." When he indicated she should follow him to his desk, she scooted back from her own. "What's up?"

"We gots uglies," he said cryptically. He grabbed and extra chair and slid it next to his. "Have a seat. I have a lot to tell you."

Sarah said nothing as she got settled next to her partner. She watched as he clicked on a few things, opening one file after another before a spreadsheet appeared on the screen. Her dark gaze scoured the hundreds of cells, some containing numbers, some full words or names and yet others, what seemed to be code.

"What is this?"

"What was on that thumb drive found in Bella's teddy bear," Mark said, glancing at her. "Sarah, these are the records of what is turning out to be a massive drug-dealing ring, starting from somewhere in Mexico all the way to Canada. I brought Dennis in," he added, meaning the most experienced narcotics officer in the department. "Dennis recognized a lot of these names and knew some of this code. He's sent a copy of this to the DEA and is opening up a whole new case on this."

Sarah brought a hand up, stroking her chin as she scanned the material before her. "This is what they were after," she said solemnly. "Why the place was torched and, I'd wager, why Shannon was taken."

"I agree. But was she involved?" Mark asked, raising bushy eyebrows as he sat back in his chair, studying her. "The sister said she'd been involved with drugs in the past and she has a record, so..."

Sarah continued to stroke her chin, no longer seeing the screen. She shook her head. "Something feels wrong here, Mark."

"Yeah? Your Spidey sense going off?" the older man said with a grizzled grin.

After a moment she nodded. "There's a couple people I need to talk to again," she said absently. Her brain spun while she pulled a plan together." As she pushed up from the chair, Mark's desk phone rang.

"Sloan." He listened to what was said on the other end, his gray eyes darting to Sarah who was looking down at him. "Yeah, we've got a case that might match her...Yeah, go ahead and send us what you've got. Thanks, bye." He cradled the receiver and stood from his chair. "We need to get some DNA."

He reached down and opened the drawer in his desk where Sarah knew he kept all their active files for easy access. He pulled one out and tossed it across his desk. Sarah looked down at the picture paper clipped to the file, a dazzling smile meeting her gaze. It was the same photo she had.

❧ ❧ ❧ ❧

"Andy, I know I left you a message, but Jill called again—" Mary jumped at the slam of her boss's office door, only able to stare.

❧ ❧ ❧ ❧

Andrew threw his briefcase onto the leather couch in his office and walked over to his desk, slamming his iPhone to the top before plopping down in the chair. His eyes were closed as his hands came up, covering his face for a moment before they fell to his lap. Glancing over at his phone, he sighed.

"Shit," he blew out before grabbing it.

❧ ❧ ❧ ❧

"You got those, sweetheart?" Nora asked, glancing down at her niece who was holding the stack of Missing flyers she'd printed out at the FedEx shipping center.

"Uh-huh," Bella said with a big nod, which made Nora smile.

"Okay, hand me only one this time, 'kay?"

With another big nod and some maneuvering, the five-year-old managed to peel off one of the pages. On it was a photocopied picture of Shannon, taken only three months before, with a description of all her vitals as well as the last day and place she was seen. Included was information to call with both Nora and Sarah's numbers.

Tucking the top of the page between her teeth, Nora tore off a piece of packing tape then taped both top and bottom of the page to the phone pole where they stood.

"Will this bring Mommy home?" Bella asked, looking up at Nora with big, sad eyes.

Nora knelt down so she was on the girl's eye level. She smiled at her, bringing up a hand to brush some hair out of those eyes. "Let's hope so, sweetie." They'd already had a meltdown that morning, Bella shattering into emotions when she saw her mother's picture staring back at her. "Come on. Let's go to the building where the nice man said we could put one on, okay?"

They made their way down the sidewalk to a local candy store called Taffy's where an excited kid—or big kid—could get any number of candies, cotton candy, flavored popcorn, and chocolates. It was a favorite for their ice cream on a hot summer day. On this day, Nora had promised Bella the choice of any candy she wanted if she helped her with the flyers, an offer no five-year-old could refuse.

Bella handed her another flyer as asked and Nora held it in place with a hand as her other hand came up with a piece of tape. She was startled when another hand appeared right above her own. She glanced over and saw Sarah.

"Hey," she said quietly, feeling a bit awkward after their last parting. "Glad you called earlier."

"Hey. Glad I caught you in town." Sarah gently took the flyer from Nora's hand. "Can we talk for a minute?" she asked, indicating Bella with a small movement of her head.

"Yeah," Nora said, hearing the seriousness in her voice. "Hey, Bella, you ready for that candy now?"

"Yeah!"

Thirty-five minutes later, the trio sat on the outside patio table, Bella happily swinging her feet to and fro as they dangled off the chair and enjoying the sucker ring Sarah had bought for her. It had taken forever for the child to choose, but she seemed quite happy with her selection.

"Did you thank Sarah for your sucker, Bella?" Nora asked, a vanilla ice cream cone in her hand.

"Thank you, Sarah," Bella said, her lips already as red as the sucker. "Are you going to find my mommy?"

Sarah gave her a winning smile. "I'm gonna try," she said, reaching across the metal lattice table to tweak Bella's nose. "I'm gonna do my bestest."

Bella giggled. "That's not a word!"

"It's not?" Sarah asked with feigned surprise. "I thought it was."

"No," Bella said with a vigorous shake of her head.

"Well, guess I'll have to work on my words, huh?"

Bella nodded, the sucker back in her mouth.

Nora watched the two interact, and it touched her heart. She knew Sarah, the oldest of seven, had several nieces and nephews, and she was well-versed in kids. Nora was charmed. "Thanks for the ice cream," she said softly, lifting her cone in emphasis.

"No problem," Sarah said with a small smile. "I'm saving this bad boy for later." She tapped the white paper bag sitting on the table, which contained a dark chocolate-and-orange truffle.

"So…" Nora drawled, eyeing her with a bit of trepidation.

"Nora," Sarah said, turning to face her. They both glanced at Bella to see she was happily sucking on her ring pop and watching a couple of birds peck at some dumped popcorn on the sidewalk.

"Did you find her?" Nora asked, almost breathless for the answer. She could tell there was something different in Sarah's demeanor.

Sarah sat back in her chair, leaning slightly in Nora's direction. "Nora, I need a DNA sample," she said quietly.

Nora felt her entire world go dark and nearly dropped her ice cream cone. If it hadn't been for Sarah reaching over and steadying her hand, she would have. "What? Why?"

"Preferably from your dad or Bella. But, it's necessary."

"I can give you one," Nora said, feeling numb. "I can't put Bella through that."

"Honestly, you, Jill, or LJ would be our last resort. Bella or Larry, Sr. is truly what we need."

It took Nora a moment to find her voice again, but eventually she nodded. "I'll talk to my dad."

"Okay. If you can get him to help us out, we'll need him down at the station for a cheek swab."

Nora nodded, brow drawn as she was deeply troubled. "Should—" She stopped as her voice cracked with her rising emotion. She couldn't let Bella see it. Clearing her throat, she tried again. "Should we stop?" she asked, nodding her head toward the stack of Missing posters and roll of tape sitting atop them.

Sarah shook her head. "I don't know. It can't hurt, right?" She reached out and gave Nora's arm a gentle squeeze and tweaked Bella's nose again. Grabbing her bag of goodies, she pushed up from the chair. "I'll see you two ladies later, okay?"

❧❧❧❧

Andrew pulled up to the house, his heart racing and palms sweating. He had no idea what he was about to face and honestly, had no idea how he was going to keep his inner turmoil together. He had as long as it took for the automatic garage door to open and for him to pull his car into his space next to Jill's to get it together.

Taking a deep breath, he killed the engine before hitting the button for the door on the sun visor-mounted remote. He gathered his things and climbed out of the car and headed into the house.

Sylvia was sitting at the island working on homework. He walked over and gave her a quick kiss on the top of her head.

"How are you?"

"I'm okay. Really crazy day, Dad."

He nodded and sighed. "So I hear. Where's your mom?"

"Upstairs and she is seriously and totally upset," she said.

He gave her arm a quick squeeze before heading upstairs to face his fate.

"Jill?" he called as he made his way upstairs to their bedroom, shrugging out of his overcoat and flipping it over his arm. Tyler's bedroom door was open and the room was empty, as was his entertainment center, wires dangling everywhere. "Oh boy," he said, continuing on. "Honey?"

"Adrienne, there has *got* to be something you can do. I am begging you," Jill was saying into her phone as Andrew entered the room. He noted his wife was pacing, dressed in black yoga pants and a fitted light blue tank top. He figured she'd just worked out or was planning to.

He sat on the padded bench at the foot of the bed to untie his wingtips, removing one at a time and peeling the black dress socks off, setting them beside him on the bench so he could toss them into the hamper in the walk-in closet. He glanced up at Jill again, following her pacing path across the huge bedroom.

"What is he facing with the school district?" she asked, looking as though she were near tears. "A hearing? What?" Her eyes closed and she covered her face with her hand. "God…You're kidding. Possible expulsion?" She flashed angry eyes at Andrew before continuing her pacing. "All right. Let me know and thank you, Adrienne. Bye-bye." She threw her phone on the bed. "He could be expelled from the district, Andrew!"

"Yeah, I got that. Let's talk about this," he said, pushing to his feet. He carried the socks to the laundry basket then walked to the center of the room, hands on hips as he studied Jill where she'd plopped down on the bed. "How did this happen?"

"Tyler and Jarrod Kinley apparently grabbed their math teacher's keys, and at lunch, they figured out which one was her car and took off. If Kinley hadn't crashed into a damn stop sign, God only knows how far they would have gone and how much more trouble they'd be in."

"Jesus," he muttered, running a hand through

his hair. "Did he take his game systems, too?"

"Hell, no," Jill raged, pushing up from the bed. "I took the damn things."

He nodded with approval. "Okay, so where is he? Your voicemail said you paid the bail—"

"He went home with my dad."

"What?" Andrew's jaw dropped. "Are you serious? You may as well have sent him home with goddamn Tiberius, Jill! That man has a flagrant disregard for anything we've tried to do with Tyler." He, too, began to pace and was tempted to rip his hair out. "How could you do that, Jill?"

"I needed you today, Andy!" Jill placed her hands on his chest and shoved, forcing him to take a step back. "Damn it, where were you? I didn't know what to do. I don't know what to do with this kid," she cried.

"So, you call the biggest ass this side of the Rockies?" he yelled, incredulous.

"I needed someone and, as usual, you weren't available."

"So," he said, voice deadly calm, "you call the first man who comes to mind, then?"

"I didn't know what to do," she said, her voice a little more than a whisper.

Without another word, Andrew nearly tore the buttons from his shirt as he removed it, tossing it into the dry cleaning basket, and shed everything else, tossing trousers and tie haphazardly in the general direction where they were supposed to go. After tugging on running pants and a tee, he snagged a pair of tennis shoes and sports socks.

"Where are you going?" Jill exclaimed, following him out of the room.

"To get my son away from that monster!" Andrew

roared. "Or, have you forgotten what he's capable of, Jill?"

"That's not fair," she whispered, tear-filled eyes wide. "That's not fair."

He couldn't bring himself to calm down or be sorry for his words. "And while I'm gone," he growled, pointing a finger at her, "I want you to figure out what the hell we're going to do about Tyler." He plopped down on the top stair and tugged on his socks then his shoes. "He's *our* son, damn it, and we have to stop blaming the school, the teachers that are so horribly mean, the dog, or the goddamn moon cycles." He glared at her where she stood nearly hugging the wall. "We've made this mess, Jill." He was stunned when he had to swallow hard to prevent his emotions and sorrow from showing. "We've made this mess."

With that, he trotted down the stairs and out of the house.

⁂

Lawrence Schaeffer, Sr. glanced down at his one and only grandson, basically the only grandkid who counted. Sure, he had three, maybe four granddaughters—he was never sure—but it was Tyler. He was the man of the bunch, the one who would continue the Schaeffer name and his legacy.

He'd brought the kid home, and now they sat in his man cave, the seventy-inch screen tuned in on ESPN. He glanced over at the boy who was slouched in a leather armchair. "Sit up," Larry, Sr. said, and when he was ignored, he leaned over the arm of his own matching chair. "I said, sit up!"

Tyler nearly jumped out of his chair but sat steel-rod straight, looking over at his grandfather with wide eyes.

Larry, Sr. chuckled, amused. "Come on, boy," he said, pushing up from his own chair, knees creaking from too many years of abuse, on the field and off. He walked over to the bar and slipped behind it, pointing to one of the stools for the almost-sixteen-year-old. "Sit your ass down."

He watched out of the corner of his eye as the boy took a seat, looking around. He had to internally chuckle as Tyler looked incredibly nervous, as though he were waiting for the firing squad.

"So," he began, grabbing a bottle of Johnnie Walker Black Label. He poured two tumblers half-full and tossed some ice into each before placing one in front of his grandson. When he saw the uncertain look in the boy's eyes, he leaned on the bar top with a large hand splayed to show its size, therefore his power. "You afraid, boy?"

Tyler shook his head and grabbed the tumbler, taking a drink.

Larry, Sr. burst into laughter as Tyler coughed, spitting some of the whiskey out to dribble down his chin. "Pathetic," he grumbled, throwing a rag at Tyler. "Clean yourself up and take a proper drink, like a man." Larry, Sr. eyed the boy as he downed his own drink. More coughing and sputtering ensued, but Tyler got most of it down. "There ya go." He reached across the bar and smacked his grandson on the back. "Feel good?"

Tyler nodded as he coughed a few times. "Damn, that shit is strong."

Larry, Sr. grinned. "A man's drink." Pouring the two another, the older man studied his grandson. He was a good-looking young man and had the potential to turn some heads with the ladies. He had dark hair like his father and the chiseled good looks Larry, Sr. preferred to think came from his line. His grandson had certainly inherited his height.

Tyler accepted the refilled drink and glanced up at his grandfather. "My dad never lets me do this." He smirked. "But he never lets me do anything."

"Look, kid," Larry, Sr. said, leaning on the bar. "What you did today was stupid, all right? But, mainly because you got caught." He sipped his drink. "You're a man, and hey, men will be men, right? That's our God-given right." He pointed a thick finger at the teen. "You remember that."

Larry, Sr. glanced up when the doorbell rang followed by a savage banging on his front door.

# *Chapter Eighteen*

Nora turned onto her father's street and into his driveway. She was surprised to see Andrew's Mercedes parked there and then outright panicked to see the two men near blows on the front porch.

"Shit," she said, gunning her car and squealing to the curb. She barely got the key out of the ignition before she ran from the car, not even bothering to shut the door. Andrew was pinned to the outside wall of the house by her father. "Dad!"

"He's my son, damn it!"

"Yeah, well then maybe you should try being a father!" Larry, Sr. shouted.

"Stop! Dad, stop this. Stop it." Using all her strength and body weight, she shoved her father away from Andrew. "Stop." A hand on the chest of each man, she glared at them both. "What the holy hell is going on here?"

"I'm here to get my son," Andrew said through gritted teeth, his normally beautiful blue eyes electric.

"Yeah, well if you'd been half a father, my daughter wouldn't have sent him home with me, would she?" Larry, Sr. growled.

Truly afraid, as she could feel the hatred streaming between her father and brother-in-law, she turned to Andrew, by far the most levelheaded of the two. "Andy," she said softly, "please go wait in your car."

"I'm sorry, Nora," he said, sparing a glance before returning his glare to the older man. "Not without Tyler."

"Okay. Then at least stand down. Okay? Please?"

Andrew nodded, even as his jaw muscles bulged. He took a step behind Nora, who turned back to her father.

"Dad." Her voice was soft but firm. "I came to talk to you, but if you don't back the fuck off, I will call the cops."

His steely gaze fell to her. "You wouldn't."

"Try me." To her relief—and surprise—he backed off, glaring at her as he crossed thick arms over his chest.

Pushing past her father, she looked left and right in search of Tyler. She was confused and frightened at the situation but knew how volatile her father could be. She also knew there was a severe hatred between him and Jill's husband, which she also didn't understand. It seemed to have started around the time Andrew and Jill married.

"Tyler?"

She glanced into the living room then kitchen only to hear someone groaning in the area her father used as his personal space. Essentially, if anyone had estrogen flowing through their bodies in great quantities, they weren't welcome. This was only the second or third time she'd ever seen into the room, and something caught her eye.

On the wall behind the bar was the typical shrine to Lawrence Schaeffer, Sr. that they'd all seen their entire lives: framed pictures from his college ball days, from the moment he signed on with the Denver

Broncos, *Sports Illustrated* covers that he dominated in the early 1980s. But, one picture that stood out, among all those of him standing beside sports legends and celebrities, was a picture of him standing with an attractive woman. To her practiced eye, Nora figured from the clothing and quality of photography at the time, the picture was likely taken in the late seventies or eighties. He was grinning like a fool as he stood next to a stunning redhead who looked just as happy.

On the surface, the picture showed nothing more than her father's typical flirtatious nature with beautiful women, but what caught her was the fact that, if she didn't know better, she thought she was staring into the face of her twenty-seven-year-old sister, Shannon.

Time stopped for Nora as she looked into the woman's expressive eyes, noted the deep auburn of her hair, her facial structure, and the slight quirk of her left eyebrow. All of these were features of her stunning youngest sister.

Without thought, she reached into her pocket and produced her cell phone. Lifting it, she clicked several shots of the picture before turning away to deal with the situation at hand.

"Tyler?" She noticed him staggering over toward the leather couch, hunched over and holding onto everything as he moved along. "Shit," she said, noting the two tumblers on the bar, both empty, and the bottle her nephew carried with him, hugging it to his side like a football. She couldn't help but snort internally thinking how proud her dad would be. She gasped as he stumbled, hitting his head on the large, bulky coffee table before falling to the floor, groaning. "Tyler." She ran over to him, tucking her phone back into her pocket as she knelt down beside the teen. His head was bleeding and he looked utterly disoriented. "Andrew!"

After some squabbling by the front door, Nora heard heavy footfalls running her way until Andrew slid around the corner. Under any other circumstances it would have been amusing, but it was anything but.

"Jesus," Andrew said, kneeling on the other side of his son. "Get a towel."

Nora jumped up and hurried to the bar, grabbing a white towel and quickly wetting it with cold water before running back, placing it over the teen's bleeding cut. She glanced up when she heard her father enter the room.

"What the hell, Tyler?" he boomed.

"What the hell were you thinking, Dad?" she demanded, holding the rag hard against the wound to stop the bleeding. "He's a fifteen-year-old boy."

"Yeah, and he's already a pansy enough as it is. There ain't nothing wrong with introducing him to some fine whiskey."

"Nothing wrong?" Andrew exploded.

"Don't mess with me, boy," Larry, Sr. said, pointing a finger at his son-in-law. "This state has a 'Make My Day' law and I sure as hell ain't afraid to use it. You're in *my* house."

Andrew stood up and walked over to him. "And don't *you* forget, old man. I know things about you that would ruin the reputation of the great Larry Schaeffer. This is *my* son."

Nora looked from one to the other, not sure what to think or where this unbelievable eruption of hatred was coming from. She decided to change the subject with the reason she'd come in the first place.

Once again, she found herself between the two men. "Andy, why don't you check on Tyler. He seems to be coming around," she said softly. When he returned to his son's side, she turned her focus to her father. "Listen, Dad, the police need to get a sample of your DNA."

"What? Why?" His stance grew aggressive, arms crossing over his chest and lips pursing into a thin line. "No."

"Dad, this is for your daughter. I don't know what's going on, but Sarah asked me to—"

"Never did like that Mexican bitch and I still don't. Turned my damn daughter into a flannel-wearing, pussy-loving dyke. No."

"Jesus, Larry," Andrew said, wiping away the last bit of blood from Tyler's wound. "It's a goddamn cheek swap."

"I don't trust those cops," Larry, Sr. said, shaking his head. "No way."

Nora was shocked by his refusal and honestly didn't understand it. "Even if it means helping your own child?" she said softly.

"My guess is, if they need DNA, there ain't no helping her."

"I can't believe you said that." She backed away from him, only to back right into Andrew. She felt his hands on her shoulders, squeezing slightly.

"Look, Larry, here's the deal," Andrew said, his voice deadly calm. "You will do this for Shannon. I'm one of two witnesses who know you gave a fifteen-year-old boy enough whiskey to knock a horse out. It has a name and it's called contributing to the delinquency of a minor."

"Get your faggot son and get out of my house," Larry, Sr. growled.

"You have exactly two hours to get down to the

Pueblo PD and give a DNA sample," Andrew said, Nora moving away from him and over to Tyler to help him to his feet. "*If* you don't, the dirt starts to fly, you got me?"

Without another word, Larry, Sr. turned and left the room.

"Two hours!" Andrew called after him.

⁂

"Hey, Sarah. Good news and bad news, which do you want first?" Mark asked, walking into the large room where he and Sarah had their desks with twenty of their closest colleagues. He walked over to her desk.

Glancing up from her computer screen, she gave him an unsure grimace. "Good news."

"We got a sample of Shannon Schaeffer's father's DNA twenty minutes ago. I sent it to the lab with a rush order."

"Go Nora," Sarah said, sitting back in her chair and lacing her fingers behind her head. "And, the bad news?"

"There was a body found in Shannon's torched apartment," Mark said soberly, perching on the edge of her desk.

Sarah's desk chair came to a springy snap as she sat forward. "What? Who?"

"Penny Garcia."

Sarah's mouth fell open and eyes wide. "The neighbor lady?"

"One and the same, and the second set of prints found on the plastic case that held that thumb drive."

"Whoa, shit," Sarah said. "Cause of death?"

"Homicide is saying blunt force trauma, but

until autopsy comes back, no clue whether she was dead before or after the fire. If no soot in her lungs, she was already dead."

"Holy cow," she said, shaking her head and staring off into space for a moment. "Has the son, what was it, Ronnie, been notified?"

"Dunno. El Paso is taking care of this. They said they'd let us know what they find out. They also talked about you and me heading up there for a meeting to see if the two cases are connected." Mark pushed off her desk, turning to head back in the direction of his desk.

"Mark," she said, stopping him. "Don't you find it curious that the only fingerprints found on the outside of that case are the stars of a missing case and a probable homicide?"

He glanced at her. "Very."

⚜⚜⚜⚜

Sylvia met Nora and Bella at the door, and she gave her aunt a quick hug and her little cousin a huge squeeze.

"Hey, kiddo," Nora said, setting the chocolate crème pie she'd brought down before helping Bella out of her jacket and shrugging out of hers. Sylvia hung them up.

"Mom's waiting for you in the kitchen," she said, disappearing.

Nora picked up the boxed pie, grabbed Bella's hand, and headed deeper into the extravagant house. "Hey," she called out, rounding the corner into the large kitchen.

"Hello." Jill stood at the counter, opening a bottle

of wine. "Want some?" she asked coolly.

"Uh, sure. I brought this," Nora said, setting the pie down on the massive island, knowing how much her sister loved a good chocolate crème pie.

Jill glanced at the pie, which Nora was removing from the white cardboard box. "Don't tell me that's from Foster's," she said, eyeing the dessert.

"Is there anybody else?" Nora said with a small grin.

Jill rolled her eyes as she poured two glasses of wine. "God, you're cruel. I guess extra spin class tomorrow." She smirked.

Nora accepted the wineglass and took a sip, smacking her lips for a moment to decide if she liked it. "Not bad."

"How much?" Jill asked, sucking some whipped cream off her thumb from slicing the pie.

"That looks good," Nora said, nodding at the piece already on a plate. "How's Tyler doing?"

Jill let out a heavy sigh and shrugged, her back to Nora. "Okay, I guess. I'm still shocked at the entire situation, to be honest." She turned with the two plates of pie, putting one before Nora and one before Bella, who had climbed up on the stool next to Nora. She smiled down at the little girl. "You enjoy that, sweetheart."

Bella grinned, picking up her fork in a fist and tucking in.

"What do you say?" Nora asked softly.

"Thank you."

Jill plated herself a piece and put the remainder of the pie in the fridge before joining the two. "Andy said things got exceedingly ugly."

Nora nodded. "You can say that again. I mean,

I knew Andy wasn't Dad's biggest fan, but I've never seen the fire come out of him like that. And, I know you're going to get all up in arms about this, Jill, but Dad acted like a complete"—she glanced down at Bella—"a-s-s. The way he talked about everyone and what he did to Tyler…Jill, there's no excusing what happened today."

"Any of it," Jill said, cutting through the rich mousse, whipped cream, and crust to take a bite.

Nora sipped her wine, studying her older sister. For years, Jill had always defended their father's actions, no matter what. It had been a point of contention between the two sisters—and LJ—more than once. She was surprised by the absolute look of defeat on her lovely face.

"What are you guys going to do about Tyler?" she asked softly, cutting her own piece, though she put the fork down on the plate when she noticed the mammoth bite on Bella's fork was about to fall into her lap. "Here, honey." She helped Bella take a smaller bite.

"Adrienne told me she thinks it's likely he'll get expelled." Jill met Nora's surprised gaze. "She said there's too much on his record, too many screwups." She set her fork down and rested her elbows on the granite countertop, her chin in upturned palms. "How did this happen, Nor?"

"How did it happen with Shannon?" Nora asked, wrapping her fingers around her wineglass. "I think it snowballs."

Jill blew out a breath and eyed her sister. "Andy said the police wanted a DNA sample from Daddy. Why?"

"Sarah won't tell me, only said it was needed. I'm scared, Jill, I won't lie."

"What will happen with…" her eyes fell briefly to a completely unaware Bella.

"I've thought about that," Nora said, reaching a hand over and running her fingers through long, brown hair. "Worst-case scenario, I want to keep her with me."

"Seriously?" Jill said with a chuckle, taking her wineglass in hand. "Miss, 'I never want kids'?"

Nora grinned. "I know."

"I hope you take this as a compliment, Nora, because it's meant as one. You've completely surprised me with how you've been with her, handled this. I was initially concerned when you said you were keeping her during all this." Jill smiled at Bella when she glanced up at her, chocolate smeared all over her mouth. "Oh, sweetie." Jill chuckled, hopping down from the tall stool and wetting a paper towel before moving over to the five-year-old and gently wiping her face. She looked over the girl's head at Nora. "You've done a great job."

Nora knew that ordinarily what Jill had said would have been meant to be bitchy or a backhanded compliment at best, but something had changed in her oldest sibling. She seemed humbled, somehow.

"Thank you, Jill." She cleared her throat at the awkward silence that filled the space as Jill moved back around to her stool and finished her pie. "Oh," Nora said, pulling her phone out of her pocket. "Do you know this woman? This is one of the reasons I came over tonight." She slid off her stool and brought up the picture she'd taken of the mysterious redhead framed on her father's wall. She moved around to stand beside her older sister and handed her the phone.

Jill studied the picture for a long moment, stroking her bottom lip, which her tongue flicked over to catch some errant mousse in the corner. "I know I've seen her before, but jeez, it was forever ago. She came around when I was…I want to say around…eight or nine, maybe. I remember she was really nice to me. It was the Christmas party that Mom and Dad always threw, remember?"

Nora nodded. "Yup."

"I think I saw her again a few years later."

"Why do you remember her so well?"

She smirked. "Because every time she was around, Mom and Dad would get into a nasty fight. I remember Dad telling me to call her Aunt Rhea or something like that. Rhea, Rita, something." She handed the phone back to Nora. "Why?"

"Now look at this," Nora said, swiping her finger across the screen of her phone to the next picture she had ready. Again, she presented the phone to her sister.

"Oh wow," Jill said, head jerking back slightly as though startled. "How did you get a recent picture of her? There's no way, she hasn't aged a bit…" She brought the screen closer to her eyes then glanced over at Nora. "That's Shannon."

Nora nodded. "Yup."

Jill slowly lowered the phone, handing it back to Nora, her wide gaze unflinching.

# *Chapter Nineteen*

Okay, lift higher, guys," Sarah said through gritted teeth, muscles straining and sweat beading between her breasts and across her forehead. "It's fifty-two fucking degrees out here and I'm sweating."

The couch finally made it over the edge of the truck. "It's in," one of her fellow men in blue blew out, letting his end of the couch go.

"God, what made that thing so damn heavy?" the other asked, bending over at the waist, hands on his knees.

"Sleeper sofa," Sarah said, a sheepish grin on her face as they groaned. "Come on, guys." She glanced over her shoulder back at the townhouse. "She's getting out, okay?"

"Yeah, yeah, fair enough. Come on, let's finish this bitch."

"So, I hear you boys needed some help, huh?"

Sarah glanced up to see a cute little blonde walking up the driveway dressed in jeans that somehow managed to show off muscular thighs and a narrow waist while still being baggy. She wore a cap-sleeved olive green tee with the sleeves of a fitted long-sleeved white tee covering muscular arms.

"Hey, Devon," Sarah said, walking toward her. It was the first time she'd seen the fire chief without her gear and not covered in soot. Her hair was short and tousled; no makeup but a tanned face with naturally cute features rounded off the portrait. "I know it's not exactly what you had in mind when you mentioned lunch, but your offer is definitely appreciated."

"Hey, no problem," Devon said with a smile and a shrug. "I was in town to see my grandfather anyway. So, how can I help?"

"How do you feel about moving a freezer?" Sarah asked with a grin.

Two hours and two showers later, Sarah sat across from Devon at Bingo Burger, an amazing burger joint where a true burger lover could get pretty much anything they wanted. The two carried their trays after their bingo order number had been called to the outdoor patio. It was a chilly afternoon, but it was quieter.

"I love these," Devon said, preparing her sandwich with the little plastic cups of condiments she'd grabbed from inside. "In the Springs we have Five Guys, which is awesome, but I love Bingo Burger, too."

"So," Sarah said, sipping from her fountain drink, their version of Coca-Cola. "You were saying you initially wanted to be a military surgeon. Not saying that being a firefighter is anything less than fantastic, but quite a leap."

"My grandpa," Devon said simply, grabbing a napkin to wipe a dribble of mustard from her lip. "He raised me. Had a stroke when I was twenty-two, so I left school to take care of him." She shrugged. "Figured joining the fire department would give me a decent wage and good bennies to take care of him."

Sarah studied her for a long time, noting the casual, easy demeanor of her companion. "That's cool, Devon," she said quietly. "A hell of a lot more than most would do."

"What about you?" Devon asked, dipping a couple fries in her ketchup-and-mayo mixture. "How did you end up in police work?"

Sarah was about to answer when her phone went off. She glanced at it where it rested on the table and put up a finger to forestall anything else Devon might have to say. "Hey, Mark, what's up?" She listened, grabbing her drink and sipping from the straw. Slowly she lowered the cup back to the table. "They were able to get a fingerprint after all? And?" She brought a hand up to her forehead for a moment. "Yeah. Okay…No, I'll do it. Bye." Sarah put her phone down after her partner ended the call. It took her a moment to catch her breath but finally she looked at Devon. "I'm sorry. I need to go."

⚜ ⚜ ⚜ ⚜

"'Beeeeeee ouuuuuur guest!'" Nora finished with a flourish, the five-year-old next to her managing to sing twice as loud as her forty-one-year-old aunt. Giggling like the child she'd swung around in a circle, Nora collapsed on the couch, Bella in her arms and just as out of breath. "You pooped me out, kiddo," she managed. After an hour of watching and singing to a wonderful children's classic, Nora was ready for a nap.

She glanced over at the dining room table when her phone rang. Tossing a giggling Bella aside onto the couch, she grinned as she stood and made her way to the phone. It was Sarah.

"Hey," she said, still slightly out of breath. "Wanna be our guest?" Her smile fell almost instantly. "What?" She glanced over at Bella who had popped up from the couch and was dancing with a newly repaired Sam. "Okay. I'll uh, I'll make the calls," she said with a heavy sigh. "See you soon. Bye."

✺ ✺ ✺ ✺

"Brady!" LJ roared, popping the whistle into his mouth and blowing loud and long. "Get over here!" When the tall quarterback reached him, he grabbed the face mask of his helmet and tugged his head down until they were eye to eye. "You pull that shit again, and I'll bench your ass, you got me?"

The player tried to nod but was held in place by LJ's iron grip. "Yeah, Coach. Sorry."

"Now get the hell back out there and show me what you got."

"What do you wanna do?" Thom, his assistant coach asked, glancing over to meet LJ's gaze. He held a clipboard where he took all the notes LJ shouted out during practice.

"Shit, I don't know," LJ mumbled, reaching up to readjust his baseball cap. He felt a vibration in his back pocket and withdrew his phone to see Nora's name on the screen. Putting the phone to his ear, he opened the call. "Sis, I can't right now. We got a shit quarter—" He was cut off by his sister's words, words that froze his heart. He swallowed hard. "I'll be right there." Turning to Thom, he said, "Take over."

✺ ✺ ✺ ✺

Andrew sat on the bench at the end of the bed, feet spread wide with elbows resting on his thighs and fingers clasped between. Jill sat in the wingback chair in the corner of the room, curled up and staring at him. He'd come home early to talk.

"So, what do you think?" she asked softly, out of ideas.

He shook his head with a heavy sigh, a hand coming up to run through thick dark hair. As Jill stared at him, she couldn't help but remember that his hair was one of the things that caught her eye that first night they met at some crazy party. So thick and shiny. She couldn't stop the small smile and looked away.

"I think we should consider military school or something, Jill," he said. "I mean, what happened with your dad the other night, we already agreed it was beyond inappropriate and just damned..." He shook his head and shrugged. "Just weird. But, it doesn't get Tyler off the hook. He has to be forced to be responsible for what he's done."

Jill agreed. She was about to speak when her phone rang. She glanced at it where it sat on the Ottoman and saw it was Nora's number. She pressed the Ignore key and turned back to him. "Yes. I..." She looked away with a sheepish smile before she glanced at him. "I have to admit, though," she hesitated, a hand raised in her own defense, "I don't want to." She couldn't help the simile at her own schoolgirl ridiculousness as her gaze flickered to Andy's hair again. But then, what else had her life become? "I've added to all this." She grew serious as she felt a deep and profound sadness fall over her like a veil. She looked over at her husband who was looking down at his manicured hands. "We need to do something. Military school or whatever."

Again, Jill's phone glowed to life, Nora's name front and center. She grabbed it.

"Nora, this isn't a good time—" She listened for a

moment and her body went cold. With nothing left to say, she whispered, "We'll be right there."

❧ ❧ ❧ ❧

Nora sat in a wooden chair with a thinly padded vinyl cover. Her heel did a better thumpa-thumpa on the floor faster than at any dance club. With a *WHOOSH*, the cold air came in through the automatic sliding door. Glancing over her shoulder, she saw LJ, Jill, and Andrew rush in. It would have looked like a sitcom if not for the fact it was her life.

Pushing up from the uncomfortable chair, she met them and their worried, confused looks.

"What the hell?" Jill said. "You said to rush to Parkview and it was an emergency. Is it Daddy? What's happened?"

Nora looked all of them in the eye. "They found her," she said softly. "She's alive."

# *Chapter Twenty*

The siblings and Andrew sat in the ICU waiting room, a nurse having gathered them up in the main hospital lobby to explain that a doctor would be around to talk to them soon. So, now here they all sat. The chairs were as uncomfortable as the ones downstairs, and Nora's heel was thumping against the floor again. She sat huddled, legs together and elbows on her thighs. She was chewing on her thumbnail, scared to death.

Glancing around the small corner they'd decided to inhabit, she saw LJ sitting with his head resting back against the wall, still dressed in his sweatpants and school logo T-shirt. His Cyclone's baseball cap rested in his lap. He seemed to be staring off into space, and she wondered what he was thinking about.

She glanced over to her right. Andrew sat with one leg crossed over the other, a hand on his knee the other stretched out on the back of the chair that Jill sat in next to him. Jill was pale and looked as though she were about to cry.

"Did anyone call Dad?" Nora asked quietly, feeling if she spoke too loud, somehow Shannon would slip away.

"I left him a voicemail," LJ said.

They all turned when someone entered the waiting room, which was decorated with carpeting, plastic and living plants, and decorative art hung on the walls. Sarah walked in, carrying a box of Starbucks coffee and a cardboard tray of paper cups and cream and sugar. She set everything down on the low-slung coffee table near LJ.

"Figured you guys could use this," she said softly, pulling the stacked cups apart and laying everything out on the table. She asked each if they wanted a cup and each accepted. She made her own cup after serving everyone else then dragged a chair from the other side of the room to the opposite side of the coffee table and sat, essentially facing the group. "How's everyone doing?"

"I think we're all in shock at the moment," LJ said quietly, sipping from his cup.

Jill set her coffee aside and pushed to her feet, walking over to Sarah, who stood. The two women embraced, Jill, squeezing just a bit. "Thank you," she said into the hug. Nora watched as Jill pulled out of the hug and held Sarah by the hands looking her over. "How on earth have you gotten even more beautiful?" She gave her a small smile. "You must have a deal with the devil."

Sarah smiled. "Well, you must have the same deal."

"Oh," Jill said, waving her words away. "It's good to see you again, Sarah. I'm sure you remember my husband, Andrew?"

"Sure do." Sarah reached over to shake his hand. "Hello, Andrew. It's been awhile. Your wedding, if I remember, but it's good to see you."

"You as well, Sarah. Thank you for all that you've done for Shannon."

Nora watched as Jill sat back down and Sarah turned to look at her before she, too, sat. They shared a lingering look for a moment. The intensity in Sarah's dark eyes was too much for Nora to take and she had to look away.

"Are you the Schaeffer family?"

Nora turned her head to see an older man enter the room dressed in suit and tie and a white medical jacket. "Yes," she said. "How is she?"

Sarah vacated her chair and stood next to Nora's chair, and the doctor sat in her place. "I'm Dr. Frederickson and I've been overseeing Shannon's transfer here via Angel MedFlight from where she was cared for at Cheyenne Regional Medical Center. Once she was identified, we were able to bring her here."

"Identified?" Andrew asked, reaching down absently to take Jill's hand in his own. Nora wasn't sure if he did that for his comfort or for hers.

"Yes. Miss Schaeffer's unconscious body was found by a worker in a landfill in Cheyenne, Wyoming."

Nora felt the blood drain from her face and a hand on her shoulder. Without looking, she reached up and felt Sarah's warm fingers curl around her own.

"Jesus," LJ whispered.

"Her condition was grim," the doctor continued. "There was tremendous damage done to the left front of her skull and the swelling of the brain was substantial. She's been put into a medically induced coma to get the swelling down and allow the brain a bit of relief from day-to-day functions."

"Is she going to survive, Doctor?" Nora heard someone ask in a voice she didn't recognize. It took a moment for her to realize it had been her own emotion-filled question.

"Well, we're working on that. Her body sustained a great deal of trauma due to what appears to be a brutal assault, as well as exposure. The landfill workers don't believe she'd been there for any longer than a couple days, but due to open wounds on her hands and arms, all of which are likely defensive wounds against her attacker, bacteria was allowed to breed. Understand this when you see her, folks."

"We were barely able to get a fingerprint from her, guys," Sarah added softly. "We honestly thought we were going to be reduced to a DNA match."

Nora nodded, that horrible day at her father's house briefly flashing before her eyes. "Can we see her?" she asked the doctor.

"I'll let you go in two at a time," the doctor said, meeting each person's gaze in the room. "But, you'll only be allowed to stay for a few minutes, and I'll require each of you to put on protective clothing that we'll provide. Shannon can't take another infection." He slapped his hands on his thighs before pushing to his feet. "Okay, thanks, folks."

Left alone with her family and Sarah, Nora blew out a heavy breath, unable to process what they'd been told.

⁂ ⁂ ⁂ ⁂

The three siblings and Andrew were guided back behind ICU doors, Nora and LJ outfitted in loose-fitting suits covering their clothes and masks to cover their faces and noses. They were led to Shannon's room as Jill and Andrew were outfitted.

The room was quiet, save for the soft beeping of the various machinery connected to the still form lying in the center of the bed. The blinds covering the one window were partially open, leaving the room a bit dim with eerie green glows from the machine readouts.

Nora moved over to the bed, almost holding her breath at what she saw. Shannon was barely recognizable. Her face was a giant bruise, features distorted, and eyes tightly closed. Her head was a cotton swab of bandaging as were both her hands.

"My God," LJ said, words muffled behind his mask. "This is unreal."

"At least she's alive," Nora responded, reaching out a gloved hand and gently touching what she presumed was one of Shannon's legs, a long bump in the blanket that covered her body.

"How are we going to tell Bella?" LJ asked, stepping behind his sister and placing his hands on her shoulders.

Nora shook her head slowly, unable to take her eyes off her little sister and the mother of a very sad little girl. "I don't know."

❧❧❧❧

Later that night, Nora sat in Bella's bed, the girl long asleep after the story Nora had read to her. Now, Nora sat with her back against the headboard and her fingers absently running through Bella's hair. She stared off into space, her mind somersaulting over what she'd seen that day in the ICU, looking down at her little sister. Her emotions ran from relief to worry to profound sadness to a sense of being lost and alone.

She turned to her niece and slowly, oh so slowly, moved off the bed. Once free from the girl's grasp, she leaned down and left a soft kiss on the side of her head. "I love you, little one," she whispered, making sure Bella was covered and comfortable.

As she headed down the staircase, she heard her phone ringing downstairs. Hurrying to where it lay on the coffee table, she saw that it was Sarah's number. "Hey."

"Hey," Sarah said. "Wondered if you wanted some company."

"Yeah, sure," Nora said, with a gentle smile. "Come on over."

"Well, uh, I'm standing at the kitchen door."

Confused, Nora walked into the kitchen and, sure enough, Sarah stood there with a sheepish grin on her face and waved, her phone still held to her ear. With a short laugh, Nora ended the call and set the phone on the kitchen table before unlocking the door and letting Sarah inside.

"Hey," Sarah said. "I saw the upstairs lights on so didn't want to chance ringing the doorbell and maybe waking Bella."

"Good call," Nora said, closing the door behind Sarah, a frigid chill in the night. "Literally." Nora watched as Sarah shrugged out of her jacket, dressed in the same casual outfit she'd worn earlier that day at the hospital. "Want some coffee?" She took Sarah's coat and hung it on the coat tree in the living room near the front door to the house.

"No," Sarah said, plopping down on the couch, a hand coming up to rest on her forehead.

Nora joined her, somehow liking that Sarah not only felt comfortable enough to show up but instantly made herself at home. The irony was, normally Nora hated when company didn't call first.

"What a day," Sarah said, her voice strained.

"You sound tired."

"I am." Sarah eyed her and continued. "It was

a busy day, and I wasn't expecting the news about Shannon."

"You don't look like you were working today." Nora glanced down at the jeans and simple V-neck lightweight sweater she wore. "You usually look like a fashion plate when you are."

Sarah grinned. "Nope." She studied her for a moment and added, "I had to move Leslie out today."

Nora's heart beat a little faster. "Oh?" she said, attempting to sound casual. "Is that a good thing?"

"It's a very good thing. We had a plan all worked out. Her dad and some cousins and friends were supposed to come over and move her stuff, but we got into a fight last night." She closed her eyes and ran her hand through her hair. "What's new?" she muttered. "Anyway, they all disappeared, and I had to call some buddies over to get her stuff out."

"I'm sorry," Nora said quietly. "Moving sucks even under the best of circumstances. Trust me, I know. After moving all over this planet ..." Nora met Sarah's long gaze. "What?"

"Are you here to stay?" Sarah asked, her tone flat.

Nora nodded. "Yeah. My wanderlust is completely gone." She looked away. "Eighteen years was long enough. Besides," she added lamely, "I've come to realize exactly how much I wasn't there for the people in my life"—she spared a glance at Sarah—"for those I loved."

"We all make choices, Nora," Sarah said gently. "So, were you glad to see Shannon today?" Obviously she was changing the subject.

"It was surreal, I won't lie. I'm so worried she won't make it through this. From what Dr. Fredericks said and how she looked, my God."

Sarah nodded. "Yeah, I know." She readjusted her body, so she was tucked into the corner of the couch, partially facing Nora. She rested her elbow on the back of the couch and her cheek against her fist. "You know, this case has gotten so much deeper and more complicated now. From a missing person's case to an arson case to a homicide case, all spread over three counties and two states."

"Homicide?" Nora asked, confused.

Sarah nodded. "Yeah. Probably shouldn't tell you this but, in Shannon's apartment after the fire, they found a body."

"Oh God," Nora gasped, lifting a hand to her mouth. "Who?" she whispered, afraid to hear the answer.

"The neighbor."

Nora sat up straighter. "Penny Garcia?"

Sarah nodded sagely. "Yes."

Flopping back against the couch, Nora let out a sigh. "God, this is getting crazy, Sarah. What on earth is all this about?"

"We don't know. Much of our case will be handed over to other units now, including the Feds." Sarah studied her for a moment, looking for all the world like that very world was resting on her shoulders. "Wanna watch a movie or something?"

Nora wasn't sure she'd heard her right initially but then nodded with a smile. "Yeah, I'd love that," she said with a relieved chuckle. "A movie would be great." She pushed up from the couch and went over to her entertainment cabinet, sitting crossed-legged in front of it. She opened the compartments where her DVDs were stowed and glared at Sarah over her shoulder. "If you make fun of me for digging out a DVD instead of Netflix or something, I'm going to remind you that you're older than I am."

Sarah giggled, popping up from the couch and plopping down next to her. "What'cha got?"

❧ ❧ ❧ ❧

Nora's eyes blinked open several times, confused as she found herself on the couch, a movie playing on the screen. She also felt a weight on top of her. It took her a moment to realize that *Ghostbusters II* was almost over, barely remembering the two decided to put the second movie in. It took another moment to realize that the weight upon her was Sarah.

Sarah's head rested on her shoulder, their bodies somehow managing to both be on the couch. She smiled, looking into that exquisite face. Bringing up a hand, she ran her fingers through long, dark hair.

"So beautiful," she whispered, noting the way the dancing lights from the TV screen played in the dark across Sarah's features. After a moment, those incredible dark eyes opened, unfocused and looking around. At last, they landed on Nora. "Hey. We both fell asleep."

"I guess," Sarah said, staying where she was for a minute. Nora wondered if she was about to fall back to sleep. Eventually and with a loud yawn, Sarah pushed off of Nora and sat up. Her yawn continued as she stretched her back out, arms over her head, and breasts pushing against the thin material of her sweater.

Nora forced herself to look away. She yawned herself then pushed to her feet. "God, what time is it?"

"Late p.m.," Sarah said, finding her way to her own feet. She let out another yawn before glancing at Nora. "That was fun."

Nora returned the smile. "Yes. I'm so glad you came over."

"I have to go. Damn, so tired."

"Come on, you," Nora said, walking over to Sarah and taking her hand to lead her toward the kitchen door, grabbing her jacket on the way. "Are you okay to drive? I can take the couch."

"Nah." Sarah yawned, "I'm okay."

Sarah shrugged into her jacket as they stood at the kitchen door. Nora looked at her and with a small smile pulled her into a hug.

"Thank you," she said softly.

"For what?" Sarah asked, responding to the hug.

"Yes." Nora let out a small laugh. She smiled when she heard Sarah's soft chuckle against her neck. "For being so good at what you do, for your dedication to this case. Your kindness," she finished softly.

"Quite a journey," Sarah said.

"Isn't that the truth?" Nora pulled back enough to look into Sarah's face. Yes, there was a stunning, sophisticated woman standing before her who, in truth, she didn't know anymore. But, in her eyes, she saw the woman she'd known—the one she'd loved and wanted all these years.

Nora had no idea how it began but the next thing she knew she was pressed up against the fridge, Sarah's kiss hot, wet, and demanding. She responded, her fingers clenched in Sarah's hair, holding them together as a war waged, first kin Nora's mouth then in Sarah's, their bodies pressed together, shoving the heavy fridge against the wall.

She was lost, floating above the farm, above her own reasoning, which came crashing down as Sarah pushed away, breathing heavily.

"God." Sarah panted, a trembling hand coming up to comb through her hair. "I'm sorry. God."

It took a moment, but finally Nora was back on planet earth and felt the coolness of the Sub-Zero against her back. She blinked several times then focused on Sarah, who seemed to refuse to meet her gaze.

"I need to go," Sarah whispered, sparing a glance at Nora. "I can't do this again, I'm sorry."

With that, she was gone.

# *Chapter Twenty-one*

## Pueblo, Colorado – 1995

Nora stood at the counter washing her dinner dishes. She'd made a meatloaf, sure to make enough for Sarah to take some to work with her. She knew her roommate didn't eat near enough, and for the difficult and stressful job she had—let alone the crappy overnight hours—a good dinner was key.

She could hear said roommate getting ready for her shift. The shower had turned off ten minutes before, and Sarah's footsteps echoed in the area of the house where the bedrooms she and Daniel used were. The sound of drawers opening and closing combined with Sarah's music, which lightly streamed through the house.

In the two weeks since that crazy game—Pumpkin Pick, Nora thought they'd called it—with Sarah's friends, she and Sarah had become more friendly. They still didn't exactly hang out, per se but they'd watched a couple movies together or at least joined each other when one of them was already watching a movie. One thing she had noticed, however, was that Sarah was spending more and more of her days off at the house. When she wasn't either at work or…someplace else, she spent her time at the house. This, however, was pretty much the exact opposite of Daniel. When he was at the house, he seemed moody and not all that friendly. Nora wasn't sad about this, as she had gotten tired of his constant flirting with her, but something had changed in him. Nora smiled to herself as she hand washed the glass she had in her hands and wondered if he'd finally gotten himself a girlfriend.

"Shit, I'm running late," Sarah said, rushing into the kitchen.

Nora glanced over her shoulder and promptly dropped the glass she'd been washing, causing a soapy splash to her face. "Blech," she spat, using her shirt sleeve to wipe her face.

Sarah wore her perfectly pressed uniform pants and shined black shoes, but she wore only an emerald-green satin bra on top. It was bad enough Nora had to live with the memory of their play during the game, but to have to see Sarah's glorious body, which she obviously liked to show, was pure torture.

Nora used all her willpower to refocus on washing dishes. "I so wish Mr. Perkins would get the friggin' dishwasher fixed," she said conversationally. She gasped when, out of nowhere, she felt a body pressed up against her back and two arms reach around her, a travel mug in one of the hands.

"Me, too," Sarah said in Nora's ear.

"Uh"—Nora swallowed hard—"want me to wash that for ya?"

"Nope, I got it," Sarah said sweetly, pressing their bodies all the closer as she took the wash rag from Nora's hand and began to wash her travel mug. "I forgot to do this when I came home this morning," she said, unwittingly sending a shiver down Nora's spine.

Nora couldn't breathe as her eyes slid closed. She knew Sarah's bra-clad breasts were pressed against her back, with so little material between them. The intimate little cocoon Sarah had created was leaving her dizzy and incredibly turned on.

"I, uh," she began, desperately trying to find a distraction from what she was feeling so as not to make a total ass of herself and do something stupid like orgasm against the cabinet. "I made you a lunch," she managed. "Meatloaf, scalloped potatoes, and uh"—she swallowed—"carrots."

"That is so sweet." Sarah tossed the travel mug and its lid into the rinse water. "Thanks, doll," she said against Nora's ear, leaving a lingering kiss on her cheek.

It was only once Sarah moved away, casually rinsing her cup and drying it, that Nora was able to take a full breath. Her heart was pounding, her palms were sweating, though she had no idea how that was possible while they were dunked in water. The pulsing between her legs was so bad she was ready to take care of it herself. She watched as Sarah grabbed the plastic container from the fridge with her lunch in it and placed it on the kitchen table next to her dried cup; then she hurried from the room.

"Jesus," she murmured, buckling her knees so she wouldn't collapse onto the floor. She took several deep breaths and turned on the cold water, splashing her face to cool off. She managed to finish the last of the dishes when Sarah reentered the room, her uniform shirt buttoned as she tucked it into the waistband of her slacks.

"Before I forget to tell you," Sarah said, fastening the pants and buckling her black leather belt, "I'm working a double so don't worry when I don't come home in the morning. I should be home sometime around four thirty or so tomorrow evening."

"Oh, man," Nora said, concerned. "That is a seriously long day, Sarah. Is that safe?"

"Eh, I'll be okay." She grabbed her travel mug and raised it with a grin. "Lots and lots of refills." Putting the mug down, she finished with her uniform and squared her shoulders. "Look okay?"

Nora nodded with a smile. "You look amazing. I'd let you rescue me," she added, blushing immediately at her comment.

"Oh, yeah?" Sarah raised a brow. "Count on it," she said, her voice nearly a purr.

❧ ❧ ❧ ❧

The next evening, Nora sat on her bed, the phone to her ear. "You guys are like friggin' rabbits!" she laughed. "Good Lord, three times a day? Planning to have like, twenty kids?" She laughed at what the response was on the other end of the line. "Wait, hang on, Jill, yeah?" she called out after the soft knock on her closed bedroom door.

Sarah poked her head in. "Hey. Oh, sorry, didn't realize you were on the phone." She began to retreat.

"Wait, it's okay, Sarah, it's Jill. What's up?" Nora covered the mouthpiece with her hand.

"I was going to ask if I could get your help with something, but it can wait."

"Nah, I'll help. Jill, I have to go."

"Hi, Jill!"

Nora grinned. "Sarah says hi. Okay, talk to you later, sis. Love you, too, bye." She reached over to hang up the phone. "She said hello back." Climbing off the bed, Nora joined Sarah at the door, pleased to see she'd made it home okay. It was admittedly strange not seeing her for the entire day. "You look tired."

"I am." Sarah nodded. "Are you any good at massages?" she asked, her eyes heavy and slightly bloodshot.

"Uh, yeah, I guess. I can give it a shot."

Sarah led the way to the kitchen table where she pulled out a chair and turned it around so she could straddle it. "I had to tackle a guy this afternoon and it fucked up my shoulder," she said with a heavy sigh. "I'm sore as hell."

"Damn, I'm sorry." She positioned herself to stand behind Sarah, whose hands gripped the back of the chair. "Which shoulder, and am I going to hurt you?"

"My right one. No, I'll be okay."

"Okay," Nora said, not entirely secure, but she placed her hands on Sarah's shoulders, realizing quickly that the collar and patches and such on her uniform shirt would get in the way. "Do you have a T-shirt or tank top or something you can put on, Sarah, so we can take this off?" she said, tugging lightly at the collar.

"Oh yeah, sorry." Getting to her feet, Sarah cringed at the movement. She made quick work of the buttons, tugging the shirt free from her pants and tossing it onto the table. Beneath it was a fitted, ribbed, white tank top. She reclaimed her seat, her back to Nora.

She looked down at the strength in Sarah's shoulders and her lustrous skin. She was about to find out what she'd always wondered: was Sarah's skin as soft as it looked? She stopped herself from groaning at the first touch. Yes, it was indeed soft, and no, it wasn't where her mind should be. Sarah had worked an incredibly long shift and was hurting. It was definitely not the time for her mind to be swimming in the gutter.

"How's your sister?" Sarah asked, resting her cheek on her hands, which gripped the back of the chair.

"Good. Now that she and Andy are engaged, a lot going on."

"No doubt. Good for them." Sarah winced.

"Are you okay?" Nora asked, concerned as her hands stilled.

"Yeah," Sarah gasped. "Right where you're at, that's where I hit. Fuck, that hurt."

"God, I'm sorry, Sarah. Maybe I should stop—"

"No, please keep trying to loosen that knot."

Nervous, but doing her bidding, Nora worked on the area, able to feel the stiff muscle beneath the skin. "I think I've almost got it," she said. "Hang in there." She dug the heel of her hand in, using her other hand for stability. She cringed when Sarah cried out in pain. "I'm sorry." She felt the knot give way so lightened her touch, easing the muscle back into pliability. "Better?"

"Oh God, yeah," Sarah groaned, the sound almost erotic. "Feels good, Nora." She moaned, moving so her forehead now rested against her hands on the chair.

Nora smiled, pleased she'd helped. Now, she allowed her hands to enjoy the feel of Sarah's skin and the muscle beneath, so strong and beautiful. Even as her hands began to get stiff and sore, she kept going, moving the massage down along Sarah's spine and even to her neck. She glanced at the back of Sarah's head as another long, languid groan sounded. She smiled.

"Okay," Sarah said at length, sitting up. "Now I'm just taking advantage." She grinned, pushing to her feet and turned to face Nora. "Thanks so much." She stepped over to her.

"Of course, anytime." She smiled up at Sarah, suddenly feeling as though all the air in the kitchen had evaporated.

Sarah took another step closer, which put them less than a foot apart. Her breath caught when Sarah reached out, placing her hands on Nora's hips, gently and silently asking for her to bridge the physical gap between them, which Nora did. She placed her hands on Sarah's forearms. Even as the world around them disappeared as she stared into Sarah's eyes, she distantly heard the front door open then close. She didn't care because her brain had officially stopped working as her gaze fell to full lips, so close to her own.

"Did you guys see that—Whoa."

Knocked out of her reverie, Nora turned to see a stunned Daniel standing in the doorway of the kitchen. Embarrassed, she immediately turned and went into her bedroom, closing the door behind her. Eyes closed, she leaned back against the door.

"Jesus," she whispered. "How does she do this to me?"

❧ ❧ ❧ ❧

After her eyes had grown heavy from a couple hours of reading, Nora had turned off her bedside lamp and crawled beneath the covers. She started, something waking her. Lifting her head from where she lay on her back, she saw a figure standing by the closed bedroom door. Realizing it must have been the opening and closing of that door, she had no idea who was there until the figure moved.

"Sarah?" she said, watching as she passed through a pool of moonlight coming through the window, noting she was dressed in a tank top and boxers.

Sarah said nothing as she made her way to the bed, pulling the covers back enough to slip beneath them and slide over to Nora.

Nora stared up at the woman who was on her side next to her, her upper body raised on her elbow. Her heart raced, her breath catching when Sarah's hand reached across her to rest on her hip. As Sarah lowered her head, her breast pressed against Nora's arm.

The first touch of Sarah's lips was unlike anything Nora could have imagined, due to both her inexperience and the nearly painful spark that erupted through her entire body. Sarah's lips teased Nora's before she gently swiped at her upper lip, silently asking for entrance.

Nora sighed as the kiss deepened, Sarah moving closer until she was fully on top of her. She gasped as Sarah's thigh pushed between her own, one of Sarah's hands reaching down to lift Nora's outside leg as the kiss grew deeper, more passionate.

Sarah slowed the kiss and broke from it, lifting enough to look down at Nora as she began to move her hips, her thigh pressing harder against Nora's saturated panties. The damp material between the legs of Sarah's boxers made contact with Nora's thigh. Moaning softly at the pleasure, she wasn't entirely sure what to do with her hands, so she simply placed them on Sarah's sides.

It took mere moments of their hips moving together before Nora's release hit, a loud gasp escaping her throat, followed by Sarah's soft sigh moments later. Sarah pressed them together and took her in a long, deep kiss, which left them both breathing hard. She looked into Nora's eyes and Nora felt herself getting wet all over again.

As Sarah undressed her, Nora's nerves began to wane. The gentle lead Sarah seemed to be taking introduced Nora to a world and pleasure she'd literally never known. Using her fingers, mouth, and entire body, Sarah brought Nora into a new landscape of pleasure, giving, taking, and ultimate trust.

As the sun rose upon the house and seeped through the blinds that never quite closed all the way, Nora's naked body was wrapped completely by Sarah's, the only sound the deep, even breathing of both women.

# *Chapter Twenty-two*

Welcome, welcome!" Kathryn exclaimed, arms open wide for her parents and her sisters. "It may have taken us a few months, but we finally got this place painted and ready to go."

"Hey, everyone," Kathryn's husband, Jeffrey said, welcoming his guests with hugs and kisses. "So glad you could make it. How was the flight down?"

"Bumpy, but we're here. It was quite the journey to find Emerald Lane. I mean, how many Emeralds can you have? Lane, Street, Court. Good night!" Jeffrey's father, William said with a grin, slapping his son on the shoulder. "So proud of you, Jeff."

"Honey, where's Billy?" Kathryn asked.

"Uh," Jeff said, looking around the large open space of the main floor. "Not sure. Probably outside with Stanley."

"You guys still have that old dog?" William asked with a chuckle. "And hey, what's this I hear that this place used to be owned by Lawrence Schaeffer, Sr.?"

"Yup." Jeffrey grinned. "One of the main reasons I wanted the house."

Kathryn rolled her eyes. "You guys and your football. I'll go find Billy."

The brunette headed to the large, sliding doors at the back of the house that led to the massive backyard. "Billy?" she said, stepping down onto the expansive patio. "The grandparents are here, honey."

"Mom," the nineteen-year-old college student called.

Kathryn could hear his voice but couldn't see him. "Billy, where are you?" Then Kathryn saw Stanley sitting dutifully by the house glancing over at her. Walking in that direction, she noticed the crawl space door was open. Delicate eyebrows lowering, Kathryn squatted down. "Billy?"

"Mom, I need a flashlight and now!" he said, his voice leaving her no room for argument.

"Okay," she said, trying to think of where her husband would have put a flashlight. Deciding to try the garage, she looked through the drawers and cabinets in his workbench, his tool box and then remembered she had one in the back of her Navigator.

Searching through the kit Jeffrey had put together for her in case of a road emergency, Kathryn found a long black flashlight, almost like what a police officer would use, and hurried back to the yard.

"Okay," she said, again squatting down. Out of the musky darkness came a hand, which she gave the flashlight to. "What's wrong?"

"Hang on. Stay there, 'kay?" Billy said, his voice getting farther and farther away.

"All right," Kathryn answered, glancing back up at the back patio to see that the family was beginning to gather there. She smiled and gave them a small wave. She cried out in surprise when a tennis ball unexpectedly flew out from the crawl space, Stanley instantly on the run to get it. "Goodness," she gasped, hand to her heart.

"What the hell?" Billy said from far under the house.

"Billy? What's wrong?" Kathryn asked, peeking

her head into the space.

"Oh my God!" Billy yelled, nearly flying out of the crawl space, eyes wide and face pale.

"Holy shit," she gasped. "Jeffrey, Jeffrey come over here."

"What's up, hon?" he asked, trotting down the patio stairs and over to where Billy lay sprawled, Kathryn squatting next to him.

Kathryn looked up and met his confused gaze. "I think something's wrong."

❧❧❧❧

Jill was numb as she walked into the house from the garage where Andrew had parked the Mercedes. Like a zombie, she made her way toward the kitchen. She heard the television in the living room and a brief glance showed her kids watching a movie. Tyler sat slouched in the corner of the loveseat while Sylvia had turned, her arm resting on the back of the couch as she watched her parents.

"What happened?" she asked.

Jill studied the teen for a moment, realizing that she and Andrew had hurried from the house without an explanation. She walked over to her daughter and, without a word, hugged Sylvia's head to her chest, leaving a kiss there. She looked over Sylvia's head and met Tyler's gaze, her son looking lazily over at her, anger burning deep.

"Come here, son," she said softly, reaching an arm out to him.

Rolling his eyes, he pushed up from the couch and moved over to the duo, a knee in the cushion next to his twin as he was gathered into Jill's hug. Her own eyes closed when she felt Andrew's long arms wrap around the entire bunch. She swallowed down the rising emotion. She'd cry later, alone.

❧❧❧❧

"Kristie! Dinner!" LJ called out as he set the table for three. He'd picked up a large pizza on the way home from the hospital.

He made his way back into the kitchen to grab drinks for everyone when he heard Kristie's booted feet pound down the stairs. He glanced over at her as she entered the room.

"Hey, kiddo. How's that report going?"

"It's a bitch," Kristie said. "Where's Mom?" she asked, helping to dole out napkins and utensils.

"On her way. She texted me as I was walking in the door."

As if on cue, the large garage door began to rise, the motor groaning until it clicked to a stop. Moments later, it was groaning again. LJ glanced in the direction of the garage as he pulled his own chair out and sat down. He and Adrienne had said little to each other since their fight a few days before.

"God, this looks so good," Kristie said, rising from her chair to eye the offerings. "Awesome, you got olives."

"Of course, what else?" LJ chuckled. "Everything I hate in life became everyday life the moment I had a kid."

"Oh, you poor, poor boy," Kristie said with a pout, making them both laugh.

"Hey, guys," Adrienne said, entering the room. She shed her jacket and purse. "Sorry I'm late. Damn budget meeting went forever."

"Dinner," Kristie said absently, grabbing a second slice and plopping it down on her plate.

LJ said nothing. In all honesty, he had nothing to say. He and Kristie never had dead silence, awkward moments, or just plain issues. In truth, he'd never gotten along with anyone the way he did with his daughter. He was grateful for her every day.

The trio remained silent as both LJ and Adrienne grabbed their slices of pizza and began to eat. LJ felt his wife's eyes on him, so he glanced at her.

"I'm sorry I got your message so late," she said softly. "I'll go see her this week sometime."

"See who?" Kristie asked, sipping her glass of Coke.

"I was at the hospital today," LJ said quietly, sparing a glance at his daughter.

"What? Why didn't you call me?" she asked, her half-eaten piece of pizza plopping back to her plate.

"They found your Aunt Shannon," LJ managed, unable to look at Kristie's soulful eyes.

"What?" she erupted. "Again, I ask, why didn't you call me?"

"Calm down, Kristie," Adrienne said.

"Honey," LJ began, "I had such little warning myself. I didn't know what was happening. But, they found her alive and she's in Parkview." He met her tear-filled gaze. With an understanding smile, he reached across the table to quickly squeeze her hand. "It's okay."

"I'll be heading there sometime this week, Kristie. If you want, you can go with me to visit."

"Why don't you wait a little bit on that one," LJ said, meeting his wife's eyes. "She's in pretty rough shape." He nodded his head in his daughter's direction. "I don't think I want Kristie to see that."

"Hello," Kristie drawled. "I'm right here. You don't have to talk about me like I'm not here."

"Sorry, kiddo," LJ said with a rueful grin.

"Is she going to be all right?" Adrienne asked, using the fork and knife Kristie provided for her to cut up her slice of pizza.

LJ shrugged, chewing a bite. "Injuries are pretty bad."

"That's terrible." Adrienne shook her head as she stabbed a piece.

"Oh, here's a heads up. Nora will be calling you. Now that we know Bella will be here for a while, if not permanently, she wants to get her enrolled in Vineland Elementary for kindergarten. It's a month into the year, and she's not Bella's legal guardian. Is there something you can do?"

Adrienne nodded. "I think so. Speaking of school," she said, a light in her dark eyes, "Martin Murphy called me today."

LJ said nothing, feeling his stomach drop as he focused on his plate of food. "Yeah?"

"George is going to retire at the end of the year, as in, winter break. They want me to start come January."

His head shot up. "What?"

The look on Adrienne's face was wary excitement. "It's my dream job, Larry."

"I know it is, Adrienne," he said quietly. That meant he had a huge decision to make and he had to make it soon. He glanced over at Kristie. "Do you want to move to Denver?"

"Hell no," the teen said, shaking her head.

"Watch your mouth, Kristie." Adrienne's voice

hardened. "Guys, you knew this was coming."

LJ sat back in his chair, crossing his arms over his chest. He studied her, brain somersaulting over what to say. Finally, he let out a heavy sigh. "I don't want to move."

"Damn it, Larry!" Adrienne slammed her hand on the table. "Why do you have to be this way?"

"Mom, it isn't fair," Kristie chimed in.

"Kristie, this doesn't concern you."

"Doesn't concern me? You're asking me to leave my high school, which I graduate from in eight months. You're asking me to leave my friends, my job—"

"And Julia," Adrienne said snidely.

"Yeah, *mostly* Julia." She shoved back from the table. "I'm not going!"

LJ watched her run up the stairs, mentally counting to five before the bedroom door slammed. He returned his gaze to the angry woman sitting across from him. "Neither of us wants to go, Adrienne. I'm not forcing our daughter to leave all she knows because you want a new job."

"A better job, Larry. What part of that don't you get? More money, more options for me. Hell, even for you."

He eyed her, his anger rising, though he did his best to not let it out. This was an extremely important moment and he knew it. He had to play it right. "You've always been ambitious," he began, his tone even. "There's nothing wrong with that. You know me, we've been together almost twenty-five years. I've put twenty years into this school, into this district, raised my daughter in this house." He waved his hand, indicating the house around them. "My sister is lying half-dead in an ICU unit and my family needs me.

More importantly"—he leaned forward, elbows resting on the table—"I need them and it's taken me a long time to figure that out."

"And, what about your family, Larry? Hmm? What about your wife? What about your daughter? Do we get to come first?"

"I am putting my daughter first," he responded. "I'm not tearing her away from her life here."

Adrienne's gaze dropped down to her plate. "So," she said quietly, "what does this mean? It's going to be a bit hard to have a marriage a hundred and twenty miles apart, don't you think?" When LJ said nothing, she looked up at him. "Or, is that the point?"

"I've been doing a lot of thinking lately, and I'm wondering exactly what kind of marriage do we have?"

"What are you talking about? We've always had a good marriage, Larry. We've provided a good life and a good home for our daughter, in case you've forgotten. And," she added, "much of that good life is from the ambition you so flippantly mentioned."

"You know, Adrienne," he said softly, his heart heavy and hurting, "your biggest problem all these years has been your mouth, the things you say. You've really hurt me."

"Oh, Jesus." She sighed, sitting back in her chair. "What are you saying, Larry?"

"I'm saying, I think you should take that job."

❧ ❧ ❧ ❧

"Come in," came the muffled response to LJ's knock.

He grabbed the doorknob and turned it, pushing open the door with his free hand. Inside the brightly painted sherbet-orange room, Kristie lay on her stomach on her bed, her tablet before her.

"Hey, kiddo," he said, walking over to her as she moved to sit up. "You didn't really get dinner, so here's some heated pizza and"—he pulled the cold can of Coke out of his sweatpants pocket—"something to drink."

"Thanks, Dad," she said, accepting the food and soda. "Won't Mom have a cow? Can't eat in our bedrooms, remember?"

He chuckled. "Yeah, well I'm not exactly worried about you spilling your Kool-Aid on the carpet again."

She took a bite of the pizza and glanced at him where he sat perched on the side of her bed. "We're moving aren't we?"

He met her gaze and smiled as he shook his head. "No. I made an executive decision. It's not right for us."

"So," she drawled, "What about Mom?"

LJ let out a heavy sigh and looked down at his hands, which rested in his lap. "I told her to take the job. What she decides to do, she does."

Kristie took another bite, chewing thoughtfully. She washed the food down with a drink of her Coke. "This is serious, isn't it?" she asked sagely.

He gave her a comforting smile. "You don't need to worry about that, sweetheart. Everything will work out fine."

# *Chapter Twenty-three*

Andrew drummed his fingers nervously as he sat at a back table in the local coffee shop, The Hanging Tree Café. He sipped his caramel macchiato as he eyed the place, making sure nobody he knew was passing by the large plateglass windows or stopping by for coffee or their tantalizing breakfast burritos.

He checked his Rolex. It was nearly two twenty. She was late and he was getting nervous. Blowing out a breath, he took another sip of his cooling coffee drink.

"I'm so sorry I'm late," Laura said, hurrying to his table, glancing over her shoulder before sitting down. "Jordan got sick at school, so I had to pick him up and get him home."

"It's okay." Andrew smiled, a bit uncomfortable and awkward. "Thanks for meeting me. Can I get you something?" he asked, lifting his own cup for emphasis.

"No, I'm fine. So, how are you?"

Andrew sensed she was as nervous as he was and that helped a bit. "Listen, I hope you don't take this the wrong way because I don't mean it as such," he began, his heart pounding and palms breaking out in a sweat. He dropped them below the level of the table and wiped them on the thighs of his trousers. "But, I think we made a big mistake."

Laura Caffey blew out a heavy breath. "I'm so glad to hear you say that, Andrew," she said softly. "I feel the same way. I have been racked with guilt ever since."

"Me, too." He let out a relieved breath. After all that this kind and sweet woman had been through, the last thing he wanted to do was hurt her further. "I love my wife, Laura. I honestly do," he said, unable to keep the pain out of his voice.

"Does she know that, Andrew?" Laura asked gently. "I mean," she clarified with the hard look he gave her. "Does she know you think she's beautiful? She's sexy? That you cherish her?"

Andrew's instinct and kneejerk reaction was to be angry and offended, but he stopped himself from reacting or saying anything for a long moment, considering what she'd asked. "Well, I'm gone all the time because I work my ass off to give her everything she wants. She's not always an easy woman to please," he added with a small smile.

"Lord, do I understand that one," she said with a matching smile. "Robert can be a bear to please. The house isn't clean enough, dinner isn't good enough or wasn't on the table fast enough. Not enough sex." She looked down at her hands, which were resting on the table. "It can be emotionally exhausting."

"I'm sorry, Laura," he said softly. "Is he the right guy for you?"

She shrugged. "What choices do I have? I'm sick, still have kids at home. I can't exactly go to work to support us, and I'm simply too exhausted all the time to be a single mom. It is what it is, you know? But you, Andrew, I think you and Jill have a chance…if you want one." She studied him. "Do you?"

❧❧❧❧

"I think you would have gotten a good laugh, sis," Nora said as gently as possible using what essentially boiled down to an adult baby wipe that the nurses gave her to clean Shannon's face, arms, and hands, which were unwrapped for bathing purposes then rewrapped. The intense antibiotic regimen she'd been put on via IV had killed the bacterial infection. "Yesterday was her first day and good Lord, that kid killed it!" She laughed, tossing the wipe she'd used into the trash can before grabbing another from the box. "Bella is a seriously cool kid." She stopped what she was doing and looked down into the still, pale face of her little sister. "She's changed my life, Shannon."

"How's our ML this morning?"

Nora glanced up and smiled. "Hey, Rachel. She's good, I suppose. Any day we no longer have to wear what amounts to a HAZMAT suit is a good day." She chuckled. "So grateful they got that infection cleared up."

"Yeah, that was pretty hairy." The nurse, dressed in bright yellow scrubs, walked over to the bed. "Hey, sweetie pie," she said to Shannon. "Looking good today, cutie." She reached out and rested a hand on Shannon's arm before raising her clipboard to record Shannon's vitals.

Nora studied the petite blond nurse for a moment. She was a sweetheart and a ball of energy and light. She reminded her quite a bit of Meg Ryan, ala, *You've Got Mail*, with the short sporty hairstyle, infectious smile and laugh, and bright blue eyes.

"How's she doing?" she asked, moving away from the bed to get out of the nurse's way. Nora sat in a chair by the window.

"Well," Nurse Rachel Quinn said, scribbling a few notes before sparing a glance at Nora. "Nothing has dropped, which is great, but I am seeing a bit of improvement in her blood pressure."

"This is good, right?"

"Yes, ma'am," Rachel said with the bright smile Nora was beginning to know her for. "I'm sure her doctor will be thrilled."

They both turned when the room door opened, and LJ stepped inside. He glanced over at Rachel and gave her a polite nod before walking over to the awaiting hug from Nora. "Hey."

"Who's this?" Rachel asked, extending a hand to the newcomer.

"This is our brother, LJ. LJ, Shannon's day nurse, Rachel."

"Hey, Rachel. Thanks for taking care of little sis, here."

"It's my job," she said with a happy smile. "I'll leave you guys alone. Have a great day."

Nora noticed that LJ, too, was watching the pretty nurse leave. Even in scrubs, it was apparent she had a very nice behind.

"Sorry I haven't been here for a couple days," LJ said, walking over to the bed where he reached out and placed his hand atop Shannon's leg. Her hands were still bandaged, though not as heavily as they had been. The bandaging on her head had also been somewhat downgraded.

"No worries. How's practice going for the Pig Skin Classic?"

LJ let out a groan and leaned down and placed a soft kiss on Shannon's cheek before flopping down in the chair next to Nora's. "I'm over it," he said flatly.

She looked at him, surprise in her raised eyebrows. She said nothing, thinking back to what Kristie had told her. "So, I got a text message the other day," she began. "Kristie says her mom is moving to Denver in a few months. Is that true?"

He nodded, letting out a heavy sigh as he reached up and adjusted his Cyclone's baseball cap. "Yes."

"So, you're moving, then?" she fished, turning slightly in the chair to rest her arm on the back of it, her hand dangling over the front.

He shook his head slowly, never leaving her gaze. "No."

She held his gaze, and when she realized there would be no more forthcoming, she cleared her throat. "What does this mean, LJ?" she asked gently.

"It means I think it's time to live my own life, make my own decisions." He looked away from her, his eyebrows falling and a small wrinkle forming between his eyes. "I'm unhappy, Nor. Have been for a long time." He spared her a glance and a small smile when Nora placed her hand on his shoulder. "You know," he continued, taking Nora's hand and entwining it with his, "watching how Dad treated Mom, to the point where she left, then watching how he treated the string of women who came through after that…" He gave Nora a hard look. "How he treated Jill…" He shook his head. "I decided a long time ago I'd never be that kind of man, that kind of husband or father. You know?"

Nora gave him a loving smile filled with the adoration she felt for her big brother. She squeezed his hand. "LJ, it's not in you to be like him. It never has been, never will be. I mean, hell, you're the best damn dad I've ever seen." She made sure he was looking into her eyes before she added, "Don't you ever, ever forget that, okay? If I ever have kids, or for however long I have Bella, I can only hope to be half the parent you are."

He let go of her hand only to take her into a tight, though awkward embrace across the chair arm. "Love you, sis."

"I love you, too."

"Is it absolutely terrible of me that I have not one ounce of respect for my own father?" LJ asked quietly.

Nora didn't answer for a long moment before she shook her head. "No. I think people learn how we treat them or how we feel about them, good and bad, you know? Love, respect, all that, it's not a given, not a privilege. At least, in my mind, anyway."

He nodded and smiled at her. "I like that. So, has Sarah been around much?"

Decidedly uncomfortable, Nora cleared her throat and sat up a bit straighter in her chair. She wasn't about to tell him about the last time she'd seen the beautiful brunette. "No," she managed, removing her hand from his as she tucked her hair behind her ear. "I mean, her part of the case is over, so..." She shrugged and tried to give a nonchalant smile. "Now it's up to the Colorado Springs police to continue the case and work with the Cheyenne folks, from what she said." She met his gaze. "What?"

"You still care, don't you?"

Nora blew out a breath and waved off his words. "Don't be crazy, LJ. That was so long ago."

"Uh-huh. You know, you never told me what happened with you guys, how it ended."

Nora let out a snort. "I did what I always do."

"What's that?"

"Run," she said bluntly.

"You guys were together for what, almost two years?"

"Yup. That guy we had as a roommate, Daniel, was finishing up his residency and was moving out. Sarah suggested she and I move out of the house, too and get our own place, you know, just us."

"And, what did you say?"

"Told her I'd gotten the internship with *Nat Geo* and two weeks later was on a plane to Australia." When she heard nothing, she glanced over at her brother who looked at her with shock. "I know," she whispered. "Shittiest thing I've ever done. Regretted it ever since." She gave a rueful chuckle. "She'll always be the one I let get away."

"You know, sis," LJ said gently, "I can hear the pain in your voice and to be honest, could still see a connection between you two. Whatever happens, even if you never see her again, the truth is, it may have never worked even if you'd stuck around."

She glanced at him, confused. "What do you mean?"

"You guys were both young. Let's just say that you'd taken her up on her offer and you would have gotten your own place. Let's even say you guys took things further." He shrugged. "You were both different people then. Who's to say it wouldn't have ended in absolute disaster? As in, to the point where you didn't get what you got this time around."

"What's that?"

"Peace," he said simply. "During these past horrible weeks, it seemed like you two found some balance. To walk away knowing that you're both okay, you both survived a painful experience a million years ago."

Though her heart still hurt, she smiled. "Thanks, LJ," she whispered, taking his hand back in hers.

❧❧❧❧

Jill carried the glass of cold water from the fridge dispenser up to the master bath. "Here."

Standing in the center of the bedroom barechested and with his belt and jeans unfastened, Robert took the water. "Thanks."

Jill walked away as he took the pain medication she'd given him. An accident earlier that day at work had left him with a massive headache. Sitting in the wingback chair in the corner, she crossed one elegant leg over the other. Robert had arrived mere minutes before, long enough to ask for the over-the-counter medication and to urinate. She had to admit, as she watched him, it bothered her that he had just been in her bathroom, using the toilet that she and Andrew used daily.

Silly as she knew it was, something inside felt different. She eyed his well-developed chest and usually she loved nothing more than to run her hands over it. His arms and thighs were muscular from decades working construction, but somehow, it left her dry today.

"So." He slammed the empty water glass onto the dresser, not even noticing the glare he was receiving for the water ring the glass was leaving on the expensive wood. "Get this shit," he continued, whipping the belt out from the loops of his jeans. "I think Laura may be fucking somebody." He tossed the accessory to the floor then plopped down on the bench at the end of the bed to begin unlacing his work boots. "What the fuck?" he said, glancing over his shoulder to meet her gaze. "You know? That's fucking daring."

Suddenly, Jill felt utterly disgusted. Pushing up from the chair, she collected his discarded clothing and shoved them at him. "I need you to leave."

"What?" he asked, eyes wide as he looked down at the collection in his hands. "Why?"

"Robert, I need you to leave," she said, her patience gone.

He smirked. "What, pussy bleed?" He dropped everything she'd shoved at him and walked up behind her, grinding his crotch into her ass suggestively. "There are ways around that, baby."

Angry and disgusted, she turned and violently shoved him away from her. "Get out!" Again, she gathered the pile of his clothing. This time, however, she stormed out of the bedroom and threw them over the rail, letting the garments flop down to the floor far below. "Out!"

He rushed past her, nearly knocking her down the stairs in his haste to get to his things. He stood in the foyer below, buttoning and zipping his jeans before grabbing his T-shirt and tugging it over his head and into place.

"You'll regret this, you bitch," he growled. "I'm sure your faggot husband would love to know who's been giving it to his slut wife."

Jill stood at the top of the stairs, flinching with the slam of the front door. "God," she whispered, hands coming up to cover her face. "What am I going to do?"

# *Chapter Twenty-four*

*The soft moan released as she gently suckled the hard nipple into her mouth, which brought a moan from her own throat. She let out a second moan at the taste of her flesh, the smell of her perfume and the feel of her nails trailing over her shoulders.*

*"Sarah..."*

"You know?"

Startled, Sarah looked across the table at her dinner date. "What? I'm sorry." She grabbed her water and took a long drink to cool down as well as bring her back to the reality of the moment and not the dream of the previous night. "He drank the entire bottle, you said?"

Devon grinned and shook her head. "Damn, Detective, methinks your head is somewhere else."

Sarah gave her a sheepish grin. "I'm sorry. A new case I'm working on, a bit overwhelming."

"Man, I understand that one."

"Ladies, would you like to look at our dessert menu?" the waiter asked, hands tucked behind his back as he looked from one to the other.

Sarah looked at Devon. "Want anything?"

"Nope, I'm good, thanks."

Sarah smiled up at the young man. "Just the check, please."

After leaving the restaurant, Sarah wove her way

through the busy Colorado Springs traffic to reach the small two-bedroom house Devon owned. Counting their first lunch, which was interrupted, this was their third date, and Sarah did like the spunky blonde sitting next to her. Even so, she was deeply unsettled by her dream.

The passionate kiss she'd shared with Nora the last night she'd been at her house had set off a firestorm of memories, feelings, and the realization of how lonely Sarah was. Even as she drove to the home of a woman she knew was interested in her, she felt alone.

Pulling up in front of the house, she glanced past her passenger to take a quick glance at it. "Cute little place."

"Thanks," Devon said, pride in her voice as she, too, glanced at her home. "Still needs some work, but I'm usually so beat on my days off that it's taking forever, you know?"

Sarah nodded. "I get it. It took me years to get my townhouse fully renovated."

"And, as soon as you're done, everything you did is out of style again," Devon said with a laugh.

"God." Sarah rolled her eyes. "Don't say that." The energy shifted as she met Devon's gaze.

"You know, you're probably the most beautiful woman I've ever seen, Sarah," Devon said softly.

Sarah's stomach turned with nerves. She wanted to run but decided to stay, see where this went. Where her mind had been at dinner and most the day was far too dangerous, and she needed to avoid it at all costs. As she'd said to Nora that night at the farmhouse, she couldn't go there again.

"Thank you. I think you're quite adorable, yourself."

Devon grinned, dimples showing. She unbuckled her seatbelt and leaned toward Sarah. Bringing a hand up, she buried her fingers in long, dark hair, slowly bringing Sarah's mouth to her own. The kiss was soft, as were Devon's lips.

Sarah allowed herself to respond to the kiss, hoping the feel and taste of Devon's mouth would distract her and help her figure out where she was to go next. When Devon's tongue teased her bottom lip, she allowed entry.

*Sarah had no idea how it began but the next thing she knew, she had pressed Nora up against the fridge, her kiss hot, wet, and demanding. Nora responded, her fingers clenched in Sarah's hair, holding them together as a war waged, first in Nora's mouth then in Sarah's, their bodies pressed together, shoving the heavy fridge against the wall.*

Breathing heavily, Sarah pulled away from Devon, unable to get the scene in Nora's kitchen out of her mind. "I'm sorry," she said softly, bringing up a trembling hand to smooth her hair back from her face. "Truly sorry."

Devon brought up a sleeve and wiped her mouth as she looked away for a moment. Dropping her arm back to her side, she glanced at Sarah. "What's wrong?"

Sarah let out several breaths before explaining. "Look, someone I once cared deeply about has come back into my life and…I'm confused."

Devon smirked. "I guess we're just one big lesbian cliché, aren't we?" At Sarah's confused gaze, she continued. "You, the dyke cop, me the dyke firefighter and then the ex comes back into the picture." She gave her a rueful grin. "All we need is a U-Haul somewhere in this story and it's complete. Well, that and if she were a corrections officer or something."

Sarah could easily hear the disappointment in Devon's voice. "I'm sorry, Devon. I truly never meant for this to happen. Never."

Devon nodded. "I know." She studied Sarah for a moment. "You loved her, didn't you?"

Sarah glanced out at the dark street before them and smirked. "Yeah."

"Well, thanks for dinner," Devon said, pushing the door open and stepping out of the Mustang. She reached over and squeezed Sarah's arm briefly before she left the car, closing the door behind her.

❧❧❧❧

Masks firmly in place, the medical examiner carefully gripped the rusted zipper with gloved hands. Tugging gently, it eventually gave and she took it all the way down the length of the oversized duffel bag, any color and design long ago destroyed by the elements.

"Everyone ready?" she asked, glancing at her audience of her assistant ME and two homicide detectives. At their nod, she pulled open the sides of the bag. She'd been doing this for more than twenty years but was surprised.

"Jesus," one of the detectives muttered, taking a step forward and glancing into the bag. "Looks like something that should be in an Egyptian tomb," he commented, voice muffled behind his mask.

"Is that tape or something?" the other detective asked, pointing.

"Yes, looks like perhaps duct tape." The ME

glanced at the questioning detective. "We'll have to get it dusted for prints, DNA, all the usual suspects."

"How long do you think it was under there?"

She shook her head. "Not sure. We'll find out more from the autopsy."

❧❧❧❧

"Ezra?" Jill called from where she was on her hands and knees scrubbing in the master bathroom. When the housekeeper wasn't forthcoming, she called for her again.

"Yes, Mrs. Lacey?" the older woman asked, peeking her head inside the bathroom. Her brown eyes opened wide as she looked around. "Um, forgive me, Mrs. Lacey, but what are you doing? I was headed in here after the kids' bathroom."

"No, it's okay. I'm taking care of our bedroom and bathroom today, okay?"

Ezra gave her a quirky smile. "You didn't finally kill him, did you?"

Jill looked up at her from her place on the floor, blowing a long strand of bangs out of her eyes. "Don't tempt me," she replied with a smile. "I called you in here to tell you about our bedroom, but would you please get those steaks into the marinade before you go?"

"Sure thing, Mrs. Lacey."

"Thanks," Jill said, returning to her cleaning.

❧❧❧❧

Andrew chewed nervously on his lip as he drove the Mercedes through the winding streets of his neighborhood. He glanced over to the passenger seat, noting the bouquet of two dozen red roses. He felt like an unsure schoolboy.

He took the final turn that led him to his street, the luxury car slowing as he drove closer to his house, noting the truck parked in the driveway.

"Who the hell?" he mumbled, pulling the car to the curb and killing the engine as he studied the vehicle. He'd never seen it before.

Grabbing the flowers, Andrew slammed out of his car and stormed up the walkway and into the house. His fury knew no bounds for what he knew he was about to see as he made his way up the long stairway and into the bedroom. He stopped cold, utterly confused when a startled Jill looked over at him from where she was putting clean sheets on the massive king-sized bed they shared.

"Andy?"

"Don't Andy me!" he boomed, throwing the flowers to the floor. "Where is he?" he roared, throwing open the closet door, seeing only neatly folded and hung clothing. "Huh?" he demanded, glaring at her as he made his way to the bathroom. "Where is he?"

"Andy, what are you talking about?" Jill asked, hurrying over to him. "Who?"

"Robert! His truck is in the damn driveway," he growled, pointing a finger toward the large window at the front of the house.

"Andy, there's no man here," Jill said, shaking her head. "I swear."

"Then whose truck is that?" he demanded, backing her up until she hit the wall, a gasp of air coming from between her lips. He was menacing her, he knew, but he was nearly seeing red with fury and jealousy. His palms were planted on either side of her head, and he could see the tears in her eyes. Somewhere deep inside, a little voice was telling him to calm down. He was scaring the hell out of her. "Who?" he asked again, though his voice had quieted the tiniest bit.

"Mrs. Lacey, I'll see you Tuesday," Ezra called up from downstairs, as if on cue. "Steaks are in the marinade like you asked."

"Thanks, Ezra," Jill called, her gaze never leaving Andrew's and her voice wavering with emotion.

Like a balloon that had been pricked with a pin, the anger and energy blew out of him and he deflated. He rested his forehead on the wall right above and next to Jill's head. The emotions of the last few weeks since he'd found out, as well as his own stupid attempt at revenge, rose within him. Unbidden, the sting of tears pricked behind his eyes.

"I know," he whimpered, a declaration in two simple words. He felt a tentative touch to his back and heard Jill sniffle.

"I'm sorry," she whispered. "I'm really sorry."

The tears came, and he held her to him, crushing her petite body to his, her fingers clawlike as she clung to him. "I'm sorry, too," he blew out.

"I love you, Andy. Damn it, I do," Jill cried.

He was unable to speak, so instead, he grabbed her face and brought her in for an intense kiss, which she immediately responded to, the saltiness of their mixed tears on his tongue. It took mere seconds for the kiss to get out of hand before, breathing hard, two pairs of hands were shoving at Jill's yoga pants and panties in one push. As she was trying to step out of those, her hands were at Andrew's fly, almost painfully tugging to get the button and zipper free.

"Ow," he gasped.

"Sorry," she said with an apologetic smile, which quickly slid off her lips as Andrew picked her up in powerful arms, her legs wrapping around his hips.

Fifteen minutes later and spent, he led her to the bed where they plopped down across it, Jill immediately climbing into his arms.

"I'm guessing those were for me?" she said.

"What?"

"The roses?"

He chuckled. "Yes. Sorry about that."

"You haven't brought me flowers in years," she whispered, head resting on his shoulder and arm slung across his stomach. He still wore his suit jacket, starched button-up shirt, and blue-and-black-striped tie.

"I know," he said, letting out a heavy sigh as he ran his fingers through her hair. "I'm sorry, Jill. I've let you down."

"No, Andy." Her voice was soft as she repositioned her head. "We let each other down."

He considered her words for a long time then asked, "How do we fix this? Where did I let you down, in your eyes?"

She lifted her head, resting it on an upturned palm so she could look down at him. "I don't know. I guess you were never here. Even when I asked you to be, there was always something else you had to do." She met his gaze. "I think at first you were working hard to build a good life for us, especially once the twins were born. But"—she shrugged a shoulder—"somewhere along the way, your career, the firm, was far more important than any of us were."

He raised a hand, running a fingertip down a soft

cheek. "You know what's ironic about that? As hard as I was working for you, for the kids, I felt like all you wanted was more and more and more. Like nothing I did was enough for you. I couldn't make enough money, couldn't give you a big enough house, all that."

"I think we need to get some counseling, Andy." She reached up and covered his hand with her own, bringing it to her lips before letting it go. "I love you so much, but I think a lot of damage has been done." Her gaze dropped. "I'm deeply ashamed of some of the things I've done," she whispered. She let out a rueful snort before meeting his gaze again. "Ironically, this situation with Shannon has made me stop and think about a lot of things."

He smiled up at her, noting how truly beautiful she was. In that moment, he saw that lovely creature he'd met at that party twenty-five years before, who had clenched his heart right then and there. "Me, too," he whispered. He brought a hand up to the back of her head and brought her down for a lingering kiss. "We have a lot to talk about, including what to do about Tyler. But yeah, I think counseling is a good idea."

❧❧❧❧

Later that night, Jill sat curled up in the wingback chair in the corner of the bedroom dressed only in one of Andrew's button-up shirts. She watched where he slept, bare chest visible as the covers were pushed to right above his waist. She studied him, noting how utterly handsome he was and smiling, feeling lucky that he loved her.

She turned her gaze to her phone, which rested in her hand. She tapped in her code then swiped around the apps until she found the file called, Black Book. Opening it, she looked in disgust at what she had once been very proud of: *Robert, Branson, Alex, James, Ben,* and *Maryanne.* Each name was someone she'd found great pleasure with, each with their own special talent.

With a few swipes and tap of her finger, the list and their collective contact information disappeared. She hit Save and was about to set her phone down. After a moment's thought and a few more swipes and taps, the app, too disappeared, deleted. She set the phone aside and shrugged out of the unbuttoned shirt before sliding back into bed.

# *Chapter Twenty-five*

*E*yes closed, a smile tipped her lips as she inhaled the lilac-scented air. Opening clear, green eyes, she looked around, noting an entire field of glorious, vivid purple flowers surrounding her. She looked down and saw that she wore a summer dress with a flowing skirt that blew gently around her legs. She was barefoot, the feel of the ground beneath her feet so soft and cool.

She began to walk through the flowers, allowing her hands to spread out and the palms to be tickled by the barest touch of the fragrant softness, almost like a butterfly's kiss. That's what her mother used to tell her when she was a very young girl.

Her mother. How had she remembered that? She'd left the family so, so long ago.

Feeling eyes on her, she turned and saw a woman walking toward her. She was dressed casually in white cropped pants and a cap-sleeved tee with red horizontal stripes. Her medium-length dark blond hair lifted slightly with the breeze, but what was most notable was the beautiful smile.

"Momma?"

"Hello, sweet girl," she said softly, engulfing her in a warm hug. "It's time."

"It's time for what?" she said, eyes closed as she allowed herself to be completely encapsulated by the love she felt radiating off the woman who held her.

*"Time to wake up."*

*"Don't wanna."* Her smile widened at the chuckle she heard, which vibrated through her body.

*"I know. Wake up, baby girl. Wake up, she needs you."*

*"I'm scared,"* she whispered, tears coming to her eyes.

*"Don't be."* The older woman pulled away enough to look into a tear-filled verdant gaze. *"I'm with you. I love you."*

*"I love you, too."*

The steady, even beeping of the heart monitor took on an extra beep then two then three before the heart rate was speeding. Green eyes flew open only to blink twice, fall closed, then slowly open again.

⚜ ⚜ ⚜ ⚜

"What the hell were you thinking, Beau?" LJ said under his breath, rereading the sentence his student used in his test question answer. "Jeez." He shook his head as he clicked the Comment function and typed out a comment for the teen to read when he received his test results file back on his school-issued laptop. "Yup?" he said at the knock on the office door as he typed his thoughts. He glanced up when the door opened. "Hey."

"Hi," Adrienne said. "Uh, can I come in?" she asked, sounding unsure.

"Yeah." LJ removed his computer glasses and tossed them to the desk as he sat back in his chair. Something had changed between them. Since he'd put his foot down and made it clear his intentions—let alone Kristie's—his wife had been quiet and perhaps even somber.

Adrienne walked over to his desk and sat in one of the two chairs before it. "Susan called."

"Okay," he responded quietly, curious what their realtor had to say. "What did she say?"

"Well," Adrienne began, her phone in her hand, which rested on the edge of the desk, "you know the open house went well on Sunday."

He nodded. "Yup."

"We have an offer." She set the phone down and leaned back in her own chair. "Apparently there's a couple who have been eyeing this neighborhood for a while, and when they saw our place, they jumped on it. Their offer is ten thousand above asking to ensure they get it."

LJ's eyebrows raised. In truth, he was surprised and felt a mixture of sadness and relief. "That's a great offer."

"Yes. Sixty-day possession. So, what do you think?"

"I think we should take it. I'll be honest, I never thought this place would sell so soon, though."

She nodded, looking down at her hand, which spun her phone like a top on the desk. She glanced up at him. "Are you sure?" she asked softly.

He met her gaze and knew that statement was as loaded as a 9mm. "Yeah," he responded just as softly, not a note of doubt in his response.

She pushed to her feet. "Okay. I'll call her back." She headed to the office door and turned, facing him. "Larry, this was never supposed to happen."

He let out a heavy sigh. "It never is, Adrienne."

※ ※ ※ ※

LJ sat in the hospital cafeteria, hands wrapped around a paper cup of cooling coffee, his tennis shoe-clad foot tapping endlessly on the tile floor beneath the table. He reached up and yanked off his baseball cap, tossing it onto the table and running a hand through his brown hair.

"You're ML's brother, right?"

He glanced up, surprised at the female voice suddenly next to him. He recognized the pretty blond nurse, though couldn't remember her name. "Hi. ML?"

She grinned. "Us nurses have been calling Shannon ML, short for the Miracle Lady. May I?" she asked, indicating the empty seat across from him, a tray of food in her hands.

"Oh, yes, please," he said, quickly snagging his cap out of the way.

She sat down, today dressed in powder blue scrubs with fat, white clouds all over them. She glanced up at him as she removed the items from her tray, which consisted of a hamburger with fries, a dish of fruit, and a soft drink. "Forgive me. I'm super good with faces but not so hot on names."

"Larry, most call me LJ, though," he said with a grin.

"Rachel. So, LJ, are you excited about the good news?" she asked, removing the top bun to squeeze ketchup, mustard, and mayo from plastic packets.

"What good news? I'm sitting down here because when I got upstairs, they asked me to wait for about an hour. The doctor was in with her. Is she okay?"

Rachel's grin was instantly infectious. "Our sleeping beauty woke up."

LJ stared at her, eyes wide and mouth hanging slightly open. "What? Are you serious?"

She nodded. "As a heart attack. Her doctor is in with her as well as a neurologist to see where things stand upstairs."

"Holy cow," he said, his grin slow but large. "But, I thought she was in a medically induced coma." He knitted his brows.

"She was. Her doctors have slowly been pulling back to get an idea of where her brain is, the healing that's taken place."

"I'll be…Excuse me for a minute." He grabbed his cell phone and quickly typed out a text message to Nora, Jill, and their father, telling them the incredible news. Putting the phone back down on the table, he grinned at her. "I can't believe she's awake. Is she okay?"

Rachel shook her head slowly side to side as she chewed the bite she'd taken of her dinner. Swallowing, she said, "Not sure, yet."

He nodded, understanding. Chewing on his bottom lip, he decided to change the subject to ease his nerves. "How long have you been a nurse?"

"Twelve years. I went back after my youngest was born," she said, sipping her drink.

"How old is your youngest?"

"Aiden just turned fourteen. Zack is twenty, though I have no friggin' idea how that happened." She laughed. "He's a mechanic and he and his fiancée, Jenny, recently opened their own business. Super proud of him. I'm telling you," she said, pointing the fork she was using for her fruit, "that kid can fix anything. Always could. Early on we knew college wasn't for him, so in high school, he started a program with the community college to get his certificate in mechanics."

"That's great," LJ said with an approving smile. "My daughter, Kristie, graduates this year. Quite honestly, other than being a pretty damn cool kid, I have no idea what she'll end up doing."

Rachel laughed and nodded. "That's Aiden. He's good at everything and nothing. But," she added with a shrug, "things have been tough on him these past five years."

"Why's that?" LJ asked, taking a sip of his coffee then grimacing at the cold liquid and setting the cup aside.

"Well, unfortunately Aiden's dad, Mason, didn't take his deployments too well. You see," she said, meeting his gaze, "after the nine-eleven attacks, he joined the Marine Corps, determined to give to his country. He was always a patriotic guy. Anyway, he was deployed three different times, and the last one was simply too much."

A bad feeling in his gut, LJ rested an elbow on the table, his slightly scruffy chin in his palm. "Oh man, what happened?"

"I came home one night," she said, her voice matter-of-fact. "I found him."

"Aw man, Rachel. God, I don't have words. I'm just...Damn." LJ was truly bothered by the situation. "That must have been horrible."

"It was," she said with a nod as she squeezed two packets of ketchup onto her French fries. "So, I kept my nose to the grindstone and focused on my boys. It's a lot easier with Zack out on his own. It's been hard on him, too, though."

"Understandable. Mason was his dad."

"Not exactly," she said with a soft chuckle.

"Uh-oh."

"Yeah. His dad was a mistake. He's never met him. Honestly, being nineteen and stupid, you think you have it all figured out." She shrugged, giving him a grin. "It all worked out."

"Damn, you're strong. I was married and barely made it happen." LJ chuckled.

"Was?"

"Uh," he hedged, noticing she was looking at his left hand and the gold wedding band that still glimmered on his finger. "Still am technically." He met her gaze and let out a heavy sigh. "I guess you can say we're separated, well in the process. She's taking a job in Denver and, to be honest, there's too much water under a very long bridge."

She grimaced. "I'm sorry. That's rough. How long have you been married?"

LJ brought up his hands, playfully counting on his fingers. He smiled when she laughed. "No, just kidding. Twenty-four years."

"Oh, ouch. Jeez, LJ, I'm sorry. That's a long time before a split."

"It is, I won't lie. But, honestly, it's been coming for a while, I think." He smiled ruefully, unsure why he was telling all this to a stranger, but it felt good to get it out and connect with someone, if even for a few minutes. "I refused to admit it to myself."

"How's your daughter handling it?"

"She's not thrilled obviously, but she's a good kid, a smart kid." He laughed as he reached out and played with the abandoned coffee cup. "I think she saw it before I did."

"Don't you hate it when that happens?" Rachel said, shaking her head. "Damn, I hate having to be an adult. It sucks."

He was about to respond when his phone went off with seemingly unending texts. He grabbed it and began to read, amused. "I'm sorry, but I have to go. My sisters are blowing up my phone." He laughed. "They're on their way."

"Thanks for the chat, LJ," Rachel said, reaching her hands across the table. "Makes my dinner break more interesting."

He smiled and took her hand, noting how soft her skin was. "Hey, glad I could be of service. See you upstairs."

※ ※ ※ ※

Nora glanced over at Jill as they headed toward the ICU waiting room, expecting to find LJ there. "Military school, honestly? What does Tyler think about it?"

"He doesn't know yet," Jill said with a nervous smile. The two women turned the corner only to find the room empty. "Where's LJ?"

"I don't know. I figured he would have been here, too." She walked over to the bank of chairs and sat down. Jill joined her.

It had been a good day. Jill had shocked Nora by calling her up and asking if she'd wanted to go to lunch. Their relationship had been bumpy for so many years, it felt good to let all that tension go for a little while. Something was different about her older sister and she couldn't figure out what it was. Finally at lunch, Jill had filled her in a bit.

To say she'd been shocked to hear about her and Andrew was an understatement. After all, they seemed as though they were the perfect family: wealthy with all the finest clothing, toys, cars, and house. They had a perfect daughter with perfect grades. And, sure, their son may have a few little scrapes here and there, but what did it matter? He was a Lacey and as gorgeous as the rest of them.

For Nora to find out—more importantly for Jill to admit—that it was all a ruse, was utterly shocking. The truth of the matter was, a year ago, even three months ago, Nora would have felt that it was the bite of karma. The second truth was, Nora had also been changed. Being trusted to care for Bella over the past weeks had humbled her. She hadn't been there much for her family and had dropped the ball with Shannon. She still wasn't entirely sure why Shannon would put her down as an emergency contact when both LJ and Jill were both already parents and settled.

Whatever Shannon's thinking was, she was grateful. That pint-sized girl had taught her so much and made her look at her life and her family differently.

"Hello?"

Nora looked at Jill, startled out of her reverie. "Sorry," she said with a grin. "Got lost in thought."

"Jesus, did you two friggin' fly here?"

They both turned to see LJ hurry into the room.

Nora laughed. "Hey. No, we were having lunch."

LJ's eyebrows rose as he looked from one to the other. "Wait, you were having lunch? As in, together?"

"Zip it," Nora said playfully. "So, how did she wake up? I thought she was medically induced?"

"Yeah, I said the same thing. Rachel told me they'd slowly been easing her off the medications."

Nora's eyebrows drew together. "When did you see Rachel?"

"Who's Rachel?" Jill asked.

"One of Shannon's nurses," LJ said, returning his gaze to Nora. "We were talking over dinner."

"Over dinner?"

"Well, she was eating I was listening." He paused. "What? Why are you looking at me like that?"

A slow grin spread across Nora's lips.

"Oh, knock it off." He chuckled. "I was waiting to get in to see Shannon, and she was on her dinner break, nothing more."

"Is she pretty?" Jill asked, leaning forward in her chair as LJ had come over to sit with the sisters.

"Yeah, she's cute as hell," Nora said.

"Would you two stop?" LJ exclaimed, holding up his left hand with spread fingers. "I'm still a married man, for crying out loud."

"Yeah, but—"

"Look, pal, yeah, I got your damn card," Larry, Sr. boomed into his cell phone as he entered the room. "No, I got nothing to say, knew nothing about that, move on…No, Monday is not good for me…Listen, Detective  Whatever-the-hell-you-said-your-name-is, I ain't got nothing to say. Barkin' up the wrong tree." With that, he punched the screen of his phone with a thick finger and shoved the phone into the pocket of his track pants. "Fuckers," he said, walking over to his kids.

"What the hell was all that about?" Nora asked.

"Nothing. Some stupid cop has it in his thick head that he needs to talk to me." Larry, Sr. flopped down into the seat next to Jill.

"About what?"

"I said nothing!" He glared at her, with a look that let her know not to ask another question. She'd seen it many times in her life. "So," he said, sitting back and resting an ankle over his knee, his arm reaching out to stretch along the back of Jill's chair. "Why the hell am I here?"

LJ stiffened beside Nora. She reached over and squeezed his knee. "To see your daughter," she said, barely squashing the temptation to strangle him. "The doctors pulled back on her medications and she woke up."

"Medications? What are you talking about?"

"Well, maybe if you'd actually bothered to show up you'd know what was going on," LJ growled.

Nora's grip on his knee became so tight he groaned slightly and tried to pull away from her.

"What was the goddamn point?" Larry, Sr. barked. "She's been in a coma! How the hell would she even know if goddamn Elvis Presley were sitting in that room with her."

"Daddy," Jill said, nearly using superhuman speed to move between the two men, their father still seated and LJ jumping to his feet. "They can only let in two at a time, so let's go take a walk and I'll fill you in, and LJ and Nora can go see her first. Okay?"

Their father pushed to his feet, meeting LJ's glare over the top of Jill's head before she led him out of the room.

"That arrogant asshole," LJ growled. He stepped away from Nora and ran a hand through his hair as he tossed his baseball cap on the chair.

"I know." Nora nodded, walking over to him. "He's not worth it, LJ." She looked up into his angry face until he met her gaze. "He's just not." She gave him a quick but tight hug. "Let it go," she said softly. "We're here for Shannon."

He hugged her back and let out a heavy sigh. "It was good to see you and Jill not trying to kill each other," he said, making Nora laugh.

❧ ❧ ❧ ❧

Murmuring. The sound of soft murmuring and a sniffle. *Do I know that voice?* She heard her name as though whispered on a breeze drifting to her ears.

*Wake up.*

*We love you.*

*Wake up.*

With all her might, she tried to force her eyes to open, willing the blackness to go away.

*That's it…*

Feeling as though her eyelids weighed two tons, she focused until at last, she felt some give. They seemed heavy and as though they'd been painted with glue. She slowly blinked, light suddenly so bright it nearly blinded her. She closed her eyes and tried to focus on reopening them.

She blinked. Before her was an extremely blurry figure, not much more than a silhouette.

"There you go, baby girl," was murmured by the figure. "Come back to us."

She tried, she tried desperately to see this person clearly, this person whose voice she knew. A woman's voice. All of a sudden, a wave of comfort and relief washed over her. The tiniest ghost of a smile touched her lips.

"Nora," she whispered. "You're here…"

# *Chapter Twenty-six*

Before entering Interview Room 3 in the Colorado Springs Police Department, Sarah took a moment. She'd received a call the night before letting her know that Ellis White, Ronnie Garcia's best friend, had been arrested on a domestic violence offense and they wanted her to come up and interrogate him regarding the Shannon Schaeffer case. Sarah was known as one of the best interrogators in her precinct, and Ellis White hated women and had not one ounce of respect for them. This would require some finesse and good acting on her part.

Understanding her role, Sarah placed the evidence box on the floor near her high heels and pulled her hair up into a messy bun, forging an image. Taking a final breath, she picked up the box and headed into the small room, which was set up much like they were in Pueblo's department: square table, one chair on one side, two on the other, and a two-way mirror with detectives watching on the other side.

Sitting inside in the single chair was a Hispanic man with shifty gray eyes. Handcuffs removed earlier at Sarah's request, he sat with his legs spread wide and a wrist dangling off the back of his chair. He was dressed in baggy jeans and an oversized white T-shirt.

"Hello," Sarah said cheerily, walking to the opposite side of the table and setting her box down at the end of it by the wall. "How are you?"

"Who the fuck are you?"

"Well," Sarah said, flopping down in the chair across from him, looking far more like Sandra Bullock's character in the early scenes of *Miss Congeniality* than the seasoned, brilliant detective many had claimed her to be. "My name is Detective Sanchez." She lifted the lid off the evidence box and pulled out a folder. "And you are…" She rummaged through some pages inside. "Mr. Sanders?" She glanced up at him. "Right? Elias Sanders?"

"Sheesh, stupid bitch. Get the fuck out and bring back that dude that was in here."

"Oh, sorry. Wrong guy." She laughed, tossing the page she held in her hand to the floor—it was nothing more than an old lunch order from her precinct. "Here we go. Ellis White." She looked at him with raised eyebrows. "Right?"

He smirked. "*If* you don't know, why the fuck should I?"

"Well, that's okay. I know who you are," she said sweetly. "So, I'm going to ask you a few questions regarding a case I'm working on, all right?"

"Look, bitch, I already told the dude before you that I ain't no wife beater. Move on."

"Oh." She waved away his words. "I don't know anything about that, so indeed, let's move on. But before we do, can I get you anything? Water? Soda?"

He smirked. "Nah. Ain't be in here long enough to bother."

"Alrighty then. Do you know Shannon Schaeffer?" she asked, watching his reaction carefully. This guy had a record and was a kid of the streets. He wouldn't be fooled easily.

"Nope," he said with an irritated sigh. "Who the

fuck is she?"

"You have a potty mouth, you know that?" she said with a grin. "She happens to be the young woman who is part of my missing person's case."

He shrugged, readjusting his body in the chair. "So? What's that got to do with me?"

"Now, I know you know Ronnie Garcia. Best friend, compadre. Your amigo."

"Yeah, so what?"

Sarah reached back into the folder and pulled out a picture. It was one of the many that Nora had provided her with. It was a smiling snapshot of Shannon, healthy and happy at Bella's third birthday party. She flipped the photo around so Ellis could see it.

"Yeah, I seen her before. What about it?"

"Well," Sarah said, tucking the picture lovingly back into her well-prepared folder. "That's Shannon Schaeffer." She eyed him. "Still going to tell me you don't know her?"

He eyed her right back, his grin maddening. He sat back in the chair, tucking his hands behind his head. "Yeah, I seen her. Neighbor bitch or something."

"Do you know where she's at?" Sarah asked conversationally.

"How the hell should I know? Why should I care?"

"There's a five-year-old little girl out there missing her mommy."

He barked out in laughter. "Why the fuck should I give two shits? Ain't my kid."

Sarah rested her elbows on the table, her dark eyes boring into his. He was attempting to play visual chicken with her and she had to laugh internally. To her, he was small potatoes. "Did you ever have sex with her?"

"No."

"No?"

"You deaf? No."

"And, what if I told you I had it on pretty good word that you had, hmm?" *Score one for Sarah*, she thought as his eyes flickered away for a nanosecond.

Quickly his shaken persona was shrugged away and his swagger returned. "Yeah, maybe we did. She was the slut of the whole building. I mean, shit, who wouldn't? I didn't remember, though. I got lotsa women I get a piece of. Can't say I didn't get a piece of that, too."

Swallowing her anger, Sarah pushed on. "You like rough sex, Ellis?" she asked casually, thinking of the DNA that had been found in Shannon's rape kit.

"Yeah, sometimes," he said, cocking his head to the side in challenge. "You offering?"

"Hmm. We'll get back to sex talk later. Do you like horror movies, Ellis?" she asked, again her folder in her lap.

"Wait, what?"

"Horror movies. You know, the bad guy kills everyone, crazed lunatic on the loose…"

"Yeah, especially the ones where the stupid bitch cop bites it."

Sarah grinned, genuinely amused as she brought out the picture she was looking for. "Glad you like them so I know I won't send you to bed with nightmares tonight. Wouldn't want that, would we?" she asked quietly, setting the eight-by-ten glossy on the table in front of him. It was important to watch his reactions to this one in particular, no matter how subtle he tried to keep them.

Centered in the picture was the burnt, shriveled corpse of Penny Garcia from where it had been lying in what was left of Shannon's living room.

"What the fuck is that?"

"I think the more important question is *who* is that?" Sarah said, producing another picture that was similar but a closer shot of the skull fracture in Penny's right temple. "Pretty ugly, huh?"

He sat back from the table and cleared his throat, looking a bit uncomfortable. "You got a cigarette or what?"

"Sure." Sarah reached into the pocket of her blazer and, prepared with the foreknowledge of Ellis's favorite brand, pulled out half a pack. She despised cigarettes and their putrid scent but had removed half the smokes, so it looked as though it was her own pack. She offered it to him then lit it for him.

As he took a long drag, she set the pack of cigarettes on the table and shoved an aluminum ashtray over to him that had been on the table already. Leaving the two gruesome pictures where they were, she produced a third visual. It was a white page with a simple drawn mock-up of the female body, much like a medical examiner would use during an autopsy. At the head, drawn in blue pen, were the specific injuries of the blow to the head, including placement and shape. She placed it in front of Ellis, directly next to the close-up photo of Penny Garcia's head.

"Look at that," she said, tapping a manicured fingernail on the drawing. "Outlines the brutality of that hit. Ouch, huh?" She shook her head as if in wonder. "Pretty amazing how close those medical folks got with that drawing. Good job showing the injuries, don't you think?" Not letting him stop to think or even take a breath, she continued. "You know the most interesting detail to me? As similar as these two are, I mean, hey, they're identical, yeah?" She stood and placed her hands on the table, leaning forward and looking him in the eye. "These belong to two different women, Ellis," she said softly, almost as though soothing a nervous animal. "These wounds were doled out as punishment, and—" She stood straight and reached into the box to produce a metal black baton often used by police or bouncers. With the firm push of a button, the button extended with a wicked snap that startled Ellis. He looked at her with wide gray eyes. "Something like this, according to experts, is extremely consistent with both cases." She gave him a saucy little grin. "Oh, don't worry, Ellis. This one isn't yours. I brought it to give you an idea of what we're dealing with. See, yours is in the lab, being tested."

"Tested?" he asked, his voice much weaker than the cocky man who'd been sitting there for thirty minutes.

"Yeah, you know, for blood, skull fragments, brain matter." She looked him in the eyes. "DNA." She let the smile drop from her lips as he shifted in his seat. "You know what else the experts have told us? From the angle of the injuries, both to the right temple with tremendous force, it was likely delivered by a lefty." She nearly laughed out loud when he glanced at the cigarette held between the two first fingers of his left hand. He quickly dropped the smoke into the ashtray.

She placed the baton on the table and reached in again, her hand resting on the thing she planned to bring out next.

"I have two more pieces of show-and-tell for you, Ellis. Ready?" When he didn't answer, she brought out the thumb drive, still sealed in the clear evidence bag. That too was placed on the table. "See…" She sat back down, looked at the dumbstruck young man, and spoke softly. "Here's how I think this happened. Let me know if I'm close. I think you and Ronnie Garcia, oh, by the way, he's having a little chat of his own down the hall," she fibbed. "You boys got yourselves into some pretty deep shit dealing with a drug cartel that had you in way over your heads. For some reason, you thought Shannon had either taken this from you"—she tapped the evidence bag—"or she was going to snitch. Here's the kicker, Ellis." She lowered her voice that much more so he had to listen closely. "She had no idea that thumb drive was in her possession."

Ellis swallowed hard and looked away for a moment, his cigarette forgotten in the ashtray.

"Do you believe in ghosts, Ellis?" she asked casually.

He blinked several times. "Wait, what? Ghosts?"

"Yeah. You see, we got hold of Shannon's phone records, including a printout of all her texts. Do you know what we found, Ellis?" She waited in vain for a response. "We found a text from Ronnie Garcia's number claiming to be Rick Stanton wanting to see her the night she disappeared." She sat back in her chair, eyeing him. "Now, here's the thing I don't understand. Ronnie told us that Shannon told *him* that the father of her daughter was dead." She stared at him, watching as he began to squirm. "One damore thing."

She reached into the folder one more time and placed another glossy on the pile that was already there. She watched in absolute satisfaction as he paled, looking much like a ghost himself. The picture was a shot of Shannon in her hospital bed, definitely worse for wear, but alive and staring into the camera lens.

"Shannon Schaeffer isn't missing anymore."

With that, Sarah pushed back from the table, startling Ellis as the chair legs screeched across the linoleum. She walked to the door and, with a sick satisfaction, opened it with the scent of fresh urine in the air.

# *Chapter Twenty-seven*

Tyler, get your butt down here for dinner!" Andrew called, holding his tie against his belly as he placed the final plate on the table. "Sylvia, would you please get glasses?"

"Sure, Dad."

"Are we ready?" Jill asked, glancing over her shoulder from where she stood at the stove.

"Yeah, honey, we made space," Andrew said, reaching down to straighten the hot pad. "Can you get that or do you want help?"

"Get the garlic bread out of the top oven, if you would."

"You got it."

Sylvia's look of confusion wasn't lost on Andrew and he internally chuckled. *I get it, kid.* It wasn't as though he and Jill had exactly been the perfect example of parents or family in the past. But, as their therapist, Dr. Kyle, had suggested, they were going to work harder than anything they'd ever worked at to get this family back on the right track.

"Okay, here it comes," Jill said, hurrying over to the table while carrying a massive glass casserole dish of homemade lasagna between two oven mitt-covered hands.

"Tyler Michael!"

"Uh-oh," Sylvia said with a small grin, setting down the fourth glass at the place setting. "Dad used his middle name. He's in deep, now."

"Sylvia." Jill's voice held a warning tone, even as a small smile twitched the corner of her mouth.

"God, this smells amazing," Andrew said, nearly drooling as he leaned over the table to take in the full gorgeous picture of his wife's masterpiece. She was an incredible cook and, as the years had gone on and their divide had grown, she'd cooked less and less. Her lasagna, one of his favorites, was an absolutely welcome sight.

"Yeah?" Jill said, giving him a side glance. "I hope you enjoy."

He grinned at her, admittedly affected by her tone, a tone that used to be only for him. "I'm sure I will." They shared a quick smile before he turned to his daughter. "Sylvia, please go get your brother."

"Okay," she said with a heavy sigh, pushing up from her chair and trotting up the stairs. "Hey, idiot!" she yelled. "Come on, dinner."

"So kind to each other." Jill smirked, taking the seat Andrew pulled out for her. She glanced over at him as he took his seat. "Are you still good with talking to him tonight about Saint John's?"

"Yeah." Andrew nodded. "I think it's a good idea."

"Dad!" Sylvia screeched.

Without thought, Andrew pushed his chair back so hard it tipped over backward. He took the stairs two at a time until he arrived at Tyler's bedroom at the top of the stairs. "Oh, Jesus!" He shoved Sylvia aside as she tried to hold her brother up. "God no, no, no…"

"What's the matter?" Jill asked, running into the room. "Tyler! God, no!"

"Call 911!" Andrew barked, grunting as he lifted

his son's weight with one arm, crushing his body against his own as he reached up to loosen the belt tied around the bar in his closet.

Freed, the dead weight fell into Andrew's arms and he lowered him to the floor. Tyler's color was gray, his lips slightly opened and eyes closed.

"Call 911!" he yelled again, only hearing someone run from the room as he began CPR. "Come on, come on," he pleaded, on his knees as he crossed his hands and did compressions on his son's chest. "Come on, Tyler. Goddamn it, come on."

Jill collapsed on the floor beside him, holding her son's hand as she sobbed. "Breathe, Tyler!"

Andrew gave him more breath before returning to compressions. Distantly he could hear the wail of sirens. He looked up across their son at Jill, terror in her eyes.

※ ※ ※ ※

Windshield wipers slapped back and forth, trying desperately to keep up with the deluge that had befallen Pueblo. Andrew felt it was as if God himself were unleashing His own tears and fear on the city. He drove with a quietly crying Sylvia at his side, following the bright red and blue lights of the wailing ambulance in front of him, Jill inside with their son.

His Mercedes veered off into the emergency room parking lot as the ambulance continued to the ER doors. Cutting the engine, he spared a glance at his daughter—she shook and clutched the edges of her shirt.

"Hey," he said softly, reaching over to take her hand. When he caught her tear-filled gaze, he forced a smile. "It's going to be okay." He leaned over and left a kiss on the side of her head, and they climbed out of the car.

❧❧❧❧

Jill sat in the waiting room holding Sylvia, her fingers running through her daughter's hair. So many emotions washing through her, she almost felt faint. She was scared, horrified at what she'd seen, knew she had to keep it together for Sylvia, and yet wanted to fall apart herself. She was so relieved to feel Andy's arm stretched across the back of her chair, his fingers absently massaging her shoulder.

"Schaeffer?"

Jill glanced over to see a man standing at the entrance of the waiting room dressed in pressed khakis and a tucked-in light blue button-up shirt. His dark brown hair was short and stylish.

"Here," Andrew said. "Tyler Schaeffer?"

The man walked over to the family. "Hello, I'm Jack Ballard, the Psych Liaison for Parkview." He sat in a chair across from the trio. "First of all, I want to tell you that Tyler will be okay. The doctors don't feel there will be any long-term problems physically from this attempt."

Jill felt her heart begin to beat again, tears of relief and gratitude stinging the backs of her eyes. "Thank God," she whispered. "Can we see him?"

"Not quite yet. I need to ask you a few questions and fill you in on what will happen next."

"Okay," Andrew said, his grip on Jill's shoulder tightening.

"Has Tyler ever tried this before?" he asked

gently, looking from Jill to Andrew and back.

Jill shook her head, bringing up a hand to swipe at a tear that managed to escape. "No, never."

"All right," he said, writing something down on the page attached to a clipboard that rested in his lap. "Is he on any type of prescribed medication?"

"No, nothing."

"And, alcohol and drugs. Does he have any kind of history with either of these? Even just experimental?"

Jill glanced at Andrew, thinking of the BS with her father not long ago. She returned her gaze to the man sitting across from her. "Tyler doesn't really hang out with his friends away from the house, and there's never been anything reported to us at school. We're not big drinkers at home, so…"

"Speaking of school, how are his grades? Any friend issues? Romantic entanglements? That sort of thing."

Andrew cleared his throat. "He's actually in the process of being expelled. He's always had issues in school, bad grades, his teachers have mentioned issues with focusing."

Jill looked down at her lap, feeling like such a failure.

"And finally, has Tyler ever been in therapy?" Jack asked.

Again, Andrew cleared his throat. "Jill and I have recently begun marriage counseling, but the kids never have, no."

"Okay. Listen, I know this is hard," Jack said gently. "Kids don't do this sort of thing for no reason. It doesn't happen in a vacuum. Tyler will be sent from here to a seventy-two-hour hold for psychological observation and evaluation. He will have therapy sessions and you guys will be required to come and join in at least one session, as well." He glanced from one parent to the other. "It's not my place to tell you what to do, but I strongly recommend family counseling once Tyler is released. Oftentimes when a child attempts suicide, it's part of a systemic issue."

Jill nodded, swiping another tear away. "Okay."

"Should you decide to go that route, I strongly recommend the Parkview Family Counseling Center. It's right down the street from here and they do some good work." He slapped his hands on his thighs before standing, clipboard clutched against his side. "You folks can go on back and see Tyler, now."

Andrew held Jill's hand as they ushered Sylvia ahead of them back through the ER to the curtained-off cubicle where Tyler lay still on the gurney in the small space. Jill let go of Andrew's hand as she walked up to her son, noting tear streaks that flowed from his eyes.

"Hi, sweetheart," she said softly, bringing up a hand and gently wiping the newest tear away. He didn't look at her, instead staring up at the ceiling. "How are you feeling?" Her eyes slipped closed for a moment when she saw the bruising at his neck from the brief, yet intense pressure of the belt. She knew this wasn't the time to lose it. Instead, her hand went to his hair, gently brushing it back from his forehead where she left a kiss.

"Why are you here?" he asked, voice gruff. Jill wasn't sure if that was the inner emotion or a result of the pressure against his throat.

"Because I love you, my sweet boy. I failed you." She felt Andrew step up beside her. "*We* failed you. I'm so sorry."

"Yeah, bud," Andrew said, his hand coming up to rest on Tyler's lower leg. "I'm so sorry. We're going to make this right, okay? I promise."

It was then that he glanced over at his dad. "Is Sylvia here?"

Jill moved aside, allowing her daughter to take her place. She watched the twins interact. Though obviously not identical and not always close, they shared a special bond that Jill had never been able to fully understand.

"Hey, idiot," Sylvia said softly, taking his hand.

"Hey, stupid," he whispered, a tiny smile on his face. It didn't last long before his face fell. "I'm sorry, Sylvie." He sobbed.

It took everything in her to not push her daughter aside and go to him, but it was obvious that only his twin could be there for him. Jill watched as Sylvia hugged her brother to her, both head to head as they cried together.

Later that night, Jill sat in Tyler's room, unable to look at the closet. Instead, she sat on his bed and hugged his pillow, which smelled like him. The tears were hot and fast as she rocked slightly, feeling as though she'd lost part of herself that night. All she could think of was her son as a baby, the surprise when she and Andy thought they were only having a baby girl. She envisioned his toothless grin at seven when he lost three of his front teeth in the same week. She recalled as he developed into a young man, looking so much like his father, except with lighter hair.

"Hey."

She looked up through her tears, happy to see Andy walking in only dressed in his cotton pajama pants. His hair was standing at crazy angles as it was the middle of the night. She'd woken from fitful sleep after a nightmare of seeing Tyler hanging again.

"Hi," she said softly, using her shirtsleeve to wipe her face and eyes.

"Here," he said, handing her a wad of toilet paper he'd brought with him.

She gave him a loving smile and used it. "Thanks."

"Surreal, isn't it?" Andrew said quietly with a heavy sigh.

"Yes. You know," Jill began, dropping the hand that held the damp paper into her lap. "I think Saint John's is a mistake." She looked him in the eye. "My gut tells us he needs us right now, and to send him away…"

"A huge mistake," Andrew finished.

Jill nodded. "Yeah. I think we need to see what our options are here."

"Listen, sweetie," he said gently, rubbing small circles over her back. "There's nothing we can do tonight. Tyler's okay, so let's go back to bed." He smiled when she met his gaze. "Okay?"

Jill nodded. "Yeah. Okay." She gave the pillow one more squeeze before setting it aside, giving it a small pat, almost as though it were her son's arm. Pushing up from the bed, allowing her husband to lead her by the hand back to their bedroom.

❧❧❧❧

"What do you think?" Jill asked, glancing over at Shannon, eyes wide and bright.

"Well," Shannon said softly, "I think it looks as good over there as it did on the table, to be honest." She chuckled. "Jill, I don't know why you're freaking out."

Jill turned to face her, hands on her hips. "You're finally out of ICU in your own room, and Bella's coming today. I want to make sure your room looks pretty."

Shannon was touched. She smiled at her oldest sister and reached a hand out for her. "Come here." When Jill walked over to the bed and sat down, taking her hand, Shannon said, "You're worried about the placement of fresh flowers in here for my daughter when I have this to answer for." She brought her other hand up to lightly touch the auburn fuzz that covered her shaved head. A roadmap of staples ran from above her right eyebrow up and across her temple to end a little past her ear. "I'm not sure what to tell her," she said.

Jill gave her a brave smile. "You tell her Mommy has a boo-boo," Jill offered, her voice catching on the last word. "You tell her that Mommy is safe and she's home."

Shannon smiled, rubbing her thumb along the back of Jill's soft hand. "Hey, don't start crying on me again," she teased, but then sobered. "Jill, it's okay. I'll get through this and I'll be okay."

Jill nodded, bringing up her free hand, which held the tissue she'd brought out from her pocket and dabbed at her eyes. "Sorry. The last thing you need is my issues, too."

Shannon laughed. "Yeah, since I've never dealt with those before."

Jill smiled and leaned over, leaving a careful kiss on the side of Shannon's head. "I'd better go. Andy will be downstairs to meet me for our visit with Tyler."

"Good luck, sis," Shannon said, accepting a

quick hug. Jill had filled her in on what had happened a day and a half ago. She'd been shocked and horrified for her nephew. What on earth could make him do something so drastic? As she watched Jill walk toward the door, something popped into her head. "Jill?"

"Yeah?" the oldest Schaeffer girl asked, turning.

"Weird question. Did Mom used to talk about butterfly kisses?"

"Butterfly kisses?" Jill asked, delicate eyebrows drawn. She looked away for a moment as though in contemplation before a smile curled her painted lips. "Yes. She used to do this funny thing where she'd get in close to your face, and with her inhumanly long eyelashes, she'd bat them against your cheek. It was such a creepy feeling." She laughed. "She called them butterfly wing kisses."

"Oh. Okay." Shannon gave her a small smile.

"Wait. The other things were flowers."

This caught Shannon's attention. "Flowers?"

"Yeah. We had a huge flower garden at the house on Emerald. Nora and I would follow her out there as she held you and she'd tell us to run our hands barely above the tops of the petals. Called the feeling butterfly kisses." She smiled and shook her head as though lost in the memory. "Jeez, I hadn't thought of that in forever. Why do you ask?"

Shannon shook her head, feeling strange. "No reason. A dream, I guess."

"Okay. Well, I'll see you tomorrow. Love you, sis."

"Love you, too."

Left alone, Shannon was exhausted. She'd been moved off the ICU floor the night before, her doctors feeling she was stable and well on her way to healing, which were their words. She was glad, so tired of being stuck in the hospital. At this point, her memories were few and far between, mostly random images and faces. The psychologist they'd had come in to talk to her, Dr. Haley Carrigan, warned her that she may never fully remember or it may all come back in one crushing avalanche of information.

All she knew was, she was tired, and she couldn't wait to see her daughter. As if on cue, the door to her room opened and the weight lifted off her heart was immense at the first sight of her little girl.

"Mommy!"

Shannon's eyes squeezed shut as she caught the bundle that flew into her arms. She ignored the pain and weakness in her muscles as she gave all she had to hold the light of her life as close as possible. "Mommy," Bella said, her little arms holding on just as tightly as her mother.

"Hey, baby girl," Shannon whispered, inhaling the strawberry-scented hair, wondering what kind of shampoo Nora had her using. She smelled like a little Strawberry Shortcake doll. "I'm here."

Shannon's eyes opened in time to catch Nora turn away, tears in her eyes. She smiled and squeezed Bella before she began to rain noisy kisses all over her freckled face, making the little girl giggle.

"You smell so good I may have to eat you for dessert!" Shannon made noisy eating sounds as she nibbled playfully at Bella's neck, sending the girl into even more giggles. She hugged her daughter close, rocking her gently. Nora turned back around and met Shannon's gaze. *Thank you*, Shannon mouthed. Nora smiled with a nod.

"Mommy?"

Shannon looked down to see big green eyes staring up at her. "Yes, baby?"

"Where'd your hair go?"

Shannon smiled, knowing questions would be coming. She reached down and grabbed a tiny hand in hers and brought it up to lightly touch the rough surface of her staples. Bella gasped.

"It's okay, baby," she said softly. "Remember when you fell off the swings that time and you got a boo-boo and had to get stitches?"

Bella nodded, looking uncertain.

"Mommy got a boo-boo," she said so quietly that only Bella could hear her, bringing them into their own world like she did during story time. "That's why Mommy went away," she added. "But, know what?"

Bella shook her head slowly.

"Mommy is getting better and she's never going anywhere ever again."

"You swear?" Bella whispered.

"I swear."

Bella held up her tiny hand, pinky sticking up. Shannon smiled and, reaching her own pinky out, hooked the two smallest fingers together.

❧❧❧❧

Nora headed out into the hall, overwhelmed with emotion. Yes, she wanted mother and daughter to have time alone during their first meeting after so long, but she also needed some air. To her horror, out in the hallway, she lost control over her fear and grief of the not knowing and then ultimately the relief after Shannon was found.

Bringing up her hands, she buried her face in

them, the tears hot and wet as they slid between her fingers. She could barely catch her breath, desperately trying not to make a scene, but she was too overcome by the emotional release to find her way to the ladies' room.

"Hey."

Startled by the soft voice and touch to her shoulder, she looked up, and for a moment, thinking it was a mirage, saw Sarah looking back at her, understanding in her dark eyes. The tears came harder as she was taken into a firm, warm embrace. She held on to Sarah for dear life, letting so much go as a gentle hand cupped the back of her head, gently guiding her to rest against a strong shoulder.

After a long moment, Nora's tears slowed then stopped. She felt stupid and stepped away from Sarah, using her sleeve to wipe her eyes. She spared a glance into concerned eyes.

"Are you okay?" Sarah asked softly, a hand still resting on her shoulder. She gasped lightly. "Is Shannon okay?"

Nora nodded, giving her a small smile. "Yeah, she's great. I left to give her some time alone with Bella." She scrubbed at her face with her hands for a moment to clear the wetness of her tears. "Sorry," she said, feeling foolish when she saw the tear stains on Sarah's shirt.

Sarah followed her gaze and smiled. "It's okay."

Nora looked at her, eyebrows falling. "How did you know where we were? What are you doing here?"

"Nurses down on ICU looked it up for me, where they'd moved her." She raised the binder that Nora hadn't noticed. "I have one final question, and it's for Shannon."

"Wait, I thought your part was done, with the case, I mean."

Sarah gave her a grin that both sent fire through her veins but was followed by ice. "We got the fuckers," Sarah said softly, looking around, Nora assuming to make sure nobody had overheard her.

Shocked, Nora stared at her. "What?" she whispered. "Who? How?"

"Hold off for now," Sarah said gently. "Let me get to her first. Okay?"

Nora nodded. "Yeah. Okay." She placed her hands on Sarah's arm to stop her, looking deeply into her eyes to make sure she had her attention. "Sarah," she said softly. "You're not going to upset her, are you? Or Bella? They've been through so much."

Sarah looked away for a moment, seeming to gather her thoughts before she looked back into Nora's eyes. "Nora, we need to finish this. Other than maybe you and your family, there isn't a person in this world who wants these bastards to pay for what they did more than me. Please know that."

Nora saw the truth in those dark eyes and nodded. "Okay. Come on."

Bella was giggling at something her mother had said or done when the two women entered the room. Nora glanced over her shoulder at Sarah, curious about how she'd react not only to Shannon's condition but to seeing her in person as a grown woman for the first time. Last she'd seen her youngest sister, Shannon had been around eight.

Bella looked at them, and with a squeal of delight, scooted off the high bed and ran over to Sarah, hugging her waist as she looked up at her with adoring eyes. "You did it!"

Sarah smiled down at her, brushing some brown strands of hair out of her big green eyes. "What did I do?"

"You found my mommy." She looked over at her mom watching from the bed. "Mommy, this is the police lady. She said she'd find you."

Nora watched, charmed and truly surprised that Bella remembered not only the woman but what she'd said so many weeks ago.

Sarah reached down and, with a loud grunt, picked up the five-year-old and held her in her arms as she walked over to the bed, depositing the giggling girl back next to her mom. "Hi, Shannon," she said, extending a hand. "I'm Detective Sarah Sanchez. I work on the Missing Persons Unit."

A few of her fingers still bandaged, Shannon took her hand as best she could and gave her a small smile. "Hi."

"Shannon, you probably don't recognize her," Nora said, stepping up beside Sarah, "but, you actually knew Sarah when you were a kid."

"Oh, okay," Shannon said, looking from Nora to Sarah.

"Listen, Shannon, I need to ask you to look at some pictures for me. Can you do that?" Sarah asked, holding up the binder. "To pick out the bad guys." She glanced down at Bella who was watching everything intently.

Shannon nodded, reaching up for Nora's hand absently. Nora took it, murmuring words of comfort to her.

"Okay. Nora," Sarah said softly, pulling her cell phone out of her blazer pocket and messing with it until she handed it to Nora, the camera activated. "Would

                    *Kim Pritekel*

you mind getting this on tape just for the record for the prosecution?"

"Absolutely." She took the phone in her free hand and aimed it to where she could get Shannon and the binder, which Sarah had set on the bed before her.

"Okay, today is Tuesday, October third, 2017. We're at Parkview Hospital with victim, Shannon Schaeffer to do a victim identification of the perps. I'm Detective Sarah Sanchez and this video is being conducted by Nora Schaeffer, the victim's sister. Okay." Sarah placed her hand atop the closed binder. "I'm going to show you a series of pictures, Shannon, six per page. Each will be numbered, so if you can, tell me the number of the picture if you see the men who abducted you and victimized you, okay?"

Shannon took a deep breath as she nodded. "Okay."

"Okay, here we go."

Sarah opened the top cover of the binder and inside were the six photos per page, as she'd promised. Each contained clear, color pictures of Hispanic men. Nora had to assume they were of that ethnicity since both Ronnie Garcia and Ellis White were, as well.

She glanced down at Shannon and could tell she was studying each picture carefully, shaking her head. Sarah turned to the next page, and Nora saw an instant visceral reaction.

With a trembling hand, Shannon touched the fourth picture on the page. "That's one," she said, emotion in her voice.

"You're sure?" Sarah asked carefully. At Shannon's vigorous nod, Sarah pulled out a Sharpie from her jacket pocket and marked an X on the corner of picture number four. "Okay, next page."

It was three pages later before Shannon had a truly bad reaction. She burst into tears and slammed her hand down on the very first photo, a Hispanic man with piercing gray eyes.

"Okay, okay," Sarah said softly, quickly marking the picture before closing the binder and moving it away. "It's okay, Shannon," she said with a comforting smile as she reached across the small space between them and placed her hand on Shannon's knee. "You did amazing." She looked up at Nora who was still filming. "Go ahead and stop now, Nora."

Nora hit stop and handed the phone back to Sarah, who tucked it back into her pocket. The two met eyes for a brief moment and Sarah nodded, Nora taking it that Shannon had picked out both men correctly.

"It's okay, Mommy," Bella said, climbing into her mother's lap. "Don't cry. Me and Oreo will protect you."

Through her tears, Shannon looked down at Bella. "Oreo?"

"My cat!"

"Nora," Sarah said softly, climbing off the bed. She nodded her head toward the door.

"I'll be right back, sweetie," she said to Shannon, leaving a gentle kiss on the top of her head before following the taller woman out of the room. Once the door was closed behind them as they stood in the hall, Nora turned to Sarah with a question in her eyes.

"She successfully identified both of them. The second one, Ellis White, we believe was responsible for the majority of the violence."

"Damn," Nora said, hugging herself as she leaned back against the wall behind her. "Okay. Now what?"

"Everything is pretty much done, now. Depending

on what these bastards do, the prosecution may ask Shannon to testify, but I don't know."

"But," Nora said slowly, "your part is over. Right?" At Sarah's nod, Nora tucked her bottom lip under her top teeth for a moment. "Will I see you anymore?"

Just then, Sarah's phone rang. "Saved by the bell," she said with a small smile before answering her phone.

Nora watched her for a moment, almost as though memorizing her striking features in case this was the last time she'd see her. Her gaze fell when Sarah ended the call.

"I have to go." She tucked her phone away and met Nora's gaze. "I'll see you around."

She watched Sarah walk away, taking Nora's heart with her.

# *Chapter Twenty-eight*

Jill saw Andrew waiting for her at the end of the hallway, right before the door that read, *Behavioral Health.*

"Hey," she said, taking the hand he extended toward her.

"Hey. Ready for this?" he asked, concern in his dark blue eyes.

Jill let out a heavy breath and gave him a brave smile. "I think so. After thirty-six hours, I'm glad we finally get to see him."

Andrew agreed as he pushed open the door, allowing his wife to enter before him. "Me, too. I'm curious what his therapist will have to say."

After signing in and fifteen minutes of waiting, Andrew and Jill were led back through a maze of hallways to a therapist's office.

"Hello, Mr. and Mrs. Lacey," said the friendly woman who looked to be in her thirties. "I'm Patricia Waylan, and I've been fortunate enough to spend some time with your son. Please come in and sit down so we can chat."

Jill was nervous as she sat in one of the chairs provided but she felt substantially better to have Andrew sitting beside her. She absently reached over in search of his hand, which wrapped around hers.

"Now, I know this has been a stressful thirty-six hours for you guys," Patricia began, taking her seat opposite theirs, a table with a box of Kleenex between them. "Tyler isn't a bad kid. From what I've been able to gather in talking with him as well as through personal observation and detailed notes from others, I think he's desperately trying to find a way to deal with, what I believe, is some anxiety." She met the gaze of both parents. "From what he told me, there has been some discord in the home for several years. Essentially, folks, Tyler has been crying out for help and feels nobody has heard him. This explains poor performance in school and getting in trouble both at school and at home."

Jill's stomach roiled. So many things flashed before her eyes, so many times she'd chosen to go out with friends rather than check in with her children. So many times she'd picked fights with Andrew to avoid having to deal with him. So many times she'd failed. She leaned forward and snagged a tissue to dab at her eyes as the therapist continued.

"I recommend Tyler be put on a mild antianxiety medication, though that will have to be prescribed by the local psychiatrist here, Dr. Powell. I also strongly recommend family counseling once Tyler is released from here." She paused as Jill blew her nose.

"Sorry," she said softly.

"No worries. The thing you have to truly understand is, this didn't happen with Tyler on his own. He's not a bad kid. He's not looking to be in trouble on a daily basis because it's fun for him. And," she added, her voice sober, "he certainly didn't attempt to take his own life because he had nothing better to do on a Monday night."

The tears began to flow in earnest as the memory of seeing her child hanging in his closet came back to her. Andrew put his arm around her and pulled her against him.

"It's okay, baby," he whispered. "Patricia, what can we do?"

"Well, one thing I saw in the paperwork you guys sent us, you had intended to send Tyler away to a private military school in Kansas. I'll be honest, though I understand where your mind and hearts were on that, I think it's a dangerous idea right now. Tyler needs to be close to home, needs to know that you care, and needs to feel stable in his home environment. I understand he's been expelled from District 70 schools, so I can recommend a few good charter schools in District 60. What I strongly recommend is a place called, Goal Academy. It's essentially framed for troubled kids like Tyler. I know many who have thrived there and I think Tyler can, too. It's accredited in multiple states, and he could even graduate ready to enter a vocational career among other options." She gave them a reassuring smile. "Any questions?"

Jill was far too overwhelmed for questions, so she shook her head, getting her emotions under control.

"No? Okay, let's go get Tyler."

❦❦❦❦

Jill, Nora, and Bella made their way into Shannon's room where she'd already been placed in a wheelchair.

"Hello, beautiful!" Jill sang cheerily walking over to her youngest sister and giving her a hug and kiss on the cheek. "Look at you." She ran her fingers over the incredibly soft auburn fuzz that was coming in nicely on Shannon's head. "You're starting to look like a Chia Pet."

"Oh, aren't you funny." Shannon laughed, playfully pushing Jill away.

"You ready to go home?" Nora asked, standing before her with hands on hips. "Well, to the farmhouse, anyway."

Shannon glanced up at her. "I'm sorry to be such a burden, Nora," she said softly.

"Hey." Nora squatted down in front of her wheelchair.

Jill watched her two younger sisters interact. She'd been a bit wistful of their relationship when they were all younger. But now, it was heartwarming. The truth was, if Shannon had to stay with one of them, there was no better choice than Nora.

"I feel better having you so close," Nora continued. "You and Bella." She smiled and reached a hand up, lovingly tapping Shannon's chin. "We can go geocaching."

Shannon threw her head back and laughed. "God, it's been so many years."

"She took Kristie to do that," Jill added.

Shannon glanced up at her then back to Nora. "Really?"

"Yup," Nora said, rising to her feet. She looked at Jill. "You want to push?"

"No, go ahead." Jill turned to the bed where the duffel bag she'd provided filled with anything belonging to Shannon—mainly gifts brought by well-wishers—waited.

"Can I ride?" Bella asked, looking from Jill to Nora to her mom.

"Come here, sweetheart," Shannon said, patting her lap.

Jill helped the small girl onto her mother's lap.

"Everyone ready?"

"Let's do this," Nora said, taking her place behind the wheelchair, her hands resting on the handles.

Jill slung the duffel bag over her shoulder and glanced back at Nora. The two shared a look and a smile. She walked to the room door and opened it with a flourish. "My lady," she said to Shannon, who was being wheeled closer to the exit.

Nora pushed her and Bella out into the hall. Jill led the way, a smile on her lips and in her heart as she saw so many familiar faces step out from the nurses' stations, rooms, and adjacent hallways, each one with a smile and thumbs up for Shannon.

"Go, Shannon!" someone called out. "Get 'em, tiger!"

She glanced down at Shannon to see tears in her eyes as she looked at the various faces. She had to wonder how many of those women and men she actually remembered. As they headed to the elevator to go down to the main floor to leave the hospital, the stainless steel doors opened, and Rachel Quinn stepped out. She held a bundle of things in her arms, as well as a bouquet of bright flowers.

"Hey, you," she said, walking to where Nora stopped the wheelchair. She squatted in front of it. "Hey, kiddo!" She reached up and playfully tweaked Bella's chin. "Miss Shannon, us nurses up in ICU have a little gift for you." She looked into Shannon's eyes.

Jill watched, her own emotions prickling at her eyes.

"See," Rachel began, unfolding a blue T-shirt. "You truly inspired all of us and you are our superhero." She opened the shirt to reveal a women's-style T-shirt with what looked similar to be the Superman logo in the middle, except instead of an "S," it was a yellow "ML." "You're our Miracle Lady and always will be." She refolded the T-shirt and handed it to Shannon along with the flowers she'd briefly placed on the floor. Standing, she bent down and gave Shannon a hug, which Shannon returned.

Jill glanced at Nora to see that she, too, was wiping away tears.

Rachel moved out of the way, waving as Nora pushed the wheelchair forward. Jill glanced at her sisters and niece then at Rachel. Chewing her bottom lip for a moment, she walked over to the nurse.

"Hey, Jill," Rachel said, her typical bright smile in place.

"Can I talk to you for a second?" Jill asked.

"Sure. What's up?"

❧❧❧❧

LJ ran a hand through his hair and let out a heavy sigh as he read what had been presented to him. He could feel Adrienne's eyes on him. Taking a quick glance at her, he sat back in his chair, the wood squeaking slightly under his weight.

"So, you're okay with this, then?" he asked. "My taking the down payment out of savings—"

"Which I then take out of the profit from the sale of the house, yes, I'm fine with it," she finished. "What about the furniture and all that?" She indicated the large house around them.

"Well," LJ began, his gaze falling to Adrienne's left hand. He noticed the absence of her wedding ring. Clearing his throat and any emotions attached to that, he focused his thoughts on their discussion. "Yeah,

I'm good with that. Uh, at one point you'd mentioned staying in the guest room of my place until the end of the semester." He eyed her. "Is that still what you want?"

"I don't know, Larry," Adrienne said quietly. "I'm not sure if that's a good idea. Mom and Dad offered me a place to stay, so…"

He nodded, not surprised. Her mom and dad had been a huge obstacle in their marriage. For some reason, they didn't seem to realize that perhaps LJ had family, too. Everything, every holiday, every special event, had to be spent with them. For reasons he still couldn't quite explain to himself, he'd allowed it.

"Okay." He reached for the pen she'd provided and flipped to the first page where he had to sign.

Later that night, LJ sat on the back porch of the house he and Adrienne brought a two-year-old Kristie home to. So much had happened behind those walls, so much good, so much bad. Absently his fingers went to the thick gold band on the fourth finger of his left hand. He twisted it back and forth, as he'd done a million times.

It was a chilly early October night, and though he loved the autumn and winter, he was cold. He simply wasn't sure where he belonged in the house anymore, as short-term as it was. He began to understand how much of a buffer Kristie had become. She wasn't home, instead spending the weekend with Nora to help with Shannon and Bella.

The immensity of Adrienne's energy was overwhelming and suffocating. He had to ask himself, why hadn't he noticed that before?

Returning his attention to the gold band he continued to play with, the expression on his face no doubt looking silly, he managed to tug it off, leaving a twenty-five-year-old indention behind. He held the gold ring up to his eyes, feeling like Frodo from *Lord of the Rings*, trying to decide what he thought of the ring.

Enfolding it in his palm, he rested his hand in his lap and looked out over the night, hearing a dog bark somewhere in the darkness. Tomorrow would be a new normal.

⁂

"All right, honey," Andrew said, giving Jill a quick kiss on the lips and his daughter a quick kiss on the cheek. "Sylvia, have fun at your friend's house. See you gals later."

"I love you," Jill said. "Bye, Tyler, love you!"

"Later," Tyler called back from upstairs.

Half his family leaving the house, Sylvia to her best friend Amber's house and Jill to meet up with her siblings at Nora's, it was just the guys. Still dressed in his work clothes, Andrew trotted up the stairs and to the bedroom he shared with his wife and quickly shed the monkey suit, preferring a warm pair of flannel pajama pants and a T-shirt from his alma mater for law school, CU Boulder.

Puffing his cheeks out before blowing out a breath, he tried to decide what he wanted to do with his time. He had noticed silence coming from Tyler's room. He knew that both he and Jill suffered a bit of PTSD where his room and silence were concerned. They'd begun checking on him at semiregular intervals, and he knew Sylvia did, too. He was sure the kid felt suffocated, but Andrew could never go through that again.

Leaving the bedroom, he walked over to the

teen's closed bedroom door and leaned his head in to listen: nothing. He rapped a few times on the wood—still nothing. His heart raced as he reached down and grabbed the doorknob, which turned easily. Pushing the door open, he peeked his head in and let out an audible breath of relief. Tyler sat at his desk with his headphones on working on homework.

Resting his head against the doorframe for a moment, Andrew gathered himself and entered the room, which to his surprise was somewhat neat—that is to say, there was basically a clear path to walk. He'd been telling Jill they needed to work on the kids about the cleanliness of their bedrooms. He was even flirting with the idea of making them clean their own rooms and bathroom rather than Ezra.

Walking up behind his son, Andrew reached out and placed his hand on his shoulder, startling the teen.

"Jesus, Dad," he exclaimed, turning around to look up at him. He tugged the headphones off his ears to rest around the back of his neck. "What?"

"How's it going?" Andrew asked, nodding toward the open laptop, a math assignment on the screen.

"Good," Tyler said with a nod. "Got an eighty-seven on that quiz you helped me with."

"Hey, great job, kid," Andrew said with a huge grin. He reached up and briefly cupped the back of his son's head. "Listen, since it's just us guys, what do you say to pizza and horror movies?" He hated the genre but knew Tyler loved them.

"Yeah? On the big screen downstairs?"

"All the better to see amputated body parts with." Andrew chuckled. "I'll order food while you finish up here, 'kay?"

"Yeah, cool."

❧ ❧ ❧ ❧

"You okay?" Nora asked softly, walking down the stairs backward as she held one of Shannon's hands, the younger woman's other hand holding on to the rail mounted to the wall.

"Yeah," Shannon said, focused on each step she took.

"Almost there."

"Mommy, you did it!" Bella exclaimed, clapping wildly as her mother reached the main floor of the farmhouse.

Nora grinned. "See? Your mom really is a superhero."

Bella giggled then rushed to her mother and hugged her legs. "I love you, Mommy."

"I love you too, sweet pea," Shannon said, looking adoringly down at her daughter.

As amazingly well as Bella had handled the entire last six weeks away from her mother, Nora noticed a huge change in her since the day she'd brought her to the hospital to see Shannon for the first time. It was as though a light had been relit in her eyes and the excitement and carefree nature of a five-year-old had returned—quite a change from the quiet, often-somber countenance of a little girl who didn't understand why her mommy had left her.

"Hey, hey!" LJ hollered from outside the glass screen door in the kitchen.

"Come on in, guys," Nora called out.

"Uh, kinda need help."

Nora looked at Shannon. "Are you okay? Stable?"

"Yeah, I'm good. Go ahead."

"Bella, make sure Oreo doesn't trip your mom."

She hurried through the kitchen chuckling when she saw LJ standing there with three large pizza boxes in his arms topped by a six-pack of Diet Cherry Dr Pepper, Shannon's favorite.

"Damn, that smells good," she said, letting him in. He hurried in and set the heavy bundle down on the counter.

"Well, hey," he said, grinning at her, "after nothing but bad hospital food for six weeks, I'm sure she'll be thrilled."

"Hey, LJ," the woman of the hour said, making her way into the kitchen, Bella holding her hand.

"Hey, lil' sis." LJ hurried over to her and took the small woman in an all-engulfing hug. "Good to see you, beautiful. Brought you Italian sausage, green peppers, and onions as promised and"—he turned and indicated the soda like a game show host—"your fave."

"And then after dinner…" Nora added, opening the junk drawer next to the sink and grabbing something from within. She whipped it out, showing it to her brother and sister right as the kitchen door opened. Jill stepped in holding a cake, its box printed with the store she'd bought it from.

"Uno!" she exclaimed.

They all turned to see her. Nora grinned.

"Hell, yeah. It's game time."

❧ ❧ ❧ ❧

Bella was curled up with Shannon on the couch, both out cold from too much pizza and laughs. Nora and her older siblings sat at the kitchen table, the card game long since pushed to the center of the table, forgotten until another day.

"How's she been?" Jill asked, indicating the direction of the living room. "I imagine it's helped to be with Bella."

"Oh, yeah," Nora said. "It's helped Bella, that's for sure. But as for Shannon, she gets tired pretty easy. The nurses told me that bacteria she was fighting did a number on her body and her immune system."

"You said they caught those bastards, right?" LJ asked, sitting back casually in his chair, arm slung over the back.

"Yeah. Shannon says she doesn't remember much, but that day Sarah came to get her to pick those pigs out of the picture lineup"—she shook her head sadly—"Shannon had a huge reaction, especially to the second guy."

"I wonder if maybe he was responsible for more of the violence or something," Jill said softly, glancing down to where her hands rested on the smooth wood table.

"That's what I wondered, too. Here's the weird thing, guys," she said, her voice almost a whisper as she was afraid of Shannon waking up and overhearing her. "LJ, remember that first day you came out here to watch Bella for me?"

"We found the thumb drive," he said with a nod.

"Yup. Sarah and I had been in the Springs talking to people, checking out places where Shannon hung out, stuff like that. We spoke to that son-of-a-bitch!" she said with a hiss, leaning forward in her chair. "And, the thing is, Sarah even told me she felt strange when talking to him. Like something was off." She ran a hand through her hair, almost crying with frustration. "We had him."

"Hey." Jill's voice was soft as she reached over and placed her hand over Nora's. "You didn't know, sweetie. As it is, Sarah got Shannon back, and they managed to figure out who did this. Sarah is trained to sense things about people, Nor. Don't be frustrated or mad at yourself. I think," she added, glancing at LJ, "all of us can say you were as much a part of solving this case as anyone."

LJ nodded. "Definitely. He reached out and took Nora's free hand in one of his and did the same with Jill's hand. The siblings locked in a chain, he looked from one sister to the other. "It's always been us, guys, the Three Amigos, remember? Always looking out for each other and always, always looking out for our baby sister." Nora met his gaze, feeling the passion in his words. "Let's never let go of that again. I mean, Dad didn't even show up here tonight. Again."

"Was he invited?" Nora asked, surprised.

"Yeah, I called him," Jill said. "Thought he might want to spend some time with Shannon outside the hospital."

"So," LJ continued, "as always, it's just us." He lifted first Jill's knuckles to his lips then Nora's. "I love you girls."

Nora let go of her siblings' hands and pushed back from the table, moving to the larger portion of the kitchen. Seeming to understand, Jill and LJ followed and the three went into what they called a "team huddle" as kids, but in all honesty was simply a moment of connection, a safe place after yet another rough day living under the roof of Lawrence Schaeffer, Sr. After Shannon had come along, the teenagers had put the toddler in the middle of their three-way hug, protecting her.

After the hug, Jill left a loud kiss on the cheeks of both her siblings before letting go. "I should get home. Nora, what can I do to help clean up?"

"Actually, Jill, if you want to get food wrapped up or trash tossed, everything else I can deal with in the morning. LJ, will you help me get these two upstairs?" she asked, indicating Shannon and Bella.

"Yeah, but you get the heavy one."

"Ha ha." Nora chuckled. "Though I have to say, I doubt there's a whole lot of difference between them these days."

"True facts."

Nora gathered up Bella in her arms, and with a slight grunt, LJ gathered their sister, holding her close as he got steady on his feet before following her up the steep staircase to the bedrooms on the second floor.

Nora tucked Bella into her bed, Oreo jumping up to find her spot on the pillow next to the little girl's head. "Night, sweetie," she whispered, leaving a kiss on the sleeping child's forehead. As she left the room, she made sure the nightlight was on and she left the door open a crack.

"Sorry I crashed," Shannon murmured to LJ as he settled her in the bedroom she was using down the hall. "But, don't forget, I won."

LJ chuckled from inside the room. "When don't you win Uno, you card shark? Good night, sweet girl. See you later."

LJ closed Shannon's door and stepped out into the hall. The two met eyes before Nora's gaze fell to the hand that still rested on the doorknob. She noticed the absence of his wedding ring. Without a word, she led the way back downstairs.

"So, guess it's a done deal, huh?" she asked.

"Yeah, guess so. We signed the papers Tuesday." LJ let out a deep sigh as they reached the kitchen where Jill was rinsing the dishes before loading them into the dishwasher.

"How do you feel about it? Thanks so much, Jill," she said, grabbing the rinsed dish towel to wipe down the table.

"It's weird." LJ loaded the leftover pizza into the fridge.

"What are we talking about?" Jill glanced at LJ over her shoulder from her place at the sink.

"We filed for divorce," he told her.

"How is Adrienne taking all this?" Nora leaned back against the wall near the table.

"Initially she was shocked I think, but it seems like that's passed. Now it's down to business. She's being pretty decent, to be honest."

"You don't think there's someone else, do you?" Nora asked quietly, unable to look at Jill. She knew her sister's past with infidelity and that she and Andrew were working things out.

LJ shrugged. "I considered it a time or two. About how cold she could be, you know? But, I don't think so. I think she's anxious to move on. She's wanted this Cherry Creek job for years, so I think she wants to get there and put all this behind her."

"What about you? Are you ready to move on?" Jill asked, shutting off the water and closing the dishwasher after the last dish went in."

He looked down at his left hand for a long moment, fingers spread before he balled his hand and looked up at her. "Yeah. I am."

With a reminder from Jill of the twins' sweet sixteen coming up on the twentieth, Nora was left alone.

⁂

"Larry, stop," she hissed, followed by a giggle, her much smaller hand reaching down to where his larger one was inching beneath her short skirt.

"You don't want that and you know it," he replied with an evil grin, never taking his eyes off the road. "Tickle, tickle, tickle," he said in a much higher voice as his forefingers felt her satin-clad crotch.

"You're so bad."

"Yeah, and you like it." He spared a glance at the little minx sitting in the passenger seat, all twenty-four years, red hair, and DD tits of her. He glanced up into the rearview mirror when he heard a siren and saw flashing lights behind him. "Shit," he muttered.

He slowed the Corvette down, hoping the black and white would pass on by. Instead, to his chagrin, the cop slowed as well.

Snatching his hand away, he pulled the red sports car to the side of the road and slowed to a stop, the tires crunching on the gravel. He glanced over at Dana. "Shouldn't take long," he assured her, leaning over and stealing a quick but rough kiss. He glanced to the driver's side window at the light tapping he heard there. Rolling down the window, he gave his most charming smile. "Well, good evening, Officer."

"Driver's license and registration, please," the man said, all business.

"Yes, sir, no problem." He grabbed his wallet from where it sat in the drink holder by the stick shift. He dug out the asked-for items and handed them over with a smile. "What did I do?"

The policeman said nothing as he used his flashlight to read the information provided. He shone his beam from the license to the driver and back. "Lawrence Schaeffer, Sr.?"

"Yes, sirree."

"One moment please, sir."

It was only when the officer walked away that he noticed the second officer posted right outside Dana's door. He didn't like this, didn't like this one bit.

"Mr. Schaeffer," the first officer said, returning to the opened window. "I need you to step out of the car please, sir."

# *Chapter Twenty-nine*

Colorado Springs, CO – Seven Weeks Ago

Thirteen hours to go…

Bella! You have to hurry, sweetheart," Shannon said, hurrying around the tiny galley-style kitchen to pour cereal into a bowl for her daughter and coffee into a travel mug for herself and not switch the two. You're going to be late."

"I'm here, Mommy."

Shannon glanced at her to make sure she matched, which she did, essentially. Bella dressing herself and picking out her own outfits was a relatively new thing and she tried to give the child a little latitude with it.

"Honey, your shirt is on backwards," Shannon said, hiding her smile as she placed the bowl of Fruit Loops on the table where Bella's booster seat was strapped to the chair.

Bella looked down at herself. "Oh." Giggling, she wiggled out of the shirt and turned it around before pulling it down over what Shannon always called her Buddha belly. "I forgot the picture goes in front."

"It's okay, kiddo," Shannon said, leaning over her daughter, who had climbed up into her booster. Leaving a kiss on the top of her head, she placed a spoon on the table next to the bowl. "You'll get it." She grabbed the brush she'd set on the table and began to brush out long, brown hair as her daughter ate her breakfast.

"You have to hurry this morning, sweetheart. Mommy has to go to work early, so Miss Penny is going to take you to school, okay?"

Bella nodded, wincing and crying owie when that motion caused Shannon to pull some hair. "Will you pick me up?"

"Yes, ma'am," Shannon said, tying Bella's hair back with a ribbon. "I'll be there." She glanced toward the tiny living room when there was a knock at the door. "Come on in, Penny" she called out.

A moment later Penny Garcia opened the door and stepped inside. "Hey, *mija*."

"Hey, Penny. She's almost ready. Thanks so much for doing this."

"No worries. Hey," the older woman said, stepping up to the table. "Don't forget Sam this time, mija."

"Sam! I can't forget Sam, Mommy," Bella gushed, whipping her hand out and catching her cereal bowl, sending leftover Fruit Loops and milk flying.

"Damn it, Bella." Shannon sighed. She glanced over at Penny. "Penny, would you mind grabbing Sam while I clean this and Bella up? I think he's on my bed." Left alone, Shannon grabbed a wet dish towel. "Bella, you have to watch what you're doing, okay?" she said, trying to minimize the irritation in her voice so as not to upset the girl. After all, she hadn't meant to do it, but Shannon still had to get her point across.

"I'm sorry, Mommy," she said, a finger hooked in her mouth.

"Got Sam," the neighbor said, the stuffed bear in her hand.

"Thanks, Penny. I don't have time to change her shirt. Am I a horrible mother for sending her to school like this?" Shannon asked, gathering Bella's lunch and small backpack.

Penny laughed. "Honey, she's in kindergarten. Half those kids go to school wearing at least some of their breakfast and most come home wearing their lunch."

Shannon smiled and squatted down to give her daughter a tight hug, which was heartily returned. "I love you, Princess. And remember, we're going to the zoo this weekend!"

"Yay!" Bella exclaimed, grabbing her lunch as she shrugged into the My Little Pony backpack her mom held for her.

"Okay. See you guys later."

Shannon watched them go, and with a tired sigh, she placed breakfast dishes in the sink to be washed when she got home. Hurrying to her bedroom, she threw off her robe and turned to the clothes she'd picked out the night before after taking her evening shower, which always saved her time. As she tugged panties up shapely legs, she noticed something a bit unusual. The box she kept tucked in the corner was pulled out a bit from the wall, the lid slightly askew. That box held everything that meant anything to her.

"Bella," she said, snapping her panties into place before making sure the lid was secured and pushing the box back into its place.

❧❧❧❧

Eight hours and thirty-three minutes to go...

"Yes, Mr. Tannon, I spoke with Robert Caffey this morning and he's put in for the permits, so he said he should be back to you in a week once he gets an answer from the city… Yes, sir, I'll let him know. Thank you, and you, too." Shannon hung up the phone and grabbed the tablet of paper to scribble out a quick note to her boss before she headed to lunch.

"Hey, Shannon, want me to drive today?"

"Nah, I got it," Shannon said.

Ten minutes later, she and her coworker, Ally, sat at Taco Bell.

"So, you want to leave, huh?" Ally asked,

"Yeah. Robert just," Shannon screwed up her face as she considered her words. She hadn't worked there all that long so wasn't entirely sure who she could trust. "I feel like he's always watching me, you know? Kind of makes me nervous."

"That's because he probably *is* watching you, Shannon. I mean, come on," the pregnant woman said, sitting back in the hard plastic seat. "You're young, you're gorgeous. Totally his type."

Shannon eyed her. "He's not…dangerous, right?"

"No, but he's good at manipulation. How'd you get hired, anyway?"

"Robert knows my sister, Jill. I guess he did some work for her in Pueblo."

"Is she rich?"

"Definitely. Total rich bitch."

Ally nodded, chewing the bite she'd taken thoughtfully. "There ya go. Robert only hires women he's either screwed or women he wants to screw or women based on suggestions from other women he's screwed."

Shannon's gaze fell to her nachos, suddenly not so appealing. She'd heard the rumors for years about Jill, the humiliation behind Andrew's back. Without question she did not want to pursue this conversation. "When are you due?"

"Three months. Thank God Alec owns half the company, and Robert knows he'd kill him if he came near me. I get to do my job in peace."

"That would be nice," Shannon said, dipping a cheese-covered chip into sour cream. She'd had to deal with unwanted advances her entire life, starting back to a time she didn't want to think about. "My lease is up in five months." She changed the subject. "I'm considering moving Bella and me back to Pueblo."

"Good God, why on earth would you go there?" Ally asked, sipping her Coke.

Shannon shrugged. "It's so much cheaper, for one. "I know more people there, for two. I still have a lot of friends there from my theater days."

"Theater days?" Ally asked with raised eyebrows. "Do tell."

"Nothing major." Shannon laughed nervously. "I did some stuff up in Denver after high school, some stuff here in the Springs and was part of the Impossible Players in Pueblo. That's where I did most of my work. Loved it."

"What, like a local community theater-type thing?"

"Exactly." Shannon looked down at her purse, which sat next to her in the plastic booth, her phone alarming a text message. Digging the phone out, she saw a number she didn't recognize but read the message, anyway.

*Unknown: Hey, Shannon. Been a long time.*
*Shannon: Who is this?*
*Unknown: Rick*

Shannon gasped. There was only one Rick she knew unless this was a wrong number or a sick joke.

"You okay?" Ally asked. "You look like you've seen a ghost."

Shannon spared her a glance before returning her attention to her phone. "Kind of have."

*Shannon: Rick who?*
*Unknown: Bella's dad. I want to see her. And I want to see u.*
*Shannon: Is this a joke?*
*Unknown: I be in town tonight. Can I come over?*

"Shannon, sorry, but we have to get back."

Shannon glanced up then at her watch. "Crap, sorry."

*Shannon: Have to go. Text later.*

⁂

Two hours to go...

"Look, Mommy. I have whipped cream on my head."

Shannon was amused, suds piled on Bella's head. The girl had always referred to soapsuds as whipped cream, and Shannon had no idea why. "Come on, sweetie," she said. "Let's get you all rinsed off so I can get you tucked in for sleepy time."

"And a story?" Bella asked, eyebrows raised in hope.

"Of course, you silly goose." She leaned forward

and nuzzled noses with her daughter.

❧ ❧ ❧ ❧

Five minutes to go…

Standing back from the mirror, ignoring how shadows from two of the five burnt-out light bulbs made her look, she saw herself in the mirror surrounded by bulbs, ready to head out on that stage. She grinned, admiring the red slash of her lipstick. She used to love her smile, but she hadn't had a lot to be truly happy about in a while. As she closed her lips, she also closed the door on the questionable choices she'd made from time to time. She hoped he wouldn't notice or mind. She hoped he still saw what he did on that stage seven years before.

"You've got this," she murmured, a smoky-eyed wink backing her claim.

Looking in on Bella once more, she stepped into her stilettos and grabbed her handbag, keys, and cell phone then headed out.

Standing on the front walkway of the floor of her apartment, she looked out over the parking lot, searching for his car. All day long, she'd been reading and rereading the texts she'd swapped with Rick. She hadn't seen him in a few years, and he'd never asked to see Bella. She was nervous, her stomach in knots.

She started when her phone signaled a text. Reaching into her bag, she saw another text from Rick.

*Unknown: This sucks. My truck broke down at the gas station at 10th and Avery. Red truck. Can u come get me? Can't wait to see you.*

Shannon smiled, knowing exactly where the gas station was. It wasn't far, and she knew Bella would be okay. She was asleep and would be alone for maybe five or six minutes.

*Shannon: Okay. Be right there.*

Shannon's high heels clicked across the parking lot until she reached her Subaru. She smiled at the little clay heart Bella had painted for her in daycare earlier that year for Mother's Day before she pressed the button on her key fob to unlock the door. Climbing in, she tugged her seatbelt across her chest before starting the car and pulling out of the dark parking lot.

She noted the gas station was pretty quiet. A white minivan was getting gas but that was about it. She drove around the side where the doors to the bathrooms were, which was a bit darker, no lights back there other than what shone from the bright lights out front over the pumps. Her stomach knotted up again when she noticed the red pickup truck parked there over by the curb.

Steering the little car in that direction, she pulled to a stop. Seeing no movement near the truck, which seemed to be abandoned, she pulled out her phone.

*Shannon: Is that your truck? I'm here.*

Shannon gasped as the driver's side door was yanked open and a large hand was instantly put over her mouth before she was even able to get a scream or cry out. She was pulled out of the car so roughly that it snapped the seatbelt, the vinyl end flapping uselessly against the doorjamb of the car.

She tried desperately to fight against her assailant but couldn't seem to get any footing as she was basically carried to the back of her own car.

"Get it open," she heard a voice growl before hearing the pop of her trunk.

Fighting twice as hard, kicking at anything she could, she landed hard into her own trunk, hitting her head against the tool kit she kept back there in case of an emergency. She couldn't think of much worse of an emergency.

The hand was removed and, as she was about to scream, she looked up into the most evil gray eyes she'd ever seen right before a fist came down and smashed into her jaw and the side of her head. Everything went dark.

❧❧❧❧

Her screams were shrill and panicked, eyes flying open but seeing nothing but the horrors that were locked inside her mind. She kicked her legs, arms flailing until she heard a thud then the cry of a child.

"Don't touch me! Don't touch me!" she yelled, tears running down her cheeks as she hit and pushed at the person who had hold of her. "Let me go!" she sobbed.

"Shannon!"

Chest heaving and mouth gone dry from near-hyperventilation, Shannon's eyes focused on the figure leaning above her, her vision slowly making out the terrified face looking down at her. "Nora?" The cries of her daughter pulled her fully out of her nightmare. "Bella? What's wrong with Bella?" She sat up, desperately looking for her.

"Hey, sweetheart," Nora said, picking a crying Bella up off the floor. "You okay?"

"God," Shannon whimpered, burying her face in her hands for a long moment, the fragments of the memory beginning to drift away like smoke. "Is she okay?" she asked softly, hands falling to the bed. "Come here, baby."

Nora set Bella on the bed, wide, tear-filled eyes looking cautiously at her mother.

"Come here," Shannon said again, reaching for her daughter. "I'm sorry, sweetheart." She gathered the sniffling child into her arms. She must have kicked her off the bed in her panic. "You okay?"

Bella nodded, her thumb going to her mouth as she cuddled up against her mother's chest.

"The question is," Nora said, climbing onto the bed and scooting over to Shannon, "are *you* okay?"

Shannon contemplated the question as she held Bella close. The smell of her strawberry-scented hair was so comforting to her. "I...I think so."

"Bad dream?"

"Dream, memory." She glanced over at Nora. "I can never go back to that apartment again, Nora. I mean"—she snorted—"Mr. Greenleaf was such a jerk, I'm sure all my stuff was sold, anyway." She felt Nora's gaze on her. "What?"

"Honey," Nora said softly, reaching out a hand to rest on Shannon's ankle. "The apartment doesn't exist anymore."

Shannon looked at her, utterly confused. "Wait, what?" She gave her a confused smile. "How long was I out?"

"No, the guys who did this to you," Nora said,

indicating Shannon's scars and peach fuzz that was beginning to come in. "Sarah thinks they were trying to destroy evidence."

"They…the ones who…"

Nora nodded. "Yeah."

Shannon had no words as she looked away, her gaze falling to the window across from the bed. She could see the tree outside the house dancing in the wind. "I…"

"Sweetie—"

"Why didn't you tell me? Why the hell didn't you tell me we're homeless, Nora? Bella and I have nowhere to go, we have no home, no furniture, no dishes, nothing. Why didn't you tell me? God!" The tears came fast and hard, falling on top of Bella's hair. She rested her cheek against her baby's crown and held her even tighter, rocking them both. "We have nothing," she whispered.

"Hey," Nora said, scooting closer. "Shannon, your therapist suggested I wait a little bit to tell you. She wanted to make sure you could handle it."

Shannon said nothing, not sure what there was even to say. She felt so alone, even as she held the most important person in the world in her arms.

"Honey," Nora said, resting her hand on Shannon's slumped shoulder. "I swear to you, we're going to get you through this. You're going to have your own life again, you and Bella."

Shannon could hear the determination and love in her sister's voice and spared her a glance. She saw in her eyes what she heard in her voice. "I tried so hard to get us a life, Nora," she whispered. "So hard."

"I know, sis. I know. It wasn't all in vain, I promise you. None of this was your fault."

Shannon's tears slowed and eventually stopped. She was so tired, more so than she had been in a long time.

"Come here," Nora said, seeming to sense her exhaustion.

Nora scooted down in the bed beneath the sheets and Shannon scooted over to her, Bella cuddled between the two sisters. Without another word or another thought, Shannon's eyes fell closed and peaceful sleep overcame her.

# Chapter Thirty

Come on," LJ muttered as he grunted to reach as far behind the dresser as he could, fingers grabbing blindly for the end of the cable cord. "Gotcha."

Bringing the cord up to the back of the new flat-screen he'd bought for his bedroom, he connected it to the correct port. He'd already hooked up the much larger TV to cable and to the moveable arm mounted above the fireplace in the living room downstairs. Though surrounded by boxes that needed to be unpacked, he knew that first and foremost, even before picking up some groceries, was getting his TV hooked up and ready.

"Ha!" he exclaimed with satisfaction as he stood back from his handiwork.

Deciding to bring in the last few boxes from his truck, he trotted down the stairs only to see Kristie and Julia coming in, boxes in hand.

"Hey, Dad," Kristie said, setting her box down on the couch, which was loaded with black trash bags of towels and linens and other boxes.

"Where do you want this, Mr. Schaeffer?" Julia Donovan asked.

"Right here is fine, Julia," he said, stepping over to his daughter to leave a quick kiss on her cheek and one on Julia's cheek, as well. "Nice to see you, Julia." He grinned at the two young women. "I kind of like this.

The deal is Julia gets to come over whenever she wants and I get to put her to work." He nodded dramatically. "I can handle this."

"Dad." Kristie rolled her eyes. "Um, can we go upstairs and unpack my room?" she asked, uncertainty in her voice.

LJ studied his daughter for a moment. Though he knew she would be eighteen soon, it was hard to admit to himself she was no longer a child, but a woman who was about to graduate high school and begin her life. "Yeah," he said softly. "But first, give your old man a hug." He squeezed her tightly to him for a moment before letting her go. "I'm ordering Chinese in about an hour."

"Awesome. Thanks, Dad!" Kristie called over her shoulder as she and Julia bolted for the stairs.

He watched them go and shook his head. Pushing all that aside, he looked around his brand new living room, and even though it was cluttered with boxes to be unpacked, furniture to be assembled, and random objects to be given a home, he was proud. Through all the current chaos, it was *his*. A brand new townhouse—nobody had ever lived there before, and there were no memories to wade through.

Crossing his arms over his chest, he nodded. "I can do this."

≈≈≈≈

"Damn," Nora said, leaving the two wrapped packages on the table with the other gifts. "These two made out like bandits."

"No joke," Shannon said, resting her cane against the table as she put down two other gifts that Nora had bought for her to give their niece and nephew for their sweet sixteen. "Are you sure I don't look stupid, Nora?"

Nora glanced at her younger sister and shook her head with a smile. "You look amazing, sis," she said, noting the simple dress she wore which showed off a beautiful figure, even if it was still a little thin. She also took in the short, spiky auburn hair. "I mean you've got an Annie Lennox circa 1986 look going on."

Shannon chuckled. "Yeah, and I was T minus four years old at the time."

"Still, very chic." Nora grinned at her, but she was able to see exactly how unsure her sister felt. "Sweetheart, you've got the face of a model and the voice of an angel. You have absolutely nothing to worry about." She hooked her arm at the crook of Shannon's, both for comfort through connection but also to give a bit of steady support to her kid sister, who was still a bit weak and shaky on her feet. "Come on, let's go party."

The venue was decorated for Tyler and Sylvia's birthday, and there were tables and chairs, tons of incredibly fragrant food, as well as a bar with nonalcoholic drinks available. Jill fluttered around to talk to the various groups, to refill drinks, or to get more of this or that. Nora was amused.

"You know, I'm pretty sure that's why you spent so much money on wait staff," she said, walking up to her flustered older sister.

Jill glanced at her almost as though she didn't recognize her for a moment before Nora was taken in a quick but tight hug. "I know," she said with nervous laughter. "Hey, you." She gave Shannon a hug. "Where's Bella?"

"She's having a playdate with a little friend from

school," Shannon said. "I figured this might be a little much for her. Too many people and no kids for her to play with."

Jill nodded and let out a breath.

"Breathe," Nora said dramatically, holding her older sister by her shoulders. "It's okay."

"I know. I want everything to be perfect for the twins. Tyler is doing so well now, and…"

Nora gave her an understanding smile. "You don't want to let him down." She gave Jill another hug. "Look," she said, pointing toward the center of the room where some folks were dancing to the DJ's music mix. "He's having a great time. He looks good, too. That kid always looked like a vampire, so pale and unhappy." Nora marveled at the handsome young man her only nephew was becoming, noting some stubble on his chin and over his lip.

"I know. Since he's been on the antianxiety medication and with our family therapy, he's flourishing." Jill smiled at Nora and Shannon. "He's doing great in school. Pulling all Bs and an A."

"That's fantastic, Jill. Truly." Nora knew full well the kid had been flunking out of school before. "Is he dating her?" she asked, noting the pretty young lady he was dancing with certainly had eyes for him.

"We're not sure and he won't say." Jill laughed. "I think so, but he's keeping it pretty close to the vest. Andy says we should let him come to us when he's comfortable to talk about it."

"Look at this group of gorgeous ladies."

Nora whipped around to see LJ grinning at her with Kristie standing behind him alongside the attractive blonde she remembered from Kristie's phone that day they'd spent together. "Hey, big guy," she said, accepting his hug. "Congratulations on the new place. When can we come over and see it?"

"Once it no longer looks like a storage unit." He laughed.

"Who's this?" Jill asked, also accepting a hug from LJ and giving one to Kristie.

Nora watched as Kristie glanced at her father, LJ giving her an encouraging smile and nod.

"Aunt Jill, this is my girlfriend, Julia. Julia, my Aunt Jill and Tyler and Sylvia's mom."

"Hello," Julia said softly, offering her hand in greeting.

Nora was so proud of her niece in that moment. That hadn't been an easy thing to do. She gave the pretty young women a huge smile of approval.

⁂

LJ stood near the wall watching the events unfolding before him. He'd eaten far more than he should and now felt tired and in all honesty, was ready to go home. Letting out a heavy sigh, he absently reached for his left hand with his right, fingers looking for the band that he would normally twist with nervous energy.

"It's strange, isn't it?"

Startled, LJ glanced to his left to see Rachel Quinn standing there. She looked lovely dressed in jeans and a fitted sweater for the cold late-October evening. "Hey. What is?"

She glanced down at his bare left hand. "Getting used to it being gone."

He followed her gaze and chuckled nervously. "Yeah. Guess so." He met her amused blue eyes.

"After Mason died, I wore mine for about a year. In all honesty, the day I decided to take it off, I thought I was going to need to call for the Jaws of Life."

LJ burst into laughter. "Isn't that the truth." His smile widened when he saw her grinning at him. His smile slowly fell, though, as confusion hit him. "Why are you here?"

"Jill invited me," Rachel said simply, raising the glass of soda she was drinking. "And hey, free food, how could I say no?"

His good mood returned. "I won't tell."

"I met your niece and nephew. They seem like great kids," she said, sipping her drink.

"They are. Tyler has had a tough go of it over the last few years, but I think he's getting it together now. I'm super proud of him."

"Is your daughter here? Kristie, right?"

"Good memory. Yes," he hedged, not sure what all he should reveal as Kristie and Julia were standing shoulder to shoulder talking to some of the twins' school friends. He glanced over at the nurse and, something in him told him to be honest. "She's over there, in the black combat boots standing with the blond girl."

"Oh my," Rachel chuckled. "I see attitude written all over that one."

"Oh yeah," he nodded. "The blonde is Julia… her girlfriend." He eyed her for her reaction to the information that his daughter was a lesbian.

"God, kids today are so lucky, you know?" Rachel glanced up at him. "My best friend, Gregory would have been so much better off if he'd been able to be himself and come out in high school. I mean, it wasn't like we all didn't know already," she added flippantly.

"Your best friend is gay?"

"As the day is long. Gregory has been like my brother since seventh grade. He and his long-time boyfriend, Gabriel, are getting married in December."

"Wow," he said, not sure what to say.

"Are you okay with Kristie being a lesbian?" Rachel asked, turning slightly to face him, pressing her shoulder against the wall.

He nodded. "Yes. Well, I mean it's taken some time, I won't lie. I have nothing against gay people. Not sure if you know it or not but my sister Nora is a lesbian. So, it's not exactly new to me. But…"

"When it's your own child?" she supplied.

He smiled with a small laugh. "Yeah. I saw all that Nora went through, and Kristie's mom isn't thrilled. I don't want to see Kristie get hurt."

"Nah, she's got you and certainly her aunt."

He glanced at her and studied her for a moment, her words soaking through him. A slow, contented smile spread across his lips. "Would you like to dance?"

❧ ❧ ❧ ❧

"Do you guys happen to have any cranberry juice?" Nora asked the bartender behind the nonalcoholic bar.

"Yes, ma'am," he said, turning to fulfill her order.

"From what I remember, that's good with vodka."

Nora glanced to her left, surprised to see Sarah standing there.

"Oh, wait, that was grape juice," she said with a smile.

Nora returned the smile, remembering well the time Sarah was referring to. The two thought it would be brilliant to get drunk one night on vodka and grape juice. Nora had never been so sick and had never mixed the two again.

"Yes, I avoid grape juice at all costs now, thank you very much."

Sarah chuckled. "Me, too. Diet Coke, please," she asked the bartender who had set Nora's juice down on the bar top. She turned back to Nora. "Sorry I'm late. I had to work then run home and change."

Nora noticed she was dressed in blue jeans that she couldn't help but notice fit her incredibly well. In all her life, she'd never known a woman who could make jeans look so good. She also wore a black long-sleeved shirt with the Pueblo Police Department emblem on it.

"I can't stay long," Sarah said. "I have an interrogation class to teach tonight."

"I see. So, crashing a sweet sixteen birthday party on the way?" Nora teased, taking her glass of juice as Sarah retrieved her soda. "Free dinner?"

Sarah grinned, taking a sip through the straw. "No, more like a little birdie invited me."

"Oh, he did, did he?"

"Yes, *she* did."

Nora grinned and shook her head as she walked away from the bar to get out of the way of other partygoers, Sarah following.

"I saw Shannon on my way in," the detective said as they found a table to sit at. "She looks fantastic. How is she doing?"

"Well," Nora said, finding her little sister dancing with Andrew. The two seemed to be in fairly serious talks. "Pretty damn good." She glanced over at Sarah, who looked comfortable and at ease. It was rare that she saw Sarah in casual clothes and it was nice. Somehow, to be sitting next to her wearing jeans and boots, she felt less unapproachable. Her dark hair was brushed to a shine down around her shoulders and framing an absolutely stunning face. Sarah caught her staring, but Nora couldn't quite look away for a long moment. Finally, she cleared her throat and concentrated on her juice as she turned back to watch the handful of pairs dancing.

☙ ☙ ❧ ❧

"So, what do you do when you're not visiting family members in the hospital?" Rachel asked as she and LJ danced to a quirky tune that he didn't recognize.

"Well, I teach at Pueblo West High School and I'm a coach," he responded, chuckling as Rachel did a fun little shimmy to the beat.

"Yeah? What do you teach? What do you coach?"

"English Literature and football."

"Oh, because those two go together so well." She laughed. "Do you like to read?"

LJ nodded. "I do, but more so I love to write." His eyes grew wide, shocked at the fact he'd told her what so few knew about him. He looked at her, waiting for the worst.

"Are you serious?" Rachel asked, her own eyes wide but seemingly for a different reason. "That's great, LJ. God, I wish I had the talent to write. I've always had crazy ideas, but admittedly, I do not have the talent to get them on paper. I used to write some pretty atrocious poetry, though."

LJ laughed, partly by what she'd said and the amusing expression on her lovely face but also from the relief that she wasn't going to rebuke him or call him down. "What do you like to do besides put broken people back together again?"

She smiled sweetly. "I love being a nurse. I love being a mom and I love to cook."

"Do you, now?" he asked. "Well, I love to eat."

She eyed him. "Well, I love to read and you love to eat. Maybe we can work something out."

❧❧❧❧

The early evening had become bitterly cold, the smell of snow in the air. Nora walked Sarah out to her Mustang, as she had to get to her class.

"I'm glad you came," she said, her words puffs of steam.

"Me, too. I always liked your family. It is a trip to see Shannon all grown up, though." She stopped at the driver's side door of her car and faced Nora. "She's turned into a gorgeous woman."

Nora nodded. "Yes. She can sing like no other, too."

"She's talented like her older sister, I see."

Nora smiled and rolled her eyes, tucking her hands into the pockets of her jacket. "I can't carry a tune in a bucket."

"No, you can't," Sarah said, her eyes twinkling. "But, your pictures are amazing."

The mention of her photography brought back a slew of memories and regret where Sarah was concerned. Nora looked up into her eyes. "I'm sorry," she said softly. "So sorry for being such a coward."

Sarah nodded, seeming to understand that Nora was talking about twenty years before. "It's okay. We were both young."

"Really young. But, it doesn't justify me leaving

like that." She let out a heavy sigh, filled with the sadness that had lived in her heart ever since. "Sometimes I think about how we could have been together for almost twenty-two years by now. Crazy to think about."

"True," Sarah conceded. "Or, we could have been a train wreck fifteen years broken."

Nora smiled. "That's kind of what LJ said."

"Great minds." Sarah took a step forward and raised her hands, cupping Nora's face. She brought their lips together for a soft, lingering kiss.

As Sarah pulled away, Nora looked at her, eyes wide. "Why did you do that?" she asked softly.

Sarah smiled. "Because I knew you wouldn't." She turned and unlocked her car door. Turning back to Nora she reached up and tucked some hair behind her ear. "I have to go."

Nora nodded, her lips tingling from the brief but vivid memory of Sarah's kiss. "Be safe."

"I will." Sarah ducked to climb behind the wheel. She met Nora's gaze. "Talk to you soon."

Nora stepped back to allow her to back out of her spot, watching as the sleek black car disappeared into the night.

# *Chapter Thirty-one*

Dressed only in bra and panties, Jill used her Neutrogena cleansing cream to remove her makeup, eyebrows lifting to create a funny expression as she worked on her eye makeup. She glanced into the reflected image of Andrew as he walked behind her in the bathroom, wearing only pajama pants.

"I am so tired," he said, walking to his sink and opening the mirrored door that revealed his toothbrush and toothpaste. "Who knew a damn birthday party could be so exhausting?"

Jill chuckled. "Me. Considering I'm the one who has thrown them for the past sixteen years."

"Hey now," he said, eyeing her in the mirror. "I'm working on being home more."

She smiled and reached over to playfully pinch his behind. "Do you think everyone had a good time?"

"Definitely." He squeezed some bright blue minty fresh goo on his toothbrush. "You did a fantastic job, baby. Everyone seemed to enjoy themselves, and I know the kids loved it."

"Did you see LJ and Rachel?" Jill asked, a devilish grin on her freshly scrubbed face.

"Is that who that was? The blond woman, right?"

"Yep. She was Shannon's nurse in ICU and"—she shrugged—"they seemed to hit it off, so I figured why not invite her. Plus, I'm sure she was happy to see how well Shannon is doing."

"Isn't it a little soon?" Andrew asked, sticking the toothbrush into his mouth to begin to brush.

"Oh hell, Andy, I truly believe his marriage was over years ago. I can't even remember the last time I saw a scintilla of affection between LJ and Adrienne. And hey, either way, he can make a new friend, right?"

He nodded as he continued to brush, Jill following suit at her own sink.

"So," he said, checking his straight, white teeth in the mirror as he tapped his rinsed toothbrush on the side of the sink. "I hope you won't be mad at me for this."

Still brushing, she glanced over at him, giving him her attention.

"You know I hired Corey Phelps, that young attorney out of Pittsburgh to help with my caseload so I can be home more often and spend time with Tyler?"

Jill nodded in acknowledgment.

"Tonight I asked Shannon if she wanted to be his assistant." He shrugged, hand resting on the marble vanity top. "You know, filing, answering phones, keeping his schedule together, that kind of thing."

Jill dropped her toothbrush into the sink and spat out the excess foam and quickly rinsed her mouth. "You did what?" she asked, using a tissue to wipe her mouth.

"Shit," he said. "I was hoping you wouldn't be mad. I didn't get a chance to talk to you first because of the part—Umph!"

Jill clung to him, her face buried in his neck. "Thank you, Andy," she whispered. She smiled when she heard his relieved sigh as he wrapped his arms around her.

"She deserves a chance to start over," he said.

Jill nodded, tears coming to her eyes. "She does." She backed out of the hug and grabbed a fresh tissue to dab at her eyes, giving him a smile, feeling foolish at her sudden emotion. "But, she still needs time to heal, to be okay."

Andrew nodded, leaning his hip against the vanity. "I know. I spoke with Mary on Friday. She's willing to help carry the load for Corey until we can get Shannon in and trained." He smiled. "She'd have a good wage and benefits."

"And some skills," Jill added.

"And some skills. I think it could be good for her, honey."

Jill was overwhelmed with love for the man standing before her. She cleaned up her toothpaste mess then turned to him, snaking her arms up around his neck. "Let's go to bed."

❧ ❧ ❧ ❧

It was late and Sarah was tired. The training had gone well, which she was pleased with. She walked into the dark, quiet townhouse. She wasn't sad that Leslie was gone, but sometimes the silence could be deafening.

Tossing her keys on the breakfast bar, she set her purse down next to them before shrugging out of her jacket to hang it in the closet. She was halfway there when she stopped, her mind leaving the home she'd had for years and heading down a quiet country lane.

She glanced back toward the kitchen, which led to the garage door and ultimately to her car. Turning away, she again headed for the closet by the front door only to stop again.

Twenty-five minutes later, Sarah killed the ignition and pulled her key free before gathering her phone and climbing out of the Mustang. She glanced at the house when she saw the porch light over the kitchen door click on.

Smiling at that, Sarah closed the driver's side door as quietly as she could, not wanting to wake anyone else in the house. She crunched her way across the gravel until she reached the cement path that led to the stairs. As she reached them, Nora pushed open the door.

"Hey," Sarah said quietly. "I'm sorry."

"Don't be. Come on in—it's a cold one tonight."

Sarah hurried inside, Nora closing and locking the door behind her. She felt stupid as she stood in the kitchen, noting that Nora was dressed in her robe. "Jeez, I'm sorry. I should go—"

"No, I'm glad you called." Nora looked into her eyes, head slightly tilted to the side. "Are you okay?"

Sarah looked down at her feet for a moment before she spared a glance at Nora. "Have you ever just not wanted to be alone?" she asked, her voice little more than a whisper.

Nora said nothing as she gave her a soft smile. She grabbed one of Sarah's hands and tugged lightly as she headed toward the living room and stairs. "Come on," she said, flicking off the kitchen light. "Let's get some sleep."

❧❧❧❧

Nora's eyes slowly opened. It was early, the sun not fully awake, nor was she. She was, however, awake enough to realize Sarah slept beside her. Lying on her back, she turned her head from her position to study Sarah's face. She couldn't get enough of the strong yet beautiful features. Sarah had always been attractive, but she'd matured into a stunning woman. Her gaze fell to full lips, so soft, so inviting.

Slowly she brought a hand out from beneath the covers and reached out, the tips of her finger finding the soft skin of a defined yet feminine jaw. She trailed along the natural line until she reached Sarah's chin, her fingertip following down along her throat to the side of her neck.

Sarah's eyes slowly fluttered open, taking a moment to focus on Nora's. Once they did, the softest of smiles touched her lips. Neither of them said a word as Sarah turned to her side, facing Nora. She reached under the covers, urging Nora to move toward her.

Nora moved into Sarah's arms, sighing as she was held against her, her face tucked into Sarah's neck. The feel of Sarah's warm body—dressed in a borrowed T-shirt and shorts—pressed against her elicited a soft sigh from her throat. She loved the smell of Sarah's skin: leftover perfume from the previous day along with the warm scent of sleep. It always amazed her how sleep seemed to have its own smell.

She wrapped her arm around Sarah's waist, her hand tucking beneath her opposite side against the mattress. Sarah nuzzled her hair, her hand running down Nora's side, getting dangerously close to her behind as it rested on her hip.

The air in the room was changing quickly, as was Nora's heart rate and her breathing. Sarah's breasts pressed right above her own, and Sarah's warm neck was so close to her lips, before Nora could stop herself, she left a kiss there. The soft sigh that resulted sent a spark shooting through her body.

Sarah's hand cupped her behind when Nora's phone rang. She was going to ignore it, but then she realized how early it was and that it was LJ's ring. He'd never call her so early without good reason.

"God, I'm sorry," she said, pulling away from Sarah. "I'm sorry." She turned over and reached to her nightstand. "Hey, this better be important." Nora lay back down on the bed with the phone held to her ear. She glanced over at Sarah who lay on her side, upper body raised and head leaning on a fist. She had to wonder how on earth the woman could look so beautiful and sexy first thing in the morning. "Turn on the TV? Why?" Nora shot up, the covers falling to her waist. "What?" She ran a trembling hand through her hair, the tears instantly coming. "What?"

Sarah sat up and moved to sit next to her, a hand on Nora's knee.

The phone slid out of Nora's hands as the sobs tore through her. She vaguely felt Sarah retrieve the phone from her lap and heard her soft voice.

"LJ, this is Sarah. What's wrong and what do you need Nora to do?"

⁂

Jill cleared her throat again as she sat in the uncomfortable metal chair, a small ledge before her and a rectangular bulletproof glass window with a small cubicle of sorts on the other side. The chair was not yet inhabited. A phone was mounted on either side of the glass, Jill's receiver still cradled.

She held onto the purse that rested in her lap, searched before she came in. Though it was simply a leather Michael Kors handbag, at the moment it was her teddy bear, a connection to the world she knew beyond the walls of this sterile, scary place.

She started at the sound of a loud buzz. In the mesh screen wall behind the cubicle she faced, she saw an officer leading someone in. That someone was dressed in what looked like orange scrubs with a white T-shirt underneath. It was her father.

Larry, Sr. was ushered into the cubicle. Once her father was safely there, the officer backed up, hand held close to his utility belt. Jill had to look away for a moment, her emotions rising as she laid eyes on him. She waited until he got comfortable and picked up the receiver of his phone before she picked up hers.

"Hey," he said.

"Hello." It was so strange to see him sitting three feet away yet they sounded miles apart. Not entirely sure what to say next, she asked, "How are they treating you?"

"Well, you know," he said, sitting as far back in his chair as the phone cord would allow. "Food sucks, but some of the guys in here are okay. Lots of questions about my days playin' ball, you know."

She nodded, her stomach churning. She cleared her throat and met his gaze. "Did you do this?" She felt guilty for asking, but she had to know. Her siblings deserved that much, too.

Larry, Sr. sighed. "Eh, Jilly, you know things between your mom and me were always difficult. She was so damn nosy, always wanted to be in my business—"

"Did you?"

Pueblo, Colorado 1992

Larry, Sr. entered the house; a song whistled from his lips. He was happy his team had won at the Pueblo Ice Arena. Football was his passion, but a gifted athlete at anything he tried, he enjoyed the amateur hockey league he played with and carried the blue-and-white duffel bag with all his gear up the stairs as he headed to the bedroom. The house was fairly quiet, a TV playing somewhere. It was nearly ten, and he and the boys had gone out for a beer after their victory.

He headed down the hallway that would take him to what was essentially the wing of the large house he shared with Judy. The double doors of the master bedroom were closed, which irritated him. He grabbed the handle of one side and shoved, the doorknob on the opposite side of the door banging into the wall behind the door.

"Why the fuck was this closed?" he asked, walking into the room.

When there was no answer, he looked around. The king-sized four-poster was still made, unlike what he'd expected, which was to see a naked Judy waiting for him. That's what he told her he wanted when he got back from the game. Instead there were two closed suitcases and a third that was open and half-filled.

Dropping the duffel bag on the floor, he walked over to the open suitcase, fingering a folded shirt on the top of the pile. "What the fuck, Judy?" he boomed, glancing toward the master bath.

The mousy woman appeared a moment later, her makeup bag in one hand and hair dryer in the other. "I'm leaving, Larry," she said in her usual quiet voice, a voice that annoyed the shit out of him. She always sounded like she was afraid of the world.

"Come again?" he said, a laugh in his voice.

"I can't do this anymore," she said, dropping her bundles into the suitcase. She didn't look at him as she continued. "I know about all the women. I know about..." She spared him a glance. "I know, Larry. About everything."

He stiffened and stood to his full, intimidating height, chest puffed out slightly. His large hands balled into fists before they were released. "What do you mean?" he asked, voice deceivingly calm.

"Larry," Judy said, emotion in her voice. "I've done everything for you that I could. I raised our children and hers."

He eyed her, a small smile on his lips. "Don't even mention her," he said.

Judy's hands seemed to move only for the sake of moving as she rearranged the items in the suitcase. "Larry," she whispered. "I saw your pictures."

He could feel the rage building.

"I can't let you do this to her anymore. To any of them. I'm leaving and I'm taking her, LJ, Nora, and... and I'm taking Shannon, too."

"You're not taking Shannon anywhere."

Like a flash, he was on her, a hand around her throat, her petite body shoved against the wall. This wasn't a new position for her to be in, but Larry, Sr. felt this was something different.

"How dare you talk to me that way," he growled. "Who do you think you are?"

"Larry," she gasped, pale hands tugging uselessly at his iron-like grip. "I can't...Larry..."

He realized she was lifted off the ground when

her feet kicked at his shins. With a growl, he moved her away from the wall only to slam her back into it, her head thudding against the drywall.

"You will never take my children from me," he said, spittle landing on her eyelashes. "You will never tell me what to do with my children. You will never get into my business again, snooping around into things you have *no* right to be in!" he roared, slamming her head against the wall with each word.

Overtaken with rage, he could no longer even see her face. He brought up his other hand to join the first, squeezing, his teeth bared with murderous intent. With one final slam, he released his hands, Judy Schaeffer falling to the ground, coughing violently as she tried to catch her breath.

"Bitch," he said, looking into her face. "You think you can threaten me?" he asked, grunting with the kick he delivered to her stomach. She cried out in pain. He kicked her again, only for her to cry out again. "Shut up!" Another kick. He heard a satisfying crack and more cries from her. "Fucking cunt."

Looking around, he spotted his hockey bag and hurried over to it, rage still driving his every move. He unzipped it and rummaged through it, throwing out sticks, pucks, pads, and one of his skates before he found what he was looking for.

The tape ripped free from the roll with the telltale sound. He tried to tear it, but his trembling hands wouldn't cooperate. He brought it up to his teeth only for some of his hair to get caught up in it.

"Fucker!"

He tore the tape free from his hair, taking a few strands with it, then managed to rip off a piece. Holding it between thumbs and forefingers, he hurried back over to a crying Judy and roughly applied it to her mouth. She tried to fight him, but he was too strong.

Getting to his feet, he began to let her have it and let her have it good. Every ounce of fury and frustration in him came out as he unleashed on the woman he'd seen as an anchor to his gleaming ship for far too long.

After several minutes, he was sweaty and panting as he looked down at the unmoving body on the floor. Blood seeped into the carpet.

"Fuck."

Picking her up like a sack of potatoes, he walked to the master bathroom and flung her unceremoniously into the bathtub so he could go back to the bedroom and clean up the mess.

On his hands and knees, he scrubbed, getting much of it, but there were still a few spots. He sat back on his feet, out of breath and exhausted. He tossed out the face cloth he'd used for cleanup, turned off the bathroom light and threw Judy's luggage off the bed. Shedding his clothing, he climbed into bed naked.

Four hours later, Larry, Sr. woke having to use the bathroom. His mind fuzzy and muscles sore, he climbed out of bed and padded to the bathroom, stubbing his toe on one of his hockey sticks. He cursed loudly as he continued on his way. Flipping the toilet lid and seat open with a loud snap of porcelain against porcelain, he groaned long and loud as he released his bladder.

He reached up a hand to scratch across his chest. His jaw cracked with the size of his yawn, and it was in the middle of that that he noticed the unmoving figure in the tub. He absently reached down to flush as he turned to look down at Judy. She was lying in the same position as when she'd been dumped, her eyes closed and dried blood plastering the side of her face.

"Judy?" he said, shoving the shower curtain farther aside. "Hey, get the fuck up." He used the side of his bare foot to lightly kick the tub. "Hey."

When there was no movement or reaction of any kind, he lowered himself to his knees on the mat in front of the tub. Reaching over, he used his thumb to lift one of her eyelids. The unseeing, bloodshot eye that met his gaze made him cringe. He fell back onto his butt, not even registering the cold tile against his naked skin as he stared at her, realization of what had happened hitting him.

"Fuck."

⚜ ⚜ ⚜ ⚜

Jill watched him carefully as he'd grown silent for a long moment. "You owe us that much, Daddy," she said quietly.

Suddenly, his eyes were filled with rage as he focused on her. "Owe you? I owe you?" he laughed cruelly. "Who took care of you after she was gone, huh? Who took care of Larry, Jr., Nora, and Shannon?"

"I did," she said coolly.

"Don't talk to me like that, Jill," he said, pointing a finger at her through the glass. "You and I have always been close. Don't throw that away."

"Close," she said, voice dull as though it was the first time she'd ever heard that word before. "We were close. Is that what you call it?"

"Jilly," he said, his own voice turning from hard and threatening to sweet and kind. "Jilly, I've always loved you, you know that. I gave you anything you ever wanted. You say I owe you, but *you* owe *me*. Right?"

"Did you kill my mother?" Jill asked, her heart hardening with every single beat, blood cooling with every inch of the journey it took through her body. "Did you?"

He studied her for a long moment, eyes unreadable, that constant little quirk in the corner of his mouth that made him look like he was constantly smirking or he knew something the rest of the world didn't. "I made us a better family," he said at last. "I prepared you to be a good mommy to those twins of yours."

At the mention of her children, Jill felt a protective hatred consume her. Her lips pursed and her eyes became void of any emotion. She took the phone from her ear, about to hang it up.

"Jill, wait!"

She returned the phone to her ear but said nothing.

"Loyalty," he said, looking her dead in the eye. "We've always been about loyalty. We're a team, you and me."

She met his gaze, and she felt the ten-year-old little girl inside, cringing at that word and all that it meant. "Go to hell, Lawrence."

Pushing back in her chair, she dropped the phone, the hard plastic swinging freely and tapping against the leg of the chair she'd vacated. The only other sound was her high heels clicking on the linoleum on her way out of the visiting room.

She winced at the pain as she literally bit the inside of her cheek to hold back the rising emotion. Hurrying up the staircase, she was passed by two chatting corrections officers in blue who nodded a greeting to her on their way down the way she'd come. Passing through the sally port where she was buzzed through the sliding metal door to the lobby, she gathered her purse from the small cube locker and headed out.

Her car sped down Highway 50, music blasting as she desperately tried to distract herself from what was threatening to bubble up and overtake her.

"Not going to cry," she whispered, shaking her head as a hand came up, fingers angrily swiping at a tear that dare try and escape. "Not going to cry."

Like a pot filled with water, forced to stay in a state of flat affect on a cold burner, the heat was slowly rising. Surprising herself, she gripped the steering wheel in both hands, her body lunging backward and forward.

"Bastard!" she screamed at the top of her lungs. "Fuck you, bastard!"

Forty-five minutes later, Jill pulled her car into the garage, Andrew immediately opening the door to the house. She didn't even close the car door before she went into his open arms, her body instantly racked by sobs as he enfolded her into his love and comfort.

# *Chapter Thirty-two*

*M*issing since November of 1992, Judy Schaeffer, wife of Hall of Famer and former NFL star, Lawrence Schaeffer, Sr. has been found murdered beneath the home she once shared with her husband and four children, though it's come out that the youngest daughter, barely more than a toddler when Judy went missing, was not, in fact, her biological child.

"You can see Schaeffer in handcuffs as he's escorted from the courtroom, all smiles as he seems to be attempting to wave to someone in the crowd, sending a thumbs up in that direction. Noticeably missing were Schaeffer's four children in court today when he accepted an Alford Plea, which essentially states he denies guilt but concedes the prosecution has enough evidence for conviction of the second-degree murder of Judy Schaeffer.

"Sentencing will take place next month, and Schaeffer will likely end up with a minimum of twenty-five years in prison, a death sentence for the sixty-eight-year-old football star. Many are calling him the OJ Simpson of the new century.

"We're told services will be held sometime this week so Judy Schaeffer can finally be laid to rest.

"Reporting from Pueblo, Colorado, Burton Blinde, CNN."

It was raining that day. Nora would never forget that. Rain in late October wasn't entirely common, but on that day, the heavens were grieving, too. Even the minister, standing in his religious finery at the front of the church, spoke about it. He said God wept for Judy, wept for her children, wept for twenty-four lost years.

Nora sat sandwiched in between LJ and Bella. Even Bella cried, cried for a grandmother she'd never known and would never know. It didn't matter that Nora's mother was not the biological mother of Shannon, therefore not the biological grandmother of Bella; her mother would have loved them both for her entire life. She had to suppose that she had, Shannon, anyway.

She stared at the beautiful chestnut coffin that sat at the front of the church, a woman who had stood five feet three inches and weighed one hundred and eleven pounds had been rendered down to a humanoid bundle that weighed less than thirty pounds.

She felt fresh tears coming, which surprised her. She'd cried more in the past four days than she had in four years. When the body had at last been released to them, her heart had broken. She'd be lying if she said dark thoughts hadn't entered her mind over the years, but she'd never even whispered them let alone asked anyone what they might think. She had simply created a fantasy in her mind that her mom was happy somewhere, finally free. But then again, she supposed that had been true all along.

❧❧❧❧

Andrew waited back at the family limo with the

kids, leaving Nora, Jill, Shannon, and LJ alone at the gravesite, the other attendees leaving the cemetery after the minister had spoken a few words and blessings.

Nora held onto Shannon's hand as she stared down at the casket, a beautiful bouquet of flowers splayed across it. She could feel the sadness of the three people who stood with her. Though nobody spoke, she could sense their anger, their hurt, their loss because she felt it, too. She and Shannon shared an umbrella as did Jill and LJ, the raindrops splattering down on the black nylon in rhythmic thuds.

Out of nowhere, song lyrics and a melody about being someone's one companion broke the silence.

Nora glanced over at the angelic voice that dared encroach upon the somber day. Shannon's gaze remained on the casket as she continued to sing "Wishing You Were Somehow Here Again," a song she'd learned so many years ago from *The Phantom of the Opera*. She watched her sing, getting lost in the voice, lost in the words and their meaning as silent tears slid down her cheeks unchecked. She heard sniffling and knew both Jill and LJ were equally moved.

At the song's finish, when Shannon sang the final words about saying goodbye, Nora reached for her and hugged her close. Shannon's head rested on her shoulder and one by one, Jill and LJ joined them, the four orphans holding each other.

❧ ❧ ❧ ❧

Standing at the limo, allowing Jill and Shannon to climb in before him, LJ noticed Nora wasn't behind him anymore. Looking around, he spotted her headed off to the east. He wondered why until he noticed a black Mustang parked at the curb of the path that meandered its way through the cemetery. Leaning against the passenger-side door, dressed in a women's-cut black suit and black overcoat, was Sarah.

As Nora reached her, neither woman seemed to say a word as Sarah gathered Nora in her arms, holding her close, Nora's umbrella protecting them both. In the hug, Sarah glanced over and met LJ's gaze. They exchanged a small smile and LJ ducked into the limo. He looked over at Shannon, who held Bella.

"Why don't you two stay with us tonight, Shannon?" he suggested softly.

❧❧❧❧

The drive to the farmhouse was quiet, Sarah's hand resting on Nora's leg the entire time, their fingers entwined. Nora stared straight ahead. The windshield wipers gently slapped back and forth as the rain slowed a bit. She could sense Sarah's gaze on her from time to time, but she was too lost in her own pain to respond.

The dirt roads out by the farm were muddy, and Sarah took the corner into Nora's driveway slow, the splashing and sliding minimal. Somewhere inside Nora felt bad, thinking she'd either give Sarah the money to wash her car or wash it herself once everything dried out.

Sarah pulled the car to a stop and turned off the ignition. They briefly locked eyes and shared a small smile before climbing out of the car. Nora didn't bother with her umbrella as they'd be inside soon enough. Seeming to have the same conclusion, Sarah followed as she hurried to the paved path and the kitchen door, using her key to let them in.

They remained silent as each shrugged out of a damp coat and stepped out of mud-covered shoes. Stepping farther into the kitchen, Nora glanced over her shoulder at Sarah, who lagged behind.

"Want some coffee?" she managed.

"Uh, sure. If you're going to have some."

Nora went about getting everything she'd need and setting it on the counter. She grabbed the glass carafe to fill with water before her hands began to tremble as fresh emotion rose.

"Hey," Sarah said, coming up behind her and taking the carafe from her before she dropped it into the sink. "Hey."

The sobs came quickly, rocking Nora's entire body. She was turned around and gathered into Sarah's arms where she cried into her neck. As reality began to come back to her, the feel of strong arms wrapped around her, a warm body pressed to hers, the tears began to slow, her emotions calming. She inhaled Sarah's perfume.

Letting out a long breath, she held Sarah tighter to her. Right then, she wanted to feel life, not grieve the death of the past few days. She left a soft kiss on Sarah's neck before she moved her head away enough to lightly touch soft lips with her own. Sarah said nothing nor did she ask questions as Nora delivered a second kiss, this one lingering.

Sarah's hands moved from Norah's back to her hips, lightly returning her kiss, tears still fresh on her cheeks. She could taste the saltiness spread from her own lips to Sarah's as the kiss continued, followed by light little touches. Nora's hands moved up into thick, dark hair that she'd been dreaming about for almost two months. She deepened the kiss as she reached down and gently pushed Sarah's suit jacket from her shoulders, blindly tossing the garment onto the kitchen table. She needed to feel the warmth of Sarah's skin through her blouse.

The kiss deepened and began to heat up. Sarah slowed it down until she gently pulled away. She looked into Nora's eyes, a question in her own. Nora knew this situation was certainly unorthodox and not exactly the way either of them would have chosen to find each other again. But, she knew in her heart this was what she wanted, what she needed.

In response to Sarah's unspoken question, Nora cupped her cheek with her hand and gave her a reassuring smile before she took Sarah's hand and led her to the stairs and finally to her bedroom. Once there, Nora quickly pulled down the bedding and turned to Sarah, who watched her, uncertainty in her dark eyes.

Meeting her gaze, Nora slowly unbuttoned her own blouse, allowing the soft material to slide over her shoulders and down her arms only to float to the floor. Sarah took in what was exposed to her then bridged the gap between them, taking Nora in a tender but passionate kiss.

Moments later, Nora let out a sigh as they lay on the bed, Sarah pressing against her, their clothing left in a heap on the floor. She pushed Sarah to her back and moved on top of her, their kiss slow and exploratory, reaffirming what was found and lost only to be found again.

She took her time exploring the softness of Sarah's skin, reveling in the sounds of her whimpers and moans, left heady by the taste of her need. She touched every inch of her, using fingers, lips, and tongue until Sarah cried out, her back arching as Nora held on, refusing to let go until a weak nudge served as a silent reminder to stop.

Leaving a kiss in pulsing volcanic wetness, she made her way back up Sarah's body, finding herself engulfed in strong arms, a languid moan escaping Sarah's throat as they kissed, the taste of their tongues mingling.

Nora was startled as Sarah suddenly completely reversed their positions. She grinned up at Sarah, who returned it before their kiss continued. She sighed as Sarah cupped one of her breasts, lips moving away from her mouth. Sarah explored her body, leaving a trail of wet, hot kisses along her throat and upper chest until her mouth replaced her hand.

Nora gasped, her head arching back as two of Sarah's fingers slid down her body and inside. Sarah left her breast and came back to her mouth, their kiss deep and wet until they were breathing too hard to kiss. Sarah remained with her as Nora got close to release, which hit her hard and fast, overwhelming her as she let out a loud gasp.

Her eyes slid closed as her body tried to calm, Sarah holding her and murmuring sweet words into her ear and through the kisses she rained down on her face. Nora moved her hands up and cupped Sarah's face, bringing their lips together for a slow and deep kiss, cementing the connection they'd made.

Sarah moved on top of Nora, whose legs spread to give her hips room. She pressed her wetness against Nora's, adjusting her hips until they were pressed intimately together, causing them both to moan into the kiss. Nora buried one of her hands in Sarah's thick hair while stroking her other hand down a strong back, and she felt the muscles moving beneath the soft skin as Sarah's hips gently thrust against her, her hands' final destination an incredibly shapely behind.

Sarah lowered her upper body so their breasts were pressed together as she continued to move with Nora. Nora knew this wasn't going to last long as her body was strung tight, ready to explode with each thrust against her. Sarah was right there with her, almost at the peak, her increased breathing and whimpers interrupting their kiss.

Nora wrapped her arms around Sarah and held her close, their mutual pace increasing, driving them closer to a second release, which was swift and loud, Sarah's cries buried in Nora's neck as Nora's cry echoed in the bedroom around them. She wrapped her legs around Sarah's hips, enfolding Sarah in all that she felt, hoping Sarah could sense it and understand.

❧❧❧❧

As Sarah drove the Mustang into LJ's neighborhood, Nora held a box of fresh doughnuts on her lap from Schuster's Banquet Bakery and a piece of mail for LJ, Nora glanced at Sarah. Their fingers were interlaced and rested on Nora's thigh. Making love with Sarah the night before had certainly been an incredible and profound experience, but waking up wrapped in her arms had healed so much damage caused over a lifetime.

Seeming to feel Nora's eyes on her, Sarah met her gaze. The two shared a knowing smile, so much in that one expression before Sarah turned into LJ's driveway. She pulled the car to a stop and tugged lightly on Nora's hand to bring her closer. They shared a lingering kiss that ended in a huge smile from Nora.

"You know," she whispered against Sarah's lips, "it's a good thing you always keep an extra set of clothes packed in your trunk."

Sarah chuckled. "Well, as a cop it's wise, and I think with you, it'll be a must."

Climbing out of the car, Sarah offered to take the doughnuts as Nora led the way up the path to the front porch. She raised her hand to poke the doorbell. Moments later Kristie answered, giving Nora a shit-eating grin.

"Oh, shut up," Nora said without the girl saying a word. She gave her a quick hug, and she and Sarah entered the house.

"Good morning," LJ called out from the kitchen. "Coffee's brewing."

"That's good because breakfast is here," Nora said, hugging LJ then Shannon and Bella. She noticed Bella was dressed in her same dress from the previous day, but Shannon was dressed in a black punk band T-shirt and oversized sweatpants. "Gee, Shannon, I didn't know you were a Paramore fan," she said dryly.

Shannon grinned. "Hey, better than wearing a dress to eat doughnuts. Luckily Kristie and I are fairly close in size."

Nora returned her smile and gave her a second hug. "Sorry," she said into it.

"Don't you be. You guys needed some time, anyone could see that." She pitted her tongue between her teeth for a second. "Hope it was good."

Nora blushed deeply and glanced at Sarah who was looking down, a hand to the back of her neck.

"So," LJ boomed, changing the subject and clearing the suddenly heavy air. "Doughnuts?"

"Oh, LJ, as promised over the phone, your mail,"

Nora said, handing him the envelope.

LJ took it, a confused look on his face. "Why would my mail go to your house?" he asked.

"Dunno," Nora said, running her finger along the bottom edge of the cardboard lid to break the tape that held the pastry box closed. "I meant to bring that yesterday, but I forgot." Nora caught Kristie from the corner of her eye and saw a look of excitement on her face, which made her question what was going on.

While LJ tore into the envelope, Nora glanced over at Sarah who was already looking at her. It amazed her how comfortable everything felt, having Sarah there, being in LJ's new home. She wasn't sure what to expect considering the events of the past few days and burying their mother the previous day, but somehow it was like a weight had been lifted from all of them. There was no sadness in the air, no stress or tension. There was just...love.

"What the..."

Nora's attention returned to LJ, whose eyebrows had drawn as he was reading whatever the letter in his trembling hands said. "I...Oh my God." He dropped the single page, which floated lazily to land on the cooking island.

Nora grabbed it and began to read silently, her heart stopping as she gasped.

"What is it?" Shannon asked from where she was helping Bella split her doughnut in half.

Nora cleared her throat and began to read aloud. "'Dear LJ Schaffer. We received and reviewed your manuscript titled, *End Game*, and we are pleased to inform you we would like to offer you a contract on your novel for publication with DeWitt Books. Please see the proposal below as well as contact information provided. We look forward to adding you to our family of authors. Sincerely, Robin Medford, Publisher DeWitt Books.'" She looked up at him with wide eyes, her mouth hanging open.

LJ ran a hand through his hair, still trembling. He glanced over at Kristie, who was beaming with tears in her eyes. "Did you do this?" he asked, wonder and shock in his voice.

"Hey, I knew you never would, so…" she quipped.

"I don't know whether to ground you for the rest of your life or give you the biggest goddamn hug ever."

Kristie giggled and walked over to her dad. "How about both?"

"Woohoo!" Shannon crowed. "Let's celebrate with doughnuts!"

# *Epilogue*

I absolutely love what Shannon has done with this place," Sarah said to Nora from where they sat at the dining room table, three leaves added for length.

Nora chuckled. "Well, baby, this place was pretty much an empty canvas when you moved out."

"Be nice," Sarah growled playfully. "I was a detective, not an interior decorator."

"Everyone, can I have your attention, please?" Shannon asked, standing from her chair at the head of the table. She was wearing a cute dress that showed off her adorable figure, her shoulder-length hair pulled back from her face. She blushed slightly as everyone looked over at her. "Jeez, I didn't think this would be quite so intimidating." She laughed nervously.

"That's what happens when it's your house," LJ laughed from where he sat next to Rachel a bit farther down the table from her.

"Yeah, yeah," Shannon said. "Okay." She blew out a breath. "Anyway, I wanted to welcome everyone here for Thanksgiving dinner. It's, well, it's always been my dream to host a holiday in my own house." She grinned. "Problem was, I never lived in anything bigger than a shoebox."

Nora laughed, remembering those days herself. For now, she looked on with pride as her younger sister continued.

"I wanted to start by saying that I am so grateful that Sarah and Nora gave me the opportunity to have such a nice home for Bella and me, and now"—she glanced over at her boss-turned-fiancé—"Corey. So, Sarah when you offered me to rent this place from you when you moved in with Nora, you truly made a dream come true. Thank you."

Nora reached over to Sarah's lap and wrapped her fingers around Sarah's, feeling a squeeze in return.

"It was my pleasure, Shannon," Sarah said softly.

"So much has happened in the last sixteen months and I know I have so much to be grateful for. So, I thought maybe we could go around the table and offer a little of what we're thankful for. So," she said about to sit before standing back up again. "That's it."

Nora chuckled as Shannon plopped back down into her chair, looking almost relieved that she'd gotten that out.

"Okay," Shannon continued. "Bella, honey, go ahead."

"Well," the seven-year-old began, giving everyone a big, toothless grin, already telling everyone how proud she was that she'd lost two more teeth. "I'm thankful for Mommy and Corey. I'm thankful for my teacher, Mrs. Epps, my cat Oreo, but mostly because I'm gonna be a big sister."

"Bella!" Shannon hissed.

"Oops! I wasn't supposed to say that. Sorry, Mommy." She turned to the rest of the table. "Just kidding."

Nora laughed along with everyone else before offering sincere congratulations to the happy couple. She liked the quiet and shy Corey a great deal. He was a hell of an attorney, she was told, but was sweet and considerate to both Shannon and Bella.

Andrew was next, still chuckling at Bella's announcement. "Well, congrats you two for starters. I guess I'm extremely grateful for my family," he said. He glanced at Jill, holding her gaze for a long moment before continuing. "I'm grateful to be married to the love of my life and mother of my kids." They shared a quick kiss. "And, I'm grateful we won the Loenstein case, right Corey?" He raised his wineglass in salute at the laughter that garnered.

Nora watched her older sister, who was silent for a moment, seeming to truly contemplate her answer. Finally, a slow and lovely smile crossed her lips. "This time two years ago I was a very different person with a very different perspective on, well, everything. I'm grateful that none of you gave up on me," she said, sparing a glance at her husband. "And, so glad to be close to my family again. I'm deeply proud of my children, Sylvia at the top of her class and Tyler, what do you kids say, is rocking it," she said, using air quotes.

Tyler looked away, blushing.

"Happy Thanksgiving everyone," she said in closing.

Nora chuckled because Sylvia looked as though she were about to be sick as she was next.

"Um," she said, looking around shyly. "I guess I'm grateful for all kinds of stuff."

"Yeah, uh, ditto," Tyler said, almost seeming to shrink in his seat.

"That's Tyler." LJ laughed. "A man of few words." He playfully punched the teen on the shoulder. "I guess I'm next. Well," he said, letting out a heavy sigh. "First and foremost, I'm so proud of Kristie. She's doing so well in college and is in her own place." He grinned past Rachel at her. "She too is rocking it."

Kristie rolled her eyes. "You're such a dork, Dad."

LJ grinned. "So I'm told, so I'm told. I am deeply grateful for Rachel," he said, the tone of his voice going from playful to filled with meaning as he looked at the adorable blonde sitting next to him. "She's truly taught me what love can be, *should* be." He smiled. "Thank you for that."

Nora reached a hand up to swipe at a tear that was about to slip down her cheek. She'd never seen her brother happier than he'd been in the past year and could think of few who deserved it more.

"Also," LJ continued, "I wanted to share with you that I'm leaving P-Dub." He paused as a round of surprised gasps filled the room. "Guys, I hate football." He let out a little laugh. "Always have. Instead, I'll be teaching English Literature at Pueblo Community College."

Nora broke out into applause. "Awesome!"

"Let's not forget that book number two is coming out next spring," Rachel added, pointing a finger at him. "Yep, this guy."

"Yay!" Kristie exclaimed. "My dad finally came out of the closet as a writer."

LJ grinned. "Yeah, yeah. Anyway, uh, yeah. Baby?"

"Well," Rachel began, "I'd like to start by saying I'm truly grateful that Shannon has recovered so remarkably well, little Miss ML." She and Shannon exchanged a meaningful smile. "But, also that everyone here has been so accepting of me and my boys, who as you all know had to head off to spend some time today with their dads' families. You guys are an amazing group of people. I honestly thought I'd hit the lottery with LJ, but never figured that would extend to you guys, too. So"—she gave everyone a blinding smile—"thank you and I truly love you all." She turned to LJ. "Especially you."

"Hey, get a room!" Sarah exclaimed, tossing a dinner roll at the kissing couple.

Nora laughed, squeezing Sarah's thigh beneath the table.

"Right?" Kristie exclaimed dramatically. "Anywho, guess it's to the lezzie end of the table now, huh?" She grinned at Julia, Nora, and Sarah. "Nah, I'm truly grateful for everything. I'm happy and have so many good things in my life." She shrugged. "Guess I just love my life."

Nora chuckled at that simple declaration, expecting so much more drama from her eldest niece.

"Well," Julia said, grabbing her water glass, "in the epic word of Tyler, 'Ditto.'"

Nora opened her mouth to speak, but Kristie zoomed in. "Let Sarah go first!"

Nora glanced from Kristie and a grinning Julia to her left, where Sarah was scooting her chair back and had fallen to one knee.

"Oh God," Nora groaned, hands coming up to cover her face. She dropped her hands and glanced at Kristie. "Did you two knuckleheads know about this?"

"Duh! Who the hell else was going to entertain your nosy ass so she could get you a ring?"

Nora laughed, shaking her head. "And, here I thought my *considerate* niece only wanted to spend the day with me." She turned back to Sarah who, sure enough, was holding an opened ring box, an exquisite gold band with inlaid diamonds inside.

"I've waited twenty-three years to ask this, but

will you marry me?" she said softly.

Nora couldn't speak, so she simply nodded, Sarah's image blurred through her tears. "Of course!"

Sarah somehow managed to get the ring onto Nora's finger as her hand was trembling terribly. She took Nora in her arms in a tight hug amidst thunderous applause and cheers.

"I love you," Nora managed to say.

"I love you, too," Sarah responded into her ear.

"Yay!" Bella exclaimed. "Now, let's eat!"

# *About the Author*

Kim Pritekel was born and raised in Colorado, where she still lives, loving the blue skies and the beautiful Rockies. She's been writing since she was a child and has created a career as both a novelist and filmmaker.
You can find out more at
http://www.kimpritekel.com/
or on Facebook

## *Check out Kim's other books.*

**Zero Ward** - ISBN - 978-1-943353-19-4

Danny Felts grew up in the heart of the Midwest on a dairy farm, expected to follow in her mother's footsteps and marry a farmer and become a mother. Danny had other ideas. As World War II heats up, she makes a decision that will change her life forever as she becomes a lie, serving with the Seabees in the Navy as Daniel Felts.

Kate Adams is about to graduate high school in her prestigious and elite San Diego neighborhood when she's dragged to the USO for a dance with friends and servicemen. There, she meets the person that will catch her eye and her heart, only for jealousy and vengeance to tear her apart.

Are Danny and Kate strong enough to win the battle within and fight for their love?

**Connection**- ISBN - 978-1-939062-24-6

Julie Wilson lives a charmed life as a beloved teacher and aunt in the small town of Woodland. Close to her brother and guardian of two adorable Yorkies, she loves her life, the only negative being ex-boyfriend, Ray who can't seem to understand the phrase, "We're done." Believing that's her only problem, Julie has no idea what hell awaits her during a normal summer afternoon.

Remmy Foster is the quirky, friendly drifter who has

never found roots after a difficult childhood, as well as the difficulties her very special gift brings into her life. Though she may call it exploring, the truth is she's running from ghosts that haunt her every step.

After a chance meeting with Julie while hitchhiking, Remmy will be thrown head first into darkness she could never have foreseen, regardless of her abilities. As the clock ticks, life and death is on her shoulders to make the right connection.

***Warning - Some scenes may be too intense for some readers.***

**1049 Club** - ISBN - 978-1-939062-97-0

Almost two hundred souls, one plane, six survivors, endless heartbreak.

When flight 1049, headed from Buffalo, NY to Italy falls from the sky, a firestorm of drama, pain, angst and sorrow ensues. Can an author, a business owner, a teenager, good ol' boy, veterinarian and ruthless lawyer survive? Better yet, can those left behind?

1049 Club is a story of survival, love, deep regret and miracles. Can the living make peace with the presumed dead? Can the presumed dead make peace with the lives and loves they thought they had before?

**Blinded** – ISBN – 978-1-943353-53-8

After a horrible explosion sends local television news reporter, Burton Blinde reeling both physically and emotionally, she walks away from her life and the dream job she was about to start at a major news network.

For six long years she hides out in a small mountain town, working at the local library, though is haunted by the life she had, including mysterious messages and gifts she was receiving before her life was turned upside down, a veritable bread crumb trail leading to the unknown.

Unable to resist, Burton begins to follow the clues, which will lead her into the darkest places of human nature that she may not be able to return from.

9 781939 062451